PASTURES
NEW

PASTURES NEW

ANN PURSER

ORION

Copyright © 1994 Ann Purser

The right of Ann Purser to be
identified as the author of this work has
been asserted by her in accordance with the
Copyright, Designs and Patents Act 1988.

First published in Great Britain in 1994 by
Orion
An imprint of Orion Books Ltd
Orion House, 5 Upper St Martin's Lane,
London WC2H 9EA

A CIP catalogue record for this book is
available from the British Library

ISBN 1 85797 059 4

Typeset by Deltatype Ltd,
Ellesmere Port, Cheshire
Printed in England by Clays Ltd, St Ives plc

Tomorrow to fresh woods, and pastures new.

Lycidas, John Milton

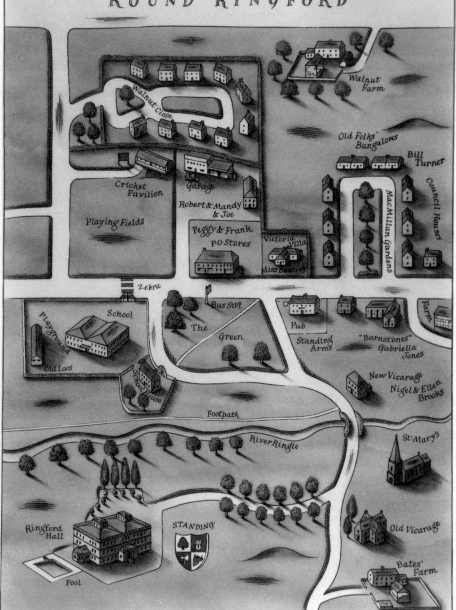

ROUND RINGFORD

Walnut Close

Walnut Farm

Old Folks' Bungalows

Bill Turner

Council Houses

Cricket Pavilion

Garage

MacMillan Gardens

Robert & Mandy & Joe

Playing Fields

Peggy & Frank P.O. Stores

Victoria Villa

Miss Beasley

Zebra

Bus Stop

School

Playground

The Green

Pub

Standing Arms

"Barnstones" Gabriella Jones

Farm

Old Loos

School House

New Vicarage Nigel & Ellen Brooks

Footpath

River Ringle

St. Mary's

Ringford Hall

STANDING

Old Vicarage

Pool

Bates' Farm

CHAPTER ONE

Peggy Palmer, of 121 Bryony Road, Coventry, West Midlands, considered herself a reasonably happy woman.

She had lived in the same house for twenty-five years, compatibly married to Frank, both of them healthy, settled, pillars of the community. It was Peggy's fifty-second birthday, and she had no reason to feel anything other than cheerful and optimistic. Walking home from her part-time job at a bookshop in the Parade, she looked forward to an evening out with Frank and a chance to wear the new blue blouse he had given her.

Her boss, Heather Marks, had kept her late talking, and she shopped quickly in the Parade before walking home. It was late summer, chillier now in the evenings, and as she opened the back door into the kitchen, Peggy shivered. She lit the gas fire in the sitting-room and settled briefly with a cup of tea, turning on the television for company.

'Frank?' she said, hearing a key turn in the front door. He's early . . . funny . . . not like Frank. She got up to greet him, kissing his cold cheek and helping him off with his gaberdine mac, noticing that he didn't glance as usual in the hall mirror to smooth his thinning grey hair.

'You're cold, love,' she said, and was surprised that he did not reciprocate her kiss.

'Anything wrong, Frank? You look . . . um . . .'

He hesitated and looked at her for a moment, and his eyes were so bleak that she began to panic. 'Frank! what is it – for God's sake tell me!'

'Peg, I meant to wait, but . . . well, you might as well know now. It's all of us, I mean, it's me – I've been made redundant.'

'What?' She shook her head, not wanting to believe what she had heard.

'Redundant . . . I've been made redundant.'

She looked at him stupidly, saying nothing, clutching at his sleeve.

'Not just me,' Frank went on, 'the whole department. They're going to contract our work out in future. They reckon it will save them money.'

His voice was strange, and he brushed Peggy's hand off his arm, as if her touch would weaken the tight hold he was keeping on himself. He walked through to the sitting-room and Peggy followed, seeking reassurance from his slender, grey-suited back, his neat black shoes, the crisp striped shirt that she ironed so carefully for him.

'There must be some mistake,' she said woodenly, 'you've been there since you left school. They couldn't do that – Mr Maddox himself said they couldn't manage without you, he said it at that party in front of everybody – how could they possibly . . . ?'

'Well, they have, the rotten sods,' said Frank with venom. He sat down heavily on the sofa and looked up at her. 'Oh Peg,' he said, and finally relaxing, he gently took her hand, pulling her down to sit beside him. His world had suddenly changed. Everything safe and familiar had taken on a shifting, unreliable aspect – what could he be sure of now? But Peggy was the same, the same plump figure sitting beside him, her pretty face framed in greyish fair curls, blue eyes anxious and dear mouth tense. She was the same, but he had changed, had failed her, and he felt deeply guilty.

'It's not necessarily the end of the world, Peg,' he said, but he knew that without doubt, in all ways, it was.

The unreality of Frank's shocking news lasted for several days. Peggy went through the motions of her regular routines in a daze, working in the bookshop, shopping, cleaning, cooking. And Frank, hollow eyed and grey faced, went to and from work at Maddox's in much the same way as usual, even won the annual championship at the firm's Chess Club, where he was Honorary Secretary and founder member.

'We shall get a good pay-off,' said Frank bitterly, 'something like a year's salary, so we won't starve. But I don't see myself getting another job easily, not at my age. We need to do some thinking, Peg.'

It was not being needed any more that hurt. He'd always worked quietly and conscientiously, maintaining the high standards he set himself, sure that he was giving value for money. And now in a matter of weeks Maddox's would manage perfectly well without him. He was betrayed, empty, squeezed of everything that made him Frank Palmer, Chief Designer of Maddox and Company.

It was Heather Marks at the bookshop who put the idea into Peggy's head, and who much later on wished she had kept her mouth shut.

'What about a business? You've got Frank's redundancy money and he's very organised and canny, and you're good with the customers here. Why don't you suggest it to Frank?'

'What kind of business?' said Peggy.

'Oh, I don't know – what do you fancy?'

Peggy thought about it. 'Well, not a gift shop, full of shiny rubbish – and you wouldn't want competition for the bookshop, would you? Still, we wouldn't have to stay round here, we could go somewhere else. Maybe move out to the country?'

'I'd think carefully about that,' said Heather.

'A village shop?' said Frank. 'Are you crazy, Peggy? Neither of us knows anything about villages or shops – '

'I do,' said Peggy, 'customers are much the same, whether they're buying books or cheese. I like customers, I get on well with them. I can sell things. It's the only thing I can do. Couldn't we think about it?'

Frank had begun to talk about scrap heaps and being finished at fifty, and Peggy knew that now it was she who had somehow to keep up the momentum of planning a future. The more she thought about running a village shop the more it appealed to her. She could see herself in a fresh apron, weighing out gobstoppers and laughing with the children.

'Could be a new start, Frank,' she said, 'fresh fields and pastures new, and all that . . .'

'Woods,' said Frank.

'What?'

'Woods, it's "fresh woods and pastures new" – might as well get it right, if that's what we're going to do.' Lethargy had taken hold of Frank, an unwillingness to talk about anything much, and this frightened Peggy more than his initial anger, increased her determination to prod him into action.

That's it then, thought Peggy, I'm off tomorrow to the estate agents to get some particulars, and Frank can come with me, has to come with me. I'm not going under, and nor is Frank, not if I can help it.

'Better take your time,' said Jim Marks, sorting newly delivered piles of novels, 'don't rush into the first one you see. Village shops are not exactly gold-mines these days. Still, Frank's head is well screwed on. Tell him to be sure to get the right one.'

'There isn't a right one for Frank,' said Peggy, 'he's full of doubts and fears, and he's not made one of his corny jokes for weeks. Well, at least we shall be doing something, not just rotting away in Bryony Road. Wish us luck, Jim.'

Jim looked at Peggy, pink faced and enthusiastic, and wished he could guarantee her the luck she and Frank were surely going to need. But he had his own worries, scraping a living from a reluctant clientele, and he patted her shoulder kindly.

'Anything we can do to help, Peggy,' he said, 'you have only to ask.'

CHAPTER TWO

'Well, it just so happens,' said Mrs Ashbourne, looking over the top of her thick, rimless half-glasses, 'there's a couple called Palmer coming this afternoon about three o'clock, just to have a look, they said.'

Doris Ashbourne, postmistress and village shop proprietor, knew very well how to whet the village appetite for gossip. Mrs Jenkins, fair of face, fat and amiable, shifted her weight from one foot to the other and waited. She had lived in the village longer than Mrs Ashbourne, and felt she had a right to know.

'Anybody else interested in buying?' she said.

The For Sale sign had been flapping disconsolately outside the shop since the beginning of November, but so far there had been no takers.

'I've said all I'm going to say on the subject,' said Mrs Ashbourne, and with impeccable Post Office tact, silently counted out the Jenkins' Child Benefit. Mrs Jenkins turned quickly, hearing a dog yap.

'Don't do that, Eddie!' she yelled at her youngest, two-year-old Edward, who was sitting in his pushchair outside the shop, stroking the Jenkins' terrier vigorously the wrong way, until its rough coat stood up and it had ventured a mock snap at the child to warn him off.

'Serves you right if he bites you!' Mrs Jenkins called, but added to Mrs Ashbourne, 'He never would, mind, he's gentle as a lamb.'

'They all say that,' said Mrs Ashbourne, pushing the pile of notes under the cubicle window.

Oh well, if that's how you feel, Doris, thought Jean Jenkins, I can see nothing more will be forthcoming today.

'Hope they decide to buy!' she said cheerily, and moved her large frame through the narrow space between display units. She emerged blinking into the clear sunlight of an early spring morning in Round Ringford.

It was a small village, most of the habitation, the school and the pub, clustering round a wide Green. A shallow, swiftly flowing river across the far side of the Green ran parallel to the main road, and was bordered by well-grown weeping willows and a footpath leading to the old stone packhorse bridge. Roofs and chimneys of a stately manor house showed above tall chestnut and beech trees, and the old houses in the village were mellow golden ironstone, sometimes banded with the greyer stone of the nearby Cotswolds. It was, to the casual eye, a peaceful place.

'Come on, then, Eddie my duck,' she said to the plump child, rewrapping him in his brightly coloured crocheted blanket, 'let's just go and have a word with Old Ellen.'

I know Doris Ashbourne is watching me, she thought, as she untied the little brindled terrier and started off across the road, the pushchair precariously unbalanced by plastic bags. Still, she wouldn't have told me if she'd wanted it kept quiet.

'Going to Tresham?' she said to the old woman waiting at the bus stop. Others were making their way across the village Green and down the main street, converging on the bus shelter, holding on to hats and clutching flapping coats, hurrying to get out of the blustery wind.

Old Ellen, a bundle of greenish black topped off with a firmly tied headscarf of doubtful colour, nodded. 'Taking the weight off me feet for a few minutes,' she said, and patted the narrow bench running the length of the bus shelter. She rummaged in an old brown, peeling leather handbag, and came up with a boiled sweet, which she unwrapped and popped into Eddie's mouth.

'You'll not be back in time to see the Palmers,' said Jean Jenkins.

'What Palmers?' said Old Ellen.

'I knew a Sid Palmer once,' said Fred Mills, who despite the cold wind had walked slowly down from the old people's bungalows, aided by his rubber-tipped stick. 'He shot hisself up in Bagley Woods.'

'Shut up, Fred, you old fool,' said Ellen, and turned to Jean Jenkins.

'Who are these Palmers, then – hurry up, gel, the bus'll be here any minute.'

'Coming to look at the shop this afternoon about three – see if they want to buy it. Doris Ashbourne didn't sound too hopeful, but then that's her, isn't it?'

Old Ellen picked up her rexine shopping bags, tightened her headscarf, and surprised everyone by announcing she was off home.

'You feeling queer?' asked Mr Mills, looking hopeful.

'Changed me mind,' said Old Ellen, 'I decided to do me shopping with Doris Ashbourne – I'll come down this afternoon with the trolley.'

'About three o'clock, no doubt,' said Jean Jenkins, with a wink at the others.

The green and yellow Tresham bus came slowly along the village street, giving time for last minute travellers to rush along to the bus stop. The scattering of passengers looked out and smiled at familiar faces in the Round Ringford queue.

'Not coming today, Ellen?' said the young driver.

'If I was, I'd be up them steps out of the wind by now,' said Ellen tartly, 'and I'm Mrs Biggs to you.'

'Might see you later, then,' said Mrs Jenkins to the old woman, and waved the bus off with a nice sense of occasion, which indeed it was, since there were only two shopping buses to Tresham each week.

'Soon be home by the fire,' she reassured a red-nosed Eddie, 'I banked it up well before we left, my duck. It should just need a tickle to bring it back to life.' Edward nodded violently, as if he understood every word.

They turned into Macmillan Gardens, a council development with sixteen houses and four old people's bungalows. With the best of intentions, the Council had used a bright stone-type material to blend in with the old houses in the village, but unfortunately Macmillan Gardens had remained a sharp yellow colour, unmellowed by time.

'There's Renata Roberts,' Mrs Jenkins said apprehensively to Edward, who was already beginning to struggle out of his wrappings, although still thirty yards from his house.

He made a passing grab at a daffodil, and his mother steered him swiftly out of reach. 'We shall have to look out for our crocuses round the back, shan't we?' she said, 'and no, Eddie! Just stay where you are for a minute!'

Renata Roberts stood at the gate of number eight, a dingy and untidy house which let down all the rest, with its heaps of scrap by the front door, and a gate permanently stuck half-open on a broken hinge. The straggly hedge had grown ragged at the top and thin at the bottom, and old Coke cans and bits of wire had worked their way through on to the pavement. Mrs Roberts had the dustbin lid in her hand, and had been tipping the remains of yesterday's meals into the bin, when she saw Jean Jenkins walking swiftly down the Gardens.

'She's got nice ankles, considering,' Mrs Roberts said to no one in particular. She was a thin, worn-looking woman, who had given up trying to maintain her rough, unkind husband and unruly children in any semblance of order.

Sandra Roberts, third daughter, aged fifteen and wearing her brother's jeans and a huge flapping T-shirt, heard her and said, 'Who do you mean, Mum? Not old fatty Jenkins!'

Jean Jenkins was still thinking about the Palmers, an unknown couple who might take over from Doris and be part of all their lives. Don't know that I'd want to do it, she thought. She saw Mrs Roberts looking hopefully at her, and crossed over to give her the news. Sandra listened in, and then slipped through the half-open gate.

'Where you going?' shouted her mother.

'Nowhere,' said Sandra.

'Put your coat on, you'll catch your death!' yelled Mrs Roberts fruitlessly, as Sandra disappeared round the corner of Macmillan Gardens.

Sandra's best friend Octavia Jones was lurking about the driveway of her house, a newly converted barn, originally owned by the squire, Richard Standing, and sold to supplement his dwindling income. Octavia's parents bought her the same uniform of jeans and T-shirts, but subtly different from Sandra's – nicer colours and better cut, flattering her emerging curves.

Octavia was hoping to catch sight of Robert Bates, the nicest of the village's young farmers, who had been carting muck up and down the street all morning. Octavia only half-listened when Sandra told her about the Palmers.

'So what?' she said carelessly.

Sandra couldn't think of a reply, knowing that when Octavia was in this mood she could be a real cow. 'Might as well be off home,' she said, but Octavia's attention had now been galvanised by the sight of a giant tractor turning the corner by the pub, and bearing down on them with a roar.

'Hey, Sandra!' Octavia was instantly animated. 'He's stopping!'

Sandra scowled, and retreated behind Octavia. She had no confidence in herself, and was self-conscious about her teenage spots. She couldn't see that her hair – if properly cut and washed – would be glossy and heavy, nor that she had inherited her poor faded mother's Italian looks, almost black eyes and finely drawn charcoal brows.

'He *is* stopping, Sandra!' repeated Octavia.

'So what?' said Sandra, getting her own back.

Robert Bates climbed out of his cab, leaving the ear-splitting tractor engine running. He found a piece of dangling chain, and tucked it up safely out of the way.

'Hi, Robert,' said Octavia alluringly, drawing a strand of silky blonde hair across her mouth. She put a foot out tentatively and rested the toe of her shoe against the huge tyre.

'Heard about the Palmers?' she said quickly, calling on the only piece of news Round Ringford had produced so far that day.

Robert nodded cheerfully, climbed into his cab and drove off. He hadn't heard a word, what with the noise of the tractor, but he knew trouble when he saw it and those two were trouble.

News of the Palmers' visit went one step further. Old Ellen called in to Victoria Villa, a solid red-brick house next to the shop, to tell Miss Ivy Beasley, before battling her way against the buffeting March wind, back across the Green to the Lodge, a tiny one-storey cottage where the floors were bricks laid on earth under the linoleum, and damp patches made strange patterns on the walls in winter.

Miss Beasley walked through to her front room and sat down in her usual watching place by the window. She saw her friend cross the road and get smaller and smaller until she finally disappeared from sight over the far side of the Green.

'And if she thinks I'm going into that shop this afternoon along with all the other nosy-parkers to gawp at some wretched strangers, she's got another think coming,' Ivy Beasley said aloud.

She subdued her short, springy grey hair with a battered old hat, and went out to fetch coal from the shed in her back yard; and, as was her custom, kept her eyes and ears open for anything useful she might pick up from the shop next door.

CHAPTER THREE

Mrs Ashbourne glanced out of the window and up towards Bates's End for the twentieth time. The sun had gone, and the wind blew scraps of paper in whorls and eddies round the Green. Pity the sun's gone in, she thought, it looks cold out there now.

'Watch pot never boils,' said Old Ellen irritatingly. 'Won't make them come any quicker, your looking out for them all the time.'

Doris Ashbourne ignored her and looked again beyond the pub, the Standing Arms, an old alehouse smartened up, with freshly painted, colourful heraldry on its swinging sign, past the ancient church with its crumbling pinnacles crowning a squat tower, and on beyond the tall stone vicarage, too big and too cold for today's impoverished clergy, and finally to where the road curled away round the corner by the farm.

This time she did see a car coming slowly down the wooded hill, disappearing from sight round by Bates's Farm, and reappearing as it crossed the narrow stone bridge over the Ringle River. It drew up, very slowly, outside the Standing Arms.

'That them, then?' said Mrs Jenkins, coming into the shop with a rush of air and setting the bell over the door jangling.

'Could be,' said Mrs Ashbourne, 'and what did you forget this morning?'

'A packet of suet, please,' said Mrs Jenkins pleasantly, ignoring the barb. 'I thought we'd have dumplings for tea, in a bit of stew left from yesterday. It'll be warming, won't it?'

'It's turned colder,' said Old Ellen gloomily, 'and there's rain in the wind.'

'You're not in a hurry, then, Jean?' said Mrs Ashbourne, 'I'll just get this order for the Hall finished.'

'No, no hurry,' said Jean Jenkins quickly, 'school's not out for a good half hour yet. Do you mind if I push Eddie inside, out of the weather?'

Doris Ashbourne saw through this one, but agreed that Eddie would be better inside the warm shop.

'They're on the move again,' said Old Ellen, peering out of the window. The car was small, dark blue and very clean, except where mud from Bateses Farm had splashed up the sides and into the shining alloy wheels.

'Perhaps it's not them,' said Mrs Jenkins, manoeuvring Eddie into a corner away from the sweets.

But Mrs Ashbourne could see the car pulling up outside the shop, and the driver opening his window, asking Octavia Jones – who just happened to have stopped to tie her shoelace – something which caused her to smile and nod towards the door of Round Ringford Post Office and General Stores.

'So this is it,' said Peggy Palmer, releasing her seat belt, and closing her map book with a snap. She looked out through the car window, now misted over with a fine drizzle, and saw a small shop, set high above the pavement, with three steps leading to the narrow door.

'Looks quite clean and tidy,' said Frank, 'not as scruffy as some we've seen.'

'That sign's been up there a long time,' said Peggy,

reading aloud from a surprisingly elegant curved and shaped signboard placed above the shop window. ' "General Stores – High Class Provisions" –that's nicely done, Frank – "Post Office, Round Ringford. Postmistress: Mrs D. Ashbourne." Can you see F. and P. Palmer up there instead?'

'Steady on, old girl,' said Frank. He and Peggy had heeded Jim Marks' advice and taken their time. It was now six months since Frank had been axed by Maddox's, but he still felt the pain of the wound and had difficulty matching Peggy's enthusiasm. He went along with her, though, because anything was better than watching old colleagues from other departments setting off for work each morning while he stayed at home, brooding.

'It's just on three o'clock,' he said, 'better make a move.'

He opened the car door and stepped out, straight into something soft and juicy, left behind after the morning's muck carting by Robert Bates. 'Oh shit!' said Frank, and Peggy giggled. 'Smell's like it,' she said, and began to laugh louder at Frank's horrified expression.

'You may well laugh,' he said, rubbing his smart brown shoe against the grass verge. 'I can see this is going to be the truly rural experience you are looking for.'

Peggy walked round and took his arm. 'Come on, Mr Palmer,' she said, 'who knows – this could be the village of our dreams.'

They stood on the pavement, unaware of the high state of tension inside the shop, and looked out over the Green at the cluster of old houses round the pub, the tiny school with its gabled school house, and the blue line of hills on the horizon. There was nobody to be seen except for a solitary old man hobbling down the street on a stick, pipe in his mouth. A ruffled brown hen with a bright red comb tipped drunkenly over one eye pecked at the grit in the gutter outside the school gate.

'It's a very small village, Frank,' said Peggy.

'And quiet,' said Frank.

'Do you think that's all there is?' Peggy said, a small note of doubt creeping into her voice.

'If it is,' said Frank, 'we shan't make our fortunes here.'

They were silent for a moment, listening to the rap-rap of the rope against the white flagpole in the school playground. Peggy watched a sudden flurry of rooks, quarrelling and swearing, rise from the tall trees in the distant park, and said, 'It's very beautiful, though, Frank . . .'

'It is indeed, my love,' said Frank, taking a deep breath, 'come on, let's investigate.'

Conversation in the shop stopped as they opened the door, and everyone turned to look at them. Frank cleared his throat and was about to introduce himself, when a crowing voice came from the corner.

'PalmersfarmersPalmersfarmers!'

Young Eddie's vocabulary was small, but he came from a long line of gossips, it was in his blood, and he had naturally absorbed the name which had been travelling round the village all morning.

Mrs Jenkins cuffed him not too gently round the ear. 'Edward! – just you be quiet.' She turned with a broad smile to Peggy, and said 'I am ever so sorry! I don't know where he thinks he got that from.'

'Don't you?' said Mrs Ashbourne wryly. She looked over the top of Old Ellen's untidy head and said as pleasantly as she could manage, 'Mr and Mrs Palmer? Glad you found us. I'm Doris Ashbourne. I'll be with you in a minute.'

'Got Mary York coming in, ain't you?' said Old Ellen.

Mrs Ashbourne had had just about enough of Old Ellen. 'Is there anything you don't know, Ellen Biggs?' she said sharply.

'Keep your hair on, our Doris,' said Old Ellen, 'I'm off then – you can send round the few bits for the Hall.' She stopped and looked at the Palmers standing awkwardly just inside the shop door. 'Not like it used to be when I was cook up there,' she said, looking at them speculatively. 'Times were when the Hall would have fifty pounds' worth of groceries every week. Doris is lucky if it's fifteen pounds now.'

She waved at Eddie, shouting at him as if he was deaf, 'Ta ta, Eddie Jenkins, be a good boy!' and left, banging the door behind her. She struggled down the steps, and stood, undecided, on the pavement for a few seconds, then turned and went along to the gate of Victoria Villa, unhooked the latch, and walked in. Ivy Beasley was waiting for her impatiently, the kettle singing on the hob.

'We shall be in the house, Mary,' said Mrs Ashbourne, 'if I'm wanted. There's no more pensions due out today, and Mrs Jenkins has been in for her benefit. It'll just be the village school turn-out – the big ones have had the day off, so there'll be no school bus.'

Mary York nodded, and slipped out of her sheepskin coat, hanging it on a hook behind the Post Office cubicle door. She was a plain girl, short-sighted and thin, and looked younger than her twenty-six years. She had anchored her hair in a pony-tail with a black elastic band, and wore no visible make-up.

'Don't you worry, Mrs Ashbourne, I shall be fine,' she said, and her smile embraced Peggy and Frank with a pleasant warmth.

Mary liked the look of Peggy, who reminded her of her mother. She's got a nice smile, thought Mary, very friendly. She's well dressed, too, better than my mum – got more idea.

Her examination of Frank was cursory, as he and Peggy began to follow Mrs Ashbourne into the house. She noted his well-cut thinning grey hair and a mouse-coloured gaberdine raincoat. His eyebrows were drawn together in a small frown, but his eyes were kind, and twinkled a bit when he smiled at her. There was a smell, though. She sniffed. Surely not him? He looked so clean.

'We'll make a start, then,' said Mrs Ashbourne, and led the way.

Two doors led out of the shop into the house, one straight into the kitchen from just under the clock, and the other into a passage, a rogues' gallery of family photographs. At the end of the passage was the front door of the house, covered with a thick, dark red curtain.

'Don't use that much,' said Doris, 'just weddings and funerals, I suppose. You might just want to wipe your shoe on the mat, Mr Palmer, I think you could have trodden in something out there – that Robert Bates was goin' too fast this morning.'

Frank meekly cleaned his shoe on the rough bristles of the mat, and caught up with the two women as they went through another door out of the dark passage, Mrs Ashbourne saying 'Mind the step!' just too late. Peggy recovered her balance, and peered into the long gloomy interior.

'What a lovely room!' she said, causing Frank to look at her in surprise. She walked down its length and turned back to look at the long central beam, huge and black, notched and pitted with age, supporting rows of cross beams like the skeleton of a fish.

'There is just this one sitting-room,' said Mrs Ashbourne, 'it's cosy when the fire's going. Me and Jack used to eat in the kitchen mostly.'

'Is your husband . . . er . . . ?' said Peggy.

'Dead,' said Mrs Ashbourne flatly.

Peggy had noticed a photograph standing prominently on top of a bookcase by the fireplace, of a smiling young man, carefully groomed, with plastered-down hair and neatly trimmed doggy moustache over a full, rather feminine mouth.

'Is that your Jack?' she said, and immediately felt she had been too familiar.

'Yes,' said Mrs Ashbourne primly, 'that is the late Mr

Ashbourne. Taken many years ago, before he . . . took badly.'

'He was very handsome,' said Peggy, trying to retrieve approval.

'Handsome is as handsome does,' said Mrs Ashbourne dismissively. 'Do you want to see the kitchen now?'

Peggy and Mrs Ashbourne disappeared back into the passage, but Frank loitered in the sitting-room, trying to register some details. Peggy was a great one for instant enthusiasm, but often she couldn't remember much at all when they got back home.

Two small windows at either end of the long room gave some light, but it was a sombre space, filled with graceless heavy furniture and ornaments not old enough to be antique. He closed his eyes and imagined him and Peggy sitting either side of the big open fireplace, curtains drawn and the wind roaring outside. He put his hand to the back of his neck, where he felt a draught, a real draught, not imagined, and shivered.

'I hope you know what you're doing, Peg,' he said.

'Frank!' shouted Peggy. 'Come and look at this!'

She was standing in a large kitchen, leaning back with her hands on the rail of an elderly, cream-coloured Rayburn cooker which gave off a warmth that was almost visible.

'Isn't it marvellous?' she said.

'I do like a larder myself,' Mrs Ashbourne was saying, and Peggy, who had never had a larder in her life, was agreeing wholeheartedly.

Frank looked round at the plain white walls, unadorned except for a trade calendar and a crooked heart-shaped corn dolly tied with a dusty green ribbon. He didn't much like the liver-red quarry-tiled floor, and looked with growing impatience out of the window where the wind blew tea-towels horizontal on a scrappy washing line.

'We mustn't be too late back, Peggy,' he said.

Mrs Ashbourne took the hint. 'I'll just show you round

upstairs,' she said, 'then we can discuss the business.'

'Now you're talking,' said Frank, and followed the women once more as they climbed the narrow stairs and went from a white-painted bedroom, with heavy white cotton lace covers and thick net curtains, to a tiny bathroom scented with a windowsill full of geraniums, and back on to the low-ceilinged landing.

Peggy looked out of the small window into the garden. 'Lovely daffodils, Mrs Ashbourne,' she said, 'are you a keen gardener?'

'Not me,' said Doris Ashbourne, noticing with relief that the sun had come out again, bringing the garden to life. 'It's more like April than March, isn't it?' she said, and carried on without a pause. 'No, it was him, he was very keen until – well, until he wasn't any more. It's a bit untidy now, but it wouldn't take much to set it straight.'

Much of what, thought Frank, having a sudden, unappealing picture of himself toiling over a spade full of heavy, wet earth. And what is all this about old Jack? Just what was it about this place that did for him? Probably setting that garden straight. If she drops many more hints I shall ask her outright.

'Who's that?' said Peggy, looking down on the bent back of an elderly woman in the neighbouring garden, vigorously wielding a chopper and splitting logs like a man. An old black felt hat covered her iron-grey hair, and her sturdy legs were planted well apart to anchor her firmly for the job in hand.

'That's Ivy Beasley,' said Mrs Ashbourne quickly, 'she's all right when you get to know her.'

The woman straightened up, hand on her back, easing the strain, and turned slowly, as if she sensed the watching eyes. She looked up, and the expression on her face sent a shiver down Peggy's spine.

Frank, noticing, put out his hand and touched her gently. 'All well, Peg?' he said quietly.

'Someone just walked over my grave!' she said, smiling weakly.

'I'll just put the kettle on,' said Mrs Ashbourne, 'and then we can have a chat.'

CHAPTER FOUR

The warmth of the kitchen and a cup of hot, strong tea restored Peggy's equilibrium. She relaxed, and found it easy to talk to Doris Ashbourne, who in her skilful way proceeded to find out more than the Palmers had intended to tell her. Frank, however, was reluctant to bare his soul to a stranger, and steered the conversation back to the shop.

'Well no,' said Doris Ashbourne, 'we didn't know much about business ourselves when we came here, but we learned. The hard way, Jack used to say. Still, there's a lot I can show you, so don't fret about that.'

She got up from the table and took the simmering kettle off the Rayburn, filling the teapot and replacing the purple and yellow striped knitted tea cosy. 'Just let it brew,' she said, patting the bunch of woolly roses on top, 'then we'll have a fill-up.'

We'll take it, Peggy wanted to say, we'll buy it now, tea cosy and all, and the simmering kettle and the big kitchen and the dark, cosy sitting-room, and the white bedroom, and the geraniums and the garden that needs straightening, and the dancing daffodils. Not sure about the neighbour, but we can deal with her when the time comes. Go on, Frank, just say we'll take it.

'We'll need to know a great many things, I'm afraid,

though you have been most helpful already,' said Frank, in his gentlemanly way.

'Ask away,' said Mrs Ashbourne, 'Mary York can stay 'til closing time, so there won't be any hurry.'

After ten minutes more of Frank's sensible questions and Mrs Ashbourne's equally sensible answers, Mary York put her head round the door and asked if Doris could spare a minute to sort out a problem in the Post Office.

Two girls were unclipping hair slides from the cards and trying them on, giggling and dropping the slides on the floor. 'Here, Sandra Roberts,' called Mary, 'you're not to take them off the cards!'

'How're you supposed to know what they look like, then?' said Sandra grumpily, and added something under her breath which Peggy did not catch.

But Mary York heard, and she stalked out from behind the counter, marched over to Sandra Roberts and snatched a hair slide from her hand.

'You can just say you're sorry, miss, or else get out of the shop,' she said, her voice sharp and her face now brilliant scarlet.

Mrs Ashbourne looked up from behind the Post Office window. She shook her head at Mary, and called across, 'Are you buying anything, Sandra? If not, don't waste Mrs York's time. And how many times have I got to tell you not to be cheeky?'

Sandra said nothing, but with her face set and mouth clamped tight shut, she walked away from Mary York over to where Peggy stood by the counter, banged down a red hair-slide, and emptied her purse so that the coins ran in every direction. Peggy put out her hands to catch the money, and scooping it into her cupped hand she put it neatly on the counter in a small pile.

She looked across at the scowling girl, who glared back at her. 'Thank you,' Peggy said, 'Mrs York will give you your change.' The girl's eyes flickered and for a moment

Peggy thought she saw tears. The dark eyes were shiny and liquid, and Peggy felt an unaccountable pang of sympathy.

'You have to watch those two,' said Mary York, not taking her eyes off them until they left the shop, 'there aren't many in this village, but those two are the worst. Poor Mr and Mrs Jones worry ever such a lot about Octavia, going around with that Sandra Roberts, but it is difficult, living in the same village and that.'

'It's not long to closing time,' called Mrs Ashbourne, 'why don't you get off home, Mary, and I'll finish with Mr Palmer here.'

Mary unhooked her coat and tied a scarf neatly round her neck. 'Would you like to have a quick walk round the village, Mrs Palmer, if you're not needed here?' she said kindly.

Peggy, encouraged by Frank and Doris Ashbourne, picked up her handbag, and followed Mary out of the shop.

'It must be strange,' said Mary, as they walked by the twitching curtains of Victoria Villa, 'having your husband home all day, after being so used to him going off every morning and not coming back until teatime.'

She doesn't miss much, thought Peggy.

'That's where I went to school,' Mary said, pointing across the road to a stone building with high windows set in its twin gables. Coloured paper tulips made a bright frieze along the lower edge of the windows, but Peggy could not see into the classroom.

'That's so the children can't see out, no distractions,' said Mary. 'They've gone home now, anyway – you missed the onslaught when you were in the house with Mrs Ashbourne. They always come straight out of school into the shop to buy sweets and crisps and it's all hell let loose for ten minutes.'

' "This building was Erected in 1868," ' read Peggy from a stone tablet high up on the wall of the school, ' "by Charles

William Standing, Lord of the Manor, for the Education of Children in the Faith and Practice of the Church of England." '

'There's always been Standings at Ringford Hall,' said Mary.

They quickened their pace against the cold, and turned across the Green, giving Peggy a clear view over to the river and its fringe of willow trees, and to the tall chestnuts in the park of the Hall. A group of small children played on climbing logs in a fenced-off corner of scrubby grass.

'You can just see the roof of the Hall over there, where that chimney is smoking – they must have a fire in the drawing room,' said Mary, and Peggy wondered at her familiarity with the Standings' domestic arrangements.

But Mary's family had all worked on the estate at one time, when the Standings were the chief employers in the village. In the rambling old stone house, with its lofty rooms and endless corridors, servants had once answered bells that jangled on the kitchen board, the cook had ruled over obedient maids, and the butler had run his household like clockwork. A team of gardeners had kept the lawns and flower beds manicured for the family and their frequent guests.

All that had now come to an end, and everything was reorganised to use as little labour as possible. The silver was no longer cleaned to a fiery sparkle, and dust could be found in unnoticed corners. The croquet lawn had lumpy dandelions and plantains, and the trees in the orchard had long since rambled out of their regimented columns.

But the elegant proportions of the old house survived, the interior kept its gracious atmosphere, and the grounds and their vistas remained wide and spacious. The old village families knew the Hall as they knew their own cottages and back gardens, and its routines were still there in their subconscious. They knew which room had the fire, without thinking.

'We'll just go up to the bridge,' said Mary, taking in the village in a broad sweep of the hand, 'then you can see the church and the vicarage, and come back round by the pub. That'll be it, really – shop, Hall, church and pub – all you need.'

Peggy looked to see if Mary was joking, but her thin face was serious. They walked past the tall vicarage, half-hidden by its forbidding yew hedge. Like the Hall, it had seen grander times. A three-storey house, with bands of gold and grey stone forming patterns on its solid walls, it had sheltered generations of parsons and their families.

'Reverend Collins has lived there for years,' Mary said, 'near retiring, he is. It's an old barn of a house – built for big families. There's a little path from the vicarage to the church called Ladies' Path, made so some old parson's daughters could walk to church without being seen by the rest of the village. Cyril Collins lives mostly in the kitchen and his study. That's a nice room, mind, books all round him and a sort of manly smell of old leather and pipe tobacco.'

This time Mary was laughing, and Peggy smiled. 'The garden looks a bit of a mess,' she said, 'it must be a lot for one man to do.'

'He doesn't bother,' said Mary, 'he just gets it scythed down in the autumn, and that's it.'

They walked on to the old bridge across the river. Peggy leaned on the parapet, smoothed by generations of village elbows, and looked down into the water. It was shallow and fast flowing, and the water so clear that she could see tiny fish darting in and out of weed growing at the edges.

She imagined the river in summer, with small boys in Wellington boots, holding jam jars with string handles, wading in the cool water. Well, she thought, at least it would be possible here.

'It is all very peaceful,' she said to Mary, turning to look back at the village.

'A bit too peaceful for some,' said Mary, 'but if you're used to it you couldn't live anywhere else.'

'Where is Mrs Ashbourne going to live?' said Peggy.

'Up in Macmillan Gardens – there's one of the old people's bungalows free, and it's been promised to Doris. They'll hold on 'til she's sold the shop.'

By the time they had walked back to the pub, and Mary had said she never went in there because her family had always been Baptists, the green and yellow shopping bus had slid slowly along the street and pulled up at the bus shelter.

'There's Fred Mills,' said Mary, 'I'd better give him a hand with his bags. Are you all right now, to find your way back?'

Peggy walked slowly, trying to imagine herself living in Round Ringford. She glanced at the window of Victoria Villa as she passed, and saw a shadowy figure behind the curtain, watching her, unmistakably watching her.

CHAPTER FIVE

It was like this the day I buried Mother, thought Ivy Beasley some weeks later. No blustery wind, just a gentle breeze stirring the willows by the river, and a warmth in the sun. It was a shame, on such a lovely day, to shovel earth on top of someone who had been your companion for so many years. Still, the vicar made a good job of it, gave Mother a decent service and a very nice little talk about her life. Some of it wasn't quite true, but you expect that. Ah well, that was a long time ago.

She shook herself, and moved her lace curtain a fraction to give her a better view of the Green, where the warm sunshine had brought out the village children, rushing about and quarrelling, making and breaking friends, fickle as puppies.

'You would have been pleased, Doris Ashbourne moving out at last,' she said, addressing her long-dead mother, as she often did, without thinking it at all odd.

'You're going barmy, Ivy,' Ellen Biggs had said. But Ivy never took much notice of Old Ellen.

'Them Palmers should be here any minute now, Mother,' said Ivy Beasley, 'Doris's things have been gone round to Macmillan a good hour ago.'

Outside the shop, which was closed, although it was a

Saturday morning, a small reception committee had formed, with several children including William Roberts and Warren Jenkins – eleven-year-old, bullet-headed sons of the village – and of course Sandra and Octavia, and Fred Mills, puffing away at his evil-smelling pipe.

The reception party had seen off Doris Ashbourne, with Warren and William carrying a few plant pots and wheeling the wheelbarrow round to her new home, and Fred Mills tactfully looking the other way when she had taken a last look at the empty house and blown her nose hard in a large white men's handkerchief.

'Are you there, Ivy?' shouted Old Ellen from the pavement. 'I've got those patterns you wanted.' No reply from behind the lace curtain, so Ellen sighed and opened the gate to Victoria Villa.

'You might as well sit down for a minute, I suppose,' said Ivy Beasley, reluctantly inviting Ellen into the front room.

'Don't want to miss the Palmers,' said Ellen, 'still, we can see them from your front window. You can see most things from here, can't you, Ivy?' she added maliciously.

'Looks like them now,' said Ivy Beasley, ignoring the smirking Ellen, and pulling her maroon cardigan well down over her dark flannel skirt, as if girding her loins against some unexpected invasion. 'That's a removals van, or my name's not Beasley,' she said.

'It's never likely to be anything else,' said Old Ellen under her breath, and she stood up to get a better view. 'Well, I'm off outside to see if there's any help needed.'

Ivy Beasley laughed at this hypocrisy. 'What do you think you could do, Ellen Biggs?' she said. 'You don't fool me – you're just nosy.'

Ellen took this in good part, put a pile of old knitting patterns down on Miss Beasley's table, and let herself out of the front door of Victoria Villa just as the furniture van arrived in front of the Post Office and General Stores.

The Palmers' blue car drew up behind the van, and Peggy

and Frank got out and walked round to the foot of the steps up to the shop. Peggy looked at the little group of watchers, and smiled her ready smile. 'Good morning!' she said, and there were one or two muttered responses.

'D'you want any help, miss?' said William Roberts, and got dug in the ribs by Warren Jenkins for his boldness. Distantly related, they looked almost like twins with their closely cropped hair, brilliantly coloured anoraks, and worn jeans.

Frank said, 'No thanks,' and Peggy said, 'We might well need an extra pair of hands, thank you.'

With little ceremony, the Palmers' worldly goods were marshalled and unloaded, and Peggy directed the personal contents of her home into strange rooms, where they looked out of place and forlorn. She had loved the squat little house more and more during the past weeks' visits, loved its thick mullions with ancient dates and initials carved deeply into the soft stone, and the trellis porch with twisted skeins of clematis.

But now, standing on what was so recently Mrs Ashbourne's landing, Peggy felt tearful and dispossessed. This wasn't her home, and she had left Bryony Road looking abandoned and the empty rooms strangely unfamiliar. She came down the narrow stairs and walked through the quiet shop.

'I told you to be extra careful!' Frank, too, was beginning to feel the strain, and glared angrily at an impassive-faced removals man, patient and experienced, hands in the pockets of his brown overalls, looking at an inlaid chess table and waiting for the storm to pass.

'Look – you've scratched the side of it – do you realise how much this table is worth?'

'That'll polish up all right, there's no depth to that scratch.'

Frank turned away, and watched with increasing alarm as his large mahogany wardrobe teetered on the edge of the pavement. It had always been much too large for Bryony Road, let alone an old cottage. But it had been the one thing Frank had salvaged from his mother's home, before the sharks had come in and cleared the lot for a tenner.

'This is a meaty one!' said the removals man, and sat down with his mate on the steps of the shop, mopping his forehead with a duster.

Frank nodded and sat down on a kitchen stool left forlorn on the pavement. He looked up and the small windows stared blankly at him, no curtains softening the black interior. Peg'll soon put that right, he thought, nobody better at making a home. He glanced up to the eaves of the plain little house, where neatly plastered house-martins' nests waited for the new season's arrivals.

They must be fond of it, he thought, to keep coming back.

Frank smoothed his hair and loosened his collar. It was odd, but he had begun to like it all much better now Mrs Ashbourne's furniture had gone. Empty houses usually looked dismal, smaller and dirtier. But as Frank directed operations and saw the rooms lighter and more spacious than he remembered, he had cheered up. That is, until he saw the careless, disfiguring scratch.

The reception party had broken up some while ago, Fred Mills off to the pub, and the two girls drifting up towards Bates's End to see if Octavia could further her pursuit of Robert Bates. William and Warren had obeyed the call of their rumbling stomachs and disappeared up Macmillan Gardens, and the village was quiet, switched off.

Frank thought longingly of Bryony Road, and wished he could shut his eyes and be transported instantly to his chess table, set up with the latest problem, in the sunny window of their sitting-room – and be interrupted by Peggy, calling him for lunch, Saturday bangers and mash . . .

A muddy Land-Rover drove slowly by on the other side of the road, and came to a halt outside the school. Not another spectator, thought Frank, we can do without that, but the door of the vehicle opened and a burly, shock-haired man climbed out. He walked confidently over to the shop, and smiled cheerfully at Frank.

'Morning!' he said. 'Bill Turner's the name – do you need a hand with that?' He pointed at the lumbering wardrobe, beached like a dying whale on the sloping pavement.

The removals man's eyes brightened, and Frank nodded and managed to raise a smile.

'Very kind of you,' he said, 'my name's Frank Palmer, but I expect you know that already.'

Bill Turner laughed. 'Got us all weighed up, I see!' he said, and lifted one end of the wardrobe as if it was an orange box. 'Come on, lads,' he said, 'heave ho!'

'Oops!' said Peggy, coming out of the shop door and nearly crashing into them.

'Hello,' said Bill, 'I'm Bill Turner, at your service.'

'That's nice,' said Peggy, cheering up, and looking at deep-set blue eyes and a warm, open smile, 'pleased to meet you.'

Bill returned to his house in Macmillan Gardens, glad that he would have some news for Joyce. He polished up in his mind the scene on the pavement outside the shop. Mr Palmer was really mad, Joyce, he rehearsed, and all over this funny little table, with a chess board on the top. Then you should have seen the wardrobe – huge, it was, and these two weedy little removals men not having a clue how to get it in the house.

He walked up the narrow path, past the front door with its small square of window, like all their windows, heavily shrouded with layers of curtains, and through the passage round to the back of the house, where he took out his key and let himself into the narrow, cluttered kitchen.

'You're late,' said Joyce, from her seat at the kitchen table.

'Not dressed yet?' Bill said, looking sadly at his wife hunched up over a newspaper spread out on the table, a cup – no saucer – half-full of cold tea by her side.

'Not feeling so good today,' said Joyce, pulling her faded pink dressing-gown closer round her. 'I might get back into bed this afternoon, see if I can get some sleep – I was awake most of the night, what with those Robertses making all that noise, and Jean Jenkins' Eddie screaming his head off for hours.'

'Have a bit of dinner first,' said Bill, and began to tidy the kitchen, emptying breakfast remains into the bin, and stacking dishes on the draining board.

'What's been going on this morning, then?' said Joyce, but Bill had lost heart and just said, 'Not a lot – the Palmers arrived at the shop, and Doris Ashbourne has settled in at number twelve.'

'Thanks very much,' said Joyce, 'a very interesting account.'

She got up from the table and limped out of the room. Bill could hear her switching on the television, and then the cheerful voice of a chat show host filled the house. He sighed, and opened a tin of baked beans, which he tipped into a small chipped saucepan and set on the gas stove to heat up.

Then there was silence again, and Joyce appeared at the kitchen doorway. He looked at her uncombed hair and grey, lined face, and said ritually, 'Would you like to go out this afternoon? I could take you for a run in the van – get a bit of fresh air?'

Joyce had not been out of the house for years, but Bill kept up the fiction that maybe that afternoon she would feel like it, would wash her face and comb her hair, put on some make-up and some of the smart clothes, now a bit out of date, but presentable, that hung neglected in her cupboard upstairs.

She drooped, and shook her head. 'You'll be off out

again, I suppose, with your latest fancy woman, whoever she is. Don't mind me, I'll just stay here and maybe kill myself. I can't think of anything else to do.'

She began to cry, and Bill walked over and put his arm round her shoulders. 'You do talk a lot of nonsense,' he said, 'you know there's no one else but you.' He tried not to notice the stale odour surrounding her, but she pushed him away violently. 'Clear off!' she said. 'Don't you touch me, never, never!' she rushed upstairs, limp forgotten, and banged the bedroom door behind her.

Peggy lay exhausted in her own bed, in a strange white bedroom, with crooked black beams criss-crossing the ceiling and blind, uncurtained windows exposing everything in the room to the quiet, black night sky above a sleeping Round Ringford.

'Frank,' she whispered.

'Yes?'

'Oh, you're not asleep yet,' she said.

'I was just dozing off,' he said, 'what's the matter?'

'Nothing, really, I just wanted to hear your voice.'

'It is very quiet, isn't it?' said Frank.

'And dark,' said Peggy, 'I miss our street lamp. I liked the orange glow – sort of cosy, wasn't it?'

'You've got moonlight instead,' said Frank, pushing the covers back and getting out of bed. He walked on his toes on the cold floor over to the window and looked out. 'Come here, Peg.' He beckoned her over to his side, and put his arm round her warm body in its thin nightdress.

The moon had emerged from behind a cloud and in its sharp, cold light Peggy could see every detail of the school building and the bus shelter, and away in the distance the river flowing silver through the willow trees. The roofs of the Hall were black against the sky, and an owl hooted to its mate up in Bagley Woods.

'Frank! Isn't it wonderful?'

34

'Last in bed's a silly bugger,' said Frank, turning and leaping towards the bed, his thin legs like spiders' under his flapping nightshirt. Peggy, not so lithe, bounced in after him and they lay cuddling up for warmth.

'It was kind of Mrs Ashbourne to come round and wish us well,' Peggy said, 'she must have been feeling a bit lost.'

She buried her face against Frank's shoulder and was quiet for a moment, then said, 'I had half hoped our friendly neighbour might offer us a cup of tea, but I didn't get one sighting – did you?'

'Nope,' said Frank, stroking her back, 'the lesser–spotted Beasley had definitely gone to ground today.'

'You are silly, Frank . . .' Peggy's voice was sleepy, and Frank could feel her relaxing, her head heavy on his shoulder. ' 'Night, Frank,'' she said, 'God bless.'

'Goodnight, Peg,' said Frank, 'God bless,' and hoped the Almighty was listening.

CHAPTER SIX

'If you don't get a move on,' said Jean Jenkins, standing rooted to the kitchen floor, cooking quantities of bacon and eggs for her family in a huge frying pan on the gas stove, 'you'll be late for school again, and your Dad'll wallop you.'

'He'll have to catch me first,' said Warren, grinning at his mother.

'And have you finished your homework? All that time you were down the shop with William yesterday – I should think Mrs Palmer was glad to see the back of you both.'

It was Warren's first year at Tresham Comprehensive, and he had felt very small and young, after being joint cock-of-the-walk with William Roberts at the village school. Once or twice he had managed to miss the bus, and this Monday morning he had that sinking feeling of another school week ahead.

Warren was bright. His teachers told Jean and Foxy that he should do very well, go to university maybe. His father, who – like his father before him – had worked on Standing's estate all his life, shook his head, believing that all Warren cared about was farm machinery and shooting rabbits, and the problems of farming that were always the same, and yet always different from season to season.

'Mr Richard says I can help with the orphan lambs –
they've got more than usual this year, ' said Warren.

'When you've done your homework,' said his mother,
'maybe you can.'

'You going down the shop this morning, Mother?' said
Warren's father, sitting down at the table and gratefully
gulping his hot, sweet tea. He was a short, stocky man
whose name was Ernest, but for as long as he could
remember he had been called Foxy. The top of his sandy-
red head just came up to his wife's shoulders, and his
features were sharp and dog-like.

'Very likely, Foxy,' said Jean, 'most people will, I don't
doubt, just to have a look.'

'She's nice, that Mrs Palmer,' said Warren, feeling the
pound coin safely hidden in his jacket pocket. 'Me and
William helped them a lot yesterday, couldn't have done
without us, Mrs Palmer said.'

'Get going!' said his mother. 'Now! And don't you hang
about waiting for that William Roberts.'

'PalmersfarmersPalmersfarmers,' sang young Edward
from his little chair in the corner. He waved his spoon about
gaily, scattering drops of golden yolk over the floor, and
laughing with delight as they were gratefully licked up by
the waiting terrier.

'Just you eat your egg, my duck,' said Jean Jenkins, 'an'
you'll grow to be a big strong boy like Warren.'

'Time those girls were up,' said Foxy. He was proud of
his family, and especially of the twins, Gemma and Amy,
who were eight and still at the village school. They lived a
self-contained, private life, content with each other's
company, communicating without needing to speak, and
not caring about friends. Six-year-old Mark, still in his
pyjamas, was sitting at the table laboriously reading the
back of the cornflake packet. 'He's my quiet one,' his
mother had said many times, and Mark smiled his secret
smile, biding his time.

'Is that the girls now?' said Jean Jenkins. But Foxy went to the front door, and was followed back by an attractive blonde postwoman, smart and businesslike in her smooth dark blue uniform.

She poured herself a cup of tea from the pot on the table, as she did every morning, and sat down, perching on the edge of a kitchen chair.

'Go on, then, Maureen,' said Jean Jenkins, smiling.

'Go on what?' said Maureen.

'Tell about the Palmers,' said Jean.

Maureen paused just long enough for dramatic effect, then said, 'Well, I thought they'd be in a bit of a flap when me and Margaret got there first thing. And Brian, of course, he rushed in and out in his usual hurry with the letters. But Mr Palmer didn't fuss, just seemed to take it all in.'

'What about her?' Jean Jenkins refilled the teapot from the electric kettle on the draining board.

'She pecked about a bit,' said Maureen, 'a bit over-excited, I think, but there wasn't much for her to do.' She sipped her tea, and held both hands round her warm mug.

'Must be funny, without Doris Ashbourne,' said Jean Jenkins.

'Very peculiar,' said Maureen, 'still, they seem eager to please, so I expect they'll do.'

'I'll be down there later,' said Jean Jenkins, 'I hope she's got some more stuff in now – Doris had run the place down a bit. D'you want another cup?'

Maureen got up from the table and brought the mug over to the sink, rinsing it and turning it upside down on the wire drainer. 'Nope, I'd better be on my way, thanks,' she said. 'There's a letter for Joyce Turner this morning – God knows who'd want to write to her . . . still, I shouldn't say nothing about that, should I?'

'No use saying anything,' said Jean Jenkins, 'all the saying's been done.'

★

The white bedroom above the shop was a muddle of clothes and shoes, not yet put away in their final resting places. Frank had been dressed for hours, wearing a neat brown tweed jacket and well-pressed grey flannel trousers. He unearthed his hairbrush from a pile of underwear, and brushed his already neat hair in front of the long wardrobe looking-glass.

'I'm shaking all over,' said Peggy, sitting at her dressing-table and holding a pink lipstick in her hand. 'How am I ever going to put this on straight?'

'Peggy, love . . .' said Frank, coming over to stand behind her, his hands firm on her shoulders.

'Well, today's the day – they'll all be in, and it will be just you and me against the massed villagers of Round Ringford.'

'You and me and Mr Geoffrey White, from head-quarters,' said Frank.

'Oh yes, Mr Geoffrey White,' said Peggy, 'I'd forgotten about him. Anyway, I'm looking forward to it really, just hope we'll be up to it.'

Frank didn't answer, but walked over to the bedroom window and looked down on to the road outside. Squeals and yells were coming from the bus shelter, where a group of uniformed schoolchildren waited for the bus. The sun was coming out, lifting the mist from the Green, and catching the shorn, sandy head of Warren Jenkins as he scuffed his way along to join his friends.

'There's that Roberts girl,' Frank said, 'is it Sandra? Sister of William, I think. Skirt's so short you can see her knickers.'

'You shouldn't be looking,' said Peggy, 'you can get arrested for that.'

Frank patted her on the shoulder. 'That's my girl,' he said, and clattered off down the uncarpeted stairs to look out for the man from the Post Office. Unlike Peggy, he

39

wasn't nervous or excited, just determined to do what was asked of him to the best of his ability.

At nine o'clock exactly, Mr Geoffrey White walked into Round Ringford Post Office and General Stores with a Monday morning face and a bulging briefcase in his hand.

'Mr and Mrs Palmer?' he said. 'I am here to help you for your first week working with our organisation – any problems arising from the day-to-day transactions can be sorted out, and I can fill you in on the informational resources of our various departments which will be there to back you up.'

Oh dear, thought Peggy, but Frank shook Mr White by the hand, and opened up the Post Office cubicle, saying, 'How about a cup of tea for Mr White, Peggy?'

'Are you Open or Closed, then?' said a loud rasping voice. Her first customer was her neighbour, Miss Beasley, who stood by the door, twisting the Open/Closed sign this way and that in her grey-gloved hands.

'Oh, sorry, Miss Beasley,' said Peggy, with a nervous smile, 'what with Mr White being here on the dot I quite forgot to turn the sign.'

'Have to get used to doing more than one thing at once,' said Ivy Beasley, 'our Doris was a genius at it. Box of matches, please.'

'Yes, of course,' said Peggy, looking up and down the shelves behind the counter where cigarettes and tobacco were stacked. Matches should be there somewhere, surely?

'In the drawer underneath,' said Miss Beasley, drumming her knitted fingers on the counter.

Peggy opened the drawers one after another, finally finding matches stacked in packets of six boxes, with a few loose ones rattling about next to bundles of string and tiny cartons of drawing pins.

'It's always the last one you open, isn't it?' she said pleasantly to Miss Beasley. 'Is it just the one box?'

'Just the one,' mimicked Ivy Beasley, 'I haven't got money to burn.'

Peggy laughed. 'That's very good, Miss Beasley,' she said. 'Will there be anything else?' Good God, she thought, I sound like Mr Grub the Grocer.

'That's all,' said Miss Beasley, unsmiling, and put the exact money down on the counter. 'Your kettle's boiling its head off,' she said, as the shrill whistle ascended the scale in a deafening crescendo. 'That's another thing for you to attend to,' she added, with a shadow of a smile. 'Good morning!'

And good morning to you too, muttered Peggy as she put the coins in the till.

Hard on Miss Beasley's heels came a brisk, smartly dressed woman, exuding confidence and professional friendliness. She smiled warmly at Peggy and introduced herself.

'My name is Sheila Pearson,' she said, addressing the entire shop as if at a meeting, 'and I am your District Councillor. I live at Casa Pera – and shall be very happy to help in any difficulties you may encounter in the course of your settling down in our community.'

'Thank you – what can I get you?' said Peggy, learning fast.

'Nothing just now,' said Sheila Pearson, 'I wonder if I could just tackle you on a very important Ringford matter?'

Peggy saw Frank look across and shake his head at her.

'Perhaps you and your husband would like to come round for a drink and we could chat some more?' continued Mrs Pearson. Frank shook his head more vigorously.

'What important Ringford matter?' said Peggy, remembering Mrs Ashbourne's warning – never say yes to anybody until they've finished explaining.

'The houses,' said Sheila Pearson, 'we have a proposed housing development, up on Barnett's Home Close, and I think it is fair to say the village is divided down the middle.'

'No it's not,' said Old Ellen, creeping in behind Sheila

41

Pearson, somehow managing to open the door so slowly that the bell didn't ring again.

'How did you do that?' said Peggy, wonderingly. 'Practice,' said Old Ellen, 'you don't always want folks to know you've arrived.'

'As I was saying, Mrs Palmer,' said Sheila Pearson, glaring at Old Ellen, 'there is considerable controversy on this proposal, and I would really like to explain it fully to you both, if you have time – shall we say this evening? Half past seven?'

'Just wants to get you on 'er side,' said Old Ellen, walking behind the display unit and picking up a packet of detergent. 'Don't take all day, then, Mrs Councillor Pearson,' she said, 'I've got washing to do back 'ome.'

Mrs Pearson shrugged and smiled at Peggy. 'Can I expect you then?' she said.

'I'm awfully sorry,' said Peggy quickly, 'but we shall be much too tired after our first day. It is kind of you, though, and perhaps another time . . .'

'If it's not too much trouble,' said Old Ellen, 'do you think I could have two slices of ham?'

'Mrs Biggs,' said Sheila Pearson, nettled, 'the new houses are a very important issue.'

'All be the same when we're dead and gone,' said Ellen, 'no need to get so steamed up.' She made a face at Sheila's retreating back.

'You getting that ham or not?' she said to Peggy. 'If I don't get back soon to that washing, half the day'll be gone and no doubt the sun as well.'

'I'm sorry,' said Peggy, 'it won't take a minute. I do apologise.'

Old Ellen was overcome. Nobody had apologised to her for many a long year, and it bowled her over. For once she was speechless, and was halfway to the door before she remembered her detergent. Peggy helped her put the packet in her shopping bag, and opened the door for her.

'There's no need for all that,' Ellen said grumpily, 'Ringford's not used to it. Best you remember that. Has Ivy been in?' she added. 'Better not try soft-soaping her – she'll gobble you up.'

Peggy waited until the door closed behind Old Ellen, looked across at Frank and began to laugh.

Mr White, however, did not laugh. 'She's right, you know,' he said, 'country people don't like a lot of fuss. They can make your life a misery if you get off on the wrong foot. I've seen it on my rounds, many a time.'

CHAPTER SEVEN

I shall have to go next door again, Mother, said Ivy Beasley to her empty kitchen. I forgot to get chocolate Digestives for when Robert comes in this afternoon. It was that Palmer woman dithering about, drove it right out of my head.

She looked out of the kitchen window at her sunny garden stretching away with its rows of spring cabbage and healthy young broad beans. She had fixed the row of sticks for her runners, and the currant bushes and apple trees were showing signs of good things to come.

I might ask Robert to give a hand in the garden this year, Mother, all this chopping and digging and weeding is getting a bit much for me. And that weedy Frank Palmer ain't going to be any use to anybody.

'Get off!' she shouted and banged on the window. A crowd of swearing sparrows flew off her neatly hoed vegetable beds, and she sighed. It's a lot to do, Mother, she said, and me not getting any younger.

It's no good feeling sorry for yourself, Ivy, said her mother's voice inside her head. Better get on with some work, do something useful.

Ivy Beasley opened the larder door, walked into the cool whitewashed interior and took out the big enamel flour bin, and placed it on her kitchen table. I'll make some rock buns, she thought, Robert always used to like them when he was a tiddler. Then I shan't have to go to the shop again today.

She took a dull metal tablespoon out of the kitchen drawer, and began to heap flour into the mixing bowl that had belonged to her grandmother. You should be glad I'm making rock buns for him, Mother – it was his grannie gave you the recipe, you said.

Without weighing or measuring any of the ingredients, Ivy Beasley swiftly mixed them to the right consistency and spooned dollops on to a baking tray, which she slid into the range oven with a practised flick.

The Bateses and the Beasleys had been good friends in her mother's time. Grannie Bates and Ivy's mother had been founder members of the Women's Institute in the village, and prided themselves on upholding the traditions of jam and Jerusalem. We could do with a few more like them now, thought Ivy, it was them sort that kept this country going.

You and Grannie Bates, Mother, she said, walking through to her empty sitting-room at the front of the house and taking up her knitting from her seat by the window, you are much missed in this village.

She looked over to the school and watched the children, fuelled by their lunch and rushing about apparently pointlessly in all directions in the playground. Seems only yesterday that Robert was playing out there, she thought, and now him a young man.

Robert Bates' mother had had a hard time when he was born, and Ivy Beasley had helped out for several weeks, terrified at first of handling a tiny baby, but growing confident and loving, and finally breaking her heart when she wasn't needed any more. But Robert the toddler had tottered towards her when others, wary of her stern expression, had hung back; and later, Robert the shabby little schoolboy with bitten fingernails had regularly called in to see her, certain of a rock bun and a mug of milk.

Now it was part of Robert's routine – cup of tea and a chat with Auntie Ivy on Monday afternoons. He missed a few at harvest time, and when he ploughed on into the night, the tractor's lights sending other-worldly beams across the field. But Ivy knew the farming year, and did not hold it against him.

'Lovely smell of cooking, Auntie!' Robert's cheerful voice later that afternoon sent shock waves through Ivy Beasley's silent house.

'Sit yourself down, Robert,' she said. 'Haven't baked rock buns for a good while – but here you are, see if I haven't forgotten how.'

Robert sat by the range fire and picked currants out of the buns like a small boy. 'You haven't lost your touch, Auntie,' he said. Ivy Beasley bent to put another log on the fire, hiding her pleasure from Robert. It wouldn't do to let him see how fond she was of him – that's the way to heartache, Mother.

'Been in next door yet?' said Robert, knowing what was foremost in Ringford gossip that day.

'This morning,' said Ivy Beasley, 'I went for a box of matches. They had the Post Office man there – that Geoffrey White – I used to know his sister over at Bagley.'

'What do you think of the Palmers?' said Robert, feeding the right question.

'Not much, so far,' said Ivy, 'like fish out of water, they are, with their townie talk and forward ways. Calling over the fence to me already, she was.'

'Auntie!' said Robert, helping himself to another rock bun. 'That's not giving them much of a chance! Weren't you in there first thing with a bunch of flowers, you being neighbours?'

'Don't you be cheeky, my lad,' said Ivy Beasley, 'there'll be no bunches of flowers from me. Folk have to prove their worth in Ringford, it's always been like that, then you don't make no mistakes.'

If you hadn't been so cautious about making mistakes, thought Robert, you might not be a lonely old Ringford spinster now. He brushed the cake crumbs from his lap and walked over to the window. 'School bus is back,' he said, 'I'll just wait until those girls have gone into the shop, then I'll make my escape.'

'After you, are they?' said Ivy Beasley with a crooked smile. 'They'll get more than they bargain for one of these days,' she added, 'pair of hussies.'

Robert watched Sandra Roberts and Octavia Jones wiggle their way to the shop and disappear up the steps, then he pecked Ivy Beasley on the cheek and walked noisily out of the house, waving to her at the window as he jumped on to his tractor and drove off down the street at speed.

There, thought Ivy Beasley, and I forgot to ask him about doing a bit in the garden. It'll do next Monday, said the voice in her head, and Ivy Beasley took up her knitting again as her house settled back into silence.

'Beats me,' said Jean Jenkins to Peggy, as she fought her way through the bus children quarrelling over the racks of sweets, 'what Robert Bates sees in old Poison Ivy – he goes in there every week, you know, never misses.'

'Must be some attraction not yet revealed to me,' said Peggy wryly, 'I can't say we've become instant friends. Robert seems a nice lad, though, he was in here earlier for some groceries for his mother.'

'Just you put that back!' shouted Mrs Jenkins across the heads of the chattering, grabbing children milling about in the shop. 'William Roberts! If you want that chocolate, pay for it – if not, put it back at once!'

She turned to Peggy. 'Hope you don't mind – thing is, you've got to catch 'em at it.'

Peggy shook her head, desperately trying to add up four separate small white paper bags full of pocket money sweets for Gemma and Amy, Mark and Eddie, all shepherded up to the counter by their mother to pay separately with handfuls of warm, damp coins.

'Mind your own business, fatty,' muttered William, but not quietly enough. Mrs Jenkins, moving fast, grabbed him by his collar and frogmarched him swiftly down the steps and on to the pavement, where she told him exactly what she thought of him.

'You are a twit,' said Warren Jenkins, as he caught up with his friend on the way home, 'she's got this fantastic hearing – better'n a rabbit, my dad says.'

'Look, bet you can't hit a moving target,' said William, aiming an idle peanut at Sheila Pearson's car passing by, 'bet she's goin' to the shop – all the nosy-parkers are there today.'

'My mum says Mrs Pearson is all right,' said Warren.

'My mum says she ought to mind her own business, ferreting about making trouble over them new houses,' said William.

'Mum says we all ought to back her up, get some new blood in the village,' said Warren.

'Blood?' said William, with an exaggerated expression of disgust. 'New blood! I didn't know she was a vampire – bloody old Mrs Dracula, *bloody old Mrs Dracula*!' He ran on ahead of Warren and disappeared into his broken-down gateway. The last Warren heard of William was a yell, as his father fetched him one as a matter of course.

Warren Jenkins shrugged. William was his best friend, but he could be very difficult at times. Best to ignore him, Mum said. Warren approached his own house, glanced at the closed curtains of the Turner windows next door and stuck his tongue out at them ritually. Then he waited for his mother to catch him up and let him in for his tea.

Sheila Pearson drew up outside the shop, as William had predicted, and consulted her list. Butter, brown sugar, eggs and a packet of white envelopes. She should have remembered them this morning, but she'd had a long chat with a friend on the Planning Committee, and had other things on her mind.

A big silver car had also drawn up and a tall, willowy woman, attractive in a pallid sort of way, and wearing a plain dark green wool dress, arrived at the foot of the steps up to the shop at the same time as Sheila.

'After you, Mrs Standing . . . Susan . . .' said Sheila Pearson.

'Thank you, Mrs Pearson,' said Susan Standing, allowing Sheila to open the door for her, 'I just have to buy a stamp. It is the new people's first day, isn't it?'

The last of the schoolchildren dawdled out of the shop, leaving the door open. Sandra and Octavia were still there, hovering round by the section of make-up and nail polishes, and Peggy – duly warned – tried to keep one eye on them, whilst counting up the pile of coppers the last child had dumped on the counter.

'A first-class stamp,' said Susan Standing to Frank, who was still closeted with Mr White in the cubicle.

'Afternoon, Mrs Standing,' said Mr White, practically touching his forelock, 'lovely day it's been?'

'Er, no,' said Susan, ignoring him completely, and continuing to address Frank, who had torn off the stamp and pushed it through to her under the cubicle window. 'No, I think I'll have a second-class stamp instead,' she said, pushing the first one back towards Frank. A draught caught it, and took it floating to the floor.

'I'll pick it up,' said Mr White, 'don't you worry, Mrs Standing.'

'Well, good,' said Frank, tired after the long day, and fed up with all this, 'thank you, Geoffrey. Are you sure you've made up your mind, now, Mrs Standish?'

'Standing,' said Susan icily, 'and no, I don't think I shall need a stamp after all. Oh, and tell your wife – er, Mrs Palmer, is it? – that Mrs Ashbourne was under weight on the apples in last week's order. We shall expect an adjustment.'

Frank frowned. 'My wife,' he said grimly, 'is over there, at the counter, so you can tell her yourself. Good afternoon.' He slammed the heavy stamp book shut, and turned away to pick up his mug of tea, now stone cold.

The silence in the shop was electric. Sandra and Octavia stopped giggling, and Sheila Pearson stood rooted to the spot, staring fixedly at a display of aftershave. Peggy, not quite sure what was going on, smiled encouragingly at Mrs Standing. Susan Standing, however, wife of the hereditary Lord of the Manor, looked to neither right nor left, and swept out of the open door without a word.

'Oh dear,' said Sheila Pearson, 'I think you've offended her. What a shame – such a sweet person.'

'No, she's not,' said Sandra, blurting it out with a very red face. 'She thinks she owns Ringford and everybody knows they ain't got two pennies to rub together.'

'Sandra Roberts!' said Sheila Pearson, horror-struck. 'Don't let me hear you speak like that again, or I shall be obliged to complain to your parents!'

'Much good that'll do you,' said Sandra. 'Just thought Mrs Palmer should know, that's all.'

'Creep,' whispered Octavia, and slipped a small bottle of scarlet nail polish into her school bag, under cover of Sandra beside her. She gave Sandra a shove, and they left the shop without going anywhere near the counter.

'You should watch those two,' said Sheila, 'they have a reputation for being light-fingered, you know.'

'What can I do for you, Mrs Pearson?' said Peggy, shifting from one aching foot to the other. She glanced at the plain-faced clock and was relieved to see it approaching half past five. Two more minutes and she could shut the door, get rid of Mr Geoffrey White – who already had his coat and hat on – and sit down with Frank in the kitchen for a post mortem.

'Just these few things, please, and I wonder if you have a minute now the shop is empty to allow me to explain the new houses issue?'

'Not a chance,' said Frank, coming out of his cubicle and rubbing his eyes. He aimed his most charming smile at Sheila Pearson, and said, 'I am sure you understand, my dear.'

'Of course,' said Sheila, 'I do get carried away – my David says I am far too impulsive. Do come and have a drink – Friday? – then we can chat at our leisure.'

Well, we can't refuse her twice in one day, thought Peggy. 'That would be very nice,' she said, 'we shall look forward to it.'

'If it hadn't been for that Susan Standish – ' said Frank, sitting with Peggy at their kitchen table and drinking, at last, a hot cup of tea. The warmth of the day had gone, a reminder that it was not summer yet, and Peggy was glad of the Rayburn's heat.

'Standing,' said Peggy, 'Susan and Mr Richard Standing, don't you remember?'

'Standing, then,' said Frank, 'if it hadn't been for her and her lousy stamp I was quite enjoying the job. Old Geoffrey White is a good chap, knows his stuff. But then that silly woman came in, treating us like servants and patronising everybody in sight.'

Peggy said nothing. She was so tired that she thought she would never get up from the table again. The day was a kaleidoscope of faces and voices, and snatches of disconnected conversation floated in and out of her mind until she felt quite dizzy.

'Mrs Pearson wants us to go for a drink on Friday,' she said, when she could think straight again, 'to talk about the houses.'

'I know,' said Frank, 'I was there, Peggy love.'

'Oh yes,' said Peggy. 'I don't really know how much you can hear in that cubicle.'

'If old George is not whispering in my ear, I can hear almost everything. Not what those girls were saying, mind you, hiding behind the displays, but then they don't mean us to hear.'

'Why did Mrs Standing sweep out like that?' said Peggy, helping herself to a shortbread biscuit from a packet on the table.

'I suppose she thought I was rude to her,' said Frank, 'but then, she was rude to me.' Their conversation was interrupted by a sudden jangling of the shop bell.

'Didn't you lock . . . ?'

'I thought you'd done it,' said Peggy.

'Anybody there?' called a deep voice. Frank scowled at Peggy, and muttered, 'Go away, whoever you are,' under his breath. But Peggy frowned and shook her head at him, so he sighed and went through to the shop.

Peggy heard him say, 'Hello Bill! You caught us on the hop – we thought we'd locked up.'

'Sorry! It doesn't matter, it'll do tomorrow,' said Bill Turner.

Peggy joined them in the shop, and – remembering Doris Ashbourne – insisted on serving him. She looked up at this tall, burly man, with his vivid blue eyes and incongruously long fair lashes, and smiled. He smiled back, and his teeth were uneven but very white. He ran a dirty hand through his hair, and said, 'Sorry, I am a bit mucky, but I've come in straight from work. Could I have a few rashers please, enough for a quick supper for me and Joyce? Thanks very much – as a matter of fact she'll give me hell if I go back without it.'

'Would you like a cup of tea – we're just having one,' said Peggy.

That's carrying customer service a bit far, thought Frank, but he remembered Bill's readiness to help on Saturday, and said, 'Come on in, we could do with a bit of livening up!'

Bill followed them into the kitchen, ducking under the low beam where Peggy had hung some dried flowers, making even less headroom. He looked round at the red-painted chairs, at Peggy's blue and white china arranged on the dresser shelves, and the prints of brightly coloured stylised flowers on the walls, and he smiled. ' 'S'nice in here,' he said, thinking how tired Mrs Palmer looked, but pretty in her pale blue check overall, 'it doesn't look nearly as dark as in Doris's day.'

'Probably the bare windows,' said Peggy, 'I haven't got curtains to fit yet, and it's a bit of a mess, but all in good time.'

'What's all this about new houses?' Frank said. 'We have been nobbled already by Mrs . . . Pearson, is it?'

'Ah, yes, Councillor Mrs Pearson,' said Bill. 'Some don't like her, but she works hard for the village and her heart's in the right place. She's very keen on John Barnett building a few new houses up at Walnut Farm.'

'She talks like a politician,' said Frank.

'Only when she's on her high horse,' said Bill. 'She tried hard to help my Joyce, but it did no good.' He finished his tea and got up to go. He looked back wistfully into the homely kitchen. 'Don't forget,' he said, 'if there's anything I can do, just let me know.'

Frank locked the shop door behind him, pulled down the window blinds, turned off all the lights and returned to the kitchen. 'Good bloke, that,' he said.

'Not very happy, though,' said Peggy, taking the tea things over to the sink to wash up. 'Now Frank, are you sure you've locked the Post Office securely, and turned on the alarm?'

'Yes, ma'am,' said Frank, with a smart salute.

CHAPTER EIGHT

Spring became early summer, and the hedgerows were full of pink campion and cranesbill, and tiny blue speedwell flowers brightening up the lush green grass. Peggy bought a book on wild flowers, so that she could identify them when she and Frank went for evening walks along the deserted railway track and the old gated road.

'I think it's a Lesser Hawkbit,' said Peggy, turning pages.

'Looks like a dandelion to me,' said Frank.

A week of brilliant sunshine had escalated sales of ice-cream and emptied the cabinet, and before Frank could get to the wholesaler Peggy had apologised so many times that she nearly burst into tears when Susan Standing came in and snubbed her with a dismissive 'It's not very nice anyway.'

'Take no notice of her,' said Doreen Price, waiting to be served and watching Peggy's expression. Doreen had come into the shop most days since the Palmers arrived, and the more Peggy saw of her the more she liked her. She was everybody's idea of a farmer's wife, round bodied and rosy cheeked. Her habitual bluntness disguised a shy wariness of strangers, but in Peggy's case this was soon overcome once she'd decided Peggy was a friend.

'Sometimes I think I'll never get it right,' said Peggy, 'there's so much to remember.'

'Do you fancy a night out to cheer you up?' said Doreen tentatively. Peggy looked at her doubtfully, and Doreen laughed. 'Don't get excited,' she said, 'I mean the W.I. meeting next week. Mind you, with Madame Standing in the President's chair you may not want to come.'

'I'll think about it, Doreen,' said Peggy, 'it's just that we have to spend most evenings doing the books and pricing stock and a hundred and one other things . . .'

And I don't want to leave Frank for a whole evening to cope on his own, she thought, not that he isn't more than capable. But she'd found him only last week sitting dejectedly with his head in his hands and the Coventry evening paper in front of him. There had been a story about Maddox's winning a big order from Japan on the front page.

'No,' said Doreen, 'the meeting's in the afternoon. I'll just drop in and see if you can get away.'

Next morning, the sun was undimmed, and burst in on Peggy when Frank drew the curtains. She awoke painfully, with a throbbing headache. In spite of taking a couple of aspirin, she felt no better and sat at the kitchen table unable to eat breakfast, holding her hand to one side of her head, and covering her eyes. When she got up and rushed upstairs to be sick, Frank knew that something was wrong.

'Better get the doc,' he said, when she reappeared, looking pale and drawn.

'He comes to Miss Beasley's today,' said Peggy, 'I could see him there, save a journey into Bagley. I'm not sure I could drive, anyway – can't see properly.'

Miss Beasley's house became the surgery once a week in Ringford. Dr Russell, senior partner in the long-established general practice in Bagley, drove through the narrow lanes at twenty miles an hour in his sleek Rover, and set up shop in Ivy's front parlour. She switched on a one-bar electric fire in winter, and in summer put a small vase of flowers on the oak drop-leaf table where Dr Russell sat to interview

Ringford patients one by one, often knowing what they were going to say before they said it.

'If you don't mind the whole village knowing what's wrong with you,' said Frank.

'The way I feel,' said Peggy, 'I wouldn't mind the whole county knowing that I've got a terrible pain in my head and feel as if I shall go on throwing up all morning.'

'Right, then that's it,' said Frank. 'Half past ten, you can be first in the queue, and then back here and straight to bed. I can cope perfectly well in the shop – you know me, Mr Grub the Grocer, always at your service.'

Peggy managed a weak smile, and patted Frank's hand. 'I'm sure it's nothing much,' she said, 'I'll be fine by this afternoon, but you could give Mary York a ring, see if she's free.'

Peggy wasn't first in the queue, in spite of being at the front door of Victoria Villa on the dot of half past ten. Old Ellen had made it five minutes earlier, and sat in a brownish heap on Ivy Beasley's kitchen chair. Seeing the doctor was a serious matter, and Ellen dressed sombrely, as was appropriate.

The kitchen had become the waiting room, and it swiftly filled up. Mrs Jenkins was there with Eddie, not at all his usual jovial self, and Fred Mills limped in – a very exaggerated limp today – aided by his stick.

Peggy sat in the corner on a piano stool, propping herself up against Miss Beasley's larder door, wondering how to stop herself being sick again. The front door opened, and Peggy heard Miss Beasley's voice, unusually pleasant in tone, welcoming Dr Russell. 'Good morning, Ivy,' said her old friend, 'how are we today? Got a kitchenful, have we?'

Ivy Beasley poked her head into the kitchen, and said, 'Ellen Biggs, you're first.'

Ellen struggled to her feet with difficulty. 'Hurry up, Ellen,' said Miss Beasley, 'Doctor hasn't got all day.' Ellen disappeared, and the kitchen went quiet. 'Shush! Be quiet, my duck,' said Jean Jenkins to Eddie, who was grizzling to himself. Eddie made an irritable grab at a cactus plant, placed exactly in the centre of Miss Beasley's small, oilcloth-covered kitchen table, pricked himself, and buried his face in silent grief in his mother's ample bosom.

Then Peggy understood why silence had fallen. 'It's me knees, Doctor,' she heard Ellen say quite clearly, and then Dr Russell's deep voice. 'Still got some pills left, Ellen?' It's not right, she thought, we shouldn't be listening, and then a great wave of nausea swept over her and she couldn't think of anything else.

A shaft of sunlight penetrated a gap in the net curtains and shone like torture into her eyes, and she covered them with her hands. She heard the door open, and thought it must be her turn. But when she looked up, it was Bill Turner looking round for a seat.

'Morning, Peggy,' he said, and took the spare chair beside her.

'Hello, Bill,' she said in a small, strangled voice, thinking that she really would be sick if Old Ellen didn't get a move on.

'You look terrible,' he said, peering anxiously into her face.

'Thanks,' she said.

'No, seriously,' he said, 'shall I get you a glass of water or something?'

'I'll be all right,' she said, 'if Ellen Biggs doesn't take too long. Must be a stomach bug, I think.'

The door opened again, and once more the order 'Next please!' rasped around the kitchen.

'Good morning,' said Dr Russell, well briefed by Miss Beasley, 'it's Mrs Palmer, isn't it?'

Peggy clutched her stomach and explained her symptoms. 'Do you want me to take anything off?' she said, and even *in extremis* wondered how that would go down with the listeners in the kitchen.

'No, no,' said Dr Russell, 'clear case of migraine, my dear. Been doing too much?'

He began writing a prescription, and Peggy swallowed hard, fighting a strong urge to be sick. 'I thought migraine was just a headache,' she said.

'Vomiting, impaired vision, dizziness, pins and needles, and more,' he said, smiling at her as if giving her good news.

'I've never had it before,' she said.

'Can strike at any time – usually times of stress, so take it easy, please. These tablets may help – but a darkened room and sleep is the best I can advise.'

Peggy stood up and grabbed the side of the table. Dr Russell looked at her in alarm. 'Can you manage, Mrs Palmer?' he said, rising to his feet.

Peggy nodded and made unsteadily for the door. 'Goodbye, Doctor,' she said lightheadedly, 'I shall be fine.' But as she got to Ivy Beasley's front step the bright sunshine blinded her and she felt the ground slipping away from under her feet.

'Never seen Bill Turner move s'fast,' said Jean Jenkins to Foxy as they sat having their dinner.

'He's a very fit man,' said Foxy, 'what was wrong with her, anyway?'

'Migraine, Doctor told her,' said Jean, clearing away the remains of liver and bacon, and setting a bowl of apple and custard in front of Foxy. He had demolished it before she sat down with her own, and he turned to Eddie, wrapped in a blanket and asleep in his pushchair in the corner.

'Just a little bug, Dr Russell said,' Jean Jenkins reassured her husband, 'once Mrs Pearson gets here with the medicine, he'll be on the mend.'

It was one of Sheila Pearson's unsung services for the village to collect medicines from the chemist in Bagley and deliver them round to people who couldn't get into town for themselves.

'What did Bill do, then?' said Foxy, waiting while Jean finished her pudding before reminding her about his cup of tea.

'He picked her up, lock, stock and barrel. She's no lightweight, but it was no more'n a newborn lamb to him. He just carried her straight into the shop, and when I went in after we'd seen Dr Russell, that Mary York were behind the counter and no sign of the Palmers.'

'Just as well Bill was there,' said Foxy, 'suppose he was after Joyce's pills.'

'She's hooked on them, if you ask me,' said Jean Jenkins.

'Better get back, still a lot of grass to get in,' said Foxy, draining his teacup and picking up his old kitbag. He looked down at the sleeping Edward, and gently touched his forehead. 'Feels a bit feverish,' he said, 'keep an eye on him, gel.'

'You'll be late, I expect,' said Jean, 'what with this good weather, and Mr Richard being up London for the week.'

'I might be back at teatime for a minute or two,' said Foxy, his big hand on his son's silky, fair hair, 'just to check up on Eddie here.'

'You might just look in at the shop,' said Jean, 'see how she is.'

No sunlight lifted the gloomy atmosphere next door in the Turners' house. Bill had changed the sheets on Joyce's bed, and put a pile of her grubby clothes into the washing machine. 'You'd never put clean things on, Joycey, if I didn't put them in the wash,' he said good-humouredly to his listless wife.

He had cleaned through the dimly lit house and dusted every inch of furniture and ornament. It was a kind of undeclared war between them, Joyce making as much mess and muddle as she could, and Bill clearing it up until no sign of her slatternly ways was visible – for a short while, anyway.

'If I don't keep up standards,' he had said to Tom Price, Doreen's husband and Chairman of the Parish Council, the only person in Ringford Bill confided his troubles to, 'we shall be finished. I know it. I dread what would happen to her.' Tom had no solutions for him, but at least provided the comfort of a listening ear.

'Ivy came in this morning,' said Joyce, her voice low and cunning.

'Oh yes,' said Bill, knowing what was coming.

'Said you played the hero in the surgery, rescued the damsel in distress.'

'Don't be daft,' Bill said, 'it was just Mrs Palmer fainted, that's all. I happened to be there and helped her back home. Did Ivy bring you some competitions to do?'

'Don't try changing the subject,' snapped Joyce, 'I suppose you think I don't know what goes on, never going out and that. Well, Mr Cleverdick Turner, I have my spies, so you needn't think you can get away with it!'

She advanced towards him, her hands like claws aimed at his face. He ducked away from her, but not fast enough, and one of her long, half-broken nails caught his skin and he felt a sharp pain.

'You bitch!' he said, and turned away, crossed the landing to the bathroom and slammed the door shut. He stood looking in the mirror at the red weal coming up on his cheek, and took several deep breaths. He deliberately unclenched his fists, and splashed his face with cold water from the basin he had just cleaned. I have to get out quick, he thought, or I shall do her a mischief.

He ran down the stairs two at a time, and without stopping to lock the back door he grabbed his bike and was opening the front gate before he heard her screams. 'Bill! Bill Turner! Come back here! I'll kill myself if you don't!' And on and on, until he was out of Macmillan Gardens and could hear her no more.

He cycled up the Bagley Road and the woods closed

60

round him, cool and comforting. Propping up the bike against a piece of broken fencing he walked through the trees, starting up young scuttling rabbits and shrieking pheasants, until he reached a familiar clearing, his refuge since boyhood. He sat down on a moss-covered tree stump and looked down a dry, rutted track to the foot of the hill and over the village.

What a bloody mess, he thought. I can't see any way out of it.

The valley of the Ringle stretched out before him in the sun, a green and pleasant land, with its bright ribbon of water and sheltering folds of hills encircling it. Why can't she be happy here, Bill thought, there's some would give their eye teeth to live in Ringford. Lots of women have miscarriages and try again. We should have tried again – I should have been firmer. But not our Joyce, oh no, she suffered more than most, certainly wasn't going through that again. Why didn't I leave her then, when she was still all right, more or less? Couldn't go now, it'd be like leaving a helpless child.

He could see the shop quite clearly, and the big silver car outside. Mrs Standing must be on her way, he thought, off to London to join Mr Richard. Won't matter if I'm a bit late back.

Wonder how Peggy is? She was really poorly when we got her up those stairs and into bed. Frank was upset . . . just as well Mary York was there, she's a good gel. Poor old Peggy cried in pain when she came to.

I could have put my arms round her again, smoothed it away, he thought, shifting off the stump and on to the green, rabbit-cropped turf, and stretching out his long legs. He pillowed his head on his hands, and with the scent of Peggy's flowery perfume and the warmth of her body still vivid in his senses he drifted off to sleep.

CHAPTER NINE

Frank and Doreen persuaded Peggy to go to W.I., Frank saying that he was quite capable of running the shop for the afternoon. 'Go on, Peg,' he said with a wink, 'go and live it up for a bit.' She had returned around teatime with a favourable report, and now sat talking to Frank, watching the welcome rain beating down the flowers, scattering the pale pink rose petals from the rambler outside the window, and running in rivulets down the slope in the yard into the old drain in the corner.

Frank moved a pawn slowly from one square to the next.

'Who's winning?' said Peggy.

'He is,' said Frank with a smile.

It was a ritual joke, something Peggy always said when Frank was working out a chess problem on his own.

'The best bit,' said Peggy, 'was when Mrs Jenkins got up and said everyone should go to the meeting about the new houses tonight. Sheila's giving one side of it, and Mr Richard's taking the anti-houses side. Susan Standing glared at poor old Jean, and brought us all back to order. Do you think we should go, Frank?'

'I thought you might suggest that,' said Frank, moving his white queen across to menace the black knight, 'how about a nice cup of tea?'

'Thank you, dear,' said Peggy, taking out her tapestry and cutting off a new piece of blue wool.

'Ah,' said Frank, and went off into the kitchen, patting

her infuriatingly on the head as he went. 'Have to look after my little wifey,' he said.

The new houses meeting was well attended, all the chairs in the old wooden village hall taken, and the debate had been lively.

'Well, you must have seen them, Ellen,' said Ivy Beasley, as she and Ellen Biggs walked back home. The rain had stopped, and a sprinkling of stars shone benevolently on the two elderly women.

'You whispered loud enough for everyone to hear,' said Ellen, 'I should think Mrs Palmer must have heard it, too.'

'Serves her right, Pushy Peg,' said Ivy, 'getting up on her hind legs and spouting on, when they've only been in Ringford five minutes.'

'I thought she were good,' said Ellen, 'short and sweet, and said very sensible things about the shop needing more custom, and that.'

'Bill Turner thought she was good, too,' said Ivy, 'practically holdin' hands, they were.'

'So you said, Ivy.' Ellen turned to cross the road and make her way home. 'If I were you,' she continued, stepping off the pavement, 'I should just watch what you say about all that. Could cause a lot o'trouble.'

'Only commenting on what I see,' said Ivy, 'no smoke without fire.'

When Sheila Pearson opened her lounge door, she found a sleeping David.

He woke suddenly, jumped to his feet and said that he had only just drifted off. He was a tall man, with gingery hair and a noble profile – hooked nose and high brow. He was also a very patient man, loved his wife and was proud of her work for the District Council. But he did not have the same stern community conscience, and sometimes found it difficult to produce the required enthusiasm for Sheila's campaigns. His father had been a nice man, without ambition, and David had inherited his father's niceness but his mother's socially ambitious nature.

'You should have heard Jean Jenkins,' Sheila said, taking off her mac.

'Tell me all about it,' said David, smothering a yawn.

'She really let rip at Mr Richard – which, considering she works for his wife, wasn't very tactful – and then told the audience very lucidly all the good reasons for having a few new houses in the village.'

'Such as what?' said David, putting a saucepan of milk on to the stove, and spooning cocoa powder into two mugs.

'Oh, all the things we've been saying for months – you know, keeping the shop open, new young children for the school, not having a village full of weekenders, that sort of thing.'

'What did Richard think of that?'

'Not much, he looked furious! But some people loved it – even old Fred was clapping and stamping his good leg when she sat down. Peggy was a surprise, too, getting up and saying her piece about the shop – Frank was dreadfully embarrassed, but Bill Turner was cheering her on – and of course I made a few points, but not nearly so effectively as those two.'

'Well done, darling,' said David, 'now drink up your cocoa and then we can get a good night's sleep.'

In the big bedroom at Ringford Hall, Richard Standing, tall and a little overweight, with untidy dark hair, looked at his sleeping wife and was glad he did not have to tell her that the meeting had not been quite the walkover he had expected.

'Richard?' muttered Susan in her sleep.

'Sshh,' said Richard soothingly, 'no need for you to wake up. Tell you all in the morning.'

But Susan was awake now, and sat up, pulling on a green silk bedjacket that had been her grandmother's. 'How did it go?' she said.

'So so,' said Richard, 'we shall know more after the site meeting next week, when brother James should help us along. No, tonight was just the usual arguments over again. Jenkins was most objectionable, I have to say; and that Palmer woman was much too persuasive.'

'You should have let me come,' said Susan, 'was Barnett there?'

'Young John was – not so young now, I noticed.'

Richard's mind began to wander, thinking of the Barnetts and John's sister Josie, much older and one of Richard's early flames. She'd had the family's red hair and a temper to match. He had been about nineteen . . .

'Come to bed, Richard,' said Susan, 'tell me more in the morning.'

Stretched out beside Susan, Richard continued to think about Josie Barnett. He drifted into a doze, and thought he saw the Ringle, sparkling in the sun, and the willow trees moving gently in the breeze. He and Josie were sitting on the bank, throwing stones into the water.

'Marry me, Josie,' he said, in a warm, thrilling voice.

'Not likely, you cheeky bugger!' said Josie, and leaping up pushed him firmly into the cold, rippling water.

'You little devil!' he shouted as he surfaced.

'What did you say?' said Susan, sitting up in bed again.

'Dreaming,' said Richard, 'sorry, old girl.'

He hadn't seen much of Josie after that, and she'd gone off and married an American. Lovely little Josie, with her flaming hair and freckled nose. He had never forgotten her, and nor had the village.

Peggy and Frank sat in the kitchen, too full of the meeting to go to bed. 'You know me,' said Frank, 'keep your head down and avoid the flak.'

'You didn't mind me speaking, then?' said Peggy.

'Did you hear old Beasley's remark?' said Frank, and immediately wished he hadn't said it.

'About me?' said Peggy, looking out of the window at

Miss Beasley's garden, as if she might be lurking by her woodpile in the dark.

'Didn't catch all of it,' said Frank, blundering on, 'but it sounded like "Pushy Peg" and there was something about Bill, too.'

'Did she really say that?' said Peggy, looking shocked. She drew the curtains, and came back to the table. 'Can't drink any more of that,' she said, tipping half a cup of coffee into the sink, 'I shan't sleep now, anyway.'

'Don't take any notice of old Ivy,' said Frank, 'I was proud of you – once you'd sat down – and Bill clearly thought you were wonderful.'

'Oh Frank, you are a dear,' said Peggy, blushing and remembering Bill's big hand over her own. 'Do you know, when I sat down and people clapped, I really felt I almost belonged to Ringford.'

Frank looked at her. 'Can't say the same myself,' he said, 'I still dream about wild nights at the Chess Club, and calm days at Maddox's when everybody just let me get on with the job in hand.'

'Frank dear,' said Peggy, taking his hand, 'it will get better, believe me. Why don't you ask about a chess club in Tresham?'

'Too far,' said Frank, 'but I might have a go at teaching Bill – he's very keen to learn.'

Peggy got up and locked the back door. 'Worth going, was it?' she said.

'I suppose so,' said Frank, 'perhaps I'll go up to the site meeting next week. Who knows, getting my shoes muddy might make me feel I belong to Ringford too.'

CHAPTER TEN

'What a day!' David Pearson looked out of the bedroom window at Casa Pera across to Bates's Farm, where Robert Bates was tinkering with a giant tractor in the yard, apparently oblivious of the pouring rain. It had begun early, a fine grey mist at first, when David had gone down to get Sheila a cup of tea, but now settled into a sullen wet day, the sky heavy and unyielding.

'Just my luck, we shall be sloshing about all over the place in Barnett's field,' said Sheila. She was sitting on the edge of the bed pulling on her tights, and David looked approvingly at her legs, one clothed and smooth and shiny, and the other still naked, brown from last year's Spanish sun. She took out of the cupboard a tailored navy-blue linen dress with white collar and piping, and held it up against her.

'What do you think, David?' she said.

'I think we should go back to bed at once, and . . .' He put his arms round her, crushing the dress, and she pushed him away good-naturedly.

'No, not now,' she said, 'go on, go and start breakfast, it's getting late.'

Early after all, Sheila arrived at the field and looked across the rain-soaked landscape towards Walnut Farm. The line of trees that gave the farm its name blew almost horizontal in the strong wind, which now flung flurries of raindrops into Sheila's face, as she waited for the others to arrive.

She used the time to marshal the arguments she would be putting to James Standing, Chairman of the Council Planning Committee, and brother of Richard. They've got it all sewn up between them, she thought, and I shall find out how.

She walked slowly down the field to the hedge which separated the site from the playing fields. The cricket pavilion roof shone with a sheet of white water covering the blue-grey tiles. It's my turn to mastermind cricket tea this weekend, she thought, there's no relief from public duty once you get on the treadmill. Still, David enjoys his cricket and it is something we can both be involved in.

'Sheila!' She looked back towards the gate, and saw Frank Palmer waving a walking stick at her and shouting something she could not hear. Why on earth has he come up here in this weather, she thought, and began to walk over to him, her wellies squelching in the soft, muddy grass as she avoided cow pats and rabbit holes.

'What time does it start, Sheila?' said Frank, as she came within earshot.

'The meeting, do you mean? Half past ten, they've put it back half an hour to give Mr Standing a bit longer over his breakfast.' She held on to her umbrella with both hands, as the wind threatened to blow it inside out.

'Now, now, Sheila,' said Frank, 'sweet reasonableness is what wins on these occasions.'

Sheila was puzzled. It was unlike Frank to show much interest in the new houses, let alone plough through wind and rain to a site meeting which he probably would be expelled from anyway.

'Just doing my bit for the community,' said Frank, reading her expression. 'Peggy had her say at the Village Hall, and it seemed only fair that I should back her up by coming along today. However,' he added, shaking water out of the rim of his trilby hat, 'I may have been mistaken.'

'I should go home, Frank,' said Sheila, 'they won't want you here, and you'll just get wet through. I'll pop in on my way home and tell you what happens, if you like.'

But cars were drawing up in the road outside the field, and Frank shook his head. 'Might as well stay now,' he said, 'I don't suppose they'll want to be out in this for long.'

Three people had collected by the gate, and Sheila noted the solid bulk of Tom Price, standing separately, to one side. Good old Tom, she thought, maintaining his impartiality. Two other men – she recognised only James Standing – began to walk across the field. The rain increased in intensity, and Sheila said, 'Come under my umbrella, Frank, you're soaking already!'

'Morning, Mrs Pearson,' said James Standing, 'though I must say it is far from good – what happened to summer, eh? I wondered whether to postpone our meeting, but there seems to be some urgency in the matter.' It was the same loud, confident voice as his brother Richard's.

James Standing was egg shaped, with no neck to speak of and narrow shoulders widening out into a big paunch which then tailed away into short legs and ridiculously small feet, at the moment encased snugly in green Wellington boots. He had pulled his waterproof hat well down over his eyes and his horn-rimmed glasses were spattered with rain.

Tom Price came over and touched Frank's arm in a friendly fashion. 'What are you doing here, Frank?' he said.

'Interested party, being the village shopkeeper, you know,' said Frank.

Tom frowned, said, 'Not sure the rules will allow . . .' and looked at James Standing.

'Certainly not,' said Chairman James, 'can't have just any old riff-raff turning up on site.'

Sheila Pearson bridled. 'He's hardly that, Mr Standing,'

she said, 'you are probably unaware that this is Mr Palmer, the new village postmaster and owner of the stores.'

'I don't care who the hell he is,' said James Standing, 'he's not allowed at this meeting – no offence, of course, Mr Palmer.'

'Then who is this gentleman?' said Sheila sharply, indicating the tall man she had seen getting out of James Standing's car.

'I am the press, madam,' said the man, 'Bingley-Smyth, editor of the *Evening Gazette*. It is our duty to the citizen to make sure that all such meetings are played out in the public arena.'

'Shut up, Tim, and don't talk such rubbish,' said James Standing. He turned to Frank, and waved his hand towards the gate. 'Perhaps you could leave us now, Mr Palmer, to get on with our business.'

He began to pull plans out of a leather briefcase, and was immediately shielded by a huge, brightly coloured golf umbrella produced like the flags of all nations by Tim Bingley-Smyth.

'Not willingly,' said Frank, 'but since Mrs Pearson has kindly offered to report straight back to us in the shop after the meeting, it seems I must accept and leave you to it.'

He squished back across the field, his shoes full of water and rain dripping out of his hat into his eyes. He felt an absolute fool, and was painfully aware of a burst of laughter from the men as he reached the gate and negotiated the thick stretch of mud, liquefied by the now torrential rain.

'Frank! Meeting over already?' said Peggy. 'You look terrible – you'll catch your death. Go and take off those wet things at once and have a hot bath – and don't say anything until you come down!' she added, seeing the look on his face.

Doreen emerged from behind a display unit and put a tin of brown shoe polish down on the counter. 'Just this, please, Peggy,' she said, 'I forgot it earlier on.'

'Not like you, Doreen, you're usually so well organised,' Peggy said.

'It was Tom, rushing out to that meeting, put me all at sixes and sevens.'

'Looks like the meeting wasn't a great success,' Peggy said, 'not for Frank, anyway. He would go, though, didn't even stop to put his boots on. I told him it wasn't the right thing.'

'It's not easy in villages,' said Doreen, 'it never was.'

A drowned-looking Sheila Pearson dripped into the shop just before lunch, and stood waiting impatiently while Peggy put three cooking apples into a bag for Old Ellen.

'You're wet, then, gel,' said Ellen, never one to shirk the obvious, and noting with some satisfaction that Mrs Pearson had her car outside and would be able to give her a lift home.

'So would you be, Mrs Biggs,' said Sheila sharply, 'if you had stood for an hour on Barnett's field, and then sat for ages in a steamed-up car being lectured by a bone-head from the press.'

'Don't know what you're talking about, dear,' said Ellen, 'but I could do with a lift 'ome if you're not goin' to be long.'

'Where's Frank?' said Sheila, looking into the Post Office cubicle, and seeing it empty.

'He's still upstairs,' said Peggy, 'I'll call him.'

'No, no,' said Sheila, 'I must get home and dry off, but I promised to let him know what happened, so I'll catch up with him later. You could just tell him it was all much as I expected – Standings United, really. Bye, then. Come on, Mrs Biggs, give me your bag and let's get you home.'

Ellen was half in the front seat of Sheila's car, when Ivy Beasley shouted from her front door, 'Ellen, Ellen Biggs, I want you!'

'I really cannot wait for you, Mrs Biggs, I'm afraid,' said Sheila, 'I must get these wet things off.'

Ellen heaved an exaggerated sigh. 'Better go and see what Ivy wants – I shall never hear the end of it if I don't.' She took her shopping bag from Sheila and began to hobble off towards Victoria Villa. As an afterthought, she looked back and shouted, 'Thanks all the same, Mrs Pearson.' Sheila drove off with relief, thoughts of steaming hot cups of coffee and fluffy, dry white towels filling her head.

'What you want, Ivy?' said Ellen, leaning on Miss Beasley's gate post and breathing heavily. 'Done me out of a lift, you did . . .'

'Don't give me that,' said Ivy Beasley, 'you'd rather have a bit of a chat than a lift home any time.' Ellen perked up, and walked into Miss Beasley's hall and through to her kitchen at the back.

'D'you want a cup of tea?' said Ivy.

'All right, but be quick about it, Ivy, I put a rice puddin' in before I come up the shop. What's all this about, anyway?'

'All in good time,' said Ivy Beasley, with a superior smile. She put two spoonfuls of tea from an old japanned caddy into a brown earthenware teapot, poured on boiling water and gave it a good stir. Then she set out two cups and saucers with spoons, a glass sugar bowl and a white pottery jug of milk. 'A teabag would do, Ivy,' said Old Ellen, looking at all this with a caustic expression. 'Don't get all this fal-de-lal when you come down the Lodge.'

'Have to keep up standards, Ellen – if we don't, there's nobody else will,' said Ivy Beasley. She poured the tea and handed a cup to Ellen, who said, 'Ta, Ivy – I can see you're in one of them moods.'

'Now,' said Miss Beasley, sitting herself down carefully in a spindleback chair by the kitchen window, 'you know our Pushy Peg . . . '

'No, no, never met 'er,' said Old Ellen, irritably, 'o'course I know her, Ivy, do get on with it!'

'Well, I think we've got trouble brewing between our shopkeeper and his wife, that's what I think.'

Ellen waited impatiently, taking birdlike pecks at the hot tea.

'Pushy Peg was talking to Doreen Price about that meeting, and said she'd had a hard time getting Frank to go up there, 'specially in all that rain. She said she was fed up with him leaving everything to her, and for two pins would boot him out,' Ivy leaned back and looked challengingly at Old Ellen.

'Boot him out? Doesn't sound like Peggy Palmer.'

'My hearin's not gone yet, Ellen Biggs,' said Ivy, 'and that's what she said. I was behind the cereals, I think she'd forgotten I was there.'

Ellen looked closely at Ivy. Her expression was bland, and Ellen did not trust her an inch. 'You sure you've not made all this up, Ivy?' she said. 'Everybody knows you got it in for Peggy Palmer.'

'Please yourself what you believe,' said Ivy, 'you've known me long enough, I'd have thought.'

'That's just it,' said Old Ellen, 'plenty long enough.'

The rain had cleared away, and bright sunshine lit up the wet roads and roofs. The big chestnut trees dripped on to Old Ellen's beige felt hat as she trudged up Bateses End, wondering why she ever had anything to do with that old cat Ivy Beasley. Doreen Price's car stopped and Doreen poked her head out of the window. 'Like a lift, Ellen? You look a bit heavy laden. I'm on my way to put roses on Mum's grave.'

It was still a couple of hundred yards to the Lodge, and Ellen climbed in gratefully. 'I was gettin' a lift with Mrs Pearson,' she said, 'but old Ivy kept me gossipin'.'

'Thrives on it,' said Doreen, 'it's a dangerous pastime.'

'Quite right, dear,' said Ellen, ''specially when Ivy's got her knives out.'

'What did she say?' said Doreen, in spite of herself.

'It was about what Mrs Palmer was telling you, it was, about wishing she could boot out that wet ha'porth of a husband of hers.'

'Ellen Biggs!' said Doreen. 'Peggy never said anything of the sort – Ivy's gone too far this time.'

'You sure?' said Ellen. 'Well, 'ere we are, thanks very much. Lovely roses, them, your mum'll be pleased, wherever she is, God rest 'er soul.'

Ellen Biggs climbed out, her good humour restored, and went down her little path humming tunelessly to herself.

'Drat!' said Sheila Pearson, climbing out of the bath and wrapping a big towel round her dripping body. 'Just when I was warming up – ' She went quickly into the bedroom, leaving wet footprints on the pale pink carpet, and picked up the telephone from the bedside table.

'Hello, Sheila Pearson speaking, who is it? Oh, hello, Frank, have you dried off now? Good! Yes, I was coming down later on to tell you. I'm pretty sure now that we are up against a considerable plot – I had a session with that Bingley-Smyth idiot, and he was very cagey! What? Yes, well, you saw them there together. And Richard and brother James are very close, you know. Drinks? Yes, love to – we could swap a few ideas . . . What time, about sixish? Lovely, yes, see you then – bye, Frank, byeee!'

Well, isn't that nice of them, she thought, padding her way back to the bathroom. She could manage to fit in a drink this evening, David too, of course, before dashing out to the Community Council meeting in Bagley.

David, arriving home at a quarter past six, was not so charmed by the invitation, having driven ninety-five miles on a business trip which had turned out to be fruitless. 'Why tonight?' he said. 'Why couldn't it wait until the weekend?'

'Oh David, please don't be cross,' said Sheila, 'you

know I always like to get things done straight away. We shall have to go in the car, it's too late to walk, and I have to rush off to Bagley as soon as we get back.'

'What about supper?' said David wearily.

'I've left you a pizza in the freezer, you only have to heat it up, dear,' said Sheila.

'Super,' said David bravely.

Sheila put on a one-woman show at the Palmers'. Far from an exchange of ideas, it was a monologue. She finally came to her conclusion: '. . . which makes me pretty sure that the reason for Mr Richard's objections is a selfish one. He plans to build houses on the field behind our house, and with Barnett's application refused, he stands a much better chance.'

David stood up. 'Time to go, Sheila, if you want to get to Bagley by eight. Super to see you, Frank, you too, Peggy – speak to you soon, both of you.' He shepherded Sheila out, still talking, and they drove off at speed, the big dark green Vauxhall squealing round the corner by the pub and nearly taking off over the humpback river bridge.

CHAPTER ELEVEN

After brooding on Ivy Beasley's mischief-making for a few days, Doreen Price decided to act. She pressed the bell at Victoria Villa, and looked anxiously towards the shop next door. She did not particularly want Peggy to see her on her way to tackle Beasley. It was hot in the sun, and she reflected that Ivy was probably keeping her waiting on purpose.

'Morning, Mrs Price,' said Ivy, wiping her hands on her apron. Doreen followed her into the front room. 'No thanks, I won't sit down,' she said, 'what I have to say won't take long.'

Ivy's eyes hardened, and she backed away from Doreen, leaning up against the dresser, next to the photograph of her formidable mother.

'Now, Ivy,' continued Doreen, 'some nasty untruths have been said about the Palmers, supposedly what she said to me, and I'm told it was you who said the untruths. So I've come to sort it out.'

'Are you calling me a liar, Doreen Price?' said Ivy.

'You seem to know what I'm talking about,' said Doreen, solid as a rock.

'Doesn't bother me,' said Ivy defiantly, 'sort out what you like. I've no interest in the wretched Palmers. Bad day when they came to Ringford, if you ask me.'

'Nobody's asking you,' said Doreen, 'and until they do, you'd do well to keep quiet.' A high colour had suffused her round cheeks.

'Nothing but trouble,' said Ivy, 'and making bad go to worse for poor Joyce Turner.'

'That's enough of that,' said Doreen, 'and don't forget, Ivy, the W.I. elections are coming up next month. You've been Secretary a long time, you know.'

Ivy Beasley followed her to the front door. 'You threatening me, Mrs Price?' she said.

'Don't be ridiculous, Ivy,' said Doreen, 'just lay off – that's all.'

She shut Ivy's gate carefully and drove off up the Bagley road. That'll stop her tricks for a while, she thought, for a little while.

The shopping bus coasted along the edge of the Green, and stopped at the bus stop opposite the shop. Two or three Ringford passengers got up and slowly clambered off, saying their goodbyes.

'Come on 'Tavie,' said Sandra, 'wake up, we're here.'

Octavia had chosen the window seat just in case she could catch sight of Robert along the road, but had dozed off in the heat of the sun shining directly on to her. The girls stood up, Octavia yawning loudly, and made their way to the front of the bus.

'Where are we going?' said Sandra. 'It's time for me tea.'

'Tea?' said Octavia. 'We've got something better than tea – come on, quickly, we don't want any of your horrible little brothers following us.'

A rickety footbridge, out of bounds to the village children and closed off with barbed wire, was Octavia's target, and she climbed expertly round the wire and skipped lightly across the swaying rotten planks.

'Hey, we're not supposed . . .' said Sandra, standing

squarely on the footpath, carrying her sports bag and frowning mutinously at Octavia.

'Scaredy cat, Sandra Roberts!' said Octavia. 'Too fat to cross the bridge, are we?'

'You're a cow, Octavia Jones,' said Sandra, reluctantly squeezing round the endpost of the bridge and all but collapsing into the water.

'Buck up, Sandra,' said Octavia, 'move yourself, do.' She led the way through a thicket and into a clearing, hidden from sight by a ring of dense thorn bushes. 'Another balloon,' said Octavia, picking up a used condom with a piece of stick, grinning knowingly at Sandra.

Sometimes I hate her, thought Sandra, she's really wicked. She sat down on the grass and looked at Octavia. 'We're trespassing,' she said, 'it belongs to Standings this side of the river.'

'And who is going to tell them we're here?' said Octavia. 'Come on, open the bag and give us drink – I'm dying of thirst.'

Sandra pulled out the bottle of red wine they had bluffed through the checkout in the Supashop in Tresham. 'You were lucky they didn't ask how old you were,' said Sandra, trying to open the plastic top. 'Give it here, stupid,' said Octavia, and expertly flicked off the cap. She took a long swig and handed it back to Sandra, who obediently did the same, grimacing at the sharp, vinegary taste.

They continued to pass the bottle, Sandra pretending to drink more than she actually took, and when it was empty Octavia lay back on the grass.

'Mmm,' she said, 'this is the life. All I need is my darling Robert . . .'

'My head feels funny,' said Sandra.

'Don't be such a baby,' said Octavia, staring up at the sky, 'if you can't be more fun than this, I shall have to get another friend, one who – '

She sat up suddenly, turned over on to all fours, and was

violently sick. She moaned and keeled over on to her side, clutching her stomach.

' 'Tavie!' said Sandra, rushing across and putting her arm round the retching girl's shoulders. 'That's it,' she said, in her mother's voice, 'bring it all up, better out than in . . .' And she comforted her and wiped her face and forehead with a handkerchief dipped in cold Ringle water, until Octavia was able to struggle to her feet and aim for home.

It was Octavia who suggested getting a can of Coke on the way, telling Peggy she felt funny because of the hot bus. And it was Mrs Ashbourne, buying some stamps and knowing about the reflective power of the Post Office cubicle window, who spotted Octavia as she slipped a tortoiseshell comb into the sports bag while Peggy was at the fridge.

'Open your bag, miss,' she said. Octavia stared at her, dumbfounded. 'Open your bag, or I send for the police,' said Mrs Ashbourne, hands on her stout hips.

'Mrs Ashbourne!' said Peggy.

Doris Ashbourne held up her hand, as if to silence anything Peggy might have been about to say. 'Give me that comb,' she said. Octavia took out the tortoiseshell comb like someone mesmerised and handed it to Mrs Ashbourne.

'Old cat,' said Sandra under her breath.

'That's quite enough of that, Sandra Roberts,' said Mrs Ashbourne. 'Now get off home before I send for the law – and you can be sure Mr and Mrs Palmer will be up to tell your parents directly. And you'd better get that smell of drink off your breath before you get home – especially you, Sandra Roberts.'

There was a stunned silence in the shop after they left. Then Peggy said, 'I feel an absolute fool, Mrs Ashbourne. Were they putting it on, just to confuse me?'

'No, no, gel,' Doris said, 'she felt funny all right, but it wasn't the hot bus. They'd been drinking, and that Jones girl had been sick. I could smell it – got very well acquainted with it when my Jack was alive. No, the stealing is by the way – I don't think Octavia Jones can help herself. They've got real trouble there. Shall you go and see the parents? You might do a bit of good in the long run.'

'Not today, Peggy,' said Frank, 'you are not going anywhere except into the garden with a nice cup of tea and the newspaper full of stories of the big wide world, which I assure you is still out there, somewhere.'

CHAPTER TWELVE

The whole of Round Ringford seemed to be out in the sun as Peggy walked along the road by the Green, with its ring of chestnuts shading the seat where the pensioners sat reminiscing and commenting on the passers-by. The pub windows were open, and the curtains blowing in the warm breeze. Peggy noted William and Warren tightrope walking on the low wall separating the pub garden from the Green itself.

' 'Lo, Mrs Palmer,' shouted Warren Jenkins, 'you goin' to the Joneses'?'

Little devils, thought Peggy, they're the ears and eyes of the village, those two.

They were right, of course. She had been greeted by several people leaning on their gardening forks or resting by idling lawn mowers, and realised that her progress was being carefully observed.

Sandra certainly saw her. Sandra had been Eddie-sitting, whilst Foxy and Mrs Jenkins had taken Gemma and Amy and Mark roller-skating in Tresham. Sandra was walking across Macmillan Gardens on her way home, but turned around, guessing that her house might be next on Mrs Palmer's list and hoping to make herself scarce, but her mother had caught sight of her and yelled, 'Sandra! Come 'ere, I want you to 'elp me.' Sandra obediently went home, with intimations of trouble on its way.

Bill Turner, cutting his front hedge in spite of protests from Joyce that people would be able to see over it, saw Peggy go by, and felt his heart lurch. Look what you're doing, you silly bugger, he said to himself, you'll cut your hand off if you're not careful.

And Mrs Ashbourne, on her way back from a cup of tea with Doreen Price, met Peggy, and said, 'Going to Joneses', are you? Good gel, they'll thank you for it.'

Gabriella and Greg Jones were in their back garden and Peggy had to walk round the side of the house to find them.

'Hello, Peggy!' said Greg, a pleasant-faced, wiry young man with a toothy smile and a hearing-aid acquired in early childhood. He had the alert, wary look of the deaf, concentrating hard on what was said to him and following every word to pick up what he could by lip-reading.

'Am I glad to see you!' said Gabriella. 'Greg's had me out here weeding since lunchtime, and my back is killing me.' She stretched and rubbed her back, stuck her fork into the flower bed, and set off across the lawn. 'Cup of tea time, Greg,' she said, 'come on in, Peggy – or would you rather sit in the sun?'

That's where Octavia gets her looks from, thought Peggy. Long silky blonde hair, high cheekbones and a narrow straight nose, a trim figure kept in shape by regular exercising and energetic games of tennis – just what I've always wanted to look like and never did.

'This is lovely tea,' Peggy said, sitting in their cool lounge, where the oatmeal-coloured curtains had been drawn against the bright sun, 'did you get this from us?'

Gabriella looked embarrassed and shook her head. 'No, there's this little delicatessen in Bagley, just opened recently, and they have a wonderful selection of teas – this is Lapsang Souchong.'

'Must tell Frank to look out for it at the wholesaler's,'

said Peggy. She knew it embarrassed villagers if she caught them out buying their supplies elsewhere, and her comment was not without a little malice. Might as well start on top, she thought.

Greg looked at Peggy apprehensively and said, 'Hope you don't mind my asking, Peggy, but is this just a social call – and I do hope it is – or did you have some reason for coming?'

He's heard, of course, thought Peggy, but then who hasn't? I might as well plough on now I'm here.

'Well, yes, it's about Octavia – I'm afraid she and Sandra have been persistently taking things from the shop and deliberately not paying for them.' She assiduously avoided the word 'stealing'.

Whether they had an inkling or not, Gabriella and Greg looked shattered. 'Are you sure, Peggy?' Greg said. 'Did you face them with it at the time?'

'The last time it happened – this week – Mrs Ashbourne was fortunately in the shop and caught them redhanded. She does, of course, have years of experience. It was, I'm afraid, on this occasion just Octavia who put a comb into her bag quite deliberately.' Thank God for Doris Ashbourne, she thought. Nobody would question her authority . . .

'Gabriella,' said Greg, 'please go and see if Octavia is still in her bedroom. She was up there earlier, playing her guitar. Better ask her to come down, and see what she has to say.'

Gabriella got up, but at that moment Octavia drooped into the room and propped herself up against a bookcase by the door.

'Ah,' said Greg, 'there you are, 'Tavie, please come and sit down. We have something to discuss with you.'

How reasonable we are, thought Peggy, beginning to be irritated by this kid-glove handling. This was not the cocky Octavia she knew and disliked, this was a child, eyeing its parents with a calculating look, waiting to see which way the wind blew.

'Darling,' said Gabriella, 'have you needed a new comb and not told me?'

Octavia's face closed up, and she shook her head. ' 'Course not,' she said.

'Then why did you take one from the shop without paying for it?' said Peggy.

'I didn't,' said Octavia.

'Mrs Ashbourne caught you with it in your bag,' said Peggy, putting her cup and saucer down with a crash on the big, shiny coffee table, and trying to keep calm.

'It was mine,' said Octavia.

'The red one?' said Gabriella, beginning to look relieved.

'No, the tortoiseshell one,' said Peggy firmly.

'She hasn't got a . . .' said Gabriella, and stopped.

'Girl at school gave it to me,' said Octavia.

Greg stood up. 'Peggy, my dear,' he said, his voice unnaturally loud, making Peggy jump, 'we're going to have to talk to Octavia alone, and then I shall certainly come along and sort it all out with you. If she has done anything silly, then we shall explain her mistake to her carefully, you can be sure of that.'

Peggy got to her feet. 'It may come to more than that, Greg,' she said, 'it is not the first time this has happened. Please let me know soon the result of your chat with your daughter. You might also like to ask her where she got the alcoholic drink which made her so sick that afternoon.' With dignity she walked into the hall, Greg half-running to keep up with her and to open the door for her to leave.

'Goodbye Gabriella, Greg,' she said, and ignored Octavia. She could not bear to look at her, to see her triumphant, lovely, sneaky little face.

Round one to Octavia Jones, I'm afraid, she thought, as she walked away and crossed the road to tackle the

Robertses in Macmillan Gardens. I don't rate my chances with the next lot very highly.

Not a soul in sight, she thought, that's odd. When I came by, it looked full of people in their gardens and chatting over their fences. Ah well, teatime, I suppose.

She walked on, trying not to look for eyes at the lace-curtained windows. She reached number eight and pushed past the broken gate, struggled through the jungle of worn-out pushchairs and collapsed tricycles, and reached the front door.

She knocked and waited. Absolute silence greeted her, and she knocked again, certain that at this time of day someone would be at home. They probably have plenty of practice at being silent, Peggy thought, when they spot the rent man coming up the path.

That was pretty nasty, she thought, I'm getting as bad as old Ivy. One last knock, then I'm going home. She was beginning to feel isolated and rather frightened, standing in this alien junkyard of a garden.

'Peggy!' She looked round, and saw Bill Turner outside his house on the opposite side of the road. 'You'll not get an answer,' he said, 'try going round the back, but be careful of the dog.'

Peggy at once felt safer for having Bill around, and giving him a wave to show she had heard, she walked round to the back of the house. Just as well he warned me about the dog, she thought, as she rounded the corner and came face to face with a snarling Alsatian. It was tied up with a thick rope, giving it a few yards' freedom, and Peggy skirted round it to find the back door standing open.

She knocked tentatively, and saw people sitting round the table in the kitchen, drinking and eating, and watching horse racing on a small television set high on top of a fridge.

'I did knock at the front,' she said, and a man she recognised as father Roberts turned round.

'We heard yer,' he said, and turned back to the screen.

'May I have a word, please?' Peggy said, determined now to carry on.

'Have as many as you like,' said Mr Roberts, 'we don't charge.'

'It is about Sandra,' she continued, 'she and Octavia Jones have been persistently taking things from the shop, and it must stop.' Brief and to the point, she thought, that's what is needed here.

There was no reaction whatever, and she added, 'I should like to think you will do something to prevent such a thing from happening again – I don't want to have to call in the law.'

Mr Roberts stood up slowly and Peggy backed away, her heart thudding. He opened his mouth, still full of bacon and egg, and yelled, 'Sandra!' at the top of his voice. In the silence which followed he continued to stare at Peggy.

She could hear footsteps coming downstairs, and Sandra appeared, looking mutinous. 'What?' she said. 'Did you hear what Mrs Palmer said?' said Mr Roberts. 'Nope,' said Sandra, 'what with you shouting, no chance of hearin' anythin' else.' She ducked with almost nonchalant ease as her father swung a clenched fist towards her.

'Did you go thieving in the shop?' he said.

' 'Course not, it were 'Tavia, not me,' said Sandra.

'There you are then,' said Mr Roberts, turning to Peggy, 'you'd best go round to them Joneses and sort out that snotty kid of theirs.'

Peggy explained that she had already been there, and they had promised to do something about it. 'But Sandra is not totally innocent, Mr Roberts,' she said, 'and she had been drinking too, I'm afraid – though perhaps she is better at holding it.'

Mr Roberts roared with laughter, and said, 'Chip off the old block! Pity she didn't save some for her dad . . .' Then his face changed, and he came nearer to Peggy, his hand raised and a finger pointing at her.

'Now look here,' he said, 'don't you come causing trouble no more. You think just because you've been here for a few months you can go around accusing people. Well, we've been here always and we belong. So bugger off now, and don't come back.'

He walked towards Peggy, who backed away hastily, ending up dangerously near the Alsatian. Caught between the two hostile figures, she began to shake, and then saw Mr Roberts' expression change again.

'What you want, Turner?' he said, and Peggy looked round to see Bill coming round the corner.

'Just come to see if Mrs Palmer needs any help,' said Bill, and taking her arm led her away and out of Roberts territory. As they crossed the road she heard Sandra's voice call out, 'Could have told you it wouldn't do no good. But I didn't take nothing, Mrs Palmer.'

Peggy was still shaking, and Bill waited with her until she was calm. 'Thanks very much,' she said, 'that's the second time you've rescued me,' and Bill smiled.

'Next time you decide to tackle the Robertses,' he said, 'best send Frank.'

CHAPTER THIRTEEN

'I saw you, Bill Turner!' screeched Joyce, grabbing Bill's arms in a vice-like grip. 'That's her, isn't it – that is the Palmer woman!'

'Joyce, Joyce,' said Bill, guiding her gently over to the sofa in the front room, where she had been peeping between the curtains to see him talking to Peggy. 'She asked me how to get an answer from the Roberts house, and I told her to go round the back. You know they never answer the front door.'

'You went in after her,' accused Joyce, huddled up in misery on the sofa.

'I heard that dog barking, and went to see if she needed help,' he said wearily. 'There isn't nothing to it, Joyce, I promise you.' But good Christ, he thought, I wish there was. I wish there was something to get me out of this everlasting gloom.

'You wouldn't go five yards to help me,' said Joyce, with blind unfairness. She got up and turned on the television set. She sat quietly watching for a few minutes, and Bill went into the kitchen to put the kettle on and prepare their tea. He buttered currant buns and made cheese sandwiches, and set them out on the kitchen table. A large pot of tea and two white mugs completed his preparations and he called Joyce. 'Tea's ready, Joyce, do you want it in there, or here?'

No answer. Sulking again, he thought and sat down at the table, starting on one of the sandwiches, shutting the kitchen door against the sound of loud pop music on the television. She had not come in twenty minutes later, and Bill steeled himself for another confrontation. He went through to the front room to persuade her to eat.

He could not believe what he saw. How had she managed to create havoc so silently? The television was still on, the sound turned up, and he supposed she had used it to mask the sound of breaking and crushing.

She was crouched in a corner of the room, hugging a red embroidered cushion and crooning to it. Every chair had been turned carefully upside down or on its side, and the drawers of the chest by the window were pulled out and emptied. All Bill's mother's ornaments were in pieces in the hearth, and all Joyce's own were intact, carefully grouped on the mantelpiece. Bill's family photographs had been pulled from their frames and ripped, and the model aeroplane his dad had given him for his eighth birthday was in pieces on the rug by the fireplace.

Joyce watched him through the strands of hair hanging over her face, like a cat in the grass, an unblinking stare, waiting for his reaction.

Bill stood and surveyed the wrecked room, the core of their lives that he had struggled so hard to keep intact, and waved his arm round it all in a gesture of helplessness and defeat. Tears began to spill out and run incongruously down his lean, outdoor face. Joyce began to laugh, clutching the red cushion closer to her and rocking it backwards and forwards. 'Bye baby bunting,' she sang in a cracked voice, 'Daddy's gone a-hunting, and now he wishes he bloody well hadn't . . .'

Bill wiped his face roughly with the back of his hand and turned away. 'I shall be back, Joyce, see what you can do to clear up,' he said, and quietly left the house, deaf to Jean Jenkins' cheery 'Hiya Bill', and blind to Doris Ashbourne's wave as she walked with Ivy Beasley up Macmillan Gardens to her bungalow home.

'Don't look so good, does he?' said Mrs Ashbourne.

'Do you wonder at it,' said Ivy Beasley, 'she'll lead him a dance once too often, if you ask me.'

Half an hour later, Bill returned, calmer after his walk over the Green and up the river path, but with his heart still heavy, and as he opened the front room door he could see Joyce curled up on the sofa, apparently asleep, and no attempt made to set the room straight.

He fetched brush and dustpan and a bucket and began to clear up. Down on his hands and knees at the hearth, picking up broken pieces of china he had grown up with, he turned suddenly and caught Joyce looking at him. She shut her eyes quickly, but not before he had seen the glee in that look.

'Your sister's night for coming over,' he said to her, ignoring the feigned sleep. 'We'd better get this room looking a bit more ship-shape.' He set the chairs upright again, and took the bucket full of broken pottery and torn-up photographs into the outhouse by the back door.

Might be able to piece some of them together, he thought. He went down the garden and into the big wooden shed where he kept his rabbits. The big, soft angoras hopped excitedly round their cages, anticipating food. Stupid things, he thought, but at least they're pleased to see me. He filled up their food and water troughs and checked the doors of their cages. He had been breeding angoras for years now, and his stock was valuable.

When he went back into the house Joyce was sitting on the sofa, the storm apparently over. She said, 'I suppose you'll be going down to those Palmers again – for your chess lesson, ho ho.'

'I shall,' he said, 'and you'll have a normal conversation with your sister, so she will go away and think everything is my fault.'

Joyce stared at him. 'Don't talk rubbish,' she said, 'she knows I'm ill. And anyway, it is all your fault.'

'You're not ill, Joyce,' he said, 'if you could just get out of here and stop brooding – '

'Shut up, Turner!' she said, her voice rising. 'You know I can't go out – you just like tormenting me! Shut up, shut up!'

'I'll put the kettle on,' said Bill, 'you've had nothing since dinnertime. You'll feel better with something inside you.'

It would be easier, he thought, as he walked slowly down Macmillan Gardens, if she was worse. Then they'd have to do something about it. But she can be good as gold if somebody comes, then they think it's me making a fuss about nothing.

He looked across the Green to where Warren and William were tumbling over and over like puppies on the summer grass. Ah well, he thought, it's a lovely evening, and I'm off to play chess with Frank – and Peggy will be there. There are compensations.

'Come on in, Bill,' said Peggy, opening the back door wide. 'Frank's got it all set up ready for you. Go through.' She was wearing a plastic apron with puffins in rows, and looked relaxed and comfortable. She picked up a drying-up cloth and swiftly dried the blue and white cups, saucers and plates, putting them away on the dresser.

'You all right, gel?' said Bill. 'Did you sort out those girls?'

'I'm not sure, Bill,' said Peggy, emptying tea leaves into the pedal bin, 'I think they might have survived better than I did! But at least I've warned the parents, and if we need to take it further they can't complain.'

'Funny about Sandra,' said Bill, propping his long frame

up on the edge of the kitchen table, 'she were a nice little thing, and she's still good-hearted if anything needs doing. I reckon that Jones girl isn't all that good for Sandra, you know how a bad apple rots the rest all round it.'

Peggy hung the drying-up cloth over the Rayburn rail, and swilled clean water round the sink. She turned to look at Bill, and was surprised at the shadows under his eyes. 'I've never really seen Sandra pinch anything,' she said, 'it's always Octavia does the nicking, but Sandra acts as cover.'

Frank called from the sitting-room, hearing Bill's voice. 'Ready for you, Bill!' Bill smiled at Peggy, touched her gently on the arm and said, 'Glad you are all right, anyway,' and went through to find Frank.

Not sure who it is he comes to see, thought Frank uncharitably, as Bill walked in. 'Sharpened up your wits, then, Bill?' Frank said. 'We're playing a straight game this evening, and no help from me until it's over.'

'Good God, boy, that'll be a quick game!' said Bill, sitting down opposite Frank. He moved his pawn forward two squares, sure at least of his opening gambit, and waited for Frank.

Several games progressed, Frank considering carefully his strategy, and Bill impulsively making what seemed the obvious move at the time.

'Not too fast, Bill,' said Frank, 'give every move plenty of thought – try to work out what's going happen four or five moves ahead.'

'That's not bad advice for life in general,' said Peggy philosophically, 'except that other people never do what you'd thought they would.' She walked round the room, switching on reading lamps and the tall standard behind Frank's chair. She leaned over the back and put her arms round his neck, giving him a swift kiss on the top of his head. 'Who's winning, then?'

I love her dearly, thought Frank, but there were no distracting wifely interruptions at the Chess Club, just peace and quiet and time to think. Still, old Bill is not exactly a challenge.

'If you do that, lad – ' said Frank, pointing at Bill's knight.

'No, hang on,' said Bill, 'you said you'd not help me until the game was finished. Let me make the mistakes first.' He moved his knight to threaten Frank's queen.

'Check,' said Frank, taking his castle across the board to menace Bill's king.

'Oh blast it,' said Bill, and moved his king into the corner.

'Checkmate,' said Frank, clinching it with his bishop. He sat back, laughing. 'You made a fatal mistake two moves back. Here, let's set it up how it was, and I'll show you.'

The telephone rang, and Peggy put down her tapestry and got up to answer it. 'Yes? Yes, he's here, Mrs Jenkins. Do you want to speak to him?' She turned to Bill, and motioned him to the telephone.

'Your wife's not too well, Bill,' Peggy said, 'her sister's been round to Mrs Jenkins and asked her to call you.'

'Sorry about that, old lad,' said Frank, as Bill put down the telephone, all animation gone from his face. 'I reckon you'd have beaten me the next game.'

'I'll be back, never fear,' said Bill, with a brave stab at cheerfulness. 'Thanks very much, Frank, and for the coffee, Peggy. Same time next week?'

'Couldn't carry on without my weekly fix of chess,' said Frank, smiling at him. 'Hope Joyce is better soon.'

'Thanks, Frank – bye then.'

Peggy shut the back door slowly behind Bill and came back to the sitting-room, where Frank was putting away the chess pieces. He looked up at her and was surprised by her expression.

'I could slap that Joyce,' she said, and jabbed her needle fiercely into the tapestry canvas.

CHAPTER FOURTEEN

We shan't see much of Robert this month, Mother, said Ivy Beasley to her quiet kitchen. A preserving pan of bubbling strawberry jam plopped and spat on the stove, and orderly rows of empty jam jars stood on the table ready to receive the lethally hot liquid.

The smell of the jam filled the house and sent her thoughts skidding back to childhood years when her mother stood in this kitchen at the stove, using the same preserving pan and wooden spoon – and many of the same jam jars, too. Some still had her mother's labels clinging stubbornly to the glass, recording gooseberries topped and tailed, blackcurrants staining the capable hands, damsons pulped and baked until they turned into a setting cheese.

I've got plenty of past to think about, Mother, but precious little future. What did Robert say after you died? Try to look forward, Auntie, there's plenty of other folk to care about in Ringford. Well, he's the only person I care about, and now he's busy with the harvest I shan't set eyes on him for weeks.

She turned on the old electric oven to a brisk heat. Yes, I know, Mother, you always made a sponge in the range, but it ain't reliable enough for me. Can't afford to have it sink in the middle with Ellen and Doris coming to tea. Not that

Ellen is much of a cook, too slap-dash. And Doris got too used to eating them sawdust cakes from the shop. Still, that don't stop them criticising.

She filled the dented black baking tins with creamy sponge mixture, and slid them carefully into the oven. Twenty minutes from now, Mother, she said, what will that be? The voice inside her head said ten past eleven, Ivy, surely you can tell the time by now . . .

Time you had a rest, Mother, said Ivy, that's right, close your eyes and have a nap. I've got a lot to do before they come. Jam'll be ready soon, and nobody would think I'd ever dusted this house.

The lumbering giant combine harvesters had gone up to the burnished fields in brilliant sunshine, filling the village with clouds of dust from the dry roads, and drowning birdsong, conversation and crying babies with their hungry roar.

'It weren't like this when we were kids,' said Old Ellen, resting gratefully in Ivy's armchair after her walk from the Lodge. 'Harvest was the best time of the year. All out in the fields, rabbits for the pot and straw for the dollies. And them stooks to play house in, d'you remember, Ivy?'

' 'Course I do, Ellen Biggs,' said Ivy, cutting slices of airy sponge cake lightly dusted with icing sugar. 'I remember that Fred Mills – he were bigger'n us – chucking handfuls of stubble with great clods of earth sticking to it. Hit me on the leg and made a graze that bled till I got home. Mother didn't half sort him out, I remember that!'

'Don't do to hark back, though, does it,' said Doris Ashbourne. 'Young Mark Jenkins is keen as mustard on them great combines. He's got models of 'em and pictures of 'em, and knows every combine round here practically by name!'

'He's a quiet one, that,' said Ellen, wiping raspberry jam off her chin with a paper napkin, 'takes after his Uncle Jim over at Bagley.'

'Jim Jenkins!' said Ivy. 'Let's hope Mark don't go the same way, then.'

'He's all right now,' said Doris, 'settled down a treat since he married that Bagley girl – and I see she's expecting . . . Trim his sails a bit, that will! Yes please, Ivy, just a small piece.'

'The three witches of Ringford,' said Warren to William, as they passed by Victoria Villa and saw behind the net curtains Ivy, Ellen and Doris sitting with their teacups, weaving spells.

'And Old Ellen had that black cat,' said William, 'that's a sure sign. They'd have chucked her in the village pond years gone by, my dad says.'

'Suppose the Ringle would do,' said Warren speculatively, 'we could lure her out one dark night.'

'She'd get you first,' said William, 'her Black Magic would protect her . . .'

They were on their way up to the Bates' harvest fields with the Jenkins' terrier, to see what he could scent out in the newly cut corn. He strained at the leash, impatient with the boys' ambling progress.

Warren pushed William into the road with a scoffing laugh. 'Black Magic is chocolates, you loony! What you give your lover, your beloved Octavia – ' He dodged and ran, angrily pursued by a vengeful William Roberts.

'He'll come to no good, that Warren Jenkins,' said Ivy Beasley, standing up and watching the two boys out of sight, 'too clever by half.'

'Nothing wrong with Warren,' said Doris Ashbourne, 'he should do well, given a chance. I reckon William's quite bright, too, but his father will beat it out of him if he can. What a difference, eh? Foxy Jenkins is one of the best, and his kids grow and flourish. Roberts is an ignorant bully, and if his kids do any good it will be in spite of his best endeavours.'

'Jean's a good gel, too,' said Old Ellen, 'she's like an old broody, shelterin' her chicks under her wings. He knows it, the child, if he's kept safe. My old mum were like that.'

'Didn't do much for you, Ellen Biggs, did it?' said Ivy sharply, remembering her own mother, possessive, caustic-tongued and forever critical.

'Now, now, Ivy,' said Doris Ashbourne, 'how about another cup of tea, it's parching weather.'

Ivy was still standing by the window, and now leaned forward, pulling the curtain a fraction to see more clearly. 'Bill Turner's a good customer at the shop these days,' she said, 'there he goes again. Can't keep away, it seems.'

'Always did come in a lot,' said Doris Ashbourne, 'Joyce never goes out, so Bill has to get the supplies. He goes into Tresham now and then, but mostly he gets what he wants from the shop. He was one of my best customers, was Bill.'

Ivy's face set. 'He's even more regular now,' she said, 'his Joyce was telling me about them chess games he has with Mr Palmer. She reckons it's a bit more than chess that Bill goes for every week.'

She picked up the teapot and found it empty. 'I'll just go and fill it up, if it will stand it,' she said, and left the room.

'She don't need to listen to what that Joyce says,' said Old Ellen in a hoarse whisper, 'she's three parts mad these days. Jean Jenkins says not many weeks pass without Joyce Turner screaming 'er 'ead off.'

'Poor soul,' said Doris, 'she's pursued by devils, as the Good Book says.'

'She'll be pursued all the way to the loony bin if she's not careful,' said Old Ellen.

'Who's in the loony bin?' said Ivy Beasley, returning with the teapot and setting it down to brew.

Ellen was fortunately saved from having to answer by the roar of another tractor and trailer passing by, shutting out the sunlight and plunging the room into temporary gloom.

Doris Ashbourne hastily changed the subject, brushing

crumbs from her lap neatly into her cupped hand and tipping them on to her empty plate. 'That was a very nice sponge, Ivy, very nice indeed.'

Sunlight and the net-veiled view of the Green returned to the room.

'Soon be Show time, then we'll all be bullied into making sponges,' said Old Ellen, 'I see they're having it at the Hall this year, that David Pearson's doing, I expect, 'im and his Mr Richard . . .'

'At least it gives the poor bloke something to do while his wife's out pestering people about new houses nobody wants,' said Ivy.

'Not heard nothing about them lately.' Ellen adjusted her voluminous pink skirt and began to heave herself out of the chair. 'I was chatting to young John Barnett yesterday – 'e says there's been some hold-up.' She was finally upright, and added, 'Thanks very much, Ivy, my turn to have you and Doris next week. And 'ere, this'll give you something to think about, young John said his sister Josie – you remember 'er, Ivy – is due for a visit from America in the autumn. "Mind you tell Mr Richard," I said, and John boy didn't half give me a look! Ta ta, then . . .'

CHAPTER FIFTEEN

There were two local newspapers, the *Gazette* and the *Advertiser*, and Sheila Pearson had nobbled the editor of the *Advertiser*, the one she considered reasonably independent and not in the Standings' pocket. It was a dull week, and though the editor was sceptical about the Ringford Mafia story she tried to sell him, he promised her he'd look into it and see what he could do. She declined his invitation to go for a drink, and tried not to back away as he sneezed all over her. She returned home moderately pleased with herself.

'Where have you been, David?' she said, finding David walking up the drive ahead of her.

'I got home early – went round to the Hall to see Richard, and we finalised a few details for the Show. He's got some magnificent onions – never seen anything like it!' David had been co-opted on to the Round Ringford Horticultural Society committee that year, and had thrown himself into it heart and soul, with the result that he had found himself doing most of the work.

Sheila bristled. 'I suppose he'll enter them as his own?' she said.

'Of course,' said David, 'why not?'

'Because they were grown by Bill Turner in the Standings' kitchen garden where Mr Richard never sets foot, that's why not,' said Sheila righteously. She put her handbag down on the kitchen table and picked up the kettle. 'Cup of tea, David?' she said. 'I'm really tired and dying for one.'

'I did have a cup with Richard,' he said casually, 'Susan brought us one in the study. Richard's a super chap, you know, Sheila, quite super. He's got all the details of the Horticultural Show at his fingertips, and some really good ideas about ways of improving it. Had a few suggestions myself, of course, and Richard was really pleased.'

Ah well, thought Sheila, better keep the editor's promise to myself. 'All set, then, for the show – all we need is good weather, it's only a couple of weeks,' she said.

'Richard's hiring a good-sized marquee, and hopes to get a celebrity friend to open the show – all helps to attract a few people from outside the village.'

'Who's the celebrity?' said Sheila, opening the biscuit tin and putting some chocolate wafers on a little flowery dish with a porcelain handle. We can have tea on the patio, she thought, make the most of the summer sun while we've still got it. She'd noticed a nippy chill in the air the last couple of evenings, once the sun went down.

'He didn't say,' said David, 'I expect he wants to keep it a surprise – he's up to all those public relations tricks, old Richard! By the way,' he added, 'he asked if you and I would like to pop in for a drink after the Show. I accepted, of course – really kind of him.'

He leaned back in his garden chair, looked beyond the velvety green lawn and over the flower beds bright with chrysanthemums and Michaelmas daisies coming into flower, away to the parkland with its spreading oaks and quietly grazing black and white bullocks. He took a deep breath and said, 'Can't beat the country life, can you, my darling? Oh yes, and how did we get on this afternoon at the mighty *Advertiser*?'

'Nothing doing, really,' said Sheila, 'bit of a waste of time.'

The pile of schedules in the shop had in fact gone down gratifyingly quickly, and Doreen Price was delighted. She had been in charge of the craft and cooking classes for years, and was weary with trying to bully people to enter.

'You're a gem, Peggy,' she'd said, 'I shall put you up for the job next year.'

And at the bus stop, Mrs Jenkins had said to Doris Ashbourne, 'Peggy asked me so nicely I couldn't refuse, never entered before, but she's got me down for strawberry jam and Dundee cake. Mind you, my Foxy says I can't be beaten where strawberry jam is concerned.'

'I shall enter a patchwork teacosy,' Doris had said, 'it has taken me three years to finish it and if I don't win first prize, I shall want to know the reason why.'

Peggy had had no luck with Frank. 'It's just asking for trouble,' he said, 'there's my runner beans out there, long and straight, bug-free and juicy, and if I put them in they're sure to win. Then where shall I be? Hated by every other gardener in the village, and labelled uppity and pushy.'

It was Sunday morning, still and quiet, with as yet no yells and squeals from children on the Green to disturb the calm. The bells had rung for early service, and Peggy had wondered about getting up and going to Holy Communion. But she couldn't get moving fast enough, and instead she assembled the makings of a trial flower arrangement for the Show. Frank had lit a bonfire at the bottom of the garden, scenting the air with woodsmoke.

'Well, I am determined to have a go,' Peggy said from under the kitchen table, crawling around with her reading glasses on the end of her nose.

'What on earth are you doing, Peg?' said Frank, seeing only the soles of Peggy's shoes.

'Looking for a pin,' she said in a muffled voice.

'I suppose it would be stupid to ask what you need a pin for?' he said, patting her bottom.

'Give over, do, Frank,' she said, emerging on her knees holding a long pin. 'It must be obvious that I'm doing a flower arrangment.'

'Not a single flower in sight,' said Frank, picking up a dried cow parsley head and giving it a shake.

'Frank, please put it down,' said Peggy. She grabbed his hand to help her and stood upright, pushing her hair back and brushing seed heads and cotton-woolly old man's beard off her skirt.

'I know, don't tell me,' said Frank, 'you are creating an exquisite table centrepiece with two dried bulrushes and an old boot.'

'You may laugh,' said Peggy, 'but it is much more difficult than you think. I have now been here an hour and a half and have created exactly nothing.' She stuck the cow parsley in a tottering spongy base, pushed it down hard, and the whole thing collapsed in a heap on the floor.

'So that's that,' she said, 'I shall just have to make a wholemeal loaf instead. I must contribute something, else Doreen will be round here after my blood.'

'Peggy,' said Frank, 'Peggy Palmer, light of my life, haven't you forgotten something this morning?'

'If you mean church,' said Peggy, 'the answer's no, I didn't forget, I just sinned. That is, I turned over in bed and thought bad thoughts.'

'No, not church, you wicked woman,' said Frank, and produced a parcel from behind his back. 'Happy birthday, dear Peg,' he said, and gave her a peck on the cheek.

'So you did remember, you rotter,' she said, smiling broadly, and taking the parcel with both hands.

She carefully took off the tape and unwrapped the birthday paper, thick white paper with gold suns, moons and stars. 'It's not from the shop, you've been splashing out,' she said, impressed.

Peggy examined a shiny new book. On the cover was a smoking gun, a lace handkerchief and a bunch of grapes. It was the latest John Gilbert mystery, a jigsaw of clues and deceptions and dodgy loopholes in the law.

'Frank,' she said with a grin of pleasure, 'you know just how to keep a wife happy and content.'

'I don't know about that,' said Frank, 'but I'm glad you like the book.'

There was a card tucked inside and she opened it. 'You romantic fool,' she said, 'how could you doubt that I'd love you for ever and ever?'

'Oh I dunno,' said Frank, 'life's full of surprises.' He walked over and kissed Peggy on the top of her head. 'Many happy returns, my old love,' he said.

'Anyone here got a birthday?' Bill Turner put his head round the back door, smiled at Peggy and winked at Frank.

'Ah, Bill,' said Frank, 'there you are – come on in and have a coffee.'

Bill stepped into the kitchen and took off his boots by the door. He walked in his stockinged feet over to where Peggy sat at the table and said, 'Shut your eyes and put out your hands.'

What are they up to? thought Peggy, but did as she was told, and felt something warm and furry put into her palms. She opened her eyes in surprise, and saw a tiny kitten, its round blue eyes startled and afraid. It mewed desperately, and she held it close to her, laughing and stroking it, and saying, 'There, there, what are you doing here?'

'Needs a good home,' said Bill, 'and seeing as Frank told me it was your birthday I thought you might take it in.'

Peggy turned to Frank, who was looking smug. 'Did you two plot this together?' she said, and Bill replied, 'Had to ask the boss, didn't I, and he said you would like it.'

The kitten curled up against Peggy and stopped trembling. 'It's purring!' she said. 'It's trying to purr!'

'It might like a drink,' said Frank, and got up to get some milk.

'No, I'll do it,' said Peggy, 'let me do it.'

She fetched a saucer and poured a little warm milk left over from the coffee. Very carefully putting down the kitten, she put her finger in the milk and rubbed it against the tiny mouth. The kitten licked her finger, then its lips, and then tentatively lapped the milk, starting back in surprise when it splashed itself with tiny drops.

'Where did it come from?' she asked Bill.

'It's a bit of a mystery,' said Bill, 'I heard it mewing from the old ruined barn up Bates's End. Took me ages to get it down from a great old beam. I reckon it'll be fine if you coddle it a bit.'

'You'll have to think of a name for it,' said Frank, 'perhaps it should be William after Bill here.'

'No,' said Peggy, 'I shall call him Gilbert, in honour of my new book. A pair of birthday mysteries.'

'Only one snag,' said Bill, 'I think he is most likely a she.'

'Ah,' said Peggy, 'well, too late now – she'll have to be Gilbertine and Gilbert for short.'

Frank and Bill fussed about in the old wash house and found a cardboard box for a bed, and Peggy tore up an old blanket and settled the kitten inside. But it wouldn't stay, and tried to crawl up Peggy's leg and get back into the safety of her arms. She picked it up, smiling and stroking its little head. 'You silly baby,' she said, and rubbed her cheek against its soft fur.

CHAPTER SIXTEEN

The *Advertiser* was out on the streets of Tresham on Friday mornings, but Sheila decided to wait for David to buy her a copy on his way home.

It's stupid, she thought, to go rushing into Tresham and spend hours trying to park the car, just for the paper. Either the editor has put something in or he hasn't; apart from selling my body, I've done all I can do now.

Drizzle spread over the village by lunchtime, and Sheila, driven indoors from her gardening, looked around for something to do. She picked up next month's Council papers, but couldn't concentrate, and turned on the television. Usual mindless rubbish, she thought, and turned it off again. Her knitting filled in another ten minutes, then she put that down and decided to wash her hair. Her brown curls fresh and bouncy, she put make-up on with great care and changed from gardening trousers into a crisp denim skirt and blue and white checked shirt.

It was half past three when she finally saw David's car turning into the drive and crunch to a halt on the gravel. She opened the front door and looked anxiously to see if David had remembered.

'Here you are, poppet,' he said. 'Hey! There's no need to snatch . . .'

Sheila walked through to the lounge and riffled through the pages, wondering for the hundredth time if she had said too much, or not enough, and wishing for David's sake that it could be anyone but the Standings she was up against.

David took off his suit jacket and went into the little cloakroom off the hall to wash his hands, humming a snatch of song, happy to be home early and looking forward to the weekend ahead. His idyll was soon shattered.

'The rotten sod!' yelled Sheila. 'He hasn't got a single word in his rotten paper.'

'Sheila, dear!' said David, emerging from the cloakroom, drying his hands on a small green towel. 'Language!'

Sheila threw the *Advertiser* to the end of the room and collapsed on the sofa, where she pummelled the cushions and sobbed loudly.

'Hey, poppet!' said David, looking at her in astonishment and dropping the green towel on to the carpet. He sat down beside her, put his hand on her shoulder and said, 'What on earth is the matter, my pet?'

'That lousy man has put absolutely nothing about the new houses in his wretched little paper, and after all that trouble I went to, ferreting about and sitting in his revolting office listening to him coughing and spitting – and what's more I think I've caught his cold.' And Sheila sneezed loudly to prove it.

'Don't be silly, dear,' said David, 'it's just because you've been crying. Here, take my handkerchief and blow.'

Sheila sniffed and blew her nose into David's pristine white handkerchief, screwing it up and giving it back to him. He hastily put it back in his trouser pocket.

'Now then,' he said, 'explain to me what this is all about. You did say, don't forget, that nothing much had come of your meeting.'

They went through the paper together, carefully scrutinising every page, but there was nothing at all on the subject of the Round Ringford housing project.

'It was probably a bad idea, anway,' said David, treading dangerous ground, 'it would have made life a little tricky in my current dealings with Mr Richard. He is being absolutely super about the Show, couldn't be more helpful.'

Oh shut up, thought Sheila. She sniffed again, ran a hand over her hair and straightened the cushions. 'Pick up that towel, David,' she said, 'I can't be going behind you every minute of the day.'

'If it's a marquee being delivered,' said Fred Mills, walking slowly up Bates's End in hazy sunshine, and stopping for breath at Old Ellen's gate, 'you can be sure it's a Thursday.' Sounds of hammering and crashing scaffolding had disturbed the village from an early hour.

'Well, it is a Thursday, you old fool,' said Ellen Biggs, sweeping leaves from her path, her skirt tucked up over a strange brown cotton shift. 'Look at these leaves, dropping already.' She leaned over her gate, and her skirts settled round wrinkled stockings and discoloured canvas shoes.

Sandra Roberts cycled slowly up to them on a battered old bike of her father's. She was brown and slimmed down from spending the sunny summer days swimming in the Ringle pool up past Prices', a deep, natural pool made by a sharp bend in the river. It had been a haunt of village children for generations, a private, secret place, not overlooked by prying adults.

Good God, thought Ellen, they'll have to watch that one soon. 'Where you off to, Sandra,' she said, 'not back at school yet?'

'Next week,' said Sandra, 'worse luck,' balancing precariously on the bike with one leg stretched out and her sandalled toe just reaching the ground.

'Keeps you outa mischief,' said Fred, 'only good thing about school, if you ask me.'

'You going up to look at the marquee?' said Sandra, and Fred nodded.

'There you are, you see,' he said to Ellen, 'I said if it were a Thursday it would be the marquee.'

'You're goin' soft in the head, Fred Mills,' said Ellen, sweeping vigorously round the corner of the Lodge and out of sight.

'You can get goin', Sandra,' said Fred, 'I'm a poor old thing these days.' He continued to hobble along, turning into the avenue of chestnuts leading up to the Hall. The sun shone through the trees, catching turning leaves and making a tunnel of dappled light.

'I'll walk with you, Mr Mills,' said Sandra, 'I ain't in a hurry.'

The two walked in silence for a while, the bike between them, and then Sandra said, 'Mr Mills, do you reckon Bill Turner is after Mrs Palmer?'

'What's that, gel?' said Fred, turning his good ear towards her.

Sandra put her leg over the bike and hopped to the other side, to be nearer to Fred's good ear. 'Bill Turner,' she said, 'do you reckon he's after Mrs Palmer? My mum was talking to Mrs Jenkins, and she said Miss Beasley had told her Bill Turner was always down at the shop.'

'That Ivy Beasley should keep her evil thoughts to herself,' said Fred Mills. 'Mrs Palmer's a good woman, if you ask me, which you 'ave, so I just advise you to spread such wicked gossip no further, Sandra Roberts.'

'Keep your hair on, Fred!' said Sandra. 'I only asked.'

'No need to be cheeky, my gel,' said Fred, 'I just reckon Bill Turner has got enough trouble with that Joyce without having any lying gossip spread about him. Be a good girl, now, and pick up me baccy pouch – it's fallen out of me pocket.'

Sandra handed him his pouch and they continued slowly up the drive, the noise of hammers and shouts of workmen getting closer all the time. 'It wouldn't be very nice for Mr Palmer, anyway,' she said, 'he's not bad, and I really like

Mrs P. sometimes. I wish she weren't at the shop, though, what with Octavia and – well, you know . . .'

'Afraid I do,' said Fred Mills, 'though it don't mean you 'as to be the same, Sandra.'

Sandra began to run with the bike, took a flying leap and landed in the saddle. 'I'm off home, Mr Mills,' she called back, 'if Old Mother Standing catches me trespassing she'll have me in the dungeons!'

Fred shook his head, relit his pipe and carried on his slow progress until he could see the blue and white marquee almost completely erected. That's a big'un, he thought, bigger'n last year. That'll be Mr Pearson, he and Mr Richard bin planning for weeks.

He propped his stick against a mossy stone urn, and watched the men for a few minutes. He had no feeling of trespassing. It had been the villagers' right since he had been a child, to watch anything going on in the park which meant a celebration. He remembered Mr Richard's twenty-first birthday, with a rowdy dance in the Hall, and supper for two hundred guests on trestle tables on the terrace. That were a good night! Except for Josie Barnett showin' up and makin' a scene because she hadn't been invited. She were a one, little Josie Barnett.

And long before that, he remembered Mr Richard's father and mother on their wedding day. That had been a grand occasion, with a feast for the estate workers and presents for all the children. Then the evening party, when everybody from the village walked in darkness up the drive and stood in the shadows, watching the fun and games in the shrubbery. Mr Richard's mother were a beauty, like a racehorse, and skittish into the bargain!

'Lost in thought, Fred?' It was Mr Richard, his sleeves rolled up and his baggy corduroy trousers resting pre-cariously on his hips.

'Good day, sir,' said Fred, 'as a matter of fact I was thinking about your father and mother on their weddin' day.'

'Ah,' said Mr Richard, 'those were good days at the Hall. They did things properly in those days.'

Fred touched his cap and said, 'Better be getting back now, sir, it takes me longer nowadays.'

'Stay here, Fred,' said Mr Richard, 'I've got the Land-Rover over there – I'll run you back, don't want you keeling over in the drive!'

Blow me down, thought Old Ellen, looking out of her window and seeing old Fred sitting snugly beside Mr Richard as they drove by on the way to Macmillan Gardens. He always were an ole chancer, were Fred Mills.

'Two days before the Show is about right,' said Peggy, 'the bread won't be too new, and it'll cut easily.'

Peggy had abandoned all thoughts of flower arrangement, and settled for home-made bread, but Doreen had persuaded her for the sake of swelling the number of entries to polish up four evenly sized cooking apples from the old tree in the garden.

'I shan't claim any credit for them,' said Peggy to Frank, setting them down on the table. 'I just picked them off the tree.'

'Yes,' said Frank, 'but it's the lovely way you pick them.'

She had put them on a blue-rimmed chalk-white enamel plate, thinking it appropriate that it was the old cooking plate that her mother had used for apple pies. The waxy green skins shone, miraculously free from blemish. Could be plastic, thought Peggy irreverently.

'Those loaves should be done,' she said, glancing at the shelf clock, 'better get them out – no burned crust will pass Miss Beasley's eagle eye.'

'Look out, Peggy!' yelled Frank, but too late.

Gilbert skittered across the floor, fleeing from imaginary predators, her eyes wild and her tail thrashing, just as Peggy withdrew the loaves carefully from the oven. Peggy tripped over the rumpled rug, and the baking tray bearing two hot bread tins flew out of her gloved hands and crashed on to the floor.

'Oh no!' she cried. 'Not the bread ruined as well!' Frank rushed to pick them up, swearing as he burned his fingers on the hot metal. The loaves, risen to a gentle dome and light mealy brown, tipped neatly out on to the floor.

Peggy took a deep breath. Gilbert had rushed into her box, brought to her senses by a very real fear of retribution. Peggy went over to her and stroked her head, saying in a soothing voice, 'Don't be frightened, little one, it wasn't your fault.'

'Of course it wasn't,' said Frank, 'I mean, who would have thought a scatty cat tearing about the floor and making bloody great mountain ranges in the rug would trip anyone up?'

'All right, Frank,' said Peggy, 'but she is only a baby . . . come on, help me salvage something from this disaster.'

Peggy picked up the loaves and placed them on a cooling tray. She fetched the feather duster from the cupboard and began to flick off dust and kitten hairs.

'Peg, you can't do that – you can't put them into the Show after they've been on the floor!'

'Can't I just,' said Peggy grimly, 'no one will know if you don't tell them.'

'But the judges have to taste a piece of each loaf,' protested Frank.

'Won't kill them,' said Peggy, unsmiling. 'If you think I'm going to bake another batch at this late stage, you are wrong. These loaves are going into the Show tomorrow, and you are going to keep mum . . . please?'

'Have it your own way,' he said, 'I just hope Miss Beasley's not judging the bread, that's all.'

Miss Beasley was known to be a fierce and unforgiving judge of the Produce Classes. The fruit cakes were closely scrutinised for a dip in the middle, jams and jellies were tilted remorselessly for any hint of not being set, and the

Victoria sponge was measured by Miss Beasley's fearsome eye for any slant or slope off the horizontal.

'Well, she is a judge,' said Peggy, 'and I don't care. Just so long as I have something to take round to the Hall in the morning, I certainly shan't expect any prizes.'

'We shall be drummed out of the village,' said Frank.

'Get your *Advertiser* here!' shouted David Pearson, opening the door of Casa Pera and wiping his dry shoes thoroughly on the mat.

'Just thought you might like to check it out,' he said, handing the folded newspaper to Sheila in the hall. 'Had a good day, dear?' He kissed her on the cheek, took off his suit jacket and went to wash his hands.

'I've been busy,' said Sheila, 'I got a call from Susan Standing to help out with setting up the flower tables. Bit of a cheek, I thought, when she usually cuts me dead.'

'Ah yes, Sheila,' said David, pouring himself a gin and tonic, 'one for you too, darling?' He began to fill a glass for her without waiting for her reply. 'But you see, she would know that we all want tomorrow to be a really super day, and I'm sure that goes for you too, if only for my sake?'

'Of course, David dear,' she said, 'and have you noticed how she always gets what she wants in the end? Any suggestion of mine was lost in her foggy disapproval, and we did everything Madam's way.'

'It's because she's a Standing, well, not originally of course, but I believe her family are even better born,' said David. 'You can't get away from it, the genuine aristocracy still counts for a lot in this country, especially with village people.'

How did I come to marry this man? thought Sheila, half-meaning it. Because I love him, she reminded herself firmly, and because he is much nicer than I am.

'They just know which side their bread is buttered,' she said, 'those that work on the Standing estate. They know jobs are hard to come by. Beats me how Bill Turner gets away with it: he was quite rude to Richard Standing this afternoon. Mind you, I sympathised with Bill, the way Mr R. was chucking his weight about.'

'Funny, that,' said David, 'I've noticed that Richard is a different chap when he is talking to his workers. He's as nice as pie to me, really quite super.'

'That must be because you are a natural aristocrat,' said Sheila, unable to resist, 'one of nature's gentlemen.'

David looked at her suspiciously, but could see no trace of a smile.

'Well, aren't you going to look at the *Advertiser*?' he said, and she nodded, idly opening it out, and saying, 'Not much point, is there, since that oaf did absolutely nothing about my story. Hey, though, wait a minute – ' She had opened the centre pages and was looking at them goggle-eyed.

'Oh my God,' she said, 'just look at this!'

David leaned over her shoulder and saw big, very black headlines across two pages: 'STANDINGS RULE RINGFORD OK?' Two photographs took up much of the space. Richard Standing and Susan stood laughing with Tim Bingley-Smyth at some evening-dress function, and in contrast there was Barnett's field, cows quietly munching grass in the summer sunshine.

The story underneath was brief. The editor had done his homework, and nothing was said that he could not prove absolutely. In fact, not much was said at all, but a lot implied that the reader could guess at for himself. The *Advertiser* had done Sheila proud.

David Pearson sat down in an armchair with a glum face. 'That's torn it,' he said, 'I don't know what on earth Mr Richard is going to say about that. It's a pity, old thing, that you could not have waited until after the Show.'

For once, Sheila was silent.

'Ah well,' David continued, 'at least it does not connect the story with you in any way.'

Sheila dumbly handed him the paper and pointed out a couple of paragraphs at the foot of the page, right next to the big splash. David read it with growing dismay.

'What's going on?' says Councillor Mrs Sheila Pearson, the hardworking representative for the area. In discussion with the editor, Councillor Pearson voiced her worries and asked for our help. What do YOU the reader think? Write in, and we will pass on your letters to Mrs Pearson.

If it had not been out of the question, David would have burst into tears. Instead, he got up and poured himself another large gin.

'Don't usually have a second,' he said, 'but on this occasion . . .'

CHAPTER SEVENTEEN

Show day in Round Ringford, and many people were up early, looking anxiously out of their windows at the sky, which at dawn had been rosy pink shading into dark, threatening red at the horizon. A chill wind ruffled the surface of the Ringle, and the willows shivered, shedding one or two twirling slender-pointed leaves into the grey ripples of the river.

'If wet, in the Village Hall?' said Doreen to Tom, as they had a cup of tea in the big farm kitchen. 'Spoke of rain,' said Tom, 'but it won't matter too much, we've got the big marquee.'

' 'at on't rain,' said Old Man Roberts, grandfather to Sandra and the rest of the brood, opening the back door and putting a set of keys down on the table. 'Mark my words, the sun'll be out by ten. Done the chickens, missus, so if that's all, I'll be getting off 'ome.'

The Prices and the Robertses had worked together for generations – the one always employing the other on the estate farm. There was familiarity and respect. Each knew exactly how far to go, and the work of the farm got done without a hitch as a result. The only problems arose when Tom wanted to introduce something new into the routine. 'Good enough for 'is father, should be good enough for 'im,' said old Roberts.

In Ivy Beasley's bedroom the black alarm clock went off with a tinny jangle. I know, I know, Mother, Ivy said, drawing the curtains and peering out. Red sky in the morning, shepherd's warning. But shepherd's often wrong, so I'm not saying nothing yet.

She dressed quickly and went down to make her small breakfast of cornflakes and toast with home-made marmalade. Robert had brought her some fresh butter from the farm, and she cut off a thick dollop, topping it off with a blob of marmalade. She chewed it thoroughly, with enjoyment. No, Mother, I'm not chewing it thirty-two times. It ain't necessary, I don't care what Grandmother said.

I wonder if I am going barmy, she thought, like Ellen Biggs says. Barmy is as barmy does, said the voice in her head.

'I'm on car park duty at one o'clock,' said Foxy Jenkins, pulling on his shirt in the tiny bedroom where he and Jean had happily occupied the big double bed since they were married. The bed had belonged to old Lord Bailee at Fletching, and Foxy had gone to the sale after the old boy died. 'Got it for thirty pounds,' he'd said proudly to Jean, bringing it back to Ringford on a farm trailer. 'Who else would want it?' Jean had said, as they sawed it in half to get it up the stairs.

'I'll help, Dad, I can direct cars,' said Warren from the lavatory, where he was holding siege against his twin sisters. 'Gemma, Amy, come and get your breakfast!' shouted Jean from the kitchen. 'And Mark, will you stop tormenting our Eddie at once, or I'll clip your ear.'

'I shall have to be on the gate from midday, Mrs Standing says.' Jean had been up since six o'clock, and she made a mental note to take an umbrella.

'What you doing with the kids?' said Foxy.

'Gemma and Amy and Mark are going with Doris Ashbourne,' said Jean, 'then once they're safe inside they can look after themselves, and Eddie can stay with me on the gate. Warren'll be with you, all right?'

'S'long as the young'uns know where to find us,' said Foxy. 'I don't want them wandering off, with all them strangers about.'

Bill had left Joyce sitting like a house spider in the corner of the kitchen, still in her grubby dressing gown, reading a women's magazine brought in by Ivy Beasley. 'This could be me,' she said, and read aloud, ' "Dear Nurse Brown, I am a lonely young woman living with an unloving husband and want to make a new start. Can you advise me?" '

'Don't, Joyce,' said Bill, 'I can't take much more.'

'Huh! you can't take much more – what about me? You're off out to the Show, enjoying yourself with all and sundry, not giving me a thought. What shall I do all day? Well, you may find I've done meself in when you get back. I know how, don't you worry.'

Bill said nothing, and cleared away the breakfast dishes. 'I'll do these when I come home,' he said, 'got to go now. Don't do anything stupid, please, Joyce.' She didn't answer him, just went on reading, and he left the house quietly, locking the door behind him as usual.

Peggy opened up the shop and felt the excitement in the air. The village was busy already, more cars than usual on the street, and she could see a stream of people making their way down Bates's End to the Hall, taking their entries in time for judging at ten o'clock.

'Looks like being a nice day after all, Frank,' she called over her shoulder. The sun had climbed out of its ominous rising, warming up the breeze and making a nonsense of the weather forecast. Now the sky promised nothing but good. Feathery high clouds, so slight and filmy that they presented no threat, hung motionless over far distant places. 'Nothing but blue skies, from now on,' sang Peggy, sweeping up the sweet papers and crisp packets, and glancing towards Victoria Villa to see if Ivy Beasley noticed.

'Never saw the sun, shinin' so bright, never saw things goin' so right,' joined in Bill, like the other half of a double act. He put a couple of letters in the post box and rode off on his bike, waving to Peggy and shouting, 'Morning, Frank,' as he went. Only he knew what it cost him to lift his spirits and sing.

Is there nothing that man can't do? thought Frank, opening up the Post Office cubicle and unlocking the safe.

'Is my white T-shirt clean?' shouted Octavia to her mother downstairs at Barnstones. Gabriella Jones hunted through the washing basket and found it, clean but unironed. 'Needs ironing,' she shouted up to her daughter.

'Oh Mum, do it for us, please,' wheedled Octavia, 'I'm meeting Sandra at ten outside the school.'

'As if I hadn't enough on my plate this morning,' said Gabriella, getting out the ironing board, and putting her basket of small cakes and pastries to one side. She had fallen under Susan's spell, and against her inclinations had agreed to help with refreshments.

'You can iron so much better than me,' said Octavia, appearing at the kitchen door in jeans and a bra. Oh dear, thought Gabriella, she's much too pretty for comfort. 'Better than I, dear,' she said, 'and put your wrap round you, 'Tavie, you never know who might come to the door.'

'Chance'd be a fine thing,' muttered Octavia, and disappeared upstairs again.

Old Ellen dressed carefully in the pink skirt, with a short-sleeved white lacy top, revealing flabby underarms and a scraggy neck. She added her best red cardigan in case it should get cold, and then took an old canvas chair into her front garden where she sat down to watch the people going by.

'Morning Ellen,' said Doris Ashbourne, carrying her patchwork teacosy carefully wrapped in white tissue, and protected by a green Marks & Spencer's plastic bag. 'Didn't you enter nothing in the show?'

'Too old,' said Ellen, 'can't stand on me feet for long enough in the kitchen.'

Doris continued up the drive, thinking Old Ellen always had an excuse for everything. 'Lazy old devil, she is,' she said, catching up Ivy Beasley, whose notepad and pen were tucked into a capacious black bag, prepared to sit in judgement on the village's best baking efforts.

'And what does she think she looks like in that get-up?' said Ivy, herself soberly dressed in grey skirt and white blouse, pinned firmly at the collar with a large black jet mourning brooch.

By lunchtime, cars were parked all along both sides of the road at Bates's End, and were filling up the temporary car park set up in the field beyond the Vicarage. 'Shouldn't get too mucky,' said Foxy to Warren, as they directed cars into long parallel lines down the field, 'ground's quite dry.' 'I liked it better last year,' said Warren, 'when it rained and we 'ad to tow all those cars off, and I helped drive the tractor.'

But there were no signs of rain now. The sun shone benevolently down on the colourful scene in the Park grounds, and though still cool under the trees, the heat on the open lawns was such that people were glad of the flurries of wind that caught tent flaps and strings of striped bunting. The traditional festive sound of the Tresham Silver Band drifted down the avenue, as Peggy and Frank, walking arm in arm, made their way to the Show. A hum of conversation, broken by shouts from excited children, grew louder as they approached the park gates, and Peggy, infected by the atmosphere, skipped a couple of steps in time to the familiar tune. Her green sunray pleated skirt swung skittishly as she moved, and Frank recalled in a flash of mixed emotion a young Peggy rockin' round the clock in the Coventry Jubilee Hall.

'Steady on, old girl,' he said, 'anybody would think you'd never been to a Horticultural Show before.' 'I haven't,' said Peggy, 'and nor have you. I'd no idea it was to be such a big do, though David Pearson has certainly been pestering everyone for long enough over it.'

'You have to hand it to him, though,' said Frank, 'he certainly knows how to do a thing properly.'

They turned into the park gate, and gave their entrance money to Mrs Jenkins, solid and colourful in a bright red dress. 'I was beginning to think you weren't coming, Mrs Palmer,' she said to Peggy. 'You'll be missing the celebrity!' Peggy felt ridiculously pleased that her absence had been noticed.

While Frank was fumbling with his change, Peggy leaned down and tickled Eddie, making him giggle. 'Isn't he good?' she said, 'sitting there in his pushchair like a little emperor!'

'He's happy s'long as he's got people talking to him,' said Mrs Jenkins.

'Who is the celebrity?' said Frank. 'It's all been a great mystery.'

'Usually means they haven't got one until the last minute,' said Mrs Jenkins knowingly.

She was, of course, right. Richard Standing had grandly promised a celebrity opener at an early committee meeting, and then had left it much too late. Telephoning around to a few showbusiness friends, he found that they had been booked up for months on the annual round of fêtes and charity events. At last he'd found a popular chat show host who'd been at school with him, and happened to be free.

'What sort of press coverage can you promise, Dicky?' said the star with the warm-hearted image. Surprised at the calculating edge to the celebrity's voice, Richard Standing had diffidently mentioned the *Gazette*, the Tresham *Advertiser*, and been wounded at the derisive laughter at the other end of the telephone. 'Actually,' said the star, 'I've just remembered I promised to take the kids to a horse show – sorry, Richard love. See you soon, bye!'

In desperation, he had asked his aged aunt, Lady Frimley,

to open the Show. In her youth, Lady Frimley had been often in the news, but now she lived a solitary life in London. A gadabout and social butterfly, her name had been linked with the most eligible bachelors in the land, even with royalty on one occasion. Her early life and colourful adventures had become legend in the Standing family, but it was a sad truth that few people in Round Ringford had ever heard of her.

Peggy and Frank wandered with the crowds down the side of the blue and white marquee, which gently swelled and flapped in the light breeze. Heads nodded in greeting, and they confirmed several times that it was a perfect day for the Show. They came to the edge of the Hall garden where a podium had been erected by Bill Turner and draped stylishly with the Union Jack. There the crowd was gathering, waiting for Richard Standing to begin his introductory speech. The members of the Studio Band from Bagley were waved into silence by their conductor, and Susan Standing drifted smilingly into view.

She was followed by her husband, who had his hand under the elbow of a tall, thin, elegant old lady, dressed in pearly grey silk, and wearing a wide straw sun-hat. This was anchored with a pink chiffon scarf tied prettily beneath her chin with a large bow. Richard Standing helped his aged aunt up on to the platform, and turned to the crowd.

'Ladies and gentlemen,' he began firmly. But only a few people in the front row heard his words, and he shook the microphone in front of him in irritation. Unfortunately his shake did the trick, and the assembled villagers were surprised and amused to hear their squire say, 'What's the matter with this bloody thing!'

Richard Standing's speech of welcome was warm. He recalled the wonderful days of the past when the Show had always been held at the Hall, and the family's old gardener had walked off with all the prizes.

'Bet that was popular,' said Peggy to Frank, who frowned at her.

'And now,' said Richard Standing, 'the moment you have all been waiting for – I would like to introduce our guest who has graciously agreed to spare some of her precious time to open our Show this afternoon.'

'Wonder what keeps her so busy the rest of the time?' said Peggy to Frank, who shook his head at her warningly.

'Lady Frimley has come down all the way from London to be with us today,' said Richard Standing.

'Big deal,' said Octavia Jones in an audible voice.

Richard glared at her and continued, 'She has been associated with the Standing family and Round Ringford for many years, and the older ones among you will remember her wonderful efforts in the W.V.S. during the war.'

One or two people coughed restlessly, and Sandra Roberts, standing with Octavia by the tea tent, said loudly, 'We was robbed! She ain't no celebrity!'

'Before I hand over to Lady Frimley,' said Richard Standing, looking furiously at the girls, 'I have a few important thank-yous to say to the many people who have helped to get this show on the road! There's Foxy and Jean Jenkins for parking cars and taking money from folk who may or may not want to pay – ' He looked round the crowd, waiting for laughter that did not come. 'And then our hardworking and impartial judges Fred Mills, Ivy Beasley, Albert Hill, and Olive Scott from Fletching,' he continued. There was polite applause, and the crowd waited, expecting one more name, one more very obvious name.

'And last but not least,' said Mr Richard, smiling at his wife, 'I must thank Mrs Standing for being so patient and wise, and keeping us all in order!' Susan shook her head self-deprecatingly and looked over the park and far away. There was no applause, and the crowd still waited.

'What about David Pearson?' said Peggy in surprise. 'Surely he deserves a mention?'

Frank looked guiltily at her. 'Forgot to show you the *Advertiser* this morning, sorry,' he whispered. 'I saw the story while you were out busking with Bill on the pavement.'

'I did see it,' she whispered back, 'but surely that wouldn't . . . ?'

Frank nodded, and put his finger to his lips, hushing her up.

Sheila Pearson, standing with David over in the corner by the shrubbery like a naughty child excluded from the party, felt her heart sink. She put her hand in David's for comfort, but he shook it away, and turning, walked with a purposeful tread out from the corner, across the front of the crowd and the podium, and headed with touching dignity for the big wrought-iron gates of the Hall.

This happened in complete silence, and since the crowd had all either read the *Advertiser*, or had been told about it, everyone knew exactly what was going on and waited delightedly for the next development.

Everyone, that is, except Sheila Pearson, who wished devoutly to be swallowed up by an earthquake, or failing that, prayed to wake up and find it had all been a bad dream.

As Richard Standing cleared his throat to continue, someone else moved in the crowd. Peggy Palmer left Frank's side and walked through villagers who fell back to make a pathway for her, over to where Sheila stood alone. 'Hello, Sheila,' she said in a clear loud voice, 'David has certainly done a grand job here.'

'Thanks,' whispered Sheila, 'thanks a lot.'

The crowd exhaled like a deflated balloon, and attention returned to Richard Standing, who was just stepping back to give Lady Frimley her big moment. Unfortunately, Bill Turner had made no guard rail at the rear of the podium, and Mr Richard stepped back too far. He disappeared neatly from sight, and Susan rushed to his aid. Lady Frimley, shortsighted as a bat, noticed nothing, but was pleased that her little joke about being 'unaccustomed as she was to public speaking' should have got such a roar of laughter.

'What a shame,' said a deep voice behind Peggy, and she turned to see Bill Turner with a perfectly straight face standing behind her.

'Bill,' she said, 'you didn't . . . ?'

He shook his head solemnly, said, 'As if I would,' and walked slowly away towards the exhibits tent.

The crowd listened politely to Lady Frimley, and then began to fragment into chattering groups, heads together and with many glances over to where Sheila still stood miserably with Peggy.

'Don't worry,' said Peggy, 'they'll soon have other things to think about, you know what Ringford's like.'

Each year there were another two or three new things to see or do. 'Spoil the Show, they do,' Fred Mills complained, 'we didn't 'ave all them extras in my dad's day.' But whole families with children came and made an afternoon of it, and this was good for the coffers in the end.

This year an alien bouncy castle, more at home at a motorway service station, and suggested by David Pearson after a journey down the M1 from a business meeting in Sheffield, had been inflated and anchored in the orchard, and squeals of terror floated over the Show grounds.

Sam Smith, the blacksmith from Fletching, had been a more appropriate suggestion from Tom Price, and Sam vigorously demonstrated his skill on a long-suffering pony in a corner of the field. Stalls of dried-flower arrangements and home-produced honey were soon doing good business, and the large refreshment tent, manned by the W.I., was as usual the best patronised quarter of the Show.

Peggy could see Frank coming over to join them, and she waved at him, anxious that Sheila should have both of them standing by her. But he was nobbled by Fred Mills halfway across the grass, and Peggy knew he was stuck for a good ten minutes.

'Shall we go and see if we've won anything?' she said to Sheila, taking her arm.

'No, thanks all the same,' said Sheila, now pale and near to tears, 'I'd better go and see where David has got to. Anyway, you shouldn't be seen with me too much or you'll be blackballed too.'

'Don't be ridiculous,' said Peggy, 'I'm sure it was just a silly oversight.'

'You know better than that, Peggy,' said Sheila, and went on with a bit more of her usual spirit, 'it's not that I mind for myself – if you take on a public position you have to expect to be Aunt Sally occasionally. No, it's David – he has worked so hard for this Show, and thinks the sun shines out of . . . well, you know. Sodding Standings . . .'

'It might have been a mistake,' said Peggy, 'maybe Richard Standing will be round with an apology . . . miserable pig . . .'

Sheila shook her head sadly, and smiled at Peggy. 'Thanks, Peggy,' she said, 'I shan't forget your kindness.' She walked off and Peggy insisted on going with her, turning back only at the big gates, and waving her an encouraging goodbye.

Frank was nowhere to be seen when Peggy got back to the marquee, and she guessed he had gone off to look at the display of caged birds, housed in another small tent round by the blacksmith. Well, she thought, he can do that on his own. She couldn't bear to look at the tiny, fluttering creatures with their baleful eyes and fragile, dry little legs.

That'll be where he is, thought Peggy, so I shall go and see how my bread and cooking apples have survived judgement by Poison Ivy.

She walked through the entrance of the marquee and saw Doreen Price standing by a stall selling gardening books and tools, and supplies for the keen flower arranger.

Doreen already had three little wicker baskets with long handles hooked over her arm, and was looking covetously at a large trug, big enough to carry vegetables for four for a week.

'Doreen Price,' said Peggy, 'what are you up to?'

'Caught me out,' said Doreen, 'don't tell Tom.' She looked round her to see who was listening, and then said, 'You did right by poor old Sheila. Tom says Mr Richard blew his top yesterday when he saw the paper, but I reckon she's only doing her job.' Susan Standing drifted by, and Doreen coloured. 'Better not say any more now, Peggy, you know how it is.'

'Where's the baking section, Doreen?' said Peggy, fed up with village politics. 'Right up the other end,' said Doreen, 'I'll see you up there in a minute.'

Peggy walked along the aisles between long rows of trestle tables, putting off confrontation with her own entries. Giant scarlet shaggy-headed dahlias vied for attention with their acid-yellow cousins, overshadowing more subtle flowers. Ah, but those roses! Dark, velvety red, and peach shading into yellow with firm dark green leaves and not a trace of black spot to be seen. The air was heavy with the scent of the roses and of late grown pastel pink, mauve and white sweet peas. As the sun warmed up the marquee and more people crowded in to look at the exhibits, Peggy's head began to swim and she stood for a while near a side opening, gulping fresh air and watching tides of people passing to and fro.

She set off again past the vegetables, marvelled at the huge onions and wondered if they were edible. 'I just love the shallots,' she said to Mary York, who stood looking at plates of sand, each with twelve tiny shallots sitting exactly vertically in a perfect circle.

'Graham's got a First for his marrow,' Mary said, 'we teased him – said he blew it up with a bicycle pump. We did laugh!'

'How beautiful!' said Peggy, passing the craft tables, well supported with babies' matinée jackets exquisitely knitted in white, pale pink, blue and yellow. A clown teddy bear boasted First Prize, and there were several rather peculiar handmade objets d'art. Don't know what else you could call them, thought Peggy. Oh, and look at that terrible necklace of shells! It would scratch you to pieces.

Sandra Roberts was standing on her own in front of the children's display of miniature gardens. Peggy, unsure of her reception, said, 'Hello Sandra, anything from your family here?'

Sandra turned to look at her, and Peggy was horrified to see a tear slowly trickling down the girl's brown cheek. 'It's not fair,' said Sandra, 'they always wins the prizes.' Peggy looked at the gardens meticulously set out in trays, with tiny stone walls and patterns of flowers and vegetables in all kinds of unlikely materials cleverly put to use. Some even had ponds with tiny bulrushes and garden seats made from matchsticks.

'The kids don't make them,' said Sandra, 'it's their mums and dads. Our Andrew made his own, but of course he don't get a prize, oh no.' She pointed to a much more roughly put together garden in a battered tin tray. A small plastic duck floated on a piece of broken mirror, and the flower beds contained only heads of wilting daisies, picked by Andrew on the Green.

'What a shame, Sandra, when he'd taken the trouble to enter on his own,' Peggy said. She leaned forward, shielding the trays from view for a minute, and very swiftly slid the red First Prize card from beside a miniature masterpiece across to Andrew's hopeful offering. 'You never know,' she said to Sandra, 'they may not notice it's the wrong name . . .' Sandra stared at Peggy dumbfounded as she walked off towards the baking tables.

Oh dear, there it was, her domed, mealy brown loaf, cut

through the middle, and exposing to the world a soggy, uncooked, inedible centre.

'Oh no,' she said aloud, 'how did that happen?' She dare not read the comment on the white card, and wished she could scoop it up and take it away, far from all eyes.

'Not quite up to standard yet, Mrs Palmer,' said a sharp voice at her elbow. She saw Miss Beasley, neat and inconspicuous in her grey skirt and white blouse, looking at her like a predatory ferret.

'You could say that,' said Peggy, 'yes, you're quite right, Miss Beasley. The Rayburn let me down, would you say?' A tiny ball of anger was gathering in the pit of Peggy's stomach, seeded by David's humiliation and now fed by Miss Beasley's smug expression.

'Just lack of experience, I expect,' Ivy Beasley said, 'it takes longer than you think to learn our country ways.'

Stupid old bag, thought Peggy, and as the anger snow-balled, she said with deliberation, 'I don't suppose dropping it on the kitchen floor helped.' She watched Miss Beasley change colour. 'You mean this loaf has been on your kitchen floor!' she said.

'Oh, I wiped off the dust and cat's hairs very carefully,' Peggy said, 'and anyway, nobody's going to want to eat it, are they?'

Miss Beasley, speechless with annoyance, stalked off towards the judges' table and Peggy could see her tackling poor Doreen Price, now writing busily on record cards and checking results.

'Nothing they can do to you now,' said Bill, coming alongside, 'except perhaps clap you in leg-irons.'

'You were listening,' said Peggy, feeling a lot better. 'Have you seen Frank anywhere? I'm not going into that bird tent after him.'

'Last seen heading for the teas,' said Bill, 'shall I come with you and protect you from any more Beasleys?'

'You can tell me where the cooking apple class is,' said Peggy, 'perhaps I've had better luck there.'

'You certainly have,' said Bill, and led her to the dishes of apples, none so shining and perfect as her own.

'Congratulations!' said Bill, and she saw with gratification the red card tucked under her plate: Mrs Peggy Palmer, First Prize.

'Goodness!' she said. 'Well, Frank says it's the way I pick 'em, but there's really more credit due to Doris Ashbourne than to me.'

'Never look a gift horse, gel,' said Bill, 'you get all of one pound for first prize. Come on, you can blow it on a cup of tea.'

'How's Joyce?' Peggy asked, as they pushed their way out of the marquee. 'Isn't she coming this afternoon? Surely she would enjoy seeing old friends?'

They were greeted by Mrs Jenkins, released from duty, with Eddie holding her hand and toddling drunkenly along, determined to stay on his feet. His white-blond hair flopped over his eyes, and he chuckled as a passing mongrel licked his outstretched ice-creamy hand. He's good enough to eat, that child, thought Peggy, dear little soul. 'Wonderful day for the Show,' she said, nodding at Gemma and Amy, identical and withdrawn in a secret game with daisy chains.

Bill's face had closed up like the sun going in, and he said, 'Joyce just didn't feel like coming out this afternoon.' He said it with such finality that Peggy let it go, thinking it was not her business to pry.

'Ah look, there's Frank,' she said, and led the way to where he sat with a cup of tea on a rickety card table set precariously on the grass.

'I went to look at the birds – feathered variety,' he said, smiling at Peggy, 'I see you triumphed with the apples.'

'I'm thinking of giving the prize to Doris,' she said, 'but maybe I'll buy you a cake instead.'

Bill took orders and went off to the tea tent, and Frank looked at Peggy seriously for a moment. 'You did well, Peg,' he said, 'I'm not a great fan of David Pearson, but that was a dirty trick of Richard Standing's, public humiliation for them both. Very easy for him to do, and very cruel, too.'

Peggy was surprised at his vehemence, and patted his hand. 'I expect it will blow over,' she said, 'most things do in Ringford.'

'Bloody Ringford,' said Frank, and got up to help Bill with the tea things.

The raffle was drawn, and the cups presented. Bill won the shield for the best allotment, and Tom Price took all the dahlia prizes. Peggy was delighted to see that Mrs Jenkins' strawberry jam had a First, and Mrs Ashbourne's teacosy had been Highly Commended.

She looked at her watch and was surprised to see that it was nearly half past four. 'Quite an afternoon,' she said to Frank as they strolled back down the avenue, William Roberts on his bike weaving figures of eight around them and taking no notice of Sandra and Octavia who tried to stop him.

'In a funny way I really enjoyed it,' said Peggy, 'not the Pearson bit, of course – but I did have a good sort-out with Poison Ivy. Quite a few people were on Sheila's side, you know . . .'

It was cool under the trees, and Frank shivered. 'Walk up,' he said, 'it'll be warmer out on the Green.'

'Did you enjoy it, Frank?' said Peggy, waving to Old Ellen at her window lookout post.

'On and off,' said Frank, 'maybe it will be safe for me to enter those beans next year.'

The springy turf of the Green still held some warmth of the day, and small knots of village people stood at their gates, discussing the afternoon's happenings. William Roberts had speeded up and was trying out circus stunts on his long-suffering bike, spurred on by Warren Jenkins and the terrier. A kind of peace had settled over the village, a glow of satisfaction at a job done well, a tradition successfully upheld.

Peggy and Frank walked slowly across the Green, watching the queue of cars now curling round by the pub and heading off towards Tresham. 'Good turnout,' said Frank, 'should have made a bob or two.'

As they opened the back door and went into the kitchen, Gilbert rushed up to meet them, and Peggy scooped her up and hugged her tightly. 'Has mummy's baby been alone all afternoon, then?' she crooned into the furry little head.

'Mummy's little baby has eaten those sausages mummy forgot to put in the fridge,' said Frank, picking up an empty plate from the draining board, and putting it in the sink. 'Do you think the cricket's still on?' he said, and walked through the passage into the living room.

Peggy heard him groan, and then shout, 'No! Oh God, no!'

She rushed into the room behind him and stopped dead. It was as though a giant hand had picked up all their belongings, tossed them into the air, and let them fall in pieces all over the floor. Peggy's tapestry work had been pulled apart, as if it concealed diamonds in the stitching, and the drawers of Frank's bureau were pulled out and tipped on to the floor, papers, books and pens in a jumbled heap. His chess pieces were scattered all around the room, and the old wooden box that contained them had been trodden on and split like firewood. Vases lay in broken shards on the floor, and lamps – sent flying in the speed and panic of the hunt – lay on their sides in pools of broken glass.

The window overlooking the garden stood open, one of its panes broken enough to allow a felonious hand to reach through and turn the latch.

Frank turned and looked at Peggy. 'As you were saying, Peggy, quite an afternoon . . .'

CHAPTER EIGHTEEN

Ivy Beasley and Ellen Biggs walked slowly down the avenue of chestnuts conducting a post mortem. 'It were bigger than last year,' said Ellen, 'more entries . . .'

'Bigger ain't necessarily better,' said Ivy Beasley. 'It's standard that counts, and there was a lot of rubbish on them tables. Doreen Price's Swiss roll was split underneath, and Mary York's elderflower wine tasted like vinegar – not to mention the soggy effort of Peggy Palmer.'

Ellen nodded, for once in agreement with Ivy. 'And that row over the kids' garden in a tray. Andrew Roberts swore he never moved that First Prize label – not that you can believe a word them Robertses say – '

'Had to give him a Highly Commended to shut him up,' said Doris Ashbourne, catching them up as they reached Ellen's Lodge. 'He were as pleased as a dog with two tails!'

Doris and Ivy walked on down the lane, and across the Ringle bridge. They stopped, as everybody always did, to look into the water. 'Looks cold, don't it,' said Ivy Beasley, with a little shiver, 'winter won't be long.' She pulled her grey cardigan closer round her chest and looked across the Green. 'Colours begin to fade before you notice it,' she said, 'another year on the wane.'

'Come on, Ivy, buck up!' said Doris. 'Think of

Christmas on the way. That always cheers me up, thinking of Christmas.'

They watched a flotilla of ducks sail under the bridge, heading for home and the safety of Prices' yard.

'The fox'll have them soon enough, long before Christmas,' said Ivy, and Doris laughed.

'Best get you home, Ivy,' she said, 'else we shall be fishing you out of there with your hair tangled in the weeds, just like that Ophelia.'

'I saw that film,' said Ivy, 'couldn't understand a word.'

The road divided, encircling the Green, and they stood at the fork, reluctant to go to their quiet, lonely sitting-rooms and feel the excitement of the day evaporating for another year. 'Pearson woman got her come-uppance,' said Ivy reflectively, and then stiffened. 'Here, is that a police car?' she said, her mood instantly changing. 'Come on, Doris, walk round my way and let's see what's going on . . .'

'PC Cowgill – may I come in?' said the young, chubby-faced policeman, as Frank opened the front door. 'Am I speaking to Mr Palmer?'

'None other,' said Frank, 'please come through to the kitchen. We haven't touched the sitting-room – you can't move in there.'

Peggy sat at the table, Gilbert on her lap, and she stroked her mechanically, looking tearfully at the police constable as he took off his cap and nodded a friendly, 'Good day, Mrs Palmer.'

'You were at the Show, I expect?' he said, sitting down at the table and taking out his notebook. Peggy nodded, and continued to stroke Gilbert, who looked up at her with glassy sea-green eyes, sensing trouble.

'Most of the village was,' said Frank, 'no doubt how the villains managed to do it without being seen.'

'You'd like a cup of tea?' said Peggy in a strangled voice, and lifted Gilbert gently off her lap. She moved like a sleepwalker, and Frank shook his head dismally at the policeman.

'Quite natural to feel shocked,' said PC Cowgill, his round pink face serious and wise, his blue eyes full of concern. 'Yes, please, Mrs Palmer, a cup of tea would go down a treat – been on duty at a race meeting this afternoon – motorbikes, not horses – real thirsty work!'

It's not like Peggy, thought Frank, to be so beaten – more likely to be off after the thieves, with her rolling pin. Still, she's had a funny day, what with old Ivy and the bread, and the Pearson fiasco. Could have done without this.

'I'll just look at the damage, Mr Palmer,' said the policeman, draining his cup appreciatively. 'Nice little cat you got there, Mrs Palmer, what's her name?'

'Gilbert,' said Peggy, with a visible effort at concentration.

'Ah, it's a him,' said PC Cowgill.

'No,' said Peggy, 'he's a she.'

'Yes, of course,' said PC Cowgill, 'silly of me, Mrs Palmer.'

He followed Frank into the sitting-room, suggesting Peggy stayed in the kitchen to feed Gilbert. They surveyed the wreckage – Frank gloomily and the policeman professionally. 'Anything missing, Mr Palmer?'

'Video, tape deck and a carriage clock that was my father's.'

'Usual thing,' said PC Cowgill, 'a quick in-and-out job.'

'Locals, do you think?'

'Could be – or the motorway thieves,' said the policeman, 'a couple of thugs from London steal a car and tear up the motorway, come off at random and end up in a small village. They try a salesman routine if the owner is in, but if their luck's in they get an empty house and are in and out in minutes. Back to London, ditch the car and no possibility of catching them. We get a lot of that.'

'Thank God they didn't try to break in the Post Office,' said Frank.

'Too much trouble, they'd know alarms were set,' said PC Cowgill, 'and I hope you won't mind my asking, but did you check the toilet?'

'They used it,' said Frank grimly.

'You flushed it away?'

Frank looked at him as if he was mad. 'Of course I did,' he said, 'don't tell me that was wrong?'

'Just that once we caught a thief who'd used the toilet and wiped his bum on an envelope addressed to himself. It were an empty house, waiting for new people to move in. He'd taken stupid things – brass light fittings and lead from the roof. We got it all back and he got done, I'm glad to say.'

'Very interesting,' said Frank, faintly impatient, wanting to get back to Peggy, 'but I'm certain there was no envelope.'

'No, no, of course not,' said the policeman. 'Any cash missing, or jewellery?'

'Peggy's jewel box has gone. Nothing really valuable, just meant a lot to her. No cash – none in the house, though a few thousand in the Post Office.'

'Can't promise we shall get it back, Mr Palmer, but we do our best and sometimes strike lucky. If it's locals, you stand more chance.'

Frank saw the policeman out, and noticed Ivy Beasley and Doris Ashbourne standing on the corner by the school. No, I can't face them, he thought, and closed the door before they could get within earshot.

Peggy had cleared away the tea things and was standing at the sink, tears plopping into the washing-up water, Gilbert miaowing at her feet. She had no apron on, and the front of her dancing green skirt was wet with soapy water.

'Could have been worse, Peg,' said Frank, 'they could have got into the Post Office.'

Peggy turned and looked at him, and her face was distorted with tears and sudden rage. 'Never mind about the bloody Post Office!' she yelled. 'What's money compared with all our precious things? – Your chess box, and my jewellery – Mum's rings and my coral beads from when I was little – who cares about the stupid bloody Post Office . . . and who the hell is that?'

Knocking on the front door stopped Peggy's tirade and Frank went to answer it. It was Sheila Pearson, still in her smart linen dress put on for the Show, looking at Frank with a face like doom. She walked in without being asked, saying nothing, and went through to the kitchen, not noticing the wrecked sitting-room through the open door.

'Sheila?' said Peggy, wiping her eyes with the back of her wet, soapy hand. 'What are you doing here? Don't tell me the burglary's round the village already?'

'What burglary?' said Sheila, and burst into tears.

Please God, let me wake up, thought Frank, guiding Sheila to a chair. Peggy stared at her, and then at Frank. He shrugged, sighed deeply and said, 'What is it, then, Sheila?'

'He's gone,' she said. 'David's gone, didn't say where, or when he would be back. He's taken a suitcase.'

There was an unbelieving silence for a minute, and then Frank began to laugh. 'Frank!' said Peggy, shocked. But Frank had snapped, and his laughter got louder and louder. He patted Sheila on the shoulder, tried to say something but choked as the mirth took over.

Sheila stood up, affronted and astonished. 'Well,' she said, 'thank you for your support, Frank, I wouldn't have believed it of you, you of all people.'

'No, no, Sheila, sit down, please,' said Peggy, 'you don't understand. You see, we've been burgled while we were out, and everything is a mess and things broken and missing, and the policeman's only just gone.' Sheila stared at her, then walked over and put her arms round Peggy and they wept loudly and sadly together.

Frank pulled himself together, and pronounced a course of action. 'I am going into the shop,' he said, 'for a bottle of good Bulgarian red, and we shall drink it now, all of it, and

137

then maybe another after that. Sit down girls. I shall not be a moment.'

Ivy Beasley, going into her back yard to bring in washing that she had forgotten in the excitement of speculation with Doris Ashbourne about the police car, stopped dead. It was half dark, and she could see into the lighted window of the Palmers' kitchen next door. Well I never, she said to herself, that beats all.

Frank, Peggy and Sheila were singing an approximation of a Russian song at the tops of their voices and dancing, arms interlocked and feet stamping on the quarry-tiled floor. Two empty wine bottles stood on the table, and Gilbert had retreated to the inside of the laundry basket, high up on top of the fridge. 'La la-la la la!' they sang in unison, and as Ivy watched transfixed they high-stepped across to the window and pressed their noses to the panes, sticking out their tongues and waggling their fingers.

Ivy retreated in terror, slammed her back door and fled to her bedroom. They've gone mad, she thought, I've a good mind to call the police. But she put on her coat and hat and stepped quietly out of her front door. It's not late, Mother, she said, I'll nip up to Doris's and see what she thinks.

CHAPTER NINETEEN

Fading summer was replaced by the brilliant colours of autumn. The fields were a bright, rich brown from the plough, with bands of iron-red earth in some places where the newly turned soil caught the sun. The avenue of glowing chestnuts had thick spongy mats of yellowy orange leaves, flattened and dirtied under car tyres and feet, until Mr Richard pronounced them dangerously slippery, and Bill Turner cleared them away and burnt them. The tall school windows followed the season with brown paper branches covered with real flame red and yellow leaves, collected and carefully pressed flat by the children and stuck on in haphazard, cheerful splashes of colour.

Conkers were collected and drilled, strings attached and battles fought. Peggy picked up a bowlful and had them on the kitchen table until they dulled in the warm, dry atmosphere, and she threw them away. Talk in the pub dwelt on darts tournaments starting up, quiz teams being re-formed, and on the best time to bring in beasts from fields where the grass was getting sparse. There was a general air of closing up, shutting down, husbanding resources and preparing for the winter.

On Ringford Green one wet, chilly Friday, Reynolds Fair arrived, as it had every autumn since anyone could remember. Gangs of shouting men set up its famous Golden Horses and swingboats, shooting galleries and coconut shies, and the noise of the generators kept Peggy and Frank, and Miss Beasley and the Joneses, awake for most of the night. But Warren and William, and Gemma and Amy, Mark and very nearly Eddie, except that his mother noticed his toddling exit in time, ran suicidally down Macmillan Gardens, across the road and on to the Green, to stare and comment, and get in the way and be shouted at by swarthy men with huge mallets and greasy overalls.

The Saturday night was fine, and Reynolds Fair did a roaring trade with most of Ringford being supplemented by enthusiasts from Fletching and Bagley, and other villages for miles around. The smell of hot dogs and frying onions was overpowering, and Mrs Jenkins forbade her children to eat 'any of that candy floss, sugary rubbish that rots your teeth'. William Roberts had money, and he bought whirls of the pink sugary rubbish for Warren and the twins, and Warren let Mark have a taste of his before coating his mouth and most of his face with bright streaks of melted floss.

Sandra and Octavia, dangerously nubile in tight jeans and candy-coloured sweatshirts, still nut-brown from some fairly determined sunbathing during the summer holidays, drifted round the fair, greeting schoolfriends and giggling and screaming on the dodgems, and getting bumped in spine-jolting collisions with boys from the Further Education College in Tresham. These lads, still a bit spotty and unsure, were out for a good time and found Sandra and Octavia attractive but elusive. The girls had bigger fish to fry – 'Robert's bound to be here,' said Octavia – but in spite of spending all evening at the fair, they did not once set eyes on Robert Bates.

Flocks of starlings gathered in huge numbers in the tall lime tree on the Green, chattering of long journeys overseas, and then with a whirlwind of wings were gone. A touch of sharp frost withered Peggy's begonias without mercy.

'First meet on Tuesday, Peggy,' said Doreen Price, gently putting down trays of fresh brown eggs on the counter.

Peggy knew what she meant, only because there had been talk of little else for a couple of weeks. Cubbing had finished, a kind of run-up to the real thing, and traditionally the Bailee Hunt had its first meet of the season on Round Ringford Green. 'Are you for or agin', gel?' said Doreen, thinking she knew the answer – in Frank's case, anyway.

'Can't stand their bottoms,' said Frank, obligingly. 'It's the way they rise in the saddle, and there's precious few of them got the figures for it.'

'You sound like Old Ellen,' said Peggy, 'but I don't know – I think they look wonderful, and I suppose foxes are very destructive. Perhaps I'll know more how I feel after Tuesday – don't think I've ever seen a hunt close to.'

The sun shone warmly on the polished flanks of the hunters and the restless churnings of the foxhounds anxious to be off. Susan Standing arrived late on the Green, making an entrance and greeting her friends. She was ravishingly transformed, animated and clear cut, incredibly elegant in pale buff breeches, sharply tailored black jacket and crisp white stock. Her riding boots gleamed, her spurs twinkled and her usual faded colouring was intensified by the excitement.

'Forelocks ready for touching?' said Frank, standing on the shop steps with Peggy.

'They do look lovely, though, Frank, just like pictures of hunts a hundred years ago,' she said.

'I don't suppose the fox cares tuppence how lovely they look,' said Frank. 'Still, nobody could accuse the hunt saboteurs of looking at all lovely, so it's difficult to take sides.'

The hunt moved off, and spectators and hunt followers drifted away. Frank had reluctantly put a few coins in the collecting bag, not sure what he was contributing to, and Peggy looked with dismay at the turf on the Green, roughened and cut up by the hunters' hooves.

'Well,' said Doreen, fresh from rewarding exchanges with neighbouring farmers' wives, 'would you rather poison them, shoot them, or give the foxes a good run for their money and a chance to outwit the hunt?'

'By "them" I suppose you mean the foxes, not the hunt?' said Frank.

'Oh, you and your teasing, Frank,' said Doreen, cheerful with the feeling that something traditional, something belonging to her and her family, a deeply rooted part of the farming calendar, had just got off to another good start. Tom, wonderfully impressive in his pink coat had moved off on his huge, powerfully built grey, and she was extremely proud of him.

'Makes me sick,' said Gabriella Jones, joining the gathering round the shop steps. People were reluctant to go home, and stayed on, savouring the midday warmth of the autumn sun. 'How could anyone pretend it is a useful job when all they're really doing is following a blood lust, chasing a small animal until it's exhausted, setting baying hounds on it to tear it apart, and then skinning its lovely, bushy tail?'

'Have you ever seen a fox?' said Doreen. Gabriella looked discomfited. 'Because they are not lovely red furry creatures with shiny button eyes and a glorious feathery tail. They are often scruffy, thin-legged, shifty-looking old rat-bags, and they smell 'orrible.'

'No reason to kill it,' said Gabriella defensively.

'You'd kill it if it'd had your chickens, killed the lot and left most of 'em dead on the henhouse floor,' said Bill Turner, pushing his way through the little crowd and into the shop. 'Some folks do talk a lot of rubbish,' he said, smiling at Peggy, who had followed him into the shop. 'Have you got any cooking apples, gel? I just fancy an apple pie tonight.'

'What about the pastry?' said Peggy. 'Do you make that?'

'Dab hand at pastry, me,' said Bill, 'I'll bring you a piece to try.'

Mrs Jenkins, holding Eddie's hand as he took enormous strides to encompass the steps, came in and stood waiting to be served at the Post Office. Frank let himself back into the cubicle, and turned over his books.

'Did you see Casa Pera's up for sale?' Jean Jenkins said. 'I saw them putting the notice up.'

Peggy was stunned. She had got used to being first in the know, and Mrs Jenkins' news took her by surprise. Funny Sheila hadn't mentioned it – but then, she hadn't seen her for a few days. She knew that David had returned home after a week or so licking his wounds at his parents' house in Birmingham, and that Sheila intended to stir up the new houses issue again.

'Yes, Mary, what can I get you?' she said, as Mary York stood undecided at the counter.

'Can't think what to have for dinner,' said Mary.

A few unfamiliar customers, visitors to the meet, came into the shop during the morning, and Peggy was still weighing sweets for William Roberts at one o'clock. 'I'll go and make a sandwich,' said Frank, 'open a tin of corned beef.'

William paid for his sweets and turned to stare at a middle-aged man who walked tentatively into the shop. He was unremarkable except for a dirty white collar and a reluctance to look Peggy in the eye, and William stared because he had never seen him before.

He stood at the Post Office window, and Peggy went over to serve him.

'Would you cash this for me, please,' he said, 'it's for my sister – baby's ill and she can't get out of the house.' He pushed a Child Benefit book under the plate-glass window.

Peggy looked at the authorisation page, and it had been signed. She began to count out the allowance, and the man shifted quietly from one foot to the other. Hearing a car door slam, she looked up and saw Sheila Pearson coming up the steps. 'Morning, Sheila,' she said, 'I've a bone to pick with you!'

She continued to check the money, and stacked it neatly into a pile. Picking up the allowance book, she prepared to tear off the necessary section, and then stopped. I suppose this is all right, she thought, hesitating, not sure what to do.

'Could you hurry, please,' said the man, 'I'm late for an appointment in Bagley.'

Sheila made a signal to Peggy from behind the man's back. 'List,' she mouthed. Peggy couldn't catch the word, and began to move the money towards the man's outstretched hand. 'The list, Peggy,' said Sheila firmly, 'have you checked Mrs Ashbourne's list of benefit entitlements?'

'Ah,' said Peggy, 'I knew there was something.' She drew the pile of ten-pound notes back again and smiled apologetically at the man. She reached for Doris Ashbourne's list of families entitled to draw benefit from Ringford Post Office.

'Here! What are you doing!' The dirty-collared man swore and pushed roughly past Sheila, ran from the shop and jumped into his car, starting the engine with a grating haste. He drove off at speed, narrowly missing the Jenkins' terrier who was ambling home down the middle of the road.

Frank, hearing the man's raised voice, came swiftly into the shop, holding the bread knife at the ready.

'What's going on, Peggy?' he said, nodding to Sheila and looking round the shop in alarm.

'Stolen Child Benefit book,' said Sheila.

'Oh, goodness,' said Peggy, 'and I nearly gave him all that money!'

'It happened to Doris Ashbourne once,' said Sheila, 'I

helped her sort it out afterwards: that's how I know about it. Didn't she warn you?'

'She warned me,' said Frank, chagrined, 'but I suppose I didn't pass it on to Peg. You all right?' he added, as Peggy came out from the cubicle, her hand pressed to one side of her head.

'Wretched migraine,' she said, 'just came on in a flash. I'll go and lie down for a minute. Oh, yes, and Frank, ask Sheila what she means by putting her house on the market and not telling us!'

Frank took over the shop, and Peggy finally emerged at teatime, her face parchment pale and huge dark smudges under her eyes. 'The pain's gone,' she said, 'but those pills make you feel almost as bad in a different way.' She stood still, looking dazed, drained, as if all her blood had been siphoned away.

Frank closed up the shop, double-checked that every lock was secure, and went back into the kitchen. He put on the kettle and made Peggy relax in an armchair in the sitting-room. They sat together drinking tea and watching Gilbert playing with a cloth mouse under the bureau.

'You're not to worry about that business with the Child Benefit,' Frank said, 'it was my fault for not telling you.'

'I don't know, Frank,' said Peggy, 'sometimes I think we're not cut out for this job. Then I swing the other way and decide we have never been so happy, and everything's turned out how we hoped.'

'Sounds reasonable,' said Frank, 'that's how most people feel most of the time, isn't it? Besides, as I said, it was my fault.'

'Tell me about Sheila, about their house,' said Peggy. Frank was pleased to see the colour coming back into Peggy's face.

'They're moving to Bagley – found a cottage and had their offer accepted. Sheila didn't say too much about it, but I gather she and David are not entirely reconciled . . . I think this is meant to be a new start. Anyway, they have to sell Casa Pera first.'

He got to his feet. 'Will you be sensible and not do anything if I go swiftly into Tresham to the wholesaler? I'd planned to get a load of Christmas stock.'

It seemed ridiculously soon to be thinking about Christmas, but Doris had said there would be nothing left by the end of October. The wholesale Festive Grotto had been set up, and already Frank's fellow shopkeepers queued at the checkouts with trolleys stacked full of wrapping paper, cards, toys, Nativity sets, tree decorations playing 'Jingle Bells', green plastic Christmas trees.

When Frank returned, heaving piles of stock into the spare room they kept for storage, Peggy was feeling better and helped him sort out the boxes and packets.

'I'm hungry,' she said, 'let's go down the pub for supper.'

One thing about migraine, thought Frank, it's like a blown fuse with Peggy. She sits on her worries, and then wham, the lights all go out and she crashes. Then peace and light are restored and she carries on, a bit flickery but gathering strength.

'I do just wonder,' said Peggy, as they walked slowly down the street past the bus shelter where Octavia was giggling with a couple of boys, Sandra nowhere to be seen, 'if Sheila had discovered more than she's told us about Standings' reasons for opposing the houses? She did say that she suspected they might have plans for the field behind her house.'

'That'd ruin more than the view,' said Frank, 'it would knock a few thousand off the value of Casa Pera. By the way, Bill Turner came in this afternoon and asked me if I would go to the planning meeting with him next Thursday. Apparently the Barnetts' plan is coming up for final discussion.'

'Why does Bill want to go?' said Peggy. She looked up at the impressive Standing coat of arms on the swinging sign and wondered what it would be like to have the burden of a great family tradition to keep up and not enough to do it on. No wonder they were so devious.

'Bill is interested, that's all,' said Frank, 'never been to a District Council planning meeting before, and nor have I, come to that. I think he's a bit shy about going by himself.'

'Can anybody go, then?' said Peggy.

'Apparently,' Frank said, 'so long as you don't say anything.' He pushed open the door of the Standing Arms and held it for Peggy to go in first. She stood uncertainly inside the door, then followed Frank to the bar. Don Cutt was in the snug, and they waited patiently. The publican seldom came into the shop, and they were not regulars in the pub, not caring much for Cutt's challenging style.

'Not much point in going to the meeting if you can't say anything, is there?' Peggy said.

'I suppose you can hear what goes on, so you know exactly how to plan an appeal, if that's possible.'

'Are you going, then?'

'If you don't need me, I think I will. It will make a change from discussing the weather with Mrs Jenkins. What are you going to have, Peggy?'

Don Cutt stood behind the bar, and Peggy smiled her most winning smile at him. 'A half of Guinness, please, Mr Cutt,' she said.

'That's right, Mrs Palmer, build up your strength, you're looking a bit peaky,' said Don Cutt, 'and a half of shandy for your husband?'

'Pint of Morton's,' said Frank nonchalantly, 'and we'll have something to eat. What can you offer us?'

They sat down in the corner by the fire with jumbo sausages and chips, and tucked in. 'I suppose this new houses thing will be Sheila's swansong, then,' said Peggy, helping herself liberally to mustard. 'You might get some fireworks at the meeting – Sheila will know she's got nothing to lose.'

'I shall bring you a verbatim report,' said Frank, mopping up tomato sauce with a forkful of chips.

'Another pint, Mr Palmer?' said Don Cutt, clearing away their plates.

'Why not?' said Frank. 'Another Guinness for you, Peggy?'

CHAPTER TWENTY

On Thursday, Frank woke up with a throat like sandpaper.
He felt hot and cold at the same time, and his head ached.

'Flu,' said Peggy, 'that's what you've got. You'd better
stay there, and I'll ring the doctor.'

'There's no need for that,' said Frank, 'this bug is all
round the village, and the doctor just says to take painkillers
and stay in bed.'

'Right, well, that's what you are going to do,' said
Peggy, straightening the quilt and plumping up pillows
behind Frank's head. I'll bring you some hot honey and
lemon, and you can get some sleep.'

'What about Bill?' said Frank.

'What about him?' said Peggy.

'I was going to the planning meeting with him, you
remember.'

'Oh yes, well, I'll give him a ring and he'll have to go on his
own.' Peggy drew the curtains to shield Frank's sore eyes
from the sun. 'It's a beautiful morning,' she said, 'old Fred is
out there on the Green, pushing at molehills with his stick.'

'Why don't you go to the meeting?' said Frank.

'Are you delirious?' said Peggy. 'Who do you think is
going to man the shop all day?' She folded up Frank's jersey
and put it away in a drawer.

'You could get Mary York to come in,' said Frank stubbornly. 'I don't like to let Bill down, and I don't think he'll go on his own.' He coughed and pulled the bedclothes up round his neck.

'It's very short notice to ask Mary,' said Peggy, 'it's not as if we have used her often. She's only taken over once or twice since we've been here.'

'All the more reason to ask her now,' said Frank. 'It's no good thinking we can cope all on our own all the time. Go and give her a ring before she goes out somewhere.'

Mary lived up the Bagley Road beyond the playing fields, in an ugly bungalow built more for economy than beauty. She answered the telephone when Peggy rang, clucked like an old hen over Frank's flu, and agreed to take over while Peggy went to the meeting. 'You're lucky,' she said, 'I should have been up at the Hall helping Ellen with the cupboards, but she's gone down with this bug as well, so I'm free.'

Peggy then telephoned Bill Turner. 'Poor old Frank,' he said in a puzzling whisper, 'still, I'd be very glad of your company.' Peggy could hardly hear him. Perhaps it's Joyce, listening in, she thought.

'All's well, then, so just you stay in bed while I'm out,' she said to Frank, taking him a bowl of oranges and a couple of farming magazines brought in by Doreen.

'Don't worry,' he said, 'I shan't be able to tear myself away from these,' and he picked up a magazine with a picture of an enormous bull on the cover.

'No point in taking two cars, gel, so long as you don't mind riding in this old crock,' said Bill, collecting her from the shop. Joyce had been difficult as usual, and wanted to know what the telephone call had been about. Bill had not risked telling her the truth, but said he had just confirmed details with Frank.

In spite of his battling with Joyce, and having to mop up a

bottle of milk she threw in his direction, he felt cheerful. Wonder if I'd feel so cheerful if poor old Frank was coming instead of Peggy? He didn't face that one, and held open the passenger door of the shabby white car for Peggy to get in.

'You look very nice today, Mrs Palmer,' he said, aware of the twitching curtains in Victoria Villa.

Peggy coloured and smiled. 'Thanks, Bill,' she said, 'I am afraid I don't have much need for dressing up these days. If I'm neat and tidy in the shop, I think that's all that is expected of me.' She eased her best jade-green skirt to prevent creasing, and unbuttoned her camel-hair jacket. 'It's warm in here,' she said.

'Heating's stuck on full, I'm afraid,' said Bill, turning the key and giving a reckless wave to the lace curtains. He turned and glanced at Peggy settling herself beside him, clicking in the seat belt and putting her handbag on the floor between her feet.

'Perhaps you and Frank should try to get out a bit more, go to the pictures occasionally?' he said.

'You're a fine one to talk!' said Peggy. 'When was the last time you and Joyce went out anywhere?'

Bill was silent, trying to remember. It was a family wedding, and Joyce made a real exhibition of herself.

'Bill?' Peggy said. 'Have I offended you?'

Bill sighed and said nothing for a few seconds. He pulled out and passed a tractor which had gone up on to the grass verge at an alarming angle for them to get by.

'No, Peggy, you haven't offended me,' he said. 'It is just very difficult at home. Over the years we've got used to Joyce being like she is. Now nobody in the village takes notice.'

'Does she ever go out?' said Peggy. 'I'd be very happy to take her into Tresham if she would like to go.'

'No, she can't do it. She can't even go out into the garden now, except sometimes at night in the summer, when everything is quiet and dark. Then it only takes a hooting owl to send her scurrying back into the house.'

Peggy looked at his big hands on the steering wheel, scrubbed clean and unexpectedly fine with a light fuzz of pale gold hairs, and wondered why he of all people couldn't fix whatever was wrong with Joyce.

'Oh Bill, I am sorry. Has she seen a doctor about it?'

'Doctors, psychiatrists, the lot, at first. None of them seemed to help, and now we've got used to our way of life and it seems the easiest way out.' If I'm not careful, thought Bill, she'll have me talking all the way to Bagley.

'Will she see people if they come to the house?' said Peggy.

'Only her sister, and Ivy Beasley and the vicar. Ivy comes in about once a week, and brings Joyce them competition books – they go through them and send in dozens of entries.'

'And the vicar?' said Peggy.

'He brings the things for Holy Communion, and says prayers with her. It seems to help her a bit. She's always calmer after he's been. But he's getting a bit past it now.'

Peggy asked him how it had all started, and heard a sad tale of miscarriage and misunderstanding between the two of them. Joyce had been very close to her mother – 'Too close, I sometimes think,' said Bill, 'and when she died Joyce got a lot worse.'

'Would she talk to me at the door?' said Peggy.

'No, I'm afraid not,' said Bill, slowing up behind a flock of sheep running and leaping in fright in front of the car. 'There they go – that's old Jack Trodd, still about I see.' He waved to a wizened little man, his weasel face surmounted by a large battered cap, a cigarette drooping from his lower lip. 'Used to work with my dad,' said Bill. The crouching sheep dog manoeuvred the flock into an open gateway.

'No, Joyce won't see many folks,' he went on, 'she's – well, she's quite jealous of other women. Goes back a long way, that does. But it's very kind of you to offer. Thanks, Peggy.' Now she knows it all, or nearly all, thought Bill.

They arrived outside the pride and joy of the District Council: the Council Offices, newly built, plain brick and parallel rows of sightless windows, secretive with their vertical blinds, and a low-angled roof of red tiles shining bland and uniform in the sun. 'Shame we all got so terrified of bad taste,' Peggy said, and Bill, having no idea what she was talking about, said, 'Mm, quite right,' and looked for a place to park.

Bill felt nervous and was anxious not to show it. He looked around and saw the reception desk, advanced on it and heard someone say, 'Bill Turner! What you doing here, you old fox?'

He turned and saw a tall, ruddy-faced man approaching with his hand outstretched.

'Rick!' said Bill, grasping the hand and shaking it enthusiastically. 'However long is it?'

'Twenty years, I should say,' the tall man said, and his eyes moved to Peggy, standing discreetly in the background. 'And is this Mrs Bill?' he said.

Bill felt a strong desire to say yes, this is my wife Peggy. Stupid bugger, he thought, pull yourself together.

'This is Mrs Palmer,' he said, 'our new village shop-keeper – we're here for the planning meeting.'

'Ah, that'll be upstairs in the Council Chamber,' said Rick, 'be starting soon. I work for Leisure and Libraries – been there since we left school. Him and me were in the same class,' he said, turning to Peggy, 'taught me more than the teachers, did Bill! We must get together, Bill, and soon, boy! Now, up those stairs and first on the left – can't miss it. Bye, then, bye Mrs Palmer – nice to have met you.'

The Council Chamber was a large room, with all its windows looking out on to the main street. The windows were open, and the hum and roar of traffic filled the room. Rows of chairs faced a dais, on which were long tables piled with box files and neatly stacked reference books.

A girl walked along the line of windows, banging them shut, reducing the traffic noise to a bearable hum. Councillors talking in groups dispersed to their chairs and the Chairman, Mr James Standing JP, strode importantly on to the dais. Either side of him, like Mafia henchmen, sat professional employees of the Council to report and advise.

'There's Sheila,' whispered Peggy, pointing to the back of Councillor Mrs Pearson's head.

'She's not on the Planning Committee,' Bill whispered back, 'but has the right to speak and vote when the application is in her patch.'

'How do you know that?' asked Peggy, forgetting to whisper.

There was a silence in the room, and Chairman Standing looked over towards Peggy. 'Could we have quiet at the back there, please? Thank you so much.' Peggy coloured and tried to disappear inside her coat.

A number of planning applications came and went, and some provoked argument amongst the Councillors. Peggy was totally absorbed by all of it – each application was a story in itself. James Standing was magisterial, reasonable and willing to listen, and then pouncing with a damning phrase, never an expression of opinion but always to the point, or a nod of approval which signified his acceptance of an argument. He could not be said to be biased.

Then it was the turn of Round Ringford, the Barnett application.

'Here we go,' muttered Bill, and Peggy shushed him, as if he was Frank, thought Bill.

The application was described and discussed, Sheila presenting some bare facts, and then James Standing said he would like to say a few words.

'If my fellow councillors do not mind,' he said sweetly, 'I should like to make a brief and objective comment. This application seems to me typical of many coming before the Committee at present, purely speculative and without relevance to the needs of the village community, merely an expression of greed and cashing in on the current vogue for country living.'

Bill was delighted to see Sheila rise to her feet.

'Mr Chairman,' she said, 'I would like to protest strongly. If I may say so, I think the chair is out of order in expressing so one-sided an opinion. As you all know, Round Ringford is in my ward, and I am well informed on the local feeling about this application. The village community as a whole is by no means against the plan, and there have been unpleasant repercussions resulting from opposing points of view.'

'Atta girl,' said Bill, and sat up straight in his chair, urging Sheila on.

'Many of our local people,' she continued, 'feel that the village needs some new blood. Houses such as these attract young families with children, and this is just what Ringford needs. We don't need all the old houses to be bought up by wealthy incomers.'

'Like yourself, Councillor Pearson?' said James Standing inclining his head with exaggerated politeness.

'And often these incomers buy just for weekend cottages, leaving the village half-empty during the week,' continued Sheila, unabashed. 'The pub and the shop need custom to keep going – it is difficult enough these days for a village shop to make a living – and I am glad to see Mrs Palmer, Ringford's shopkeeper, is interested enough to be here today.'

She smiled encouragingly at Peggy, who bravely smiled back. Sheila continued making point after point to support her case, and there were nods of approval all around her.

'She's bloody good,' said Bill, admiringly, and Peggy nodded.

'If only David could see her now,' she whispered.

Sheila came neatly to the end of what she had to say, and sat down. A vote was taken, and by a large majority the planning application was approved.

As they left the Council Offices, Bill and Peggy were joined by Sheila.

'Congratulations!' said Peggy warmly, and Bill put out his hand to shake Sheila's.

'I am afraid there will be some who won't be so pleased,' Sheila said, 'but then I shall not be around much longer to have to put up with them.'

'More's the pity,' said Peggy, 'and who will fight for Ringford when you are gone?'

'There's always someone to take your place – a lesson it's as well to learn early,' said Sheila. 'You know David went off in disgust for a while – well, he hasn't really forgiven me, and I think if we stay in Ringford there are too many reminders.' She opened the door of her car and turned back to look directly at Peggy.

'It's my only hope, really,' she said, 'and I don't want to lose David – he's all I've got. You have to hang on, don't you?'

Revving up her engine with unnecessary force, she drove off at speed.

'Not many like her around,' said Bill, helping Peggy into the car. 'Do you fancy a cup of tea, or must you get back?'

'Better get back,' said Peggy, 'Frank will be dying to know what's happened.'

Bill drove back to Ringford slowly, prolonging the journey. It won't do, he thought, it just won't do.

CHAPTER TWENTY-ONE

The whole of Round Ringford knew the result of the planning meeting long before the *Advertiser* brought out a front page story headlined STANDINGS OVERTHROWN! Mr Richard was said to be furious, and Susan had told Mrs Jenkins, who was looking cocky, that it was a very good thing that that dreadful Mrs Pearson was moving away.

Frank, weak from his forty-eight-hour flu, spent Sunday in an armchair by the fire, reading the national newspapers, and irritably refusing to discuss Sheila's triumph any further. Peggy had been so pixilated with excitement after the meeting, and Bill had come galumphing up the stairs to tell Frank the result, waking him up from a restless, feverish sleep.

All right for them, he had thought resentfully, I just hope they get the bug. That'll cool them down.

Now he suggested to Peggy that they have a moratorium on anything to do with new houses. 'Let's talk about Christmas instead,' he said, 'we have to think about a seasonable sales offensive.'

'We're not exactly Selfridges,' Peggy said, 'it will have to be something simpler than living, breathing window displays.'

He must be feeling better, she thought with relief. She'd

had enough of Frank's irritable snapping, but knew it was a by-product of flu, and was patient with him. I shall have to feed him up, she thought, looking at his pale thin hands holding the newspaper, he hasn't much in the way of reserves. Lots of shepherd's pie and carrots, that's what he needs.

She went into the kitchen to give Gilbert her supper, and was surprised to find that the little cat was not there. Gilbert had soon got used to the cat-flap in the door and turned up regularly as clockwork for her food.

'Gilbert!' she called, opening the back door. 'Gil-bert-iney!' There was no sign of her, and Peggy shut the door, thinking she must be out hunting. She was a great mouser already, and brought corpses in to deposit them proudly at Peggy's feet. 'Oh, how could you, Gilbert,' Peggy said, but Gilbert only answered with a 'perupp' and threw the dead body into the air over and over again until she became bored with it and left it lying in the middle of the floor.

'No sign of her,' Peggy said to Frank, 'perhaps I'll go to Evensong, and she'll probably have turned up by the time I'm back. If you hear the cat-flap before then, you can feed her. She's bound to show up soon.'

Only a handful of people attended Ringford church, and the Reverend Cyril Collins sometimes preached to a congregation of three or four at the Evensong service. The evening was damp and mild, wisps of mist in the air hung over the Ringle, and Peggy set off with her summer mac over skirt and jersey. Pity they don't wear hats any more, she thought, I'd like to go to church in hat and gloves, and sit in the front pew and have my servants in pews at the back, waiting to hand me into my carriage after the service.

Ah well, I'll make do with a lift from Mr Ross in his turquoise Mini if it's raining when we come out.

Mr Ross lived up the Bagley Road in a house with big windows and mock Tudor beams in the gables. His garden was a model of neatness and order, and he and his wife were seldom seen, except for attendance at church and a ritual walk with their black and white butterfly dog on Sunday afternoons. Peggy knew them slightly from their occasional visits to the Post Office, but knew that they did most of their shopping at the Supashop in Tresham.

'Evening, Mrs Biggs,' Peggy said, falling in with Old Ellen as she rounded the Green, 'are you coming to church?'

Ellen shook her head. 'Time enough for that when they carry me in on the bier,' she said lugubriously. 'I'm off to see Fred Mills. He's bin a bit off for a day or two – had this flu bug – so I'm taking him some raspberry jelly. He's a great one for jelly and custard, slips down easy.' She left Peggy at the end of Macmillan Gardens and stumped off towards the old people's bungalows.

Mrs Ashbourne, shutting her garden gate and on her way to church, met Ellen, exchanged a few words, and hurried on to catch up Peggy. 'Bit dampish,' she said, 'but not cold.' They turned down towards Bates's End and the church, the bells still ringing a measured peal. 'Robert's taken over from his dad ringing the bells,' said Doris Ashbourne, 'it's getting too much for the old man.' 'Maybe Frank could learn how,' said Peggy, 'when he's better.'

They crossed the bridge, paused to look down into the water as always, and noticed islands of twigs and fallen leaves clogging up the swiftly flowing current. 'Bill will have to do a bit of clearing out down there,' said Doris, 'he does it most years.'

The single calling bell with its frantic high note speeded up their pace, and they walked up the flagged path, through the darkness of the porch and into the airy church just as Mr Collins appeared in a crumpled white surplice to go to his seat in the chancel.

Whitewashed walls lightened the interior, and high above the arches of the aisle hung the dark, sombre-coloured hatchments of long-deceased Standings. Four steps led to the narrow chancel, setting it apart in its ancient sanctity. Bleached stone flags, worn smooth by generations of penitent villagers, approached the altar, with its plain silver cross on a pure white cloth. Above, an exuberant burst of Victorian stained glass, jewel-bright, played its part in refreshing the weary and heavy-laden.

Doris Ashbourne took her customary place next to Ivy Beasley, and Peggy was beckoned into the Price pew to sit by Doreen.

The Parochial Church Council had not allowed the introduction of new words or music into the evening service, and the thin voices sang 'Now lettest thou thy servant depart in peace,' much as Round Ringford had heard it for hundreds of years.

I wonder if they were real people, Peggy thought, looking at the wickedly carved heads acting as bosses for the graceful arch ends. A plump-faced monk, with straight haircut and bald tonsure, a relic of Catholic days, half-smiled with a knowing leer into the congregation. High up in the chancel arch were a pop-eyed, bearded king and his hawk-nosed queen, complete with crowns, lording it over their subjects with patronising stares.

'Have you seen the little Devil?' whispered Doreen, following Peggy's gaze.

'Where?' said Peggy.

'O Lord, shew thy mercy upon us,' intoned the vicar.

'And grant us thy salvation,' said Doreen Price devoutly, adding breathily behind her clasped hands to Peggy, 'he's up there on the ledge over the pulpit.'

'O Lord, save the Queen,' continued Mr Collins.

'And mercifully hear us when we call upon thee,' chorused Doreen and Peggy, 'and he's always in a different place, though nobody moves him,' whispered Doreen.

Peggy looked up and could see a carved stone head with grinning devil face, resting on its severed neck on the ledge Doris had pointed out. Two little horns sprouted from its brow, and its ears stuck out at right angles from its head.

The effect was comical and evil, like a child gone seriously astray. Peggy shivered.

'O God, make clean our hearts within us,' chanted the vicar, and Peggy answered with fervour, 'And take not thy Holy Spirit from us.'

Mr Collins preached an undemanding little homily about loving thy neighbour, and Peggy looked across the aisle to where Miss Beasley sat bolt upright, her black felt hat pulled down squarely over her expressionless face.

Difficult to love that old trout, thought Peggy.

The cool church cleared her mind and she concentrated on the vicar's words for a while, then drifted away again as she looked at the rusty red chrysanthemums, smelled their strange pungent scent, and thought of Doreen, sitting next to her, her hands peacefully folded in her lap, so secure and sure of her place in the world.

I could sit here all evening, thought Peggy, but Mr Collins was bringing the service to a close.

'The grace of our Lord Jesus Christ,' he said, raising his hand in benediction, 'and the love of God, and the fellowship of the Holy Ghost, be with us all evermore. Amen.'

Peggy left the church in a mellow mood, having said a prayer for the safe return of Gilbert and feeling that she had a great deal to be thankful for. Doreen hung back to talk to the vicar, and Peggy fell in with Mr Ross, who had been sitting at the back, having walked to church in the quiet, damp evening.

'Still pleasant weather, Mr Ross,' Peggy said, walking beside him.

'Yes indeed, Mrs Palmer,' he said politely.

'It makes you feel glad to be living in such a beautiful village, doesn't it?' said Peggy, still buoyed up by a sense of well-being.

She looked across to the Ringle where the mist was rising higher and creeping across the Green, shrouding the willows. The dark woods on Bagley Hill were still visible as a black wall, protecting the village against marauders. As the daylight died, uncurtained windows in Macmillan Gardens and the house next to the village Hall shone yellow, beacons for returning pilgrims.

'Ah, well, that depends how you look at it,' said Mr Ross, and Peggy turned to look at him, surprised at the sharpness in his voice.

'We have lived in Ringford a long time, Mrs Palmer,' he continued, 'and when we came here we chose the site of our house particularly carefully. We had always lived in crowded streets before, and the view across the fields to Walnut Farm seemed like magic to us.' He tapped his twisted barley-sugar walking stick smartly on the ground, underlining his words.

Peggy began to see his drift.

'My wife and I have been so happy here, lived our own life with nobody interfering, and now, with those houses going up opposite us, it will all change. It won't matter so much to you,' he added, and with a final crack of his stick, quickened his pace, drawing ahead of her and marching smartly across the Green towards the Bagley Road.

Peggy walked home alone, chastened by Mr Ross's outburst, and now aware that Miss Beasley and Mrs Ashbourne were a few steps behind and deliberately not catching up with her. By the time she reached the Post Office Stores her mood had changed, and she snapped, 'Well, where is she, then?' when Frank told her Gilbert had still not appeared.

Frank looked surprised, and said, 'Don't worry, Peggy, she'll turn up, cats always do.'

'Unless they've been run over, or caught in a trap, or . . .' Peggy went out into the back garden and called for Gilbert again. There was no sign, no familiar rustle in the undergrowth as the little cat forced her way through thick shrubs and honesty gone to seed. Peggy began to worry.

Gilbert was still not fully grown, and – probably because of her precarious start in life – had a nervous disposition.

'I shall have to go and ask old Beasley,' she said to Frank, 'Gilbert might have got shut up somewhere in her garden.' It will give her some satisfaction to know Gilbert is missing, I'm sure, Peggy thought, still, she might have seen her going off in some direction, give us a clue to where she might be.

Peggy went out of the side gate of the Stores, and along the path to the front door of Victoria Villa. She could see a light shining through the glass half-moon over the door, and pressed the white china bell-button.

There was no reaction at all, and yet, thought Peggy, she is surely at home, I saw her going through her gate only ten minutes ago. She rang again, a long one this time, in case Miss Beasley was out in the yard getting in coal. She had scarcely taken her finger off the button when the door opened smartly.

'There's no need to go on with the bell, Mrs Palmer, I heard you the first time. Can't just drop everything and run, the minute someone gets impatient at the front door, can I?' said Miss Beasley, still in her churchgoing coat and hat.

She's not going to ask me in, that's for sure, thought Peggy, so began straight away with her question about Gilbert. 'She's usually safely indoors by this time, you see,' she said, 'and I am worried that something may have happened to her.'

'Plenty of cats about, one gone missing won't matter all that much,' said Miss Beasley, shaking her head.

'Hey, look out!' shouted Peggy, amazed to see Gilbert shoot out of Miss Beasley's hall, worm her way through the grey stockinged legs and out of Victoria Villa as if pursued by the Hound of Hell.

'That's her!' said Peggy, turning round to follow the little tabby before she reached the road. 'I'd like to know exactly what she was doing in your house, Miss Beasley, and why you lied to me!' Peggy was tense with anger, and could have said much, much more to Miss Beasley, but Ivy, her face closed and forbidding, rapidly retreated into Victoria Villa and shut the door with a crash.

Peggy chased after Gilbert, and several times reached down to pick her up, only to grasp empty air as the terrified cat shot off again into the dusk. Fortunately she ran into the Post Office garden, and Peggy was able to quieten her with her voice before picking her up and carrying her, trembling, into the kitchen.

Frank looked up from the kitchen table, where he had begun to put out bread and cheese and tomatoes for their supper. 'Ah, there she is,' he said, 'where did you find her?'

Peggy told him, barely able to contain her fury. 'Ivy Beasley's not right in the head!' she said. 'She must have known Gilbert was in her house.'

'What are we going to do about that woman?' he said, pulling out a chair for Peggy to sit down.

'Well, I don't care about her, she can be as unneighbourly as she likes,' said Peggy, 'but if she is going to start interfering in our lives, then we have to do something about it.'

'Would you like me to go and have a word?' said Frank, rather hoping Peggy would refuse this tentative offer.

'No, no,' said Peggy, 'it wouldn't do any good. We shall just have to make it quite clear to her that we won't stand anything like tonight's little trick again.'

'Well, I can do that,' said Frank reluctantly. 'Just leave it to me.'

Mrs Jenkins came out of the Post Office Stores next morning and passed Frank emerging from Victoria Villa. He looks a bit funny, thought Mrs Jenkins, perhaps he's not got over his flu yet. It takes a long time to shake off the flu, she reflected. Or it could be something else . . . wonder what he wanted with old Beasley? Ah, well, that Frank is a close one, you never know what he is thinking.

She walked off up towards Ringford Hall and her Monday morning's cleaning for Mrs Standing. Sometimes she wondered how she was going to manage the dusting and scrubbing in a house built for a dozen servants at least. Monday morning was the worst of her two days a week. She had had the children all weekend, and then her sister and family always came to tea on Sunday afternoon, and they usually stayed up late watching television.

Jean had left Eddie with Doris Ashbourne, who loved to have him for the short time his mother was up at the Hall. In the school holidays Sandra Roberts had offered to take him out for a walk any time, but since Jean had to pay Sandra, it wasn't a very profitable alternative. And Doris would never hear a word said about money.

An upstairs window at the pub was wide open, and as Jean passed by, Don Cutt leaned out dangerously to fix a telephone wire that had come adrift in the high wind. 'Off to work, Jean?' he shouted. 'Give 'em my love!'

Jean couldn't be bothered to answer him, and continued wearily across the bridge, flattening herself against the low stone wall as Robert Bates went noisily by in his huge tractor. She reached in her bag to bring out a couple of pieces of stale bread to throw to the ducks. They half-flew, half-paddled at top speed to snatch it, quarrelling and splashing in the fight to be first.

Cyril Collins was leaning on the church gate staring into space. He jumped, startled by her greeting as she went by, and called after her, 'Morning, Jean my dear, how's the family?' Jean answered him pleasantly, and noticed that he had on two pairs of spectacles, one pair on his nose and the other clamped to the top of his balding head. No smoke came from the vicarage chimney, and Jean wondered if he was keeping himself warm. Old people got cold so easily, and there was a nasty penetrating chill in the morning air.

She turned into the chestnut avenue, shadowy and damp, which seemed to stretch endlessly before her. 'Them sheep look just about as knackered as I feel,' she said aloud, looking through the great tree trunks into the park, where scattered sheep grazed dumbly on the sparse grass. 'They could do with a good scrub,' she said, 'get rid of that 'orrible sheep-shit under their tails, what's left of 'em.'

She plodded on up the avenue, shifting her heavy bag from one hand to the other. My legs ache before I start, Jean thought, making her way round to the back of the Hall, and letting herself in to the old scullery with the key the Standings had given her. She plugged in the electric kettle, rubbing her hands in the chill of the huge, echoing kitchen.

The Standings had given up keeping the Aga alight now that Ellen had got old and arthritic and came up to the Hall for only a couple of hours at a time. There was no sign of Ellen this morning, and Jean Jenkins wondered if she was still poorly with the flu. She would call in at the Lodge on her way home to see if she needed any shopping.

The house was quiet, no sound of human voices or even dogs barking. Old Hodgson, the aged butler, must have taken them for a walk.

'Yoo hoo!' she shouted. 'Anyone at home?'

Her voice echoed in the barnlike kitchen, but no one answered. She shrugged and took the kettle to make herself a fortifying cup of tea before she started work. Adding two spoonfuls of sugar – for energy, she thought – she sat down at the table with a sigh to drink it.

The big door, covered in shabby green baize, leading into the passage to the dining-room, swung open and Susan Standing appeared. 'I see you are working hard,' she said, with no preliminary greeting.

'Good morning, Mrs Standing,' said Mrs Jenkins politely. 'I am a bit early, if you look at the clock.' She glanced at the big old shelf clock on the dresser, and was relieved to see she was, in fact, about five minutes early.

'Plenty to do,' said Susan Standing in her remote voice. 'The kitchen floor needs a good scrub this morning. Mr Richard was out shooting yesterday with his brother, and they marched straight into the kitchen with muddy boots.'

Oh no, that means rows of corpses dripping in the larder, thought Mrs Jenkins with a shudder. She didn't like pheasant, and anyway, since the Standings never gave away any of their booty, she was not likely to benefit from yesterday's massacre.

As Susan Standing walked to the green baize door, she turned back to look at Mrs Jenkins, who had risen to her feet. 'Oh yes, I was going to say to you, Mrs Jenkins, that we were most surprised to hear that you had supported the application for Barnett's new houses. Most surprised.'

She vanished, and Mrs Jenkins stuck out her tongue at the swinging door. She pulled on the rubber gloves that she brought with her and filled a plastic bucket with soapy water. The scrubbing brush was old, with a few remaining bristles, discoloured and worn down – like Fred Mills' teeth, thought Jean Jenkins. I could do with one of those squeezy mops, but you bet old meany wouldn't get me one.

It took her a long time to clean the dried mud off the old tiles, and then rinse off the soapy water.

I'll just go and dust the drawing-room while this dries, she thought, then I can make a start with the Hoover. It was always tricky if Mr Richard was at home. He hated the sound of the cleaner and would ask her to leave the carpets until he had gone off to London, or round the estate with his dogs. But he had passed her in the avenue this morning, swished by in his car without a wave. She assumed he had gone for the day, and had wished him good riddance as he turned out into Bates's End.

She looked speculatively round the big room, thought it could do with a good lick of paint to freshen it up – all those fraying curtains and faded chair covers – and began to dust the fragile ornaments, blank-faced shepherds and shepherdesses, and Staffordshire dogs with staring eyes.

I wouldn't give you tuppence for any of these, she thought – give me my little mice and birds, they're close on alive. She was just getting into a nice rhythm with the duster when Susan Standing appeared.

'Mrs Jenkins, come with me, if you please,' she said, beckoning with her forefinger.

Mrs Jenkins followed with a sigh, still holding her duster.

Susan Standing led her back to the kitchen and pointed at the floor. 'Do you call that a clean floor?' she asked, and before Mrs Jenkins had time to reply, added, 'because I don't. You will have to do it again.'

Jean Jenkins stood motionless, her solid legs apart and her hands clutching the duster. She relied on the weekly money from the Standings, meagre as it was, but she had had about as much as she could take from Susan Standing. If she hadn't had a hectic weekend, if she had gone to bed earlier, if Gemma hadn't been sick in her bed in the middle of the night . . . maybe she would have said, 'Yes, Mrs Standing,' and meekly washed the floor again.

As it was, she marched up to the kitchen table, put her duster down firmly, and said, 'No, I won't do it again. Do it yourself.'

She then turned, pulled on her coat, put the door key down on the table with a bang, said, 'You owe me last week's money – I'll send our Warren for it,' and walked out.

Outside in the stableyard, Mrs Jenkins had second thoughts. What was Foxy going to say? His wages were low, and they needed any extra money Jean could earn.

'I'll soon get another job, Fox,' she rehearsed under the falling chestnut leaves. 'There's a limit to how much a girl can take.'

★

Richard Standing, weary from a day in London and looking forward to a large pink gin, walked into the drawing-room to find his wife Susan in tears.

'What on earth is wrong, my darling?' he said. Susan very seldom showed her emotions, and almost never talked about them.

She got up from the sofa and went to stand by one of the long windows that looked out across the park, misty now in gently falling rain. She dabbed at her eyes with a small handkerchief and said in her faraway voice, 'Sometimes I wish we could sell this place, sometimes I hate it.'

Richard Standing was shocked. 'But I thought you loved the gardens and the peace and tranquillity . . .'

'Stuff the peace and tranquillity!' Susan said, stamping an elegant foot on the faded Chinese carpet. 'I'm quietly rotting away in this godforsaken village, while you buzz up and down to town to your secret assignations!'

He ignored this, and gradually teased out the story of Susan's quarrel with Mrs Jenkins, and was sympathetic. 'Don't worry, Susan,' he said, 'we are perhaps well rid of her. She has been causing quite a stir in the village over the new houses, encouraged by that Pearson woman, and is likely to be uppity now they've got their planning permission.'

'I wish I had never heard of Round Ringford,' said Susan, not at all mollified. 'I'm sick of new little houses and new little people and new little ideas. I just wish my father was alive and I could go back and start again.'

She turned towards Richard and her face for once was vivid. 'If I hadn't married you,' she said, 'just think what I might have done.'

Richard Standing said nothing, felt her anguish and did not know how to help her. 'Can I get you a drink, darling?' he said.

CHAPTER TWENTY-TWO

Mrs Jenkins had been right about Frank. He had looked funny because he felt funny. He had decided to tackle Miss Beasley first thing, while he was still almost as angry as Peggy. I shall go now, he goaded himself, before I go off the boil.

He found Ivy Beasley in her back garden, pegging out some washing. He tried not to look at the voluminous bra and the long-legged, pale green knickers. He remembered his mother wearing knickers like that, and immediately felt at a disadvantage.

'Can I have a word, Miss Beasley?' he said in as pleasant a voice as he could manage.

'I can't stop you,' said Miss Beasley, digging into her peg apron for another peg.

'Perhaps in view of what happened with our cat, you could explain to me why you dislike us so much,' said Frank. Best to come straight to the point, he thought.

'I don't know nothing about your cat,' said Miss Beasley, side-stepping the other half of Frank's question. 'It must have got into my house through the window at the back. I'd be glad if you'd keep it out of my garden and my house, nasty little thing.'

'You know perfectly well, Miss Beasley, that it is not

possible to keep a cat strictly confined, and in any case, I am quite sure she would stay as far away from you as possible. Cats are very sensitive, and always know if they are not welcome.'

Miss Beasley said nothing, but kept her back turned to Frank and continued to hang out her washing. A well-patched pillowcase caught the fresh wind, and blew out of her hand and straight into Frank's face. It was cold and wet, and he gasped.

'Miss Beasley!' he said, clutching the pillowcase and glaring at her. 'Was that deliberate? I hope not! But I shall say what I came to say: since we have been in Ringford you have been consistently unpleasant and have made my wife very unhappy at times. If we have done something to offend you, please tell us, but otherwise, I shall be glad if you will treat us with normal courtesy.'

Miss Beasley turned round and stared at him, her face screwed up and full of hate.

'Get out of my property!' she hissed at him. 'You think you're so wonderful, coming into our village and thinking you can take over, you and your high-and-mighty wife – you should lock her up out of temptation's way, too! Get out, go on, get out!'

Frank did not even notice Mrs Jenkins as he made his way home. He climbed the steps into the shop wearily, and found Peggy serving Doreen Price and chatting to her about a poster Doreen held in her hand.

Peggy looked at Frank and knew that he had had a hard time with Miss Beasley. His pale face was drawn, and she felt a pang of concern. The flu had knocked the stuffing out of him – maybe I should have gone to see old Poison Ivy, she thought.

'Hello Frank,' said Doreen cheerfully, unaware of undercurrents. 'I've just asked Peggy to put up this poster for the Jumble Sale in a fortnight's time. We are having one in the Village Hall to raise money for the fireworks.'

Frank won't like that, thought Peggy. He loathed fireworks, considered them dangerous and a menace to children. When he was little, one of his cousins had lost an eye in a firework accident, and he had been terrified. He had had nightmares and had not been able to get his cousin's screams out of his head.

'Good idea,' he said, nodding his head, and disappeared out of the shop into the house. Well, thought Peggy, he must have been upset by Beasley. Clearly had no idea what Doreen was talking about.

Doreen packed her groceries into her big egg basket and paid over cash. 'The Bonfire Party is very popular,' she said, 'it was Sheila Pearson's idea originally, and has really caught on. Most of the village goes to it. Thanks for putting up the poster – thought you didn't display them any more? Still, this is special . . . bye Peggy, bye Frank!'

'All right, let's have it, what did Ivy have to say?' said Peggy, following Frank into the kitchen.

He was sitting at the table staring at nothing, and for a moment did not answer her. Then he looked up at her and said, 'It isn't easy, is it, Peg?'

She frowned, puzzled, and asked him what he meant.

'You're better at it than me, this village life,' he said. 'I am a lazy man, on the whole, and it's really hard work living among such a small, inward-looking lot. Half the time I know it's not really me, I'm just acting the part.'

Peggy was taken aback. 'It's the flu,' she said, 'it always leaves you depressed. And you're not a lazy man! Another few days and you'll be fine again. I shouldn't have let you go into old Beasley's lair – what did she say, anyway?'

Frank was about to give her an expurgated version when the shop bell jangled.

'There you are, you see,' he said, 'we don't even have time to talk properly any more.'

It was Doris Ashbourne, buying her TV stamps, and

apparently with time to spare. She leaned up against the counter and looked at the poster Doreen had left.

'Would you like to help at the Jumble Sale?' she said to Peggy.

'Well, it depends,' said Peggy, her mind still on Frank.

'You worried about Ivy Beasley?' Mrs Ashbourne said. 'She organises it, but you don't need to take no notice of her. You can help me on the bric-à-brac if you like?'

Peggy thanked her, and agreed that if the date was free – she would consult her calendar in the kitchen – she would love to help her.

Mrs Ashbourne smiled at her, asked after Frank, and departed. Peggy wondered why she should be making such an obvious effort to be nice, and then forgot about it as a car stopped outside the shop and two men got out and climbed the steps.

'I wonder if you can help me?' said the first man, politely. 'I am looking for Walnut Farm – a Mr John Barnett,' he said.

Peggy directed them up the Bagley Road, and told them to turn right beyond Mary York's bungalow. 'You can't miss the turning,' she said, 'there is a biggish house opposite, and a long line of trees leading down to the farm.'

She watched them turning their car round, and wondered who they were and what they wanted. She supposed they would be something to do with the new houses, and called out to Frank, asking if he knew who they might be.

There was no reply from the kitchen, and she went to look, wanting him to take over the shop whilst she made the bed and tidied up. He wasn't in the kitchen, and didn't answer when she shouted for him in the garden.

She watched Miss Beasley scurrying back into her house and wondered what had been said between them.

The bell jangled once more from the shop, and she returned to pay out a pension to Fred Mills. 'You're looking a bit pale, Mr Mills,' she said, 'are you feeling better? You know we'll always bring the pension round if you don't feel up to coming out. Frank had the bug, and he's not really right yet,' she said.

'Just seen Mr Palmer off for a walk,' Fred Mills said, 'he do look a bit weedy. Looks how I feel!' His laughter turned into a cough, and he hobbled out of the shop in a cloud of tobacco smoke that was doing him no good at all, and clearly contravened the No Smoking notice prominently displayed.

Why didn't he tell me he was going for a walk, thought Peggy. What is going on this morning?

Her next customer was Bill Turner, full of the two men he had just seen marching about the Home Close field up at Walnut Farm. 'They had their green wellies on, and seemed to be doing a bit of measuring,' Bill said. 'They certainly haven't wasted much time. Still, I suppose with the winter coming on they want to get going as soon as possible.'

He saw Peggy's eyes following the trail of mud he had left from the door to the counter, and apologised. 'I am sorry, gel,' he said, 'I've been down at Bateses, giving Robert a hand with his pig yard.'

Peggy's nose wrinkled. 'I can tell that,' she said delicately, putting her hand up to her face. 'Just leave the door open when you go out,' she said, 'the smell of pig muck doesn't do a lot for trade, Bill.'

Frank did not return until lunchtime, and he looked a lot more cheerful. The long walk up towards Bagley and along the old railway line had taken away the worst of his gloom. He'd seen dozens of rabbits, startled squawking pheasant and chattering blackbirds, and a big old dog fox ran off without alarm as he pulled back long brambles from the path. 'Was that Bill?' he said, climbing up the shop steps and pausing for breath at the top.

'Yes,' said Peggy, 'can you smell him?'

During their snatched lunch, Frank leaned over and took Peggy's hand. 'Sorry Peg,' he said, 'don't take any notice of me. We're fine, you and I, and always will be.'

'Now then,' said Peggy, 'how about a night at the glorious moving pictures? There's a good film on at the Regal, Bill says, and it would do us both good.'

'Well, if Bill says so . . .' said Frank, and went to serve in the shop.

What a neat and tidy couple we are, thought Peggy, catching sight of herself and Frank in a shop window as they walked from the car park to the cinema. He, thin and wiry in his gaberdine raincoat and greenish trilby hat, his small feet nimble in good brown brogues; she, plump and quick in a blue tweed skirt, sensible shoes and her navy jacket.

Nothing very adventurous there, she thought, though I suppose it could be worse. At least Frank seems to have cheered up.

'Did you bring Gilbert in before we left?' she said.

'Of course, she was safely curled up in her box, fast asleep,' said Frank, 'didn't even notice when we left.'

'I do love her, don't you, Frank?' said Peggy, tucking her hand under his arm.

'Don't be daft, Peg,' he said, 'it's you that I adore.'

CHAPTER TWENTY-THREE

All week Robert Bates and Bill Turner and a trail of children had been going round the village collecting up jumble. Gemma and Amy had put slips of paper in every door, announcing the Jumble Sale and asking for old clothes, bric-à-brac, books, old records and tapes, garden equipment – 'Anything gratefully received – you donate it, we'll sell it!'

Doris had asked Peggy to help, partly because she needed help, and partly because she was beginning to think Ivy's vendetta had gone on long enough. She remembered only too well being the victim herself when she and Jack had moved into the shop all those years ago. Ivy had been a youngish woman then, but her strike was just as swift and her tongue equally sharp.

'I'll call in for you at nine o'clock,' Doris had said to Peggy, 'we shall do most of the sorting in the morning, though a lot of mine is ready priced. Not the nicest of part of moving house, I must say.'

It had been raining relentlessly since dawn, and the water coursing down the slope outside the shop had formed a small lake in the road. Doris noticed the gutter clogged with leaves, and made a note to mention the blocked drain to Frank. The village street was empty and the continuous rain had formed silvery puddles in hollows on the Green. Andrew and Mark'll be down here shortly, thought Doris, splashing about in their wellies.

An unfamiliar car came slowly along past the school, and Doris Ashbourne looked closely at it. A woman's pale face stared at her from the passenger seat, a pretty face with dark eyes and reddish hair cut short. Doris frowned. 'Who's that?' she said to Peggy, who had joined her. 'I know that face.' 'Never seen her before,' said Peggy, and they set off with umbrellas up, through the rain.

The house next to the Village Hall had just changed hands, and the big garage door was open. Inside, Octavia Jones was deep in conversation with a girl of her own age, the pair of them leaning casually against a sporty red car. A pleasant-looking lad with dark curly hair was polishing the already gleaming bonnet.

'New people,' said Peggy, 'haven't met them yet.'

Doris laughed. 'Nice not to be the "new people" any more, isn't it?' she said. 'They seem all right so far – three kids nearly grown up. One of them has chummed up with the Jones girl – bit rough on our Sandra, really.'

The Village Hall was a hurricane of activity. All the trestle tables were set out to form a square with a big space in the middle. There were heaps of clothes everywhere, and Doris stepped over them to reach her pitch on the far side of the hall.

'Come on, Peggy, let's get started. Looks like we've got some good stuff here.'

'Give me an idea on pricing,' said Peggy, 'I haven't done a jumble sale before.'

'Get what you can, is my motto – it's not like the shop. A bit of tinker's blood helps, like Jean Jenkins over there. She can be a real devil over a bargain. Still, I'll give you a rough idea and then you're on your own.'

Peggy picked up an old LP, Petula Clark grinning with youthful exuberance from the dog-eared, tea-stained cover. 'She was Frank's favourite,' she said, 'never liked her myself.'

'Oh yes,' said Doris, 'I forgot to tell you about first pickings. Being a helper, you can put aside anything that you want, but you have to get someone else to price it – stops fiddling. I should think ten pence for that?'

'Done,' said Peggy.

She watched Bill, his hair plastered down by the heavy rain, stepping over the piles of worn jerseys and outsize underwear, children's clothes too small and too worn out to hand down, old evening dresses and cricket boots. Doris saw his face when he noticed Peggy, and she worried for a minute.

'Here we are!' he said, dumping the box at Peggy's feet. 'I bring you treasures of the Orient – well, not really, just Madame Standing's chuck-outs. I'll be back shortly with some more.' He strode off, and Ivy Beasley, checking a pile of old hats, watched him go.

Doris started on the box from Ringford Hall, and pulled out pieces of chipped and cracked china. It was old, decorated with blue flowers and birds. She piled it up on the table and said to Peggy, 'Don't let this go too cheap – dealers come, you know, and they're after anything like this. Old Ellen sorts it out up at the Hall, and she gets a bit carried away sometimes.'

'You mean dealers actually come to Ringford Jumble Sale?' said Peggy.

'Oh yes, they get to know the ones to go to. If there's a big house in the village, they know it's always worth going to the jumble sales, just to see what the nobs have chucked out.'

Peggy pulled out a large vase, shaped like a Greek urn, with a smudgy dark blue pattern and gilt rim. 'What about this, then?' she said.

Mrs Ashbourne took it from her and tipped it up to look underneath.

'Well, Doris,' Ivy Beasley said, coming over and completely ignoring Peggy, 'shall you manage, once the rush starts?'

' 'Course I shall, Ivy,' said Mrs Ashbourne, 'and I've got Mrs Palmer to help me.'

'What's this, then?' said Ivy Beasley.

'Came from the Hall,' said Mrs Ashbourne, 'I was just having a look at it.'

'I'll have it,' said Miss Beasley, 'how much?'

Oh no you don't, Ivy Beasley, thought Doris Ashbourne, I know your game.

'This is a bit special, I reckon, Ivy,' she said, 'we shall have to find out a bit more about it.'

'I'll give you a pound, and think yourself lucky,' said Ivy Beasley.

'I've got a book at home,' said Peggy, 'it tells you how to identify pottery marks. It might give us an idea? I could bring it back first thing this afternoon.'

Miss Beasley turned and looked at her, as if noticing her for the first time. 'We don't need none of your books,' she said. 'We've always managed before, and made a good profit. So no thanks.' She marched off, the urn still in her hands.

'Right-o, Ivy Beasley, war is declared,' said Mrs Ashbourne, stepping out from her pile of junk and heading off after Miss Beasley. Peggy could see the confrontation in the cloakroom at the back of the hall, and then Doris returned, bearing a smile of triumph and the urn.

'I've said she's got to wait until we know,' she said. 'We don't want to miss a good opportunity to make a bit, do we?' And she smiled very kindly at Peggy.

The urn was tucked away under the table, and Peggy checked the mark again. It was very simple, with the outline of a crown and below it two entwined letters, an "O" and a "B".

Peggy rushed home at lunchtime, and with a quickly

made ham sandwich in one hand and the pottery book in the other, she looked for the OB mark. 'Oakby Bank Pottery! Here it is, Frank, it says it's quite rare and fetches good prices at auction.'

'You'll get dreadful indigestion, Peggy,' said Frank, 'for goodness' sake slow down.'

Peggy sat at the kitchen table and tried to eat slowly. But her excitement over the vase bubbled up again, and Frank decided to take over.

'Here,' he said, 'give me the book, and I'll ring old Sam Cohen in Coventry – he'll know all about it.' He disappeared and Peggy could hear him talking on the telephone.

'Looks like you've got a nice piece,' he said, reappearing, 'Sam says two hundred and fifty pounds at a rough guess.'

Mrs Ashbourne received the news with glee, and they had just set the vase in a prominent position on the stall when Richard Standing marched into the hall and looked fiercely about him.

'Ah!' he said. 'There it is – I'll just take that back, Doris, there's been a mistake.'

'No indeed, Mr Richard, once an item is given it ain't possible to retrieve it. You must come and buy it back this afternoon if it's so important to you.'

'Important? I'll say it's bloody important! You stupid woman, it is not just important, it is extremely valuable. I don't know what Ellen can have been thinking of to give it to the collector. Who was collecting from the Hall, by the way?'

'Bill Turner,' said Mrs Ashbourne.

'I might have known it!' said Richard Standing. 'Bloody man cannot mind his own business!'

'I'll thank you to watch your language,' said Miss Beasley's grating voice as she came up behind the irate squire. With Peggy on his left, and a group of determined women on his right, he was surrounded.

'I repeat, Mrs Ashbourne,' he said, 'that vase is worth a great deal of money and I must have it back – now!'

'Two hundred and fifty pounds,' said Peggy coolly.

'I beg your pardon?' said Richard Standing. 'I don't think I asked for your opinion.'

'Two hundred and fifty pounds,' repeated Peggy, 'that is how much it is worth – I have that on very good authority. It seems to me that unless Mr Standing is prepared to pay that sum under our first pickings rule, he will have to relinquish the vase.'

'I'll be damned if I pay for my own vase!' spluttered Richard Standing. 'I shall be back very shortly with my solicitor.

'And,' he shouted as he left the Village Hall, 'don't you dare sell that vase until I return. I shall make you refund every penny!'

Silence followed his departure. Peggy looked round the hall at solemn faces. Then muffled laughter came from the kitchen, and she saw a tousled grey head appear over the counter of the hatch, a large, round face creased with mirth.

It was Ellen Biggs, and she had been hiding there all the time.

'I think,' said Mrs Ashbourne, 'the best thing we can do is raffle it.'

Mrs Ashbourne pulled a piece of white card from one of the boxes under the table. She wrote quickly, in her round, shopkeeper's hand.

CROWN OAKBY VASE – EXTREMELY RARE AND VALUABLE
KINDLY DONATED BY MR AND MRS RICHARD STANDING
Get your Raffle Tickets here – £1 each, six for £5

'Doris,' said Peggy. 'What on earth will he say?'

But there was no time for Mrs Ashbourne to reply. At the thumbs-up sign from Doreen, Miss Beasley unlocked the Village Hall doors with a flourish, and a tide of people swept in as if through floodgates.

The first half hour of the sale was total anarchy. The carefully sorted clothes were tossed up and down until they were back in jumbled heaps. Most of the stock on the bric-à-brac stall sold in the first ten minutes, and Peggy was nudged a couple of times by Doris Ashbourne as she served a dowdy-looking man and woman, selling them an unbelievable forty-eight raffle tickets. 'Dealers,' said Mrs Ashbourne, under her breath.

The crowd thinned a little, and Peggy's heart sank as she looked across the Village Hall and saw Richard Standing coming in the door, accompanied by a mousy little man carrying a briefcase.

'Here we go,' said Doris Ashbourne, 'it's him or us. Stand firm, Peggy.' She braced herself, and put a restraining hand round the neck of the urn.

Richard Standing and his solicitor reached the table, and as he read the white card his face deepened to a richer shade of purple.

'You will stop this at . . .' he began in a hoarse voice, when he was interrupted by a slender, attractive middle-aged woman, her smooth reddish hair cut short to flatter her small head on a narrow neck. Her tartan kilt and soft creamy jersey emphasised curves in all the right places.

She looked hesitantly around the hall, and found the peson she was looking for.

'Richard, darling!' she said, walking over and flinging her arms around his neck. He stared at her, then took her hands and looked closely at her, all the colour draining from his face.

'Well I never,' said Mrs Ashbourne, 'it's that Barnett girl, her that pushed him in the Ringle! Who'd have thought we'd see her again.'

It was indeed Josie Montrose, *née* Barnett, who after jilting the very young Richard Standing, had married a rich

American she met in Birmingham and not been seen in the village since.

The Village Hall was agog. Many of the women remembered Josie, and those who didn't were quickly brought up to date.

'Richard!' she said, with the faintest of American accents. 'How wonderful of you to give that lovely old vase. I must buy lots of tickets and hope I win it. Here . . .'

She handed a pile of banknotes to Peggy, who began busily tearing off cloakroom tickets. 'We've reached our target,' she whispered to Doris, and then said to the stranger, 'do you have a telephone number to leave with us?'

'Oh, just put the Hall,' said Richard Standing grandly, and putting his hand under Josie's elbow he guided her gently towards the tea tables. The sale returned to a quieter hum of business being done, and the women discreetly looked away from the tea corner – except for the occasional irresistible glance.

'That's torn it!' said Doris Ashbourne, looking towards the door.

Peggy followed her gaze and saw Susan Standing wafting into the Village Hall. She was carrying her little Yorkshire terrier, and stopped to buy an entrance ticket and to chat with the vicar, who stood drinking one cup of tea after another and wolfing down home-made cakes as if he hadn't eaten for weeks.

Those watching, and that included most of the people in the Village Hall, saw her turn and knew that she had seen Richard and Josie, blind to their surroundings, deep in animated reminiscence.

CHAPTER TWENTY-FOUR

Josie Barnett Montrose – as she was now calling herself – stayed in the village with her elderly parents for a couple of weeks, and during that time the big silver car was seen in all kinds of unlikely places.

'They were parked in a gateway up on the Bagley Road late last night,' said Doreen, collecting two pounds of spicy pork sausages for the men's dinner, 'I saw them when I was coming back from choral practice. He really should be a bit more careful, in his position.'

'What about Susan Standing?' Peggy asked. She made a note in the book of things they needed to restock: ham, string, butter, matches. 'Does she know about it – and if so, does she care?'

'Oh yes, she cares all right,' said Doreen, 'and I have no doubt she knows all about it. Unfortunately, since Jean Jenkins got the sack we don't get the gossip from the Hall. But there's no flies on Susan Standing, for all her wambly ways.'

Susan Standing sat at her dressing-table, staring at herself in the looking-glass. Her face was pale, paler than usual, and her soft mousy hair had not been brushed. What a mess, she thought, I suppose I must tidy myself up and do something.

But so what? There was absolutely nothing that had to be done by her, nothing that if left undone would affect anybody in any way. What a completely useless life, she thought.

And now there was this Josie woman, making her feel even more useless. Richard has lost his wits, she thought, but if he cared even a little for me, he would not have risked making me the laughing stock of the county. No fight left? she heard her much-lamented father say, no daughter of mine gives up without a fight.

Her hairbrush gleamed up at her, the silver back, engraved with her initials, winking in the reflected sunlight. She took it up in a sudden movement, and threw it with some force across the room. It landed on the soft carpet with a thud, and she got to her feet.

'Right, Richard my boy,' she said aloud, 'if it's excitement you want, you shall have it.'

She walked firmly out of her bedroom, across the landing and down the curving stairs.

'Are you listening, Mr and Mrs Hodgson?' she shouted as she went. 'Because there may be something worth listening to shortly!'

Feeling much better, she marched to the telephone and dialled her mother over at Bagley.

'Mother? I'm coming over this afternoon, shall you be there? I have a little job for you to do. Are you good at car-spotting?'

'Must you go back next week?' whispered Richard Standing, his nose buried in Josie's expensively perfumed neck.

He had taken her out to dinner at The Bull at Bagley, and now they were parked high up on the hilltop, the car's lights extinguished. Round Ringford lay before them, spread out in the moonlight, with the bulk of the Hall showing sternly through the trees. Far beyond the village the sky was lighter, the horizon blackly red, reflecting the urban sprawl of Tresham, but Ringford was at peace, safely enclosed in its tree-ringed hollow.

A warm glow came from the car's tape deck, where a soft voice crooned quietly into the night.

'It's just like when we were kids, isn't it, Dickie?' said Josie.

'Makes me feel nineteen again,' said Richard, stroking her hair, and nuzzling against her warm skin.

'I still get homesick for Ringford,' said Josie, 'I wish I could stay longer, you know I do. But Ted is getting fed up – ringing me up all the time and asking when I'm going back. And now an airline ticket arrived this morning, with next Friday's date on it. So that's that – I daren't upset him too much, because of his heart.'

'His heart?' said Richard, one hand boyishly unbuttoning her blouse.

'He's had one attack, and is on pills all the time now. His doctor says he has to be real careful and not to get upset. So there we are, Dickie darling, our days are numbered.'

'All the more reason to make the most of them,' said Richard Standing, breathing faster. 'Can you make it up to London for a couple of days before you go? We have this little flat just off Baker Street, and we could be completely alone.'

'What about Susan?' said Josie, patting her hair.

'Oh, she's quite happy with her dog and her good works in the village,' said Richard, and turned Josie's face towards him.

Behind them a car came over the top of the hill and illuminated the entwined lovers clearly in its brilliant headlights.

'Christ!' said Richard. 'Can't they dim the bloody things!'

His angry words were interrupted by Josie, who straightened her clothes quickly and sat bolt upright.

'It's stopped!' she said, panic in her voice.

They heard a slamming noise, and then Richard was cooled by the night air as his door was wrenched open and a figure stood outlined by the romantic moon.

'How pathetic!' said Susan. 'How sordid and pathetic. Get out, the pair of you.'

It was then that Richard noticed the gun.

'Susan!' he said. 'What on earth are you doing?'

Susan laughed. 'I think it is more a matter of what you and this middle-aged slut are doing, isn't it? Mind you, it is no secret, Mrs Josie bloody Barnett Montrose. Everyone is thoroughly enjoying the gossip – except, of course, me.'

She lifted the shotgun and aimed. Josie screamed and Richard threw himself on the ground. But Susan was not aiming at either of them. She expertly peppered each tyre of the silver car in turn, and smiled at the satisfying crack and hiss as they flattened to the rim.

'Now you can walk home, Richard and Josie, childhood bloody sweethearts,' Susan said calmly. 'Hand in hand, why don't you? How sweet.'

She turned away and climbed back into her car, started the engine and drove off towards Ringford, giving them a cheery wave as she went.

Bill Turner had been to see Joyce's sister over at Bagley, and they had talked endlessly about Joyce and what could be done to help. As usual, their talk had gone round and round in circles, and Bill had left feeling deeply depressed.

He drove slowly back to Ringford, thinking about his early days with Joyce, when they had been happy enough with their life together. Lots of people don't have children, he thought, and seem to be content. Look at Frank and Peggy, they are close as doves, and don't need anybody else.

He came over the top of Bagley Hill and began to cruise down into the village. He noticed the big silver car parked in a gateway, and thought what a silly bugger his boss could be. Then he reflected that given the opportunity, he'd be no saint, either. His headlights picked up a man and a woman, walking in single file at the side of the road, heads down and faces shielded from the light.

'Well, well,' said Bill, drawing up beside the man and opening his window. 'Mr Richard, sir, have you had trouble with the car? Can I give you both a lift?'

They sat together in the back of the car and Richard Standing tried to bluff his way out, offering the most lame excuse. 'Just happened to see Mrs Montrose in Bagley,' he said, 'and of course there are no buses.'

'Of course,' said Bill, with a smile, 'but how did you manage to get four punctures at once?'

Bill dropped Josie off at Walnut Farm, and Richard Standing got out with her. He put his head back in Bill's car, and said, 'Mind your own bloody business, Turner.'

'There's gratitude,' said Bill with a snort of laughter, and drove off home, feeling quite cheered up.

CHAPTER TWENTY-FIVE

*There will be a meeting of the Fireworks Committee
in the Village Hall on Wednesday evening, 7.30 sharp.*

'Do you mind, Mrs Palmer?' Robert Bates had brought in
the notice, his beguiling smile encouraging Peggy to relax
the rule on posters once more. 'Some of them forget, see.
Thanks very much.'

'I see you've got a big bonfire built already, Robert,' said
Peggy. 'Frank and I walked by on Sunday, and saw a huge
heap of wood in the long field.'

'Always have a good fire,' said Robert, 'that's the bit I
like best – it'll be bigger yet!'

'They've got me down for sausages,' said Peggy, 'I'm
looking forward to it.'

He walked over to the door and held it open for Peggy's
next customer.

'Good morning, Mrs Palmer, lovely morning, isn't it?'
Susan Standing walked smartly into the shop and put an old
wicker shopping basket down on the counter. Robert made
a face behind Susan's back. It wasn't a lovely morning, it
was cold, foggy and the roads were slippery with black ice.

'A pound of ham,' Susan said, 'and a pound of Cheddar
cheese. That should keep him going for a few days.'

'I'm sorry, Mrs Standing, I didn't quite catch . . . ?'

'I said,' Susan replied firmly, 'that that should keep him going for a few days. I mean Mr Richard, and I refer to the fact that I shall not be back for at least two weeks. Ellen will no doubt be sending an order later this week, and will keep an eye on the larder.'

She took the packets of ham and cheese and put them in her basket. 'Will you book those, please, Mrs Palmer?' she said, and left the shop, humming a little tune.

'Well, what was all that about?' said Frank, looking up from stamping parcels in the Post Office cubicle.

'Remember what Bill told us about giving Mr Richard and that Josie a lift that night? Well, I reckon that's what it is all about,' said Peggy.

'Is madame going away, then?' said Frank.

'She said she wouldn't be back for at least two weeks. If ever, if you ask me.'

'Oh dear,' said Frank, 'wasn't he just having a bit of fun? That Josie was very attractive . . .'

'You would naturally say that!' said Peggy. 'Anyway, Josie's not the first, according to Jean Jenkins. He's got a fancy woman in London, she says.'

'A fancy woman!' Frank roared with laughter, leaning backwards on his stool in the cubicle until he nearly fell off.

'Whatever made us think that village life would be a quiet retirement?' he said. 'Every day a new earth-shattering revelation!'

'Talking of shattering earth,' said Peggy, not in the least put off, 'did you see the lorries up at Walnut Farm? It's a terrible mess – poor old Mr Ross, I do feel sad about him.'

'Well, you can't build houses without making a mess, especially when the weather begins to turn,' said Frank, looking up at the plain-faced clock. 'Is it coffee time yet?'

'Makes me feel quite guilty for having supported the plan in the first place.'

'Oh, Peggy dear,' said Frank, 'you can't be loved by

everybody. Sooner or later you're bound to make an enemy or two.'

'Well, I certainly have an enemy in old Poison Ivy, she hasn't been in the shop at all lately. Yes, all right, I'll go and make the coffee.'

Frank frowned, serious now. 'Ivy Beasley is a dangerous woman,' he said, 'it's best to ignore her – and even that is risky.'

'Don't be silly, Frank, she wouldn't do anybody any real harm, surely?' said Peggy.

'A great deal of harm can be done by a word or two planted in the right ear,' said Frank. 'Fortunately, most people take Miss Beasley with a pinch of salt.'

Frank had gone up to the garage and Peggy was out in the stockroom, when the shop door opened, and she heard a man call, 'You open, or what?'

She went quickly in to see the owner of the unfamiliar voice leaning across the counter and reaching for a packet of crisps. He was young and goodlooking, with roughly cut fair hair and weather-brown skin, and he was wearing workmen's clothes and huge, very muddy boots.

'Got any filled rolls, love?' he said to Peggy.

'Sorry,' she said, 'I don't get much call for them. I can do you a sandwich, though,' she added helpfully, 'with ham or cheese.' What is good enough for Mr Richard is good enough for this young man, she thought.

'Thanks,' he said, 'I haven't got much time though, if you could be a bit slippy.'

He wandered about the shop, picking up bars of chocolate and cans of Coke, while she hurriedly made sandwiches in the kitchen. Her mind was working fast. This lad was almost certainly from the building site, and if she could get a regular supply going to the workmen it would be a useful increase in trade.

'There you are, then,' she said, wrapping the sandwiches in greaseproof paper and putting them in a bag.

'How much, missus?' said the lad.

Peggy thought for a few seconds, then fixed a reasonable price, and added up the purchases.

'You from the Walnut Farm site?' she said.

'Yep, we've got a big job on there,' he said, 'and the weather is not helping. Still, better than working in Tresham.'

'Might you want some more sandwiches tomorrow – or I could get rolls?' said Peggy with an encouraging smile.

'Why not?' said the lad. 'If these are good, I could get you a contract!' and he clumped off good-humouredly out of the shop.

'Well done, Peg,' said Frank. 'How about a round of cheese and pickle for this manual labourer?'

The young lad was as good as his word, and next day he came in around midday with a scrubby bit of paper in his hand and read from a list of orders for sandwiches.

'Some of them would rather have rolls, if you can do them,' he said, 'but sandwiches will do for today.' Peggy cut and spread, and filled with ham and cheese, and this time put in a bit of mustard and pickle.

By the time the lad had collected up sweets and drinks, the total was very useful, and Peggy felt quite excited by the possibilities. I could get Doreen to make some pasties and see how they go down, she thought. After all, the men were going to be in Ringford for some time.

'What's your name?' she said, feeling that he was young enough for her to ask.

'Sam,' he said, 'least that's what everybody calls me. My real name is Felix – thanks to my daft dad, but Mum always called me Sam and it stuck. See you tomorrow!'

'Bye Sam,' said Peggy, 'mind how you go.'

CHAPTER TWENTY-SIX

Sandra Roberts had for the last few days been getting off the school bus at Walnut Farm, although it was nowhere near her house, and she had to walk through the village to reach home.

Peggy had been blackberrying along the hedge by Mr Ross's garden, and seen her once or twice. She had wondered if Sandra and Octavia had quarrelled and were avoiding each other.

Mr Ross had come into the shop specially to tell Peggy about the blackberries, an oblique peace offering. He was a kindly man, and his wife had said it was no good fussing about the new houses. They would have to make the best of it.

'You could collect a few more and make a pie,' said Frank one afternoon when the late sun picked out remaining leaves and warmed them into a last flickering of life. 'We shan't get many more good days.'

'Late blackberries are not supposed to have much flavour,' said Peggy, 'but I suppose I could mix them with apples and lemon, jolly them up. Will you manage?'

'Of course I shall – your Sam's been in for his supplies, and the next momentous event is likely to be the return of the school bus, so off you go.'

There weren't many berries left, and Peggy had to reach over to find those worth picking. Never mind, she thought, it's peaceful up here, even with the bulldozers going. The Ringle stretched away into the distance, a winding silver thread, its valley quiet in the low sun with a patchwork of fields, the hedges newly cut, and here and there a copse of poplar and ash. No wonder Mr Ross had chosen this spot for his house.

'Damn!' she said, pricking her thumb on a thorny bramble. She put down her basket of blackberries and sucked the sore place.

'Hurt yourself, Mrs Palmer?' called Sandra from the other side of the road. She had got off the bus, and was walking over to where Peggy stood just inside the field.

'It's nothing, Sandra, thank you,' said Peggy, taken aback by this friendly approach.

'Them farm kids are wild,' said Sandra conversationally, pointing to three boys charging off down the farm track, coats flying and school cases thrown from one to another as they ran. Somebody whistled, once, and then again, a signal. Sandra heard it and turned, waving a hand and whistling in reply.

What is going on, thought Peggy, and then saw young Sam approaching. Sandra said, 'Ta ta, Mrs P.,' and crossed back to the farm track to join Sam. They walked away, hand in hand, and turned into the playing fields through a gate that led into the sports pavilion.

Oh no, thought Peggy, she is much too young for that. I wonder if Sam knows how young she is?

'Just your suspicious mind,' said Frank, when she returned and told him what she had seen.

'But I have seen her there before, obviously waiting for someone. Pity it has to be young Sam, he's such a nice lad.'

'All your geese are swans,' said Frank, 'including this old tabby here.' He picked up Gilbert, and scratched under her chin. She began to purr very loudly, and he laughed. 'Just an old farm cat, aren't you, Gilbertiney, but we love you.'

'I suppose you would say it is none of my business,' said Peggy, irritated.

'No, I would say they were probably interested in each other, and he was walking her home along the footpath.'

'What footpath?'

'The one that leads round the back of the allotments and comes out at the corner of Macmillan Gardens,' said Frank patiently.

Peggy sighed. 'I expect you're right,' she said, 'I shall soon be Poison Ivy's rival for chief gossip.'

But later that week Doreen came into the shop with the eggs, looking abstracted. 'I like your new overall, Peggy. Blue suits you, matches your eyes.'

'Thanks,' said Peggy, batting her eyelids in mock flirtation.

But Doreen had something more important to say. 'Have you heard?' she said.

'Heard what?' said Peggy, taking the trays of eggs from her.

'Old Roberts has walloped Sandra, and then gone off after that lad from the building site.'

'Not Sam!' said Peggy.

'Yep, I just met Roberts – or should I say, I just got out of his way as he shot through the village in that old van.'

'Frank!' called Peggy, unbuttoning her overall and taking down her anorak from the hook by the door. 'Come in and hold the fort, would you – I'm just going up to Walnut Farm.'

Doreen stared at her. 'What on earth has it got to do with you?' she said.

'What's this about?' said Frank. 'Ah, hello Doreen.'

'Doreen will tell you,' said Peggy, and shot out of the door at speed.

It was left to Doreen to explain to Frank, and he was considerably annoyed. 'If only Peggy would stop to think before she acts,' he said, 'she may find she's gone too far this time.'

Peggy arrived up at the farm puffing and blowing, and red in the face. She found Roberts' van parked by the building site, and heard him shouting at the foreman.

'Get the little sod over here,' he yelled, 'I'll break his neck.'

The foreman beckoned Sam across, and Sam walked slowly over to where Roberts stood with his head forward and his fists clenched. Peggy picked her way over the mud and joined the three men, her unsuitable shoes heavy with the wet clay soil.

'What do you want?' said Roberts, swinging round to face Peggy.

'I think I may be able to help,' she said reasonably.

'We don't want none of your nosy help,' said Roberts, 'clear off and mind your own business.'

Peggy said nothing, but stood her ground and looked at the foreman for the next move.

'What's it all about, then?' he said. 'We've got work to do here, so hurry up and get it sorted out.'

'It's our Sandra,' said Roberts, 'and this bugger here.' He indicated Sam, who had a faint smile on his face.

Don't smile, Sam, thought Peggy, it'll be a red rag to Roberts.

'I ain't done nothing,' Sam said with a shrug. The other workmen had stopped the bulldozer and were staring across at the scene.

'Do you know our Sandra's only fifteen?' yelled Roberts. 'I'll have your balls off, you randy little sod!'

'It's nothing to me,' said Sam, and turned to walk away.

'Come back here,' said the foreman. 'Is it true what this bloke says?'

'I just walk Sandra home,' said Sam, 'she's lonely, poor

kid, got no friends. And I'm not surprised, with a father like that.'

Roberts made a lunge towards him, slipped in the mud and missed his target. Peggy put herself between them.

'It's true, Mr Roberts,' she said, 'that's what I came to tell you, I've seen them when I've been up here blackberrying. They just walk back to Macmillan along the footpath.'

'Very kind of you, Mrs P., but I can fight my own battles,' said Sam.

Workmen were gathering round now, and the foreman had had enough. 'Made a mistake, mate,' he said to Roberts. 'Best be off now, and apologise to your Sandra. Get back to your work, Sam – I don't want to hear no more. Go on, lads, party's over.'

'She had one walloping!' shouted Roberts, as he backed away. 'If I so much as catch him smelling round, he'll get one too – and no Mrs bloody Palmer to hide behind!'

'You've made yourself look absolutely ridiculous!' said Frank. 'Rushing off after a boy young enough to be your son.'

'Frank!' said Peggy, shocked.

'Well?' said Frank, white-faced.

'It is you who are being absolutely ridiculous! Don't you see it is just because he is young enough to be my son that I went?'

Peggy knew that she had been impulsive and probably silly, and that the story would go round the village with a number of unfortunate interpretations put upon it.

'He is young enough to be my son,' she repeated, 'and I knew I could probably help. I thought it important to try.'

'Important?' said Frank. 'It may be important to the people concerned, but it really is nothing to do with us. I'd hate to see you turning into an interfering old bag like Ivy Beasley.'

Frank's voice grew louder in annoyance, and Peggy was alarmed.

'Don't, Frank, please don't,' she said, trying to placate him. 'I know it was silly of me to go, but it wasn't any worse than silly.'

Gilbert jumped off her chair and began to miaow loudly.

'She wants to go out,' said Peggy, 'and the door is shut.' She walked through to the kitchen and Gilbert followed her, disappearing through the cat-flap with relief.

On Monday morning Sam came into the shop with his usual bounce, and reeled off a list of sandwiches and rolls needed for the men's dinner. Neither of them mentioned the scene on the building site, but as he turned to leave the shop, he said, 'She doesn't have much of a life, you know, with her rotten family.'

'They are a funny lot to get mixed up with, Sam,' said Peggy mildly, pleased that at least he had broached the subject.

'It was nice of you, Mrs P.,' he said, as he opened the door, 'thanks.'

I'm afraid you are the only one who thinks it was anything but foolish and interfering, thought Peggy. Frank had been cool ever since, and Doreen had made it quite clear that she thought Peggy had been mistaken.

'No good can come of trying to put the Robertses right,' she said. 'They've lived in this village for years, and never been any different. We just let them get on with it.'

Bill was mild but serious. 'I did warn you, Peggy,' he said, 'that you should leave it to Frank. I wasn't there to rescue you this time.'

Peggy had had enough advice, and was particularly nettled at this. 'I didn't need rescuing,' she said, 'I got out quite safely, and all in one piece. Anyone would think Roberts was Ringford's Jack the Ripper. He's just an ignorant bully, that's all.'

'Peggy, Peggy,' said Bill, 'so he may be, but he has lived here a long time and . . .'

'I know,' said Peggy, 'don't tell me, I'd be better to leave things be.'

Frank came in from the garden and he and Bill settled down to a game of chess. They were soon totally absorbed, and Peggy flounced out of the room and shut herself in her bedroom.

Now even Bill has turned against me, she thought. I've broken the first law of the village – not minded my own business. Ah well, I don't suppose anyone will even think about it by next week – it'll be some other story going round.

I wonder, though, she thought, as she stretched out on the bed and opened a book, I wonder if my first reaction was right. Sandra's changed a lot, and you couldn't blame Sam entirely, not with those Robertses.

CHAPTER TWENTY-SEVEN

Ellen Biggs opened the door of her Lodge to admit Ivy Beasley and Doris Ashbourne, who had walked down the lane together. It was Ellen's turn to give them tea, and they squeezed into her tiny sitting-room, taking off their coats. Ivy wrinkled her nose at the smell of damp floors and musty corners.

'See you've got a good fire, Ellen,' said Doris, 'it's very parky out there today.'

'That's rotten wood from the Hall,' said Ivy, 'I had a load from Robert, and it burnt twice as good.'

'Twice as quick, too,' said Ellen, 'pity we 'aven't all got young men who come calling with loads of wood . . .'

'Don't be daft, Ellen,' said Ivy automatically. They had had variations on this conversation before. 'I'm nearly a blood relation – have been his auntie since he was born.'

They settled down, Doris in a battered old wing chair by the window, and Ivy sitting on the edge of a small sofa with sagging springs and a faded green cover rubbed threadbare on the arms.

'What about that young man up at the site?' said Ivy. 'Did you hear about my neighbour charging up there on her white horse? Stupid woman.'

'He's a nice lad, though, Ivy,' said Doris Ashbourne,

'very polite if you meet him in the street. Peggy does sandwiches for them all up there, a nice bit of extra business.'

'Shouldn't go pokin' her nose into other people's lives, though,' said Ellen, 'specially them Robertses.' She set out cups and saucers, plates and milk and sugar, on a small rickety table, and went back into her kitchen for the teapot.

'He's a devil, that Roberts,' said Doris, 'I hear him sometimes, shoutin' at that poor wife of his, his voice carryin' right round Macmillan.'

'Made it yourself, did you, Ellen?' said Ivy Beasley, She knew perfectly well that the chocolate sandwich cake had come from the shop, but could never resist getting a rise out of Old Ellen.

'Naturally,' said Ellen grandly, 'slaved all mornin' with that icing. D'you want a piece or not, Ivy?'

The cake was cut, and tea poured into old china cups that had seen better days up at the Hall. Ivy Beasley turned her cup round and drank from the unchipped side with obvious distaste.

'Heard one or two harsh words next door since that site affair,' she said, taking a bite from the chocolate cake and brushing fragments of the brittle icing off her skirt.

'Makes me wonder what you heard when me and Jack lived there,' said Doris crossly. 'Ain't you got nothing better to do than eavesdrop, our Ivy?'

'I can't help it if the Palmers are yelling at each other when I'm hanging out the washing, can I?' said Ivy.

'It'll soon be firework day,' said Doris, changing the subject. 'You going up, this year?' she said to Ellen. 'I could come to collect you, and we could walk up together if you like.' She knew Old Ellen had never liked fireworks, was frightened of the spitting sparklers and banging rockets.

'No need, I shall be all right,' said Ellen, 'I'm so deaf now I can't 'ear them like I used to – I'll just go up and see the bonfire and 'ave a cup of soup. You going, Ivy?'

'Robert's asked me to help with keeping the children in order,' said Ivy.

'You'll be good at that,' said Ellen, 'taking your broomstick, are yer?' She cackled and rocked in her seat.

'What's up with you today, Ellen?' said Doris. 'You sharpened your tongue before we came, no mistake.'

Ellen got up and put another log on the fire. She bent down with difficulty, resting one hand on her knee to support her unwilling back. 'Old age, Doris,' she said, 'that's what it'll be, old age. I'll just fill the pot and we'll have seconds.'

'Come on, Eddie, my duck,' said Jean Jenkins, lifting her chubby son into his pushchair. 'Just time to nip down the shop for some biscuits. They'll be back from school soon, scratchy as usual. We don't want to be caught without biscuits to sweeten them up, do we?' She bent down and gave Eddie a noisy kiss on his rosy cheek, and set off down Macmillan Gardens.

'I'd better have me benefit,' she said, 'I been trying to save it up for Christmas, but since I got the push from the Hall we are a bit pinched.'

'I'm sure you could get another cleaning job,' said Peggy, putting two packets of chocolate fingers into a bag, 'why don't you put up a card in the window here, and advertise for a week or two?'

'I will do, Mrs Palmer,' said Mrs Jenkins, 'if those new people at Casa Pera don't want any help. I'll try them first.'

'New people?' said Peggy.

'Yep, I saw Mrs Pearson yesterday, and she says they've sold. A couple from London, so she says, and he means to travel every day.'

'Travel to and from London every day?' said Frank, looking up.

'So she said, Mr Palmer, though he's welcome to that,' said Mrs Jenkins. 'Mrs Pearson said something about a new stretch of motorway coming somewhere near this area, and that will make all the difference, she says.'

'Good heavens,' said Peggy, 'I hadn't heard about that! Perhaps we should do some finding out, Frank?' Frank was halfway up a step-ladder replacing one of the neon tubes. It had been flickering for several days and Peggy said it gave her a headache.

'It won't matter what we do,' said Frank, 'if they want to build a motorway near Round Ringford it won't matter a damn what we think.'

The door opened with a warning jangle, and Sheila Pearson came in. 'Just been talking about you, Sheila,' said Peggy, 'were your ears burning?'

Sheila smiled. 'Nothing can touch me now, Peggy,' she said, 'we've exchanged contracts and shall be off in a couple of weeks.'

'Jean here says you know something we don't,' said Peggy. 'What's all this about a motorway?'

'Oh, it has been on the cards for ages,' said Sheila, 'but now they have set a date for next year to make a start. I shall believe it when I see it, but the rumour has been enough to send up the house prices in this area – luckily for us.'

'Will you and David be here for the fireworks?' said Frank, stepping down carefully, the old tube held like a javelin at the ready. He was apprehensive, always felt the same as firework day approached. 'I shall be glad when it's over,' he had said to Peggy.

'Oh yes, we shall be there,' said Sheila, 'after all, it was my idea in the first place. Not that I got any thanks for it at the time, just a lot of carping and criticising.'

'I remember that,' said Jean Jenkins, 'old Ivy kept on about everybody'd always had their fireworks in their own back yards, and we didn't want no changes made by newcomers – 'er usual old song.'

She lifted Eddie up and sat him on the counter, and Peggy took hold of his little sticky hand. Jean smoothed his hair down tidily, and added, 'If you tried to stop the Bonfire Party now, there'd be a riot!'

'You have done very well by the village, Sheila, from what we've heard,' said Peggy, and Mrs Jenkins nodded in agreement.

'Mm,' said Sheila, 'well, they will have to find a new District Councillor – I shall be living in a different ward, and shan't stand again. I think I'd better concentrate on David for a bit . . .'

'If you're not going to be our Councillor any more, Mrs Pearson,' said Mrs Jenkins, 'will there be an election?'

'Yes, if more than one name is put forward,' said Sheila, 'there's always someone waiting to fill the place.'

'Why don't you have a go, Mrs Palmer?' said Mrs Jenkins, with a smile. 'I'm sure you could speak up for us.' Eddie had twisted round on the counter and cuddled up to Peggy, knowing that sometimes nice Mrs Palmerfarmer gave him a biscuit.

Frank looked up and caught Peggy's eye. She grinned at him, and said, 'I think I've plenty to do here. Maybe when we've been in the village a bit longer.'

'That's my girl,' said Frank, and in those few words the air cleared between them.

Frank brought back huge packs of sausages from the wholesaler, and Peggy separated them out and put them in rows in roasting tins. 'They are best done in the oven, I think,' she said. 'I wish they didn't look so fleshy, though. It's like pricking dozens of swollen fingers.'

Robert Bates had been going up and down the village all week with tractor loads of brushwood, old mattresses and great pieces of rotting tree. The children had made a huge floppy-limbed guy and stuck him in a wooden box pram outside the school gates with a collecting tin next to him.

'He's been there all week – he wouldn't have lasted two

hours unguarded in Coventry,' said Frank, 'and by the way, I think I recognise his hat, Peggy, don't I?'

'They got it from the jumble,' she said innocently, 'looks good, doesn't it?'

'What time do they need you?' said Frank. 'I explained to Doreen that I'd rather not be there – not sure if she understood.'

'You're not the only one who doesn't like fireworks,' said Peggy, 'and anyway, Gilbert will need looking after. You'd better keep her in and close the cat-flap.'

Bates's field looked wonderful. The bonfire had been lit, and by the time Peggy arrived it was going well. Its heart was already a burning, fiery furnace. Shadowy figures were silhouetted against the orange-red glow, helpers piling on more branches and sending out huge jets of sparks as the wood landed on the leaping flames.

Each child was given a packet of sparklers on arrival, and most of them squealed with pleasure as the dead grey torpedoes burst into glittering showers. Bates's long field was a blaze of flickering light, and Peggy thought she had never seen anything so exciting. She made mental notes, storing up the details to tell Frank when she got home.

She pushed her way through the crowds of people over to the table where Doreen and Jean and Doris Ashbourne were putting out plastic cups ready for soup. Great pans of bubbling vegetable broth were simmering on a glowing barbecue grid, and Peggy's sausages were placed there to keep warm.

'Well done, Peggy,' said Doreen, 'it'll be all hell let loose in a minute when we start selling.'

Peggy lined up with the others, waiting for 'Food's ready!' from Doreen to unleash the rush. She looked across to the fire and could make out the big, burly figure of Bill Turner, heaving tree trunks on to the top of the fire. He makes it look easy, she thought. That must be David

Pearson over there, talking to Foxy Jenkins. And there's Robert, setting off the rockets. Everyone's here, well, nearly everyone.

'All the same price, then, girls,' shouted Doreen, 'cup of soup, sausage in a roll, mug of squash, or can of Coke – thirty pence each. Are we ready, then?'

Peggy shouted 'Yes!' along with the others, and for the next ten minutes had no time even to look up from the table. Surely there must be more people here than live in Round Ringford? Probably brought their friends and relations from other villages, she thought. Well, it's certainly worth the trip.

'Soup and a sausage, please, Mrs Palmer,' said a familiar voice, and she looked up to see Bill smiling through a very dirty, smoky face. She served him, and he stood by the table eating his sausage from one hand and having slurps of soup from the mug in the other. 'Never tasted anything as good as this!' he said. 'It's the same every year – marvellous!'

It might have been a tradition in the village for hundreds of years, thought Peggy, the way it looked and everything going like clockwork. Nobody would think it had been started by Councillor Mrs Pearson, and with some opposition at that.

'Is Sheila Pearson here?' she asked.

'Yep, she's over by the fence there, keeping children at bay. She's got Ivy Beasley helping her – she'd put the fear of God into anybody.'

A great whoosh silenced everybody for a minute, followed by a chorus of 'Ahhh!' as a gigantic shower of golden rain fell from the night sky.

'Never fails, does it?' said Bill. 'It's the one thing that stays just as good as when we were kids.'

'Frank hates fireworks, his cousin had a nasty accident with one when they were little,' said Peggy, 'that's why he hasn't come.'

'I thought I'd not seen him,' said Bill. He hesitated. 'There's no chance of my Joyce coming out, as you can guess,' he said, 'she's probably in the broom cupboard by now.'

Peggy smiled at him so sweetly that his heart contracted, and he choked on his mug of soup.

The grand finale was bursting out now, a surprise for the party, carefully prepared by Robert Bates. 'The Catherine wheels weren't much good,' he said to Peggy, as he came up for a quick bite, 'they never go properly, but this looks quite impressive, doesn't it?'

He proudly surveyed his signing-off message – 'GOOD NIGHT!' – as it twinkled and sparked on the wooden frame.

'More farworks,' shouted Eddie Jenkins, and everyone laughed and applauded, taking up Eddie's cry – 'More farworks, more farworks, Robert!'

Bill Turner hushed them and called for three rousing cheers for Robert Bates, and all the helpers. Then Bill stepped forward and raised his hand for silence.

'Just a last few words, if I may,' he said.

'What is he up to?' said Doreen, glancing at Peggy.

'You all know,' said Bill in a loud voice, 'that Sheila and David Pearson are leaving us, and moving to Bagley. I'd just like to say on behalf of us all a big thank you – specially to Sheila – for all they've done for the village, and hope they won't forget us but come over as often as they can.'

There were cheers and whoops, and Peggy could see Sheila over in the corner with David's arm round her.

'This firework do,' said Bill, 'was Sheila's idea, and it was a very good idea. We hope you'll be with us again next year, both of you.'

At this point, Gemma and Amy Jenkins walked forward holding awkwardly between them a somewhat battered bouquet of chrysanthemums wrapped in cellophane and tied with a bow of wide yellow ribbon. They held it out to

Sheila, who took it gently. Peggy could see in the light of the fire, still burning vigorously, that Sheila was weeping.

'They always do everything together,' said Jean Jenkins proudly, 'them twins.'

The crowd left the field slowly, and some of the children continued to rush round the fire, whooping like Red Indians and throwing plastic mugs at each other, until they were told to go home. The flames slowly died down, and Robert and Bill smothered glowing embers, making them safe for the night.

Now the light of the fire had gone, the cold moonlight took over, and the black sky retreated into a measureless distance as pinpoint stars appeared.

'That's all done, then, boy,' said Bill, and Robert nodded. 'Went quite well, I reckon,' he said, 'though I says it as shouldn't.'

Peggy helped to clear up the debris, and collected her roasting tins together. 'What a wonderful party, Doreen,' she said, 'best firework party I've ever been to.'

She turned, hearing Warren Jenkins' voice shouting in panic, 'Mr Turner! Mr Turner!'

'He's over there,' said Peggy, 'but you mustn't go near the fire. What's the matter?'

'It's Mrs Turner,' gasped Warren, 'she's screaming and screaming, and nobody can get in to her. Can you go and tell him, quick!'

'Oh my God,' said Doreen, 'what now?'

She and Peggy both ran across the field, shouting as they went. 'Bill, Bill! Come over here, quickly!'

Peggy's heart went out to Bill as she watched his face change. He rushed out of the field and disappeared off towards Macmillan Gardens at top speed.

'Come on, Peggy,' said Doreen, 'we might be needed. She's a difficult woman.'

'Come in my car,' said Peggy, 'it will be quicker.'

They arrived at the Turners' house in Macmillan Gardens to find a crowd had gathered. As they got out of the car they could hear the screams. Peggy shivered, hearing pure terror in Joyce's voice. Doreen got firmly out of the car and pushed her way through the crowd. 'Out of the way,' she said, 'what are you all doing here anyway?'

Bill had just let himself in the back door, and Peggy saw the lights come on, but the screams continued. Doreen disappeared into the house, and in a few seconds there was a merciful silence.

Best thing I can do is stay here, thought Peggy. Then I can give Doreen a lift home. The crowd split up, and the children went off shouting and hitting each other, sorry that the entertainment was over. It had been quite a bonus after the fireworks finished, and they were reluctant to go home.

Peggy sat quietly in the car and stared at Bill's house. What could have gone through that poor woman's mind to make her scream like that? Poor old Bill, too, he had a lot to contend with. And he'd been so happy, making his speech to Sheila and David, and building the fire with such gusto.

She saw Doreen coming out of the house, and leaned out of the car window to call her.

'Thanks for waiting,' said Doreen, settling herself with a sigh in the passenger seat.

'What was it?' said Peggy.

'You won't believe it,' said Doreen, 'but some little horror pushed a lighted firework through the Turners' letterbox, and it exploded inside. Joyce was demented, and no wonder.'

'How did you quieten her down so quickly?' said Peggy.

'It was Bill really, he grabbed her and held her tight. I just told her to shut up, and be quick about it.'

'Oh,' said Peggy.

'Yes, well,' said Doreen, 'she was in my class at school, and I were class prefect. She were noisy, even then.'

CHAPTER TWENTY-EIGHT

'High time you got going on the Christmas display,' said Mrs Ashbourne, coming into the shop and blowing on her fingers to warm them up. The wind was in the north-east, and blew down the Ringle valley with an icy determination to freeze everything it encountered.

'Ah yes,' said Peggy, 'we were going to ask you about that. Would you like to give us a hand?'

'No, I wouldn't,' said Mrs Ashbourne pleasantly enough. 'I don't mean to be rude, but if I help it won't be yours, will it? And you might have some good ideas of your own.'

'Quite right, Doris,' said Frank, 'we shall put our thinking caps on and come up with something irresistible.'

'We could move all the furniture to the back end of the sitting-room,' Peggy said, 'and have a special Christmas display up the front end. People could go through and browse?'

'Mmm,' said Frank, 'people like Sandra Roberts?'

'Don't give a dog a bad name, Mr Palmer,' said Doris rather stiffly. 'Sandra is not a bad girl – it was that Octavia Jones led her astray, if you ask me. Now they don't go about together any more, Sandra has been more like her old self.'

'Even Octavia hasn't pinched anything lately,' said Peggy, 'at least, if she has she's getting better at it.'

'Sandra's pretty busy with young Sam,' said Frank, 'I saw them walking hand in hand down the street last night. It was dark, so I suppose they thought it didn't matter.'

'She won't come to any harm walking hand in hand,' said Peggy practically. 'Just depends what comes next. Old Roberts must be biding his time.'

There were some days now when the weather was too bad for the workmen on the building site, and Sandra wandered about the village looking lost. When Sam did come to work, he waited for her quite openly at the end of Walnut Farm's drive, and she was a different girl. It is wonderful, thought Peggy, how love transforms people.

'Anyway,' said Peggy, 'we could keep an eye on things from behind the counter, or just open the Christmas room when we're both here.'

Frank protested that their privacy was finally going to be sacrificed completely, but Peggy persisted, saying it was only for a few weeks, and could give them useful extra business. 'You've got me there, Peggy,' he said, 'if we don't take a useful profit in the next few weeks we shall be below break-even for the year. So I give in, I capitulate, I surrender – the Christmas room it shall be.' He made a theatrical flourish, put his arm through Doris Ashbourne's, and danced her round the shop for a few reluctant steps.

'You don't seem too worried about the financial situation,' said Doris, 'is it really bad?'

'What will be, will be, me hearties,' said Frank, 'trust in your old Captain Palmer to see you safe into harbour.'

'What is 'e on about,' said Old Ellen, struggling up the steps and into the shop. ''Ere, it's cold enough for snow, our Doris.'

'Speaks of it,' said Doris, 'best be off home and stoke up the fire. You too, Ellen, you don't want to be out in this wind more'n you need.'

Peggy and Frank spent a whole weekend setting up their Christmas room, and Frank entered into the spirit of it, decorating the black beams with tinsel, and putting a silver Christmas tree in the window to attract attention.

By the first week of December, most of their Christmas stock was unsold. Peggy was still optimistic, saying that most people left things to the last minute, and then they'd be in, buying up everything.

But Frank had seen the carloads of Ringford families in Tresham, laden down with plastic bags from the Supashop, looking faintly embarrassed when they caught sight of him. He did not say much to Peggy, but he wondered if he'd chosen the wrong things from the wholesaler. Next year, he'd let Peggy get the Christmas stock – she had a much better eye for what would sell in Ringford.

'Never mind,' Peggy said, sensing Frank's disappointment at the end of another day when nothing had been sold from the Christmas room. Village children, well wrapped up against the cold winds and penetrating rain storms of December, burst into the shop and told Peggy what Father Christmas would bring them. William and Warren laughed cynically, but confessed that they too would be hanging up their dads' old socks. But none of the items on Father Christmas' lists, carefully pencilled on torn-out notebook pages, were purchased from the village shop.

'It is our first year, and we shall learn from our mistakes,' said Peggy. 'Bill said Mrs Ashbourne never made much out of it, anyway.'

'Why didn't she tell us, then,' Frank said. 'And since when was Bill our financial adviser?'

'Don't be sniffy, Frank, we were just chatting and it came up. I have heard you talking to Bill about the shop, so why shouldn't I?'

Frank did not know why, but he knew he felt disgruntled.

It was dark around four o'clock now, and the shop shed an apron of light on the pavement outside. The only other illumination in the High Street was a new, unpleasant lamp, supposed to keep burglars away from the school, and the bright spotlight high up on the pub wall.

'Have you seen the torch, Frank?' called Peggy from the kitchen, as Frank locked up the shop, drew the blind over the window to keep out the cold wind, and turned out the lights. 'What do you want it for?' he said.

'I'm going carol singing,' answered Peggy. 'The W.I. always goes, collects for a different charity every year.' She pulled on a red woolly hat and fur-lined gloves, and picked up the torch Frank had found on a shelf under the sink. 'Shan't be long, love,' she said. 'Start supper without me if you get peckish.'

She blew him a kiss, and went off humming 'The First Noel' a little off-key. Frank winced, but called 'Have a good time!' as she went out of the back door. He wasn't too sure about Christmas, and secretly wondered whether it wouldn't be rather nice to stay in a luxury hotel somewhere and have delicious food sent up to their room, and not emerge until Christmas and New Year were safely out of the way. But Peggy loved it all: tree, presents, carols, turkey and Christmas pudding, friends round for drinks – the lot, with knobs on.

Frank turned on the local television news, and listened to a tale of woe from the weather forecaster. Black ice would make the roads dangerous, and there was a possibility of snow before Christmas. That will please my Peg, thought Frank, she'll be in heaven. He sat down with the newspaper and Gilbert jumped on his lap, kneaded his legs painfully for a minute or so, then settled down to sleep. The fire crackled, and Frank felt himself drifting off, the newspaper slipping to the floor.

He awoke with a start, hearing knocking on the back door.

Blast, he thought, just when I was having a bit of peace. He turned off the television, and walked through to the kitchen to find Bill already inside, stamping his muddy boots on the doormat.

'Hello Frank!' he said cheerily. 'I've come to keep you company. Peg said she was going to the carol singing. All the women are out there, giggling like a bunch of schoolgirls.'

He doesn't wait to be asked in these days, thought Frank grumpily. There's nothing worse than being woken up when you've just dozed off. Now I suppose I've got to make conversation for hours.

Bill seemed not to notice his cool welcome, and talked on, taking off his coat as if he meant to stay. Frank reluctantly asked him to come in by the fire, and the two of them sat down in the warm sitting-room.

'Could we have a game of chess?' said Bill. 'If you feel like it, that is.'

As they set up the chessmen, Bill said, 'Does Peggy ever play chess with you?'

Frank said she didn't. He added that games bored her and she would much rather read a book or watch television. 'Besides which,' he said, 'we would probably argue all the time about the game – a bit like when I taught her to drive.'

'I tried to teach Joyce once,' said Bill. 'She thought it would do her good to be able to get out of the village now and then on her own – be more of a free agent.'

'What happened?' said Frank, moving one of his pawns forward to start the game.

'She didn't have the confidence,' Bill said, 'it wasn't too bad round the villages, but as soon as we got into town she would panic, and I'd have to take over.' He sat hunched over the chess board, staring at the pieces.

'Perhaps it would have been better with a proper driving instructor?' said Frank.

'Couldn't afford that, Frank,' said Bill, 'not on what old Standing pays me.'

'Oh,' said Frank, 'oh I see. Your move.'

They played without speaking for a while, and then Bill said, 'Did you and Peggy not want any kids?'

Frank bridled. What was it to do with Bill Turner whether he and Peggy wanted kids or not? He grunted, and it could have been yes or no. Bill nodded anyway, and continued to talk about families and about how Joyce would have been different altogether if she had been able to have children.

'Bill,' said Frank finally. 'I can't concentrate on the game and listen to you at the same time. You'd probably find it better to think about the game, if you don't mind my saying so.'

Bill looked chagrined, and nodded. 'Sorry,' he said, 'it's just that I can't talk to many people about Joyce and that, and when I get started I can't stop. Sorry, Frank.'

I am a miserable sod, thought Frank, poor devil has a rotten time with that wife of his. And he'd do anything to help us both – especially Peggy. Well, that's it, isn't it, he thought, looking at Bill's strong hand hovering over the chessmen. I'm jealous, jealous of his friendship with Peggy, and ashamed to admit it.

Bill looked across at Frank. 'Your move,' he said, 'and if I'm right you've got me cornered.'

Frank made the inevitable move, and ended the game. 'You wouldn't want me to let you win, would you?' he said. 'That wouldn't do you any good at all.'

'Oh Christ no, boy,' said Bill, laughing. 'You can beat me now hands down any time, but that's not to say you always will!'

'No,' said Frank seriously, 'you are probably right.'

The weather forecast had been accurate, and Round Ringford was a uniform white hollow, dotted with dark contrasting houses and the Ringle frozen over, for once quiet and still. The fields were smooth and featureless, and trees stood out stark against the snow. Peggy put out food for the birds, and chattering sparrows chased away a pair of greenfinches and a tiny wren, who lived in the ivy on the shed roof. The sparrows in turn fled scolding as Gilbert prowled round eating up all the pieces dropped under the bird table.

'Typical cat,' said Frank, 'she wouldn't dream of eating that stuff if we put it in her bowl.'

'Have you noticed the blue tits and blackcaps come very early in the morning, before the sparrows are around?' said Peggy.

'Early birds,' said Frank wisely, 'catch the worms.'

The strange snowy light filtered through the shop window and competed with the coldness of the neon strip. Peggy did a stocking-up tour round the shelves, making notes in the little book. 'We are completely out of currants and sultanas,' she said.

'There won't be any more needed now before Christmas, surely?' said Frank. 'All the cakes and puddings are made.'

'We're also out of mincemeat,' said Peggy, 'and a lot of people make their mince pies on Christmas Eve.'

'You want me to get more supplies, then?' said Frank, not relishing a drive into Tresham.

'Better had,' said Peggy, 'we don't want to let down our regulars.'

'I'll go this afternoon,' said Frank, 'and be back before dark.'

After lunch, Frank made a list and was about to leave when a whole string of people came in, some wanting difficult transactions at the Post Office, and others catching up on last-minute presents, just as Peggy had predicted. She emerged from the Christmas room smiling.

'That's better!' she said. 'There's not a lot left in there now.'

Frank tidied up the Post Office counter and went to get his coat.

'Don't be long, Frank,' said Peggy, 'and take care on those roads.'

It was twilight by the time Frank turned into the country

road on his way home, more an absence of light than real darkness, and roadside barns loomed up unexpectedly as he drove slowly on. He passed a farmhouse huddled under a smooth whitish grey thatch of snow, its slate roof showing blackly around the warm chimney stacks. It was difficult to tell where the fields ended and the sky began, and there was something unsettling about the strange, unfamiliar land-scape. Drifts of snow disguised landmarks so that Frank was unsure at times where exactly he was.

He turned on the car radio for company, and listened to a quiz programme, professional wits having fun with the current news headlines.

I must be tired, thought Frank, it doesn't seem as funny as usual. He shivered, and found himself thinking about his conversation with Bill the night before. Wonder what'll become of him and Joyce. Probably just drag on, poor bugger. Thank God for Peggy.

He peered out of his windscreen, now beginning to frost over as the cold intensified with the fading light. He found it difficult to see, and as he rounded a corner, he marked down a large oak tree coming up on his right and knew that he was nearly home.

'What on earth's that?' he muttered, and as he got closer saw a big black carrion crow roughly tearing apart a squashed rabbit in the middle of the road. It hopped clumsily to one side, jet black against the snow, and Frank swerved to avoid the macabre feast, feeling too late the ice under the wheels.

He was sliding, skidding across the road and unable to control the car. The boxes of stock in the boot moved to one side and increased the car's momentum. Frank wrenched at the steering wheel, and as he did so he knew he was doing the wrong thing. He felt the car tipping, the impact as it crashed into the tree, and then he felt no more.

'That's all folks, for this week,' said the jolly quiz chairman, 'over and out!'

217

CHAPTER TWENTY-NINE

Robert Bates had been up the Bagley road and round the lanes with his tractor and snow plough, clearing drifts and making sure the isolated cottages were supplied with all their needs.

As he came back towards the village, he saw something at the side of the road, just by the big oak, crooked and out of place in the pale darkness. Then he saw it was a car. Christ! he thought, that's Mr Palmer's car! He stopped his tractor and stalled the engine in his alarm.

Jumping down and feeling the slippery road under his boots, he went over to the car. He could hear voices. Thank God, he thought, they're alive, anyway.

But as he got close, he realised it was the car radio, still working and sending out unheeded messages into the half-light of the snowy landscape.

'Oh God, no,' he said, as he saw the figure flattened against the steering wheel, its head twisted at an impossible angle. He felt panic rising, and tried to open the door, but it was stuck fast. 'Oh God, no,' he repeated, and wrenched violently at the door, shouting at the top of his voice.

'Open, you bugger, open!'

The door did not move, and he stumbled round to the passenger side, where he was able to open the door immediately. He reached over and touched Frank's face, unmarked and unmoving. It was cold, colder than Robert's hands, and he knew Frank was dead.

'Oh Christ, oh God,' said young Robert, 'what do I do now?'

The radio churned out the news, reports of bad weather and accidents. Robert felt for the knob in the darkness and turned it off. He sat in the passenger seat in the sudden silence for a few seconds, his head in his hands.

Then he got out of the car and stumped over to his tractor. He pulled out a couple of warning cones from the half-dozen he had put in for emergencies, and set them up in the snow by the crumpled car. He climbed back into his tractor cab, started the engine and, tears streaming down his face, headed for Ringford.

Peggy was putting down a saucer of fish for Gilbert when she heard the side gate open.

That must be Frank, she thought, and turned towards the back door.

But there was a light tapping, and Doreen's voice called out, 'Peggy? Peggy, are you there?'

Peggy walked over and opened the door, wondering why she did not come straight in as usual. She looked out and saw Doreen, and to her surprise a policewoman in uniform behind her.

'Doreen?' she said, alarm mounting. 'What's happened, is it Frank?'

The two women came into the kitchen, and the policewoman shut the door carefully behind her.

Doreen looked at Peggy without speaking. Peggy backed away, as if trying to avoid what was coming. Doreen followed her and silently put both arms round her in a big hug.

'Yes,' she said, 'it is Frank, my dear. He's had an accident up the road – skidded into a tree.'

Peggy's head began to swim, and she clutched Doreen in terror. 'He's all right though?' she said, and knew from the way Doreen tightened her arms that he was not all right, that he was dead.

After that, the policewoman and Doreen had trouble holding on to Peggy, who escaped into violent hysterics, throwing herself from side to side of the kitchen, banging herself without feeling anything, desperate to erase this unacceptable intrusion. Finally she quietened down, and they got her into a chair by the kitchen table.

'You're coming home with me now,' said Doreen, in a quiet, motherly voice. 'We'll tuck you up nice and warm, and the doctor will give you something to help you sleep. Tom's taking care of everything.'

The policewoman checked on the locks, and put out all the lights except the one by the back door. Peggy allowed herself to be shepherded across the kitchen, and just as the policewoman was closing the door behind them she stopped.

'Gilbert?' she said, in a voice nothing like her own. 'What about Gilbert? She hasn't finished her supper . . .'

'Don't worry,' said Doreen, 'she'll use the cat-flap, same as always. We won't let any harm come to her.'

'But how will Frank get in – he didn't take a key,' said Peggy, still in the strange voice.

The policewoman shook her head at Doreen, and they wrapped Peggy's coat closer round her and moved her off slowly down the path to the gate.

By morning, the small population of Round Ringford knew that there had been a dreadful tragedy. A little group had formed outside the shop: Mrs Ashbourne, Jean Jenkins and the twins, kept home from school because of coughs. 'Can't wait here long,' said Mrs Jenkins, 'the cold air don't do them any good.'

'We shall soon know,' said Doris Ashbourne, 'you are

supposed to open the Post Office, whatever – I remember that.'

At five minutes to nine, Mary York appeared. Her face was pale and serious, and she said, 'Morning,' as if it was difficult getting it out. She had a piece of paper in her hand, and carefully stuck it with tape to the outside of the shop door.

'What does it say, Mary?' called Mrs Ashbourne, standing square and muffled in scarf and woolly hat in the cold morning air.

Mary shook her head dumbly, unlocked the door and retreated into the shop.

Mrs Jenkins marched up the steps and peered at the bald, black writing, and read it aloud: ' "Shop closed today, due to bereavement. Post Office open usual hours." '

She sniffed, and rubbed at her eyes with the back of her knitted gloves. 'Come on, girls, it'll be warmer inside.' But it wasn't, it was icy cold. Mary put on the neon lights which flickered and steadied, but did not warm up the air.

'There's a heater behind the counter,' said Doris Ashbourne, 'I'll put it on for you.'

Mary unlocked the Post Office cubicle and opened books and drawers, making ready for business.

'Know where everything is, Mary?' said Mrs Ashbourne helpfully.

Mary nodded, and finally spoke. 'It's easy really, Mr Palmer was very methodical.' Mention of Frank's name seemed to lessen the tension. It was as if permission had been given to speak of him.

'It were instant, weren't it?' Mrs Jenkins said to Doris Ashbourne. 'He couldn't have known nothing, young Robert said.'

Gemma and Amy coughed in unison, and Mrs Jenkins frowned at them. They were so well wrapped up that only their eyes were showing. One could have been a shadow of the other. 'Put your hand over your mouth when you cough, my ducks,' she said.

'Who's looking after Peggy?' said Mrs Ashbourne.

'Doreen Price,' said Jean. 'She's the best person – they're good friends, Peggy and Doreen.'

'There's no family to speak of,' said Doris Ashbourne, 'I remember her saying when they first came that they just had each other.'

This was said flatly, with no trace of false emotion, but silence fell again as the terrible sadness of it all sank in.

'You next, Doris?' said Mary York, and Mrs Ashbourne stepped forward. She handed in her pension book, and waited for Mary to count out the notes. The shop door opened, and everyone looked round nervously.

It was Miss Beasley, looking defiant.

'Good thing everything hasn't ground to a halt,' she said in her grating voice. 'I need some stamps, Mary.'

'Wait your turn, Ivy,' said Mrs Ashbourne, frowning at her. 'Have you seen anything of Mrs Palmer? I expect you came round last night?'

Doris Ashbourne know perfectly well that Ivy Beasley had not been anywhere near until this moment, but she did not intend to let her off the hook. Doris never gave up hope that in spite of Ivy's stiff, unforgiving nature, she would one day surprise her with a generous act.

'She won't want no visitors,' said Miss Beasley. 'Best left alone to grieve for a time. Nobody came near me when Mother died, not a soul.'

'That's because you locked your door and wouldn't answer to a soul,' said Mrs Ashbourne. 'We're not all like you, Ivy, and I for one am going up to Prices' this afternoon to pay my respects.'

Miss Beasley shrugged and turned away to look out of the shop window. 'It has always been unlucky, this shop,' she said. 'Look what happened to your husband, Doris,' she added, with a sly look at Mrs Ashbourne.

'Watch it, Ivy,' said Mrs Ashbourne sharply, 'just watch it.'

The shop emptied, and Mary York sat on the Post Office stool, looking round at the tidy little cubicle, Frank's tiny empire. It would be strange not to see his neat head bent over the books of stamps and allowances any more. What would Peggy do now, she wondered. It would be a lot for one person to manage, as Mrs Ashbourne had discovered. Mind you, Peggy was a lot younger than Doris Ashbourne had been when her husband died.

I suppose I could make a cup of tea while there's no one about, thought Mary, and left the cubicle, locking the door behind her. She went into the kitchen, and saw Gilbert crouched in front of the Rayburn.

'Here, pussy, here!' said Mary, but Gilbert stared at her, and then spat and ran swiftly past her into the shop.

'Gilbert!' called Mary, running after her. She knew Peggy was very strict about the food regulations, and never allowed animals in the shop.

Gilbert stopped at the cubicle door and miaowed loudly, asking to be let in.

'You can't go in there!' said Mary, and knew that the little cat was looking for Frank.

Oh dear, thought Mary, I'm going to cry. She pulled out a handkerchief and wiped her eyes, blew her nose and wished she could go home.

She picked up the cat and took her back into the kitchen, gave her a saucer of milk and shut the door. She made the tea, and hearing the shop door bell ring, she took the steaming mug through into the Post Office.

Sheila Pearson stood uncertainly by the plate-glass window.

'Morning, Mary,' she said, 'I've come over to see how things are. Gabriella Jones phoned me this morning with the terrible news.'

They talked for a few minutes, and then Sheila asked

Mary if she thought Peggy would want to be left alone today.

'I've no idea, Mrs Pearson,' said Mary, 'I'm a bit at sea with all this, not having lost anyone near and dear, as you might say.'

'I suppose I could go up to Prices' and have a word with Doreen – she would know what to do,' said Sheila, turning to leave.

'How you getting on in Bagley, Mrs Pearson?' said Mary politely.

'Early days, yet,' said Sheila, 'but we've just about got the cottage straight. You must pop in if you're passing.'

Mary said she would, though they both knew she wouldn't, and Sheila went out to her car.

Peggy sat in the warm farm kitchen and watched Doreen laying the table for the midday meal. Smells of roasting meat filled the room, and Peggy felt another wave of nausea coming on.

'You'll not be feeling hungry, I expect,' said Doreen, reading her thoughts. 'Still, better try and get something down you – no sense in starving yourself.'

Peggy's thoughts were still tumbling about, nothing coherent, and over and over again she saw in her mind the dark blue car folded up against the oak tree, Frank's body limp and lifeless against the steering wheel. After her first uncontrolled outburst of weeping, she had not cried again. She felt quite numb, as though it was all happening to someone else.

I suppose the tablets the doctor gave me are still working, Peggy thought, and stared at the newspaper Doreen had put on the little table by her side. The print was fuzzy, and she could not read more than a sentence without her thoughts wandering off again.

'Peggy,' said Doreen, 'could you finish laying the table while I just go and call Tom – he's up the yard – shan't be a minute.'

Doreen left a pile of cutlery on the tablecloth, and disappeared.

Peggy got to her feet and stared at the table. Come on, woman, she thought, you know how to lay a table, it can't be that difficult. Mechanically she put out the knives and forks, and spoons across the top. I wonder if she has glasses out? I don't know where they are kept.

Peggy opened one or two cupboard doors until she found the glasses and a water jug. She put the glasses on the table, and filled the jug from the old brass tap. It was as if she was directing her body to move around from a point high up above the room. She felt disconnected, unreal.

The door opened and Doreen came in, breathless from running. At her heels one of the farm cats slipped in quickly in the hope of a quick snack and a sleep by the fire.

Something clicked into place in Peggy's brain, and she said, 'Gilbert! I must go and feed her!'

'Mary's taking care of that,' said Doreen, 'don't worry.'

'But she will be lonely and upset, wondering where we are!' said Peggy, reaching up to lift down her coat from the back of the door. 'I must go now, poor little thing, whatever must she be thinking?'

Doreen frowned. 'Won't it wait until after dinner?' she said.

'No, no, she might run off and try and find us,' said Peggy, anxiety mounting. 'I'll come back, after I've seen to her.' She looked round the kitchen, and then at Doreen, and her eyes were dark smudges in her pale face. 'Sorry, Doreen, I have to go now,' she said, 'I'll be all right.'

Tom stumped into the kitchen and took off his boots by the door. 'Where's Peggy?' he said.

'Gone home,' said Doreen, looking worried.

'What!' said Tom. 'By herself?' He began to wash his hands in the kitchen sink, scrubbing them with an old nailbrush.

'Yep, that's what she seemed to want,' said Doreen.

'Shall I go after her?' said Tom. 'I could pick her up in the car.'

'No, I don't think so,' said Doreen, 'I think we'd best let her be for a little while. I'll go down in an hour or so and see what's happening. After all, no harm can come to her. Mary's down there all day.'

Doreen and Tom sat down to their roast pork, but neither had much appetite.

Peggy did not have far to walk, but to her it seemed like miles. She came out of the frozen, rutted farmyard into the street, where the gritting lorries had left swathes of loose, dirty gravel, now piling up at the sides of the road. There was a light shining in the Jones' window, and she could see figures moving around inside. It looked warm, busy, homey. The pub chimney had a thick plume of smoke, and Peggy imagined a roaring log fire in the bar, people sitting companionably over their drinks. She felt very much alone.

As she passed Macmillan Gardens she looked along the rows of houses and dreary winter gardens, and noticed Sandra Roberts emerging from her gate. Sandra saw Peggy and stopped, hesitated, and then ran slipping and sliding down the path until she caught up with her.

'Sorry, Mrs P.,' said Sandra, 'well, you know . . .' Peggy found she could not reply, so she nodded, and Sandra went back up the other side of the Gardens and vanished into the Jenkins' house.

I suppose everyone is having lunch, thought Peggy, that's why it is so quiet. It was a grey, misty day, and the cold penetrated her coat and her light shoes. She shivered and pulled her coat collar up round her ears. Perhaps she was being foolish, should have stayed in Doreen's warm kitchen, instead of walking down a cold, empty street the day after the death of her husband.

She stopped short. The death of her husband, she repeated to herself. The death of Frank, the death of Frank

Palmer. Frank was dead, dead today and tomorrow and every other day, until she too was dead.

Peggy looked wildly round, and then began to run. She ran, almost falling once or twice on the icy pavement, until she reached the shop. I can't face it, she thought, and went through the side gate and into the garden.

The back door was locked, and she banged on it, yelling, 'Let me in! It's my home, let me in!'

Mary York heard her screams, and rushed to unlock the back door. Peggy nearly fell into the kitchen, and Mary caught her. Gilbert, sitting disconsolately on Frank's chair, jumped down and rushed across to greet her, rubbing herself round Peggy's ankles.

Peggy picked her up and buried her face in the little cat's soft fur. 'Gilbert, Gilbertine,' she said, 'he's not coming back any more, what are we going to do?' Tears flowed faster, and Peggy sat down on Frank's chair, cradling Gilbert in her arms.

'Can I get you a cup of tea, Peggy?' said Mary, wiping her eyes behind her thick glasses.

Peggy shook her head, and motioned Mary to leave her. Mary went back into the shop and closed the door, feeling completely useless. Still, I can help in here, she thought, if anybody else comes in. After the first rush, there had been no one. She pulled out a packet of sandwiches from her bag and sat slowly eating egg and tomato, wondering what she would do if she went home and found Graham had been killed in an accident. Then she put the thought from her, terrified that thinking about it might make it happen, wondering if disaster was catching.

The telephone rang, and Mary picked it up.

'Hello, Mary,' said Doreen Price's familiar voice, 'is Peggy all right? Do you think she wants me to come down yet?'

'I'll just ask her,' said Mary, 'she's in the kitchen.'

It all sounds so normal, thought Mary, and it isn't. Peggy

was standing by the sink, opening a tin of catfood, while Gilbert purred and miaowed around her legs.

'I'll speak to her,' said Peggy, and picked up the telephone receiver. She apologised to Doreen for rushing off, and said she was all right, not to worry, and not to bother coming down. 'I think I'd like to stay here now,' she said, 'it is easier, somehow, and the more I stay away the more difficult it will be to come back, don't you think?'

Doreen reluctantly agreed. 'I'll give you a ring later to see if you're still all right,' she said.

The afternoon passed, and the light slowly went from the grey winter sky. Peggy looked out of the sitting-room window, and saw the bean poles that Frank had arranged so carefully. Dried strands of beanstalk still clung to one or two poles, and the whole unsteady wigwam leaned sadly to one side in the snow.

Peggy heard Mary York locking up, and her light footsteps crossing the shop floor as she came through to say goodbye.

'Thank you very much, Mary, we – I – couldn't have done without you,' Peggy said, and impulsively kissed the embarrassed Mary on the cheek.

'Yes, I shall be all right,' said Peggy, answering Mary's anxious question, 'and there's lots of people I can ring up if necessary. Goodbye now, you did say you could come tomorrow? See you then . . . bye . . .'

Peggy switched on the sitting-room lights and drew the curtains. It was very quiet, and she wondered whether to put on the radio. It seemed inappropriate somehow, and she sat down and picked up a book. But what is appropriate? I'm lost, she thought, starting a new job with no previous experience. She could not concentrate on the book and put it down. She stood up and went over to the table, where on the day they moved in she had put the photograph of her and Frank on their wedding day.

She was standing looking at the picture, feeling a pain so sharp that she put her hand up to her chest, when the sitting-room door opened, and Bill walked in.

'Back door was open,' he said, and stood looking at her uncertainly.

'Come in, Bill,' Peggy said, putting down the photograph.

They stood looking at each other for several seconds, and then Bill tentatively put out his hand. 'I'm really sorry, gel,' he said, 'he were a good man.'

Peggy asked him to sit down for a minute, and Bill took care not to sit in Frank's chair. In the quiet room Peggy talked in fits and starts. Bill did not say much at all, but she was able to ask him one or two questions about the accident. He gave her short, straight answers, and then asked whether she would be all right by herself in the house.

'Oh yes, I think so,' said Peggy, 'and I've got Gilbert, haven't I?'

'I could come back later on, after Joyce and me have had our tea,' said Bill, 'just to make sure you are all locked up and safe.'

'Best not, Bill,' Peggy said, 'but thanks for suggesting it.'

CHAPTER THIRTY

The next few days passed in a featureless blur for Peggy. Mary York came in each day and took over the Post Office. On Peggy's instructions she put up a notice to say the shop would reopen in several days' time. Peggy had said this would be enough time for her to organise everything, and then she would need something to do.

Tom Price sent for the Co-op undertakers, and two dark-suited men came to see Peggy. They were so kind, she thought, and knew exactly the right things to say. The Reverend Cyril Collins visited her, and sat quietly in her sitting-room, encouraging her to talk about Frank. She had never been able to see why Doreen liked him so much, but now she appreciated his spiritual strength and the humility of his offering of comfort and advice.

The funeral was arranged for Friday morning at ten-thirty, and friends were asked to come back to the Stores for coffee. Peggy was not at all sure she wanted this ritual wake, but Doreen said it was customary, and it always did everyone a lot of good.

'How do you make that out, Doreen?' said Peggy.

'It just does, that's all – leave it to me, Peggy dear,' said Doreen.

Peggy was happy to leave a great deal in Doreen's capable

hands, and trusted her absolutely. She did not go into the shop during the day, and found that she could spend hours just sitting with a cup of tea and thinking about Frank.

Deep in her armchair by the fire, listening to the whine of a cold wind threatening more snow in the village, Peggy replayed scenes from their life together, like an old magic lantern slide show.

Their first meeting was at the table tennis evening at the Youth Club, Frank lithe and quick on his feet. His partner was Peggy's best friend, and she had been mad when Frank asked Peggy to go out with him. Their first date had been to see a film at the County Cinema on the corner of the Market Place, with Frank arriving much too early, dressed neatly in a sports jacket and flannels, his tie tightly knotted and the corners of his shirt collar turning up.

I had my best grey dress cleaned specially, Peggy remembered, and bought a new red belt to cheer it up. Mum said it looked like a school uniform, but I knew I looked smart. Frank said so, said he didn't like girls to be overdressed.

Gilbert brought her back to the present, miaowing to be fed, and Peggy gave her some catfood from the shop. 'I'll get you some fresh fish next week,' she said, 'when Ernie has been round.' Ernie was the fish-van man, who claimed he went every day at the crack of dawn to Grimsby for his fish. 'You can't get any fresher than that!' he said, but Peggy doubted his word.

Nothing tastes as good as the six pennorth of chips we used to buy from the fish and chip shop after the pictures, eaten hot from the newspaper on the way home. When the chips were finished, Frank used to hold my hand in his greasy one . . . pushing his bike awkwardly . . . walking me home through those back streets to Mother . . . widowed Mother . . .

Peggy opened her eyes and realised Doreen had come in, and was sitting in Frank's chair, opposite her own.

'I remember the first time he kissed me,' she said to Doreen, who smiled.

'We had been to see *Roman Holiday* with Audrey Hepburn and Gregory Peck,' Peggy said, 'and when we got back to my house Frank leaned his bike up against the fence and very fiercely kissed me! I think he must have made up his mind that the time had come, and hell or high water tonight was the night!'

Doreen said nothing, but smiled encouragingly and put another log on the fire.

'My mum thought he was wonderful,' Peggy said, 'she was always asking me to bring him back to supper or tea, and when we said we wanted to get married she burst into tears of relief. I suppose she felt extra responsible, being a widow and having no husband to . . .'

Peggy's voice petered out, and her eyes filled. 'I'm a widow now, aren't I, Doreen? It'll take a bit of getting used to.'

The morning of the funeral was fine and bright, and in a sudden thaw much of the snow had melted. The sun shone on lingering patches on the fields and in the ditches, and in shadowy places where the sun did not reach it was still cold and wintry. The ground had been hard for old Grandfather Roberts to dig the grave, and his son had given him a hand. Gravedigging had been the Roberts family prerogative for generations, and although they no longer attended church, they were jealous of their right to lay the village dead to rest.

'Didn't like the bugger much,' said old Roberts to his son, who nodded agreement, 'but I wouldn't have wished him dead.'

'She'll be on her own, now,' said Sandra's father, 'need a bit of help with the shop, unless she sells up.'

Grandfather Roberts said, 'Bill Turner'll give her a hand, I shouldn't wonder,' and he smiled maliciously.

They finished digging the neat rectangle with its little hillock ready to be shovelled back over the coffin, and stretched out a green cloth to cover the indecent freshness of the living earth. 'Wonder if it'll be a big turn-out?' said Grandfather Roberts.

His son shook his head. 'No family to speak of, so they say,' he said.

But he was wrong. The village people had walked steadily down the street and over the bridge, joining up in groups by the lych gate. Mrs Jenkins and Foxy, on their own for once, the children parked with their grandmother over at Bagley; Doris Ashbourne, in a warm grey coat with black gloves and a grey knitted beret pulled well down over her ears. Old Fred Mills, his pipe left at home, hobbled along with his stick, and Mr Ross caught up with him at the bridge, remarking on the thaw and the sunshine.

Ellen Biggs had walked painfully over from the Lodge and was already sitting at the back of the church, huddled in a corner of the pew, not wanting to be reminded of mortality, but never dreaming of staying at home. And Mary York, head down, terrified of making an exhibition of herself by crying, walked swiftly down the aisle and sat next to Ellen.

'Look,' whispered Jean Jenkins to Foxy, 'that's Mr Richard! That's a surprise – I thought he didn't hit it off with the Palmers.' But Richard Standing knew his duty as squire of the village, and walked with dignity down the aisle and took his seat in the family pew.

The bell tolled for Frank Palmer. His old friend and chess opponent Bill Turner tolled it for him, thinking of their short friendship and wishing he could put back the clock. Never thought I'd be pulling the rope for Frank, never in a million years. He could hear a quiet hum of conversation as the church waited. Better watch out for the undertaker's signal, he thought, should be any minute now.

The church was full, a good crowd from Maddox's

233

swelling the congregation. But there was one more to come. Brisk and correct in a black coat and felt hat pulled well down, came Miss Beasley. She acknowledged Robert's smile, marched to her usual pew, caused the people sitting there to jostle one another to make room for her, and then knelt down, saying a lengthy private prayer.

' 'Ow could you, Ivy, after all you've said,' muttered Ellen Biggs.

Bill ceased his tolling, and silently squeezed in next to Mary York. He watched the open door of the church, and heard the vicar's voice intoning the familiar and awesome words, 'I am the resurrection and the life, saith the Lord . . .'

The coffin appeared, borne by the kindly Co-op undertakers, and the church seemed – as always – to hold its breath. On the coffin was a single wreath of red roses, and Bill thought how small the wooden box was, how little to show for the life of Frank Palmer. Then he saw Peggy, with Tom Price holding her arm, and her face told him that Frank Palmer had his memorial there, in her utter desolation.

Tom and Doreen had organised two little speeches, testimonials to the good character of Frank Palmer. He won't need no references where he's going, thought Bill. Tom spoke of Frank's efficiency and dedication to the Post Office, giving the village a reliable service and keeping alive the tradition of pension day – a social occasion as well as a lifeline for the old people of the village.

A senior executive from Maddox's who had climbed the ladder with Frank, stood up and talked of Frank's loyalty and devotion to the company, his enthusiasm for chess and his willingness to be involved in many aspects of the life of the workforce, which Maddox's liked to think of as an extended family.

Didn't stop them turfing him out, though, thought Bill, probably the start of all this.

Peggy had chosen 'He who would valiant be, 'gainst all disaster', for the final hymn, and the optimism in John Bunyan's simple words filled Bill momentarily with hope. 'We know we at the end, shall life inherit,' sang the congregation, and he watched from the back of the church as Peggy's head lifted up and he knew her eyes must be looking at Frank's coffin, quiet and still on the bier before the altar.

By the time Peggy walked back into the Post Office Stores, she had had enough, and just wanted to retreat into her bedroom and shut the door. But Doreen gave her plates of cakes to hand round, and there were faces to remember from the old days, and reminiscences to be got through.

'Doreen,' she said, as the last farewells had been said, 'did I see Miss Beasley in church?'

'Yep, she was there, the old bat,' said Doreen. 'I suppose we must think charitably that she wanted to pay her respects. But I'd rather see a little goodwill to the living, wouldn't you?'

Peggy did not know what she would rather see. Her mind was crowded with snatches of conversation and images of the day. Competing now with the crashed car came pictures of the funeral, and the worst moment of her life – the earth symbolically thrown to commit Frank's body to the cold, frosty ground. Frank . . . !

Doreen looked closely at her, and said, 'You'd best sit by the fire now, Peggy, and close your eyes for an hour or two. Doris Ashbourne and me will be in the kitchen washing up, and if you want anything you just call.'

Peggy protested that she should help, but Doreen would not hear of it, and shutting the door of the sitting-room quietly, went to tackle the dishes.

Peggy looked at the silver Christmas tree, carefully placed by Frank in the window to attract the customers. In a couple of weeks, thought Peggy, it will be Christmas.

What should she do on Christmas day? How would she get through it all by herself, and what would be the point of it all? What would be the point of anything, without Frank?

Gilbert jumped up on to her lap, purring, pleased at this unexpected opportunity to have Peggy to herself in the middle of the day. Peggy stroked her automatically, and closed her eyes. She would never be able to sleep, she knew that, but at least she would not have to speak to anyone for a while. She could pretend to be asleep if Doreen came back.

'. . . hath but a short time to live, is cut down, like a flower,' she heard the vicar's rolling voice from the graveside. Funny that, I'd never thought of Frank being like a flower.

Two minutes later, Peggy was asleep.

CHAPTER THIRTY-ONE

The coffin was rapidly disappearing under a shower of earth, and Peggy stood holding Tom's arm, looking down into the grave. What was that voice, faint under the sound of stones landing on the wooden coffin? There's someone knocking! Frank! Frank! Peggy tugged at Tom's arm and tried to tell him. But she could make no sound. She tried again, hearing herself shouting in her head, as the knocking grew louder and louder, and the coffin was all but covered in earth.

Tom stood staring across the valley, and the mourners all turned and looked away from Peggy. The vicar shut his prayer book, and also turned away.

'Frank!' screamed Peggy, but no sound came out of her mouth.

Then she was awake, her heart pumping, her face wet with tears, and her body soaked in sweat. The knocking came from downstairs, and she realised that she was in bed, it was early daylight and someone was trying to attract her attention.

She pulled on her dressing-gown and pushed her feet into slippers, grabbed a comb and ran downstairs, combing her tousled hair as she went.

It was Brian the postman, and Maureen and Margaret, all

three of them standing on the top step by the shop door, peering anxiously through the window.

'God, she looks awful,' muttered Margaret to Maureen, and they tried not to stare at her as she fumbled with the locks and finally opened the door, apologising profusely.

'Where has Mary got to?' she said. 'She should be here by now. I do hope she's all right – come on in, I'll put the kettle on.'

They set to work with their usual efficiency, and told Peggy to relax, not to worry about them. It was the first time Peggy had really come face to face with the routine of the Post Office since Frank's death, and she felt inadequate and lost, missing Frank's self-assurance.

But the two women and Brian got on quietly with the job, coming briefly into the kitchen when they had finished to have a quick cup of tea.

'Very sorry, Peggy,' said Brian, 'if there's anything I can do . . .'

'I was thinking,' said Maureen tentatively, 'maybe you'd like to come round and have a cuppa with me one afternoon, after the shop's shut?'

'That's very kind of you, Maureen,' said Peggy.

Then they were gone, with their routines to follow, taking the security of their daily lives for granted.

What do I do now? thought Peggy. Everyone else is starting the day, just carrying on, knowing what comes next. I could go back to bed, nobody would care. I suppose I'd better get some breakfast, though, feed Gilbert. It is too early to ring Mary York. I wonder what happened to her? Nothing wrong, I hope.

Mary York answered this herself, by rushing into the kitchen full of apologies for forgetting to set the alarm and oversleeping, and then finding her bicycle had a flat tyre, and having to walk.

'Don't worry,' said Peggy, 'perhaps it was a good thing. I've got to get used to it sooner or later. I might come into the shop for an hour or two this morning, just to tidy up and make a list of stock needed.'

Then she remembered she had no car to get the stock from the wholesalers, and that reminded her that there was the car insurance to sort out, and final arrangements to be made with the solicitors. With jobs in view, jobs that needed her to sort them out, she felt better, and went upstairs to change the sheets on the bed.

Her spirits plunged again when she put the sheets in the machine and realised that she was washing off the last traces of Frank. The pillow cases still smelt of his aftershave, and she held them close to her cheek before shoving them quickly into the machine and turning it on. Frank, Frank . . .

When Doreen came over in the middle of the morning, Peggy had got the vacuum cleaner going, and the windows of the sitting-room were wide open, letting in fresh, cold air.

'You're busy!' said Doreen.

'Better being busy than feeling sorry for myself,' said Peggy. 'My mum used to say that thinking was the worst possible thing you could do. She didn't tell me how to stop myself thinking, though. Funny, I haven't thought of Mum for ages, and now she seems to pop up all the time.'

'She was very sensible,' said Doreen. 'When are you opening up the shop again? One or two people have asked me, and I said I thought next Monday.'

'I think I might start tomorrow,' said Peggy, 'there's no sense in moping about, and it will give me something to do. Frank used to say he was a lazy man, but in fact he believed in keeping busy, said it kept the demons at bay . . . one or two demons round here at the moment, Doreen.'

The tears were close again, and Doreen looked out of the window at the wintry garden. Neat and tidy as always, Frank had cut back the shrubs and pruned roses so that the winter winds would not damage them. The bare earth had

239

heaps of horse manure ready to be spread around to nourish the soil for next spring's planting. You could see where Frank had stopped work, his tidying and preparing. The rest was neglected, waiting for attention. 'You'll need some help with this in the spring,' she said, 'perhaps Bill will give you a hand. He and Frank were good friends, weren't they – Bill will miss those chess games.'

Peggy was grateful to Doreen for not skirting round the subject of Frank's death. Mary York had seemed scared stiff of mentioning it, and had immediately changed the subject once her condolences had been made.

'Frank used to get cross with him,' said Peggy, 'poor old Bill would talk about other things while they were playing, and Frank always liked to concentrate on the game.'

'Bill is a good bloke,' said Doreen, 'he'll stand by you. Mind you,' she added bluntly, 'you'll have to watch it, you know what the old tabs will say.'

Peggy stopped dusting and stared at Doreen. 'What will they say?' she asked.

'Oh come on, Peggy,' said Doreen with a smile, 'you don't need me to tell you what they will say about a woman on her own and a nice-looking chap like Bill Turner!'

Peggy felt sick. She knew Doreen was right, but the thought of Miss Beasley gossiping about herself and Bill was horrible. 'Well, I shall just have to do without his help, then,' she said abruptly to Doreen.

'Don't be like that, Peggy,' said Doreen, 'I didn't mean to upset you. You know me, in with both feet, but it's best to nip these things in the bud.'

'What things!' said Peggy loudly.

'Nothing, just busybodies like old Poison Ivy, not giving them the chance for a nice juicy bit of gossip, that's all.'

Peggy calmed down. 'I can do without the likes of Ivy Beasley at the moment,' she said, 'but I don't mean to be cross with you, Doreen.'

'I must dash,' said Doreen, 'the vet's coming this

morning to see to one of the cows. I might ask him to give me the once over, too!' she yelled as she left.

Peggy smiled wanly, and finished dusting the sitting-room. She shut the windows, feeling the freezing air filling the room. The sky looked heavy and yellowish-grey.

'More snow this afternoon, I'm afraid,' said Mary York, coming in to tell Peggy that old Dr Russell had been in, inquiring after her.

'I told him you were getting over it,' said Mary, taking Peggy's breath away.

By Christmas Eve, Peggy had established a new routine, but it was all she could do to keep on top of the work and manage on her own. She no longer had Mary York working for her, knowing well from conversations with Frank that they could not afford it. She remembered Doreen's warning, and avoided having Bill in the house, asking him only to collect supplies from the warehouse for the shop. A new car would be ready for her after Christmas, and she looked forward to the independence it would give her.

Doreen and Tom were always ready to give a hand, as were her other friends, and Peggy came to realise that her shock at Frank's death was being cushioned by the village itself. She went to tea with Maureen in the stone cottage by the pub, and Mrs Jenkins asked her round to Macmillan Gardens, where she sat in the small room surrounded by children, all on their best behaviour, eating wonderful cakes and listening to Jean Jenkins chattering about school politics, and the doings of her various brothers and sisters over at Bagley.

Mr Ross had left a bunch of carnations from his greenhouse on the back doorstep whilst she was out. Peggy telephoned her thanks, and heard Mr Ross's account of his sister's untimely death at the age of six.

Young Robert Bates had come in several times for

groceries and cans of Cola, and in his shy way had said how sorry he was. 'I shall never forget finding Mr Palmer that way, never in my life,' he said, 'now, if there's anything you need doing, Mrs Palmer, you just ask.'

Even Richard Standing, seen less and less around the village since his Susan had departed, came into the shop and in a stiff, formal voice expressed his regret.

Peggy began to wonder if it would ever end, whether one day she would get through the long hours without having to live through the nightmare once more. And yet I can't bear it when people won't talk about Frank, she thought, I want to talk about him, it keeps him alive for me.

'Are you going to Midnight Mass?' she asked Doreen, on the morning of Christmas Eve. Doreen and Tom had invited her to spend Christmas Day with them, and she had accepted, not because she really wanted to, but because she could not face the day alone.

'We always do,' said Doreen, 'it doesn't seem like Christmas without going. Tom comes along with his cronies after a few glasses of good cheer at the pub, and their singing is chronic! I can pick you up on the way, if you like?'

'Well, could you give me a knock?' said Peggy. 'And then I can decide at the last minute.'

She made up the fire after closing the shop, and settled down with a sandwich to watch early television. The programmes were full of Christmas celebrations and parties, and endless commercials for toys costing the earth.

It has all got out of hand, she thought. A visitor from Mars would not know that the festivity had anything to do with the birth of Jesus Christ, Saviour of the World. She switched channels and there, as if refuting her thoughts, was a little news item from a village school in the region. The Nativity Play was being performed in an ancient church, and proceeds of the collection would go to orphaned children in the latest East European disaster.

Peggy watched the little Mary led gently by a desperately

serious Joseph to a school chair set up in a rickety stable, straw covering the cold tiles of the church floor. The closely wrapped doll tipped backwards as Mary sat down, and she grabbed it by a leg and settled it with a motherly shake into her meagre lap.

As the play proceeded, Peggy thought about babies. Why had she and Frank been so stupid about not asking for help? It was just that there always seemed to be plenty of time, until suddenly there wasn't, and it was too late. We could have adopted, she thought, if we'd faced up to it sooner. Any one of those bewildered, innocent war orphans would have been glad of a good home. There have always been children needing homes. I wouldn't be so alone now, she thought.

The news item came to an end before the play had finished, a flavour of Christmas being all that was required. Peggy switched again, and an unfunny situation comedy used up half an hour of relentless studio laughter. Peggy felt more and more miserable.

She turned off the television, and wondered what to do next. Hours to go before Midnight Mass, she thought, perhaps I should just go to bed and forget all about everything. I could take a sleeping pill. In fact, I could take several, and make sure that I forget all about everything for ever.

It was then that she saw Frank.

He was sitting in his chair, one leg crossed neatly over the other, his hands folded in his lap, and he was looking at her, smiling.

'Frank!' she gasped, jumping up from her chair and backing away.

He said nothing, just smiled more broadly, and lifting up his hand, blew her a kiss. Then he was gone.

Peggy rubbed her eyes, and stared at the empty chair.

Her heart was racing, and she felt cold. She sat down again, but this time she sat in Frank's chair, and thought she felt his warmth. Was it you, Frank, she thought, did you really come back to stop me doing anything stupid?

She began to cry quietly, and without speaking pleaded with God to let Frank come back, and for her to wake up and find it had all been a bad dream.

But nothing more happened, and the only sounds were of car doors slamming as revellers began to arrive at the pub for some serious drinking.

Peggy reached for the telephone. She dialled, and waited.

'Doreen?' she said. 'Can I come over, and sit with you until it's time for church?'

Doreen's kitchen was warm and bright with Christmas decorations. Cats slept in the chairs, and two smelly spaniels grunted in their baskets. The clock on the wall ticked loudly, and Doreen's knitting needles clattered out of time.

'You should get started on some knitting or sewing – take up your tapestry again,' said Doreen, 'I can't sit here and do nothing, even when the telly's on.'

The time passed, the two women chatting desultorily, and Peggy felt her calm gradually restored. By the time Doreen got up to fetch coats and scarves for the church service, Peggy had screwed up enough courage to tell her about Frank.

Doreen showed no surprise. 'Like as not you'll see him again,' she said, 'for a while. Then no more – he'll be able to go in peace.'

CHAPTER THIRTY-TWO

The Price family had had a pew in church for generations. It was two rows back from the front, and now that the old box pews had been replaced by modern ones, pale pine where there had been dark oak, there was little distinction between rich and poor, master and servant.

In the days of the box pews, when families were enclosed in their own little space, warmed and private, Grandpa and Grandma Price had sat with their large family in full view, the bored little ones swinging their legs and nudging each other, and Grandpa daydreaming of the roast and Yorkshire pudding waiting for him back at the farm.

Must have looked much the same then, except for the pews, thought Peggy, looking round at the tall Christmas tree, spangled with lights. The crib scene in the corner had been set up by the Sunday School, with its chipped plaster figures of Joseph and Mary and the Christ child, lovingly handled and placed into position in the stable by generations of children in Round Ringford. Swags of holly and ivy decorated the tall narrow windows, and the font had been filled by Doreen with white chrysanthemums and holly-berried branches – a warm welcome for churchgoers as they came in the door.

The Standing pew was occupied already. The back of Mr

Richard's head was unmistakable, large and round, dominating the smaller, softer head of Susan, returned for Christmas with the children.

'Doreen,' Peggy whispered, 'she's back, then?'

Doreen nodded. 'Togetherness for Christmas,' she said, 'wonder how long that will last.'

Peggy watched as people filed in, some of them seen in church only two or three times a year. The regulars looked at them smugly – this is our church, you are just casual attenders. God can tell the difference, don't you worry.

The service began, and the Reverend Cyril Collins said his prayers and made his announcements at a cracking pace. Long past his bedtime, thought Peggy. Doreen looked round at the door anxiously, until it finally opened and Tom Price, Foxy Jenkins and Robert Bates made their deliberately sober way into their seats.

'About time too,' Doreen hissed, and the congregation smiled.

The service was well under way when the door opened again, and in came a straggling group of young people. Peggy recognised among them Sandra and her brother Andrew, and also young Sam, looking sheepish. There were giggles as they were ushered swiftly into a seat at the back of the church by Mr Ross, who frowned them into silence.

Carols were sung lustily, and the air gradually filled with the pleasant aroma of alcohol and cigar smoke still clinging to those who had spent the evening in the pub. The girls continued to giggle from time to time, and Peggy saw Ivy Beasley turn round and direct one of her sharpest looks at the young people.

'What does Poison Ivy do for Christmas?' Peggy whispered to Doreen.

'Stays at home, I think,' answered Doreen, 'and has a happy time being miserable!'

Peggy smiled, but she thought for the first time about the

loneliness of Miss Beasley's life. Ivy Beasley had devoted herself to nursing her mother, and then been left alone, nobody needing her, and with very few friends. Her own fault, of course, thought Peggy, but who knew what resentments and hurts lurked beneath her stern bosom? And God knows I feel sorry enough for people living on their own.

Perhaps I should make a New Year's resolution, to be nice to Miss Beasley and make her my friend. Peggy silently shook her head. I've got enough troubles of my own, what with the business and everything, without taking on Ivy Beasley, she thought. And anyway, she probably likes being the village scourge – gives her some reason for getting up in the morning.

'Glory to the new-born King!' sang the congregation, and bowed their heads as the vicar blessed them all and wished them a happy Christmas. The church clock, on cue, struck twelve and everyone shook hands and smiled their greetings. Peggy found herself receiving special attention, and was warmed by the goodwill shown by people who never even came into the shop.

'Come on, Peggy,' said Tom, 'let's away home for a nightcap!'

She spent the night in Doreen's tiny spare room on a single bed which sloped with the floor, and felt that but for the tightly tucked blankets she would have fallen out. She was prepared for a sleepless night, but quickly dozed off. Several times she awoke to see the moonlight through the tiny window, and once she saw Frank again. He was standing at the foot of the bed, still smiling and holding out his hand.

This time Peggy was ready for him, and said, 'Hello, Frank – are you all right?' He nodded and once more blew her a kiss, just as he always had when going off to work at Maddox's. In seconds he was gone again, but Peggy turned over in her narrow bed feeling comforted, and drifted back to sleep.

CHAPTER THIRTY-THREE

Snow had fallen heavily again in the night, and Foxy Jenkins had been out early, sweeping the path to the washing line and knocking the ice out of the terrier's bowl, filling it up with fresh water. Other gardens were still piled high with uncleared snow, their owners happy to leave it like that until the thaw. Gaunt black bits of metal stuck up through drifts haphazardly piled in the Roberts' garden, and a leaning snowman peered drunkenly over the fence. Darren Roberts, home for Christmas for a few days, was already scraping snow from Mrs Ashbourne's path, and as he saw Bill Turner emerge from his gate he shouted a cheery 'Merry Christmas!'

Bill walked up to have a word, wrapping his woollen scarf tighter round his neck to keep out the keen wind. It was always windy round the old folk's bungalows. They seemed to catch the gusts of air that blew unimpeded up the valley until they reached Round Ringford.

'Pity they didn't think of that before they built these places for old people,' said Bill, and they talked of County Council stupidity for a while, until Darren said, 'You and Mrs Turner going over to Bagley for the day? The road was quite clear when I came over last night.'

'No, no,' said Bill, wondering why Darren bothered to

ask, 'Joyce doesn't get out much these days. We shall just have a quiet day on our own. We've got the turkey in the oven.'

He thought of their quiet day on their own, and wished it could be different. Joyce's sister invited them over every year, knowing it was a formality and that they would never now accept. Bill always cooked the dinner, insisting on all the trimmings, although Joyce ate little and kept up a constant sniping about the waste. Bill had bought a small ready-cooked pudding from the shop, and was off to pick a sprig of holly for it from the bush that grew up by Mr Ross's house on the Bagley Road.

He also wanted fresh air, finding the house claustrophobic with Joyce's mania for keeping windows tightly closed, and curtains permanently drawn across. He took deep breaths as he turned into the High Street and walked along past the Post Office. The air was clean and restoring, and he wondered if Peggy was up and about. There were no signs of life and he thought she had probably gone away for the Christmas holiday.

He didn't remember her saying she was visiting anyone, but then she hadn't talked so much to him lately. It was almost as if she was avoiding him, and he hoped he had not offended her in some way. She was probably still suffering from shock, he thought, which was only natural. He himself found it difficult to realise that Frank had gone. Bill had treated himself to a chess set for Christmas, and a book of problems which he could work through by himself.

If I miss Frank, he thought, what must it be like for Peggy?

Cutting a couple of pieces of holly from the bush, he heard voices behind him. He saw Sandra Roberts and young Sam from the building site walking through the snow, kicking the powdery drifts and stopping every now and then to kiss lovingly, careless of onlookers.

They turned down the footpath that led back to

Macmillan Gardens, and Bill followed them slowly, thinking unhappy thoughts. He and Joyce had been like that once, and everything had seemed possible. She would not let him touch her now, not even a friendly cuddle, and he missed the physical contact. I never touch a living soul, he thought, except by accident. I suppose the last time was when I picked up Peggy when she fainted outside Ivy Beasley's.

He remembered her soft skin and warm breath when he put his face next to hers to check her breathing. He saw her lovely, triumphant smile when she turned to him at the end of the planning meeting. His pulse quickened, and he thought grimly that this would not do. But he knew that Peggy was his sort, that he felt at ease with her, and he was sad that now she seemed to be pushing him away, just when he knew he could help her.

'You following us, Mr Turner?' said Sandra Roberts, but she was smiling.

Bill had not realised that his pace had also quickened, and he was now catching up the pair of lovers.

He had known Sandra when she was a cheerful, plump little baby in the Roberts pushchair, holding out her arms to him, laughing and wanting to be picked up.

'I'm here to arrest the pair of you, Sandra Roberts,' he said, 'for cluttering up the public highway.'

He fell in beside them, and they walked slowly back to Macmillan, chatting about Christmas and the snow.

'What does your dad say to young Sam here?' said Bill to Sandra.

'He's got used to it now,' said Sandra, 'my gran said we were better off where Dad could see us, better than skulking in the bushes! So Sam comes home with me now. Dad daren't fetch me one when Sam's around.'

Perhaps I should put your gran to work on my problems, thought Bill, as he waved them goodbye and turned into his own garden. He had put a holly garland tied with scarlet ribbon on the front door, but Joyce had taken it down, saying it attracted attention. You wouldn't know it was Christmas from the look of our house, Bill thought, and with a sigh opened the door and walked into the dark hallway.

Miss Beasley made up the fire in her small grate, and sat down to wait for her dinner to cook. She had treated herself to a small piece of beef, and the roasting smell was wonderful. Potatoes browned in the meat pan, and she had picked fresh Brussels sprouts from the snowy garden.

She looked at the tabby cat curled up on the hearth rug and smiled to herself. Gilbert, she thought, what a stupid name for a she-cat. I shall call her Tibbles, and when she comes in here she can have a sensible name.

The fire sent out a glowing piece of wood, and the cat shot back, startled out of sleep. Ivy Beasley picked her up and sat down again, the tabby now purring loudly as she settled on Ivy's lap.

'Deserted you on Christmas Day, has she?' said Ivy Beasley. 'Well, you shall have some dinner with me.'

The beef was nearly done, and she set a single place on the polished table in her small dining-room. Then she fetched an embroidered table napkin, which she folded and put beside her knife, fork and spoon, and turning to the oak corner cupboard she took out a wine glass, one of two, Bohemian crystal and very fine. On her way back to the kitchen she switched on the single bar electric fire in the dining-room fireplace.

'Where did I put the corkscrew, Mother?' she said to the empty chair by the range. Think where you had it last, said the voice in her head, and Ivy remembered the drawer where she had put it away last Christmas. She pulled the cork from a bottle of Australian red wine which had been on special offer from the Supashop, and carefully poured the browny-red liquid into her glass. She took an experimental sip. It warmed her immediately, and she smiled at the cat.

'I could get to like this too much!' she said, and set down the glass.

There were some crumbly pieces of beef at the side of the serving dish, and she put these on a saucer with a little mashed potato. She called the cat, who – following her nose – was quick to find the food.

Miss Beasley had heated up a Christmas pudding made last year in a batch of three, and she smothered a generous helping with whipped cream – Bates's best – not forgetting to give the cat her share on a clean saucer.

As she was washing up she saw from her kitchen window that Peggy had returned. 'Hasn't forgotten you after all, Tibbles,' Miss Beasley said, and quietly opened the back door.

'Gilbert! Gilbertine!' shouted Peggy, and the cat ran out of Miss Beasley's house and through the hole in the hedge, licking her lips as she went.

'You're soon back,' said Doreen, as Peggy came into the farm kitchen, stamping the snow off her boots.

'It was a waste of time going down to feed Gilbert,' said Peggy to Doreen, 'she didn't seem at all hungry.'

'Could be she's missing Frank,' said Doreen, 'cats are funny animals, you never know what they are thinking.'

I'm not sure I know what you are thinking, either, thought Doreen, looking at Peggy's cold, rosy face. You are doing just a bit too well, for a woman not long lost her husband.

'Tom and the son-in-law have gone up for a sleep,' she said to Peggy, 'would you like to have a bit of nap?'

Peggy shook her head. 'I don't think I would sleep, thanks,' she said, 'I thought I might go out for a walk, clear my head. It's not at all bad out there.'

'Do you want me to come with you?' said Doreen, and

seeing Peggy hesitate, added, 'I do have a lot of clearing up to do, if not.'

'Doreen, I am sorry – I've been useless, drifting about when you're so busy! Let me help with the clearing up and then I can go for a walk after that. There will still be plenty of time.'

'It'll be dark early,' said Doreen, but she didn't insist, thinking that perhaps the menial job of clearing away the Christmas dinner would be a good thing for Peggy.

'I've been thinking,' said Peggy, picking up a drying-up cloth and starting on the row of draining glasses.

'You know what your mum said about thinking,' said Doreen, her red, capable hands busy in the washing-up water.

'Yes, well, there comes a time,' said Peggy, 'when someone's got to do a bit of thinking if the shop's to be kept going. I can just about afford to pay Mary York to come in for a few hours each week on pension days, then I think I could manage the rest,' she said.

'What about collecting new stock and that,' said Doreen. She lifted the blue and white turkey plate, dripping soapy suds into the sink, and put it very gently on to the draining board. 'Careful with that, Peggy,' she said, 'belonged to Tom's grandmother. She had it for a wedding present.'

'I think you'd better dry it, then,' said Peggy.

'Go on, then, about the shop.'

'Well, I think Bill would collect stock for me, especially if I pay for his petrol, and I am pretty strong for the lifting. I used to do it anyway, Frank's back not being a hundred per cent.'

They continued to discuss Peggy's future in amiable agreement, and the pile of dirty crocks diminished until they were all done.

She seems a lot more relaxed, thought Doreen, nothing like a bit of good old-fashioned washing up to calm you down.

And then, much to Doreen's surprise, Peggy put on her coat, turned to her friend and said, 'I must get back in time for Frank's tea . . .'

Peggy stopped speaking and her face went blank. Then she began to cry, and Doreen led her to a chair by the table. She silently handed her a piece of kitchen paper, and drawing up a chair next to her, put her arm around Peggy's shoulder. 'That's it, gel,' she said, 'let it go, you'll have to have a good cry now and then. It's best that way.'

As she walked across the snowy Green, and down towards Bateses End, Peggy tried to collect her thoughts. Most of the time she found she could organise herself quite well. There were plenty of jobs to be getting on with, and when the shop had been open the days went swiftly enough.

'I wish Christmas had not been so close, it would have been easier without all of that,' she said aloud. Then she reflected for the hundredth time that if it had not been Christmas, and if she had not asked Frank to go to the warehouse on such a dreadful day, the accident would not have happened.

She crossed over the Ringle, and stood looking down at the fast-flowing water. It was frozen again at the edges, and grasses poked out through the ice. She thought of the young Josie Barnett and Richard Standing, and wondered whereabouts they had been when Josie gave Richard the push. The water was quite deep under the bridge, and it wouldn't be very pleasant to struggle out of that weedy stretch.

She thought of the possibility of drowning, of disappearing for ever under the cleansing water, surrounded by flowing water weed. But it wouldn't be like that, would it, she thought, I'd gasp for breath, and choke and splutter, and even if I wanted to drown, instinct would make me try and save myself.

'It would be too cold for you, Peg,' said a voice. Peggy

did not even look round. She knew it was Frank's voice, and that he was still with her. She didn't answer, did not seek him, just smiled and walked on up the road towards the church.

Frank's grave was a soft, white mound in the little cemetery. Peggy had taken away the dead flowers a couple of weeks ago, and the headstone had not yet been delivered. She stood at the foot of the mound, and allowed her mind to empty, not knowing how many minutes she stood there.

Then quite clearly she heard her own voice say, 'He is not there any more,' and she looked up to see Frank walking away from her across the snow, leaving no footprints. He was half-turning as he walked, and she saw that he smiled. He waved, and then blew her the customary kiss. And then he vanished.

She did not see him again after that, not at all, not anywhere.

CHAPTER THIRTY-FOUR

'It's the arsehole of the year, January and February,' said Fred Mills, leaning against the shop counter, his pipe clenched between his teeth, but unlit, showing respect for the dead. He was well wrapped up against the cold wind, his dark blue duffel coat down below his knees, and a red and blue scarf – knitted somewhat erratically by Ellen Biggs – wound several times round the hood, so that his old face peered out like an elderly pixie.

'I know what you mean, Mr Mills,' said Peggy, putting his ounce of tobacco into a bag, 'there doesn't seem much to look forward to.'

Mr Mills shook his head. 'There's always something to look forward to, missus,' he said, 'if it's only a nice cup of tea.'

Peggy smiled, but her spirits did not lift. She had had a bad couple of weeks after Christmas. I'm not sure I need any more advice and sympathy, she thought. In fact, it would be nice to get on with every day as it comes, and not have to repeat yet again that yes, thank you, I am getting on fine, and no, I am not too lonely, because I've always got Gilbert for company. But of course I am lonely – what do they think?

Now there was this letter from Post Office headquarters,

accompanied by a leaflet saying 'Illegible Figures Cause Errors!' with a little homily about writing clearly and keeping inside the column lines.

It's worse than school, she thought, except you can't go home to Mum to make it better. She had already been let off a fine for making a mistake in the weekly balance, and official lenience would not last for ever. Sooner or later she would have to get it right every time, like Frank did, every week.

Trouble is, thought Peggy, when several people come into the shop at once, and one of them wants the Post Office, I need to be in two places at once.

'You should get a permanent assistant,' said Jean Jenkins hopefully, but Mrs Ashbourne, waiting patiently at the Post Office window, said, 'It wouldn't stand it, the shop takings wouldn't cover that – not unless Peggy's doing a lot better than I did.'

She is right, thought Peggy, it was fine when Frank was here and we were not taking wages. But if I had to pay someone full-time, there just wouldn't be enough in the kitty.

David Pearson had come over from Bagley to help her with her books, and show her how to do the weekly accounts. 'Keep them up to date, my dear,' he had said, 'and you will know where you are. And if you want any help with chasing the slow payers, give me a shout – especially if it's the Standings. I'd enjoy debt-collecting from them . . .'

Contrary to Doreen's forecast, Susan Standing had not gone away again after Christmas. She came into the shop more often than before, and seemed quite keen to engage Peggy in conversation. After the usual condolences on the death of Frank, Susan had asked Peggy about her past.

'What did you do before you came to Ringford, my dear?' she said.

'Worked in a bookshop,' said Peggy, 'but it was only

part-time – it was child's play compared with running the Post Office.'

'I imagine you don't have much spare time,' said Susan, looking absently out of the shop window. 'But anything's better than boredom, you know.'

Boredom with money is better than exhaustion without any, I should have thought, Peggy said to herself, standing first on one foot and then the other. She had taken to putting her aching feet in a mustard bath at the end of the day, and sometimes it was all she could do to get her supper. Some days she was so tired she had no appetite, and then made do with a cup of tea and a couple of biscuits. She knew she had lost weight.

Even the belated good news that the police had finally caught the Show day thieves, two teenage lads from Tresham out for an afternoon's entertainment, failed to cheer her up. It did not seem to matter any more. It wasn't the same, without Frank to share the pleasure of their home.

The snow had all but gone, with only pockets of it lurking in hollow places and in deep ditches. Everywhere was wet and soggy, and Gilbert's paws made tiny fresh footmarks on the tiled kitchen floor as fast as Peggy mopped them up. Gilbert's timetable had changed since Frank had gone. Peggy noticed that she was always absent around teatime, and did not come in for her supper until Peggy had settled down for the evening in front of the fire.

'I suppose she's still pining for Frank,' said Peggy to Bill, when he brought her a pile of boxes from the wholesalers. 'She never eats all her supper these days.'

'She looks plump enough,' said Bill, dumping the boxes on the kitchen table. 'I don't think you need worry about her getting enough to eat.' He knew very well that Gilbert was visiting Miss Beasley on a regular basis, and resolved to say nothing to Peggy.

'Thanks, Bill,' said Peggy, not offering him a cup of tea. 'I suppose she couldn't be . . . ?'

'In pod?' said Bill. 'Highly likely, I should think. A cat'll get itself in kitten at a very young age. Did you not think of having her fixed?' He smiled at Peggy, wishing he could stay.

'Oh no,' said Peggy quickly, 'I don't mind her having kittens, at least one or two litters.'

'They're not so easy to find homes for,' said Bill, 'don't forget she could have four or five kittens at a time.'

'I'll manage,' said Peggy, 'I can always put a notice in the shop.'

'Well,' said Bill, 'if there's nothing more I can do for you, I'd best be off home.'

Peggy desperately wanted Bill to stay. Many times in the past she had made him a cup of tea and they had sat companionably round the kitchen table, waiting for Frank to come back from Tresham.

Now she remembered Doreen's friendly warning, and kept Bill at arm's length.

She felt the eyes and ears of the village were constantly directed towards her, waiting for something to happen. What are they waiting for? Do they expect me to collapse in the street, run out shouting for help when I can't balance the books? Grab the first man who comes along and carry him screaming to my bed? Grab Bill?

She had become public property, and because so much had been given to her in support when she needed it, now there was something owing.

I need to get away from Ringford for a few days, Peggy thought, it is all getting on top of me. I can't see it any more, it is all too close.

'You need a break,' said Bill, reading her thoughts. 'I know I'm not the one to advise, but you could do it. Mary York could manage the shop for a short while, and we'd all rally round. Why don't you go back to Coventry and see a few friends?'

Peggy sighed and said she would think about it. She thought of all the things she would have to do before she could leave, and decided to abandon the idea at once. And yet the thought of talking to someone outside Ringford was very appealing.

But if she did go, who could she stay with? The Markses, she thought, I could go and see them. Jim Marks was still keeping his head above water in his bookshop, and she was sure Heather would happily give her a bed for a few days. They had been on very good terms when Peggy worked there, and Heather had offered more than once to put Peggy up if she wanted to visit.

The evening was fine, with a clear, starry sky that promised frost, and Doreen Price decided to walk from the farm to a special W.I. Group meeting in the Village Hall. There was no sign of Peggy, and on her way back she saw a light burning in the shop. She knocked on the door, and Peggy nervously opened it.

'Oh, it's you, Doreen, come in,' she said.

'Where were you tonight, Peggy?' Doreen said. 'It was quite a good meeting, we had that doctor from the cottage hospital to talk about the kidney machine.'

'Too much to do here,' said Peggy, wiping her dusty hand across her forehead and leaving a dark smear. 'I have to get the new stock priced and put out on the shelves while there's nobody in the shop.'

She looked at Doreen, and smiled at her anxious face. 'I don't mind, really, Doreen. Makes a change from watching the telly all evening – there's such a lot of rubbish these days . . .'

'Yes, but tonight there was W.I.,' said Doreen firmly, 'and whilst that may not be the most exciting evening you could think of, at least it would be better than spending it in a dismal, cold shop pricing tins of beans.'

'I know, Doreen, I know,' said Peggy quickly, 'it was just that I forgot, honestly, I really did forget. Half the time I don't know what day of the week it is. Bill says I should get away for a few days.'

'Very good idea,' said Doreen, 'though coming from him it's a bit rich.'

'I don't think it's his fault that they don't go anywhere,' said Peggy defensively, and then was annoyed to feel herself flushing. She turned away, and headed for the kitchen, calling Doreen to follow her.

'Look at that cat,' she said, 'does she look pregnant to you?'

'Yep,' said Doreen, 'no doubt about that. And not much longer to go. You'd better get your few days away before she produces! Give or take ten days, I would say.'

'I think I might go,' Peggy said, 'I feel I can leave now for a little while. Not long, of course, because of Gilbert. Funny, isn't it – I couldn't have gone straight away, though some people said I should. I felt Frank was still around, somehow.'

'And now he isn't?' said Doreen gently.

'Not in the same way,' said Peggy. 'Come on, Doreen, keep me company with a little nightcap – I'll make us a hot toddy. I often have one, it helps me sleep, when it's oblivion I need.'

She picked up Gilbert, supporting her weighty stomach with one hand. 'Just you wait until I get back, though, Gilbertine,' she said, 'you'll need me at the lying-in.'

'Afternoon, Mrs Palmer,' said Ellen Biggs, passing by the shop where Peggy was cleaning the outside of the big window. She's lookin' better, thought Ellen, poor soul.

Ivy Beasley was ready and waiting for Ellen, and together they walked up Macmillan Gardens to Doris Ashbourne's little bungalow.

'Don't know how you can live here,' said Ivy, 'after that house with the shop. Mind you, you could get rid of a lot more stuff, that would make you a bit of space.'

'Oh shut up, Ivy,' said Mrs Ashbourne, 'if you can't be pleasant, don't say anything.'

Ellen Biggs looked at Doris in amazement. She was usually such a diplomat, from her days in the shop. What was eating her?

'I want a serious word with you, Ivy,' went on Doris, 'so you'd better take off your coat and hat and sit down.'

'I ain't come here to be nagged by you, Doris Ashbourne,' said Ivy, 'you just say what you've got to say and I'll be off home.'

' 'Ere, now,' said Ellen, 'what's all this about, Doris? Can't we just sit and have our tea as usual, and then you can say whatever it is that's botherin' you.'

Doris sniffed and disappeared into her kitchen. Ellen nodded at Ivy Beasley, who reluctantly took off her coat, but not her hat, and sat down on the big sofa which filled one side of the sitting-room. The gas fire spluttered and popped, and Ellen pulled up an upright chair as close as she could get.

'Always seem cold these days,' she said, and rubbed her hands together. Ivy said nothing, and the silence made Ellen feel uncomfortable. 'That's her and her Jack on their wedding day,' she said, pointing to a photograph hanging on the wall over the fireplace.

'I know it is, you goop,' said Ivy, 'how many times have we been here?'

'What you been doin', Ivy,' said Ellen, abandoning polite conversation, 'to make her so cross?'

'I ain't done nothing,' said Ivy, as Doris came back into the room with a tray of teacups and saucers, small sandwiches with the crusts cut off, and a Battenberg cake with its pink and yellow windows and a rich, sweet marzipan covering. Ellen's eyes brightened – perhaps it wasn't going to be so bad after all.

'That's just it, Ivy,' said Doris, 'that is exactly it. You haven't done anything at all to help that poor woman who is after all your neighbour, and aren't we supposed to love our neighbours as ourselves?'

'I don't see what it's got to do with you, Doris,' said Ivy defensively. 'I remember when your Jack died, you managed perfectly well.'

'I had to, didn't I?' said Doris fiercely. 'Because my next-door neighbour Miss Beasley didn't offer a single helping hand, not once.'

Ivy bridled. 'You was very proud,' she said, 'didn't seem to need no help. If you'd asked, I would have given you a hand, you know I would.'

'Um, can I 'ave a sandwich?' said Ellen.

' 'Course you can, Ellen,' said Doris Ashbourne, pouring out rich brown tea into flowery cups. 'Tuck in, and help yourself to sugar.'

'Surely you remember what it's like, losing someone close to you?' continued Doris, handing Ivy her cup of tea. 'You can't think straight, and the last thing you do is ask for help. Well, I've had my say, and if I don't see some charity on your part, Ivy, then you can stop these teas of ours – or else leave me out of it. I'd go so far as to say it fair sickens me.'

She got up with the teapot, and vanished into the kitchen to fill it up with hot water for second cups. Well, she thought, I've said more'n I meant to, and that'll probably be it as far as Ivy's concerned. She's not a forgiving person.

But the threat of ending their periodic get-togethers was a serious blow to Ivy. She would never have admitted it, but she looked forward all week to the afternoon when the three of them met up. God knows, I spend most of my time talking to a dead woman, she thought, I shall have to pacify Doris, calm her down.

'Dare say you're right, Doris,' she said placatingly, 'I been really busy lately, what with Robert coming in for his dinner while his mum and dad've been away. Time goes by so quickly, don't it?'

No it doesn't, Ivy Beasley, thought Doris, and you know it doesn't. Still, at least you ain't walked out in a huff, so I suppose some of it might have struck home.

'My time's almost run,' said Ellen sadly, looking at the glowing pink and blue of the gas fire, 'doubt if I'll see through another winter.'

'That's foolish talk, Ellen Biggs,' said Ivy, 'you're strong as an old donkey, and just about as daft.' She cut herself a piece of window cake, and attacked it with relish. 'Don't tell me you made this, Doris,' she said, and then hastily added, 'it's very nice, mind.'

They sat and ate in silence for a few minutes, looking from the sitting-room's vantage point down Macmillan Gardens. It was one good thing about the Council's siting of the bungalows: they had a perfect view of comings and goings in the Gardens, and could keep tabs on everyone.

'There's Bill, coming home for his tea,' said Doris.

'Suppose it'll all be spread out for him on a dainty cloth, the kettle boiling and the pot warmed,' said Ivy.

'Thought you were Joyce's friend, Ivy?' said Ellen. 'You ain't got nothing nice to say today.'

'Joyce makes me tired,' said Ivy, 'it don't matter how much you try to help, she throws it back at you.'

'Well, at least you tried,' said Doris meaningly.

'D'you want them sandwiches finished up, Doris?' said Ellen, scooping up the last two and putting them on her plate, and turning to Ivy Beasley, added, ' 'Spect you see Bill Turner going in next door to you quite a bit?'

'You wouldn't want me to gossip, would you?' said Ivy smugly. 'I wouldn't dream of sayin' anything nasty. Yes, thank you, Doris dear, another piece of cake would go down a treat.'

CHAPTER THIRTY-FIVE

'Mary,' said Peggy, 'I'm thinking of taking one or two days off – going to Coventry to see some friends – could you manage the shop on your own?'

It was a lovely, springlike day, and Peggy had woken up feeling for the first time since Frank died that she must get up and get going.

She had heard birdsong in the early morning, as if for the first time. Sparrows under the eaves of the house had woken her, and she had seen that it was already light, the sun shining through the bedroom curtains and showing up cobwebs in the corner of the ceiling. It was almost spring and she hadn't noticed, hadn't seen the small daffodil spears poking through last year's rotting coppery ferns, or chestnut buds bursting with tightly curled pale leaves. She had been blind to the red haze over the woods that would soon change to a dozen shades of green.

But now I'm awake, she thought, and looked at Mary for an answer. Mary's eyes were doubtful behind her thick pebble lenses, but she said she was prepared to have a try. 'Doris Ashbourne is always there if I get in a muddle,' she said.

'I shan't be that far away, anyway,' said Peggy, 'and I can always come back if there is an emergency.'

Heather and Jim Marks were delighted to hear from Peggy, and insisted that she come as soon as possible. They had last seen her at Frank's funeral, and had gone back to Coventry worrying about what was to become of her.

'I can't imagine her living on her own and running the business,' he said to Heather. 'I bet she'll sell up – it would never surprise me to see her back in Coventry one of these days.'

Heather was not so sure. She tried to imagine what she would do if Jim suddenly vanished from her life, but could not put herself in Peggy's place. Nothing would be the same, she could not even guess what she would do.

'It will be very nice to see her, anyway,' she said, 'and just watch you don't lecture the poor girl.'

'As if I would,' said Jim, and finishing his breakfast coffee prepared for work.

Two days later Heather was watching from the shop window, waiting for Peggy to arrive.

'She says her new car is white, and she has – to her shame – a small fluffy kitten swinging in the back window,' said Jim.

'There she is,' said Heather, and then, as Peggy got out of the car, 'oh Jim, she looks so thin!'

Peggy had been feeling very odd as she drove through Coventry to the suburb where she and Frank spent so many years. She carefully avoided the street where they used to live, making a detour that took in the shopping parade where she had bought supplies every week, and then to the Marks' bookshop.

I wonder if this was such a good idea, she thought, as she pulled up opposite the shop. I wish I could go home. But as she opened the bookshop door and was enveloped in hugs from Jim and Heather, she relaxed.

'Thank goodness you've come!' said Jim. 'Heather has been back and forth looking for you ever since breakfast time. And now you're here, Peggy, and we are so pleased to see you.' He stooped his tall, lanky frame and gave her another smacking kiss.

Peggy and Heather went upstairs to the sitting-room, and talked nonstop until lunchtime, when Jim rushed up with a broad grin and said he had a big order from the new school in Beechwood Avenue. 'That will save our bacon for another month,' he said. He hasn't changed, thought Peggy, never really grown up.

'You girls can go off for the afternoon, leave me to it,' said Jim, and so after lunch Heather suggested a walk in Beechwood Park.

It was all that remained of a large, gracious estate which had originally surrounded a big house, long since demolished. There were wide avenues lined with huge beech trees, and in summer tame squirrels swung from one tree to another in boisterous loops.

'It's not so cold here as it was when I left Ringford this morning,' said Peggy, 'the wind can sweep up that valley and freeze your ears off.'

'Ah, it was cosier in Bryony Road, wasn't it,' said Heather, thoughtlessly.

Peggy had not allowed herself to think of the past. It was difficult, since every landmark, every street corner turned into another memory of Frank. She tried to keep the conversation on the present, asked questions about the bookshop and compared notes on the retail trade with Heather.

'I can see your problem, Peggy,' said Heather, 'I don't know whether one of us could do the bookshop on our own – but we haven't employed anyone since you left, and I am not sure we could afford it now.'

'If I didn't have the Post Office it would be possible on my own, but the fact is a lot of people come in just for stamps and pensions and things, and then remember they want something else. With no Post Office, I think my customers would be reduced to about half a dozen.' Peggy smiled, thinking of Fred Mills and Old Ellen, and chubby Eddie Jenkins.

They had wandered to the far end of the park, the afternoon fading into dusk. A factory hooter sounded, harsh and loud, close by.

'That's Maddox's!' said Peggy, turning to Heather. Her face had lost its colour, her smile vanished.

'Oh, I am sorry, Peggy,' said Heather, cursing herself for being so insensitive. 'I hadn't noticed the time, and now here we are on the wrong side of the park. It must be five o'clock if Maddox's are coming out. Come on, we can catch a bus that will take us to the end of our road. There's one! Run, Peggy!'

The hooter had brought the past back to Peggy with a vengeance. She sat with Heather on the top deck of the bus, silent and thoughtful. Maddox's had been so much a part of their lives for so many years, and now, back here in Coventry, Frank was more vivid in her mind – the real Frank, the one whose life was happy and busy, and who knew exactly who he was and what was required of him.

'It wasn't the right thing for Frank, you know,' she said to Heather, who looked at her anxiously. 'Going to Round Ringford, I mean,' Peggy continued, 'he never really liked it as much as here. He pretended to sometimes, just to please me, but I knew he never felt it was home.'

'And you?' said Heather. 'Did you feel the same?'

'No, I love it – at least, I did love it until Frank died.'

Peggy was silent, and Heather did not say anything more, waiting for Peggy to continue.

'Oh, there were nasty moments, of course,' said Peggy, 'and one or two nasty old tabs who weren't very welcoming. But once we'd settled in and found some friends – or at least, I'd found some friends – it seemed as if we'd always lived there.' The bus trundled slowly through suburban streets of identically built, neatly kept houses, each one made individual by the personal touch of its owner. I'm talking about Ringford as if it's already something in the past, thought Peggy.

'No friends for Frank?' said Heather.

'Only Bill,' said Peggy, 'and he isn't really Frank's sort. He is more my kind of person . . .' She tailed off, thinking about Bill.

Heather rose to get off the bus. 'Come on, Peggy, we're nearly there, time for a cup of tea,' she said.

'Well, thanks a lot, both of you, you've been a great help.' Peggy waved from her car until she could no longer see Heather and Jim in her driving mirror. Her three days had straightened things out for her. She'd been able to see it all much more clearly. She had watched the Markses in their bookshop, and saw how much easier it was with two. Her doubts about managing the Post Office Stores for much longer had been confirmed. And anyway, she was not even sure now that she wanted to carry on.

She stopped at traffic lights on the outskirts of Coventry, and took a quick look at herself in the mirror. A thin face looked back at her, with lines beginning to make creases round her eyes and mouth. Frank wouldn't recognise me, she thought. Heather says I'm not eating properly, and she's probably right.

I'm too tired to eat, by the end of a day in the shop. And anyway, eating on my own is a miserable business. Supper with Frank was the best time of the day, talking about the shop and who'd been in, and what they'd said. Now it's just a case of fuelling the machine. Still, I suppose it won't run for ever on a quick sandwich.

'I'd better sell up,' she said aloud, driving slowly down the Ringford road. She remembered the first journey she and Frank had made to the village, and how they had stopped at the top of the hill looking down into Bateses End. Her eyes filled, and she could not see properly. She stopped the car, and fumbled for a tissue from the box on the back seat.

Shadows of clouds chased across the village and fields below, just as it was a year ago. The church stood solidly in its nest of black yew trees, and Bates's old sheep dog was a tiny moving dot, chasing his flock across the glebe field. The school playground came alive as children swarmed out, their red jerseys vivid splashes of colour. Barnett's site was hidden behind the cricket pavilion, and the neat rectangle of Macmillan Gardens looked, as always, at odds with the curving street and the crooked old houses.

It looks the same, exactly the same, Peggy thought. Why is there no mark on it to show for all that has happened? I could go back to Coventry, and find a house somewhere near Heather and Jim. I could help out in the bookshop again, for no money if they can't afford me. It wouldn't be starting again from scratch, I'd soon pick up life there – find things to do, and get in touch with old friends. I think I'd feel a bit nearer to Frank.

She looked down at Ringford, tiny and still. No one will miss me after I've gone, and Ivy Beasley can persecute someone else.

The car moved slowly down the hill and into the village. Peggy felt the treacherous excitement of one who has made a big decision.

Tomorrow, she thought, I shall ring the estate agent, and put the Stores up for sale.

CHAPTER THIRTY-SIX

She has managed perfectly well without me, thought Peggy, carrying her suitcase through the shop and watching Mary York serving Old Ellen with a quarter of a pound of butter and two bananas.

' 'Ad a good time, Mrs Palmer?' said Ellen. 'We missed you.'

Don't believe you, Ellen, thought Peggy. Out of sight, out of mind, always somebody else to talk about.

'Thank you, Ellen, yes, it was a nice break.'

'Be with you in a minute, Peggy,' said Mary York, 'must be nearly closing time.'

I wonder if Mary and her Graham would like to buy the shop, thought Peggy. But Graham York had a solid, respectable job in Tresham, and would not be likely to leave it. They were not the kind to take a risk, thought Peggy. But then, you could have said that about Frank – and then again, look where it landed him. I wonder if my lips move when I talk to myself.

Peggy checked with Mary on what had been happening, and then watched her as she rode off on her bike up the Bagley Road. Off to get tea for Graham, thought Peggy, lucky Mary.

Well, where's my Gilbert, there's always Gilbert. No

sign of her indoors, and as the cat was now very barrel-shaped, Peggy thought she could not have gone far, and went to look for her in the garden.

'Gilbertine!' she called. 'Come along, pussy, Mummy's back!'

She thought she heard an answering cry, and followed it to the wash-house across the yard. It was nearly dark already, and she opened the door and peered inside.

She could see nothing at first, but when her eyes became accustomed to the dark she made out the pile of Frank's old gardening clothes in the corner. She had not yet had the heart to take them to the dump – they were not good enough for anything else, but it would be another little death. A loud miaow came from the pile, and Peggy went over and bent down to look.

Gilbert was there, certainly, and purring very loudly. 'What's that you've got there, Bertie?' Little moving bundles were making tiny mewing noises and pushing into Gilbert's fur as she lay on her side gazing up at Peggy.

'Oh, Gilbert!' she said softly. 'They've arrived! And you managed all by yourself, you clever girl.' She put out her hand and tentatively stroked the top of Gilbert's tabby head. The cat's green eyes shone, and she curled protectively round her kittens, continuing to purr.

Peggy felt tears running down her face, and wondered why, why for God's sake was she crying? She backed out of the wash-house, as if having confronted something holy, and bumped straight into Bill Turner.

'Bill!' she said. 'Gilbert's had her kittens! I can't see how many, but she looks fine and I'm just going to get her some milk, and isn't it exciting?'

Bill followed her into the kitchen, smiling indulgently. He had seen so many litters of kittens in his life, and – though he would not mention this – drowned so many, that the news did not delight him half as much as seeing Peggy so animated and pleased. Her face was pink and tear-stained, and her hair stuck out in all directions. He thought he had never seen her look so beautiful.

'Do you think I should move them into the kitchen? Will they be warm enough out there, Bill? What do you think?'

'Leave her be, Peg,' he said, 'animals choose their nests, and it is best to let them stay. She'll keep them warm with her body, but you must take food and drink to her for a few days. She won't leave them.'

'I am so glad you came in,' said Peggy, 'I would have done the wrong thing on my own, I'm sure. Oh, I do wish Frank could be here . . .'

Bill's face clouded for a moment, and then he said, 'We do miss him, don't we? Always will, I expect.'

For the first time, Peggy understood that Frank's death had caused a gap in Bill's life. I've been so busy with my own grief, she thought, as if Frank had mattered only to me. Bill had taken to Frank. All those games of chess, and conversations in the shop. Peggy looked directly at Bill, and took a deep breath.

'Bill,' she said, 'can you spare a few moments? Have you time for a cup of tea?'

Puzzled, Bill sat down at the table and watched Peggy as she poured boiling water from the simmering kettle into the old brown teapot, and set out two cups and saucers. She poured out the milk and tea, and passed a cup to Bill.

'Two sugars, isn't it?' she said, handing him the sugar bowl.

He spooned sugar and stirred his tea, saying nothing, waiting apprehensively.

'Bill, I think I owe you some kind of explanation,' said Peggy. 'You probably think I have been rather rude and ungrateful, never asking you in, or offering you a cup of anything.' She coloured, and wished she had not started on this, but she persevered.

'You have been so kind, and I hadn't thought – was too

selfish to think – how upset you must be yourself about Frank. The fact is, I was warned off.'

'Warned off?' said Bill, frowning.

'Well, sort of,' said Peggy, 'it was Doreen who said now I'm on my own I should watch out for gossips in the village. Specially with old Poison Ivy living next door.' Bill's frown deepened, but he said nothing.

'So I did what she advised. I hope you understand . . .'

'Only too well,' said Bill quietly. 'Doreen was right. I've had trouble myself with the tattlers not minding their own business and making double out of everything they think they see.'

He looked at Peggy, and then reached out his hand. She hesitated, then slowly put hers into the big palm. 'It's all right, gel,' he said, 'I'll not make things difficult for you.'

He squeezed her hand, and then let go and stood up.

'But,' he said, 'that doesn't mean I'm going to stay clear like some frightened rabbit. You need my help, Peggy, and you shall have it. And old Beasley can like it or lump it. And if she makes trouble, just let me know and I'll sort her out – there's one or two things about her she wouldn't want known!' He laughed, leaned over and put his fingers gently against Peggy's warm cheek.

'Take care of the little mother,' he said, 'I'll be back tomorrow to see how they're going on.'

After Bill had gone, Peggy sat for a long time at the kitchen table, thinking about her decision to sell.

Mr Gray, from Lambwith & Kitchener, Bagley estate agents with a big commercial department, said that he would come over to Ringford to have a good look over the Post Office Stores, give Peggy an idea of how much to ask, and assess her chances of selling quickly.

'It's just that now I've decided, I would like to make the move as soon as possible,' she said.

Mr Gray explained that at the moment small businesses

were not moving very fast, but that she had certainly come to the right people to stand the best possible chance of a good sale.

Well, they all say that, thought Peggy, and asked if he could come over after shop hours when she would have time to talk to him. She also hoped that she could keep the news from the village for as long as possible.

'Did you see Mr Gray's car outside the Post Office?' said Jean Jenkins to Foxy at breakfast. It was still half-dark outside, and the light in the small kitchen was shrouded in swirling frying fumes.

'Open the window, gel,' said Foxy, 'it's fuggy in here.'

'Fuggywuggy,' said Eddie, from his high chair, where he was happily making a thick soup with his cereal and a spoonful of Marmite surreptitiously stirred in by brother Mark.

'Quite right, my duck,' said Jean, laughing from her usual station by the frying pan on the cooker. 'Anyway, Foxy, did you see the car? It's that big black one – not his, it's Mr Lambwith's. I recognised it.'

'You mean Sandy Gray, from Lambwith's?' said Foxy. 'Well, that means only one thing, my duck, she's goin' to sell.'

'Leave that Marmite alone, Mark!' said Jean. 'Well, she never said nothing last time I was in. I shall just ask her outright – she'll answer me straight, Peggy will.'

'D'you think Bill knows? said Foxy.

'Search me,' said Jean, 'that ain't none of our business. Could be that her friends in Coventry pushed her into it – she's only just come back, y'know.'

'She'd be a fool to go,' said Foxy, 'Ringford's her home now. She's done well, and folks like her. You wouldn't catch me going back to a smelly old town, after Ringford.'

'Ah, well, you're a Ringford lad, Foxy boy!' said Jean,

275

cuffing him lightly round the ear in affection. 'Now then, Eddie, what have you got there?'

'If you don't mind my asking, Peggy,' said Jean Jenkins, 'are you thinking of selling up?'

'Ah,' said Peggy, 'how did you know, Jean? I've only just decided myself . . .'

'Recognised Mr Gray from Lambwith's, didn't I,' said Jean straightforwardly. 'It don't take much nous to put two and two together there.'

'Oh dear,' said Peggy, 'well, yes, it's all a bit too much for me without Frank.'

Mrs Jenkins nodded sympathetically, and unwrapped a lolly for Eddie. ' 'Ere you are, my duck, don't get it all over you. We've all been wonderin',' she continued, 'what you would do.'

Peggy opened a drawer under the counter and brought out a small towelling bib. 'You left this last time you were in,' she said, tying it round Eddie's fat neck. 'Nobody asked me,' she continued.

'Well, they wouldn't, would they,' said Jean, 'you ought to know Ringford by now, we bide our time.'

'I hope I shall get someone nice to take it on,' said Peggy, feeling guilty already.

'The new lot at Casa Pera were asking about it,' said Mrs Jenkins, wiping round Eddie's sticky mouth with a doubtful handkerchief from her mac pocket.

'But they've only just moved house,' said Peggy, looking at Jean Jenkins in amazement.

'They was always looking for a village shop to buy, they said. Couldn't find one they liked, and moved to Casa Pera instead. No, Eddie Jenkins, leave that alone!'

'What are they like?' said Peggy. 'They've only been in once or twice, and then on a Saturday morning when the shop's busy.'

'Don't see much of them,' said Jean, 'but they seem all

right. Mr Osman goes up and down to London every day – he's welcome to that – and she's got some job that takes her away for days at a time. I did see her this week, though, and that's when she said about the shop. They do pay regular, that's one thing – better than the Hall.'

'Here, Eddie, come with me and I'll wipe your hands in the kitchen,' said Peggy. She picked up the plump little body and took him off, while his proud mother packed her purchases in a large green shopping bag. Peggy stood Eddie on a chair up to the sink, and soaped his hands, showing him how to turn the taps and letting him have a swish round the sink to rinse off the soap.

Look at her, thought Jean Jenkins, she should have had kids, then it wouldn't be so difficult for her now.

Peggy was busy with allowances and pensions when Doreen burst into the shop. Seeing Peggy occupied with a queue at the Post Office window, she wandered impatiently round the shelves, until the last one had been served.

'Right, Mrs Palmer!' she said, banging her hand flat against the counter. 'What's all this I hear about you selling the Stores?'

'It's true,' said Peggy, 'I was going to tell you . . .' She tailed off into embarrassed silence, aware of Doreen's hurt expression and hating herself for not having considered her most loyal friend.

'Well, I do think you might have had a word with us first – there must be a lot to think about before you decide a thing like that?'

'I did think about it, Doreen, I did an awful lot of thinking while I was with the Markses. Being away from Ringford made it easier to look at it squarely.'

'So after three days in Coventry you have decided to leave us?'

'Not necessarily,' said Peggy, beginning to feel she did have a right to decide her own future, 'but I do have to give up the shop. It is just a case of not enough business to employ someone, and too much to do for one person on their own. After all, Doris Ashbourne found the . . .'

'Doris Ashbourne is twenty years older than you,' said Doreen bluntly.

'I know, I know,' said Peggy, 'but you saw how many people were at the Post Office window just now – supposing someone had come in, needing to be served in a hurry at the shop counter?'

'Well, I don't know,' said Doreen, shaking her head, 'there must be some way of working it – you just haven't given us a chance to think it out.'

Peggy was tempted to say that it was nothing to do with 'us'. It's my shop, I have to run it, and it is my life – what's left of it.

But she said nothing more, and with an unhappily cool atmosphere between them, Doreen left the shop. Peggy, who was beginning to see that there was yet another side to the cosy womb of village life, felt her good mood evaporating.

She got to the end of the day with difficulty. Everyone who came into the shop seemed to have heard the news, and felt it was their right to know every detail. She finally locked up with a sigh of relief, and went to see to Gilbert and her kittens.

'Life is simple for you, Gilbert,' she said, 'you've got it right.'

Peggy felt restless, not able to settle down for the evening, bored with television and no appetite for supper. Bill had not come in again, and she missed him, wondering if he had thought better of his bravado and had decided not to risk the village gossips.

I'll go for a walk, get some fresh air, she thought, putting on her anorak and boots. Maybe I'll feel hungrier when I get back.

Some light lingered in the sky, marbled bands of pink

278

and blue in the dark grey of approaching night. Peggy crossed the road and set off over the Green towards the river. The Standings' silver car purred round by the pub and up towards the Hall. She could see the shapes of Richard and Susan sitting familiarly beside one another, and wondered if they knew how lucky they were to be two, instead of one and alone.

Self-pity's no good to anybody, Peggy thought, pulling her jacket closer around her, and tying a scarf round her ears where the wind nipped them. In the far corner of the Green, she saw a movement by the swings.

'Who's that?' she said aloud. It surely couldn't be a child out on its own?

She walked round the outside of the fence until she was close to the swings. There was somebody sitting there, her back supported by the chain and one foot up on the seat. Peggy could smell cigarette smoke, and suspected it was Sandra Roberts.

'Sandra!' she said. 'Is that you?'

'What if it is?' said a sullen voice.

'Well, I know it's none of my business – I'll say it before you do – but it is very cold for sitting on a child's swing in the dark.'

'It's not dark,' said Sandra.

'Oh, all right,' said Peggy, 'don't blame me if you freeze to death.'

She turned away and continued her walk towards the river. She had gone a few paces, when she heard Sandra call.

'Mrs P.!'

'What is it, Sandra?' said Peggy, irritated.

'Come back a minute – I'm sorry . . .'

Peggy walked back to the swing and said, 'Well? Make it snappy, I'm getting cold.'

Sandra began to swing a little, backwards and forwards. She threw the cigarette stub on to the grass, where it smouldered and went out.

Peggy sighed. She walked round the playground and sat down on the swing next to Sandra, pulling her scarf tighter round her ears and pushing her hands into her pockets. She too began to swing gently back and forth, and waited for Sandra to say something.

'It's Sam,' said Sandra, 'and my dad. I don't know what they'll say. My dad'll probably kill me.'

Peggy's heart sank. 'Why?' she said apprehensively.

'Can't you guess?' said Sandra. 'I think I'm in the club.'

'Oh, bloody hell,' said Peggy, and was surprised at Sandra's hoot of laughter.

'Well, well, Mrs P.,' she said, 'I never thought that's what you would say.'

'It's not funny,' said Peggy huffily, 'you caught me by surprise. It is surely very serious?'

Sandra sobered up, and said, 'Yeah, it is. That's why I'm sitting here. You did ask me.'

'You haven't told Sam?'

'Nope, not yet. He won't know what to do. He's only eighteen, and I'm just sixteen. And my dad'll kill me,' Sandra repeated.

'How sure are you?' said Peggy.

'Pretty sure,' said Sandra, 'I'm three weeks overdue. I was just wondering whether to get rid of it when you came along. So you are the first to know – that's an honour, isn't it?'

'Oh, don't be silly, Sandra,' said Peggy, 'if you are old enough to get pregnant, you'd better try behaving like an adult.'

'Silly to get rid of it, do you mean?'

'You know perfectly well that's not what I meant, and anyway, getting rid of it is not as simple as that.'

Sandra pushed the toe of her shoe into the ground, and then let herself swing to and fro again.

Peggy heard a sniff, and peered closely at the whitish face. 'Are you crying?' she said.

Sandra looked at her, her face just an outline in the near-dark. 'Of course I'm bloody well crying,' Sandra said, 'wouldn't you bloody cry?'

Peggy got off the swing and stood next to the girl, putting an arm round her shoulder.

'What am I going to do?' sniffed Sandra.

'I don't know,' said Peggy, 'but we shall have to think. What you are not going to do is stay out here and get pneumonia. Come on, you can come back with me and have a hot drink.'

Sandra slid off the swing and allowed herself to be guided back to the path, and they headed across the Green towards the Post Office Stores.

Peggy was about to show Sandra the kittens, and then thought better of it. Might not be the most tactful thing at the moment. Maybe later. She put her key into the back door, and saw a piece of paper lodged under the knocker. She took it out and opened the door.

'Come in, Sandra,' she said, 'sit down there by the Rayburn.'

Peggy put on the kettle, and then looked at the unfolded piece of paper. It was a petrol invoice, and a message had been scrawled across the back in pencil.

'Called as promised – will try tomorrow. Bill.'

So he had called after all. Peggy tucked the note under the candlestick on the mantelshelf over the Rayburn, and Sandra watched her every move, like a wild animal caught in a trap.

'Relax, Sandra, for goodness' sake,' said Peggy, 'I'm not going to shop you to your father – or to Sam, for that matter. That's your job. But perhaps we can think of a few sensible things for you to do, for a start.'

They sat for a while at the kitchen table, talking and trying out various courses of action for Sandra, and the colour began to come back to the girl's face. She had just agreed that she would have to go to the doctor, and that maybe the best person to tell after Sam would be her grandmother, when there was a sharp knock at the door.

Sandra shot up from the table and looked round wildly. Peggy motioned her to sit down again, and went to open the door.

'Mrs Palmer?' said an unfamiliar voice, and Peggy looked closer to see who it was. 'My name is Osman, just moved in to Casa Pera,' the man continued, 'could you spare me a moment?'

Peggy opened the door wider, and as Mr Osman stepped into the kitchen, Sandra slipped by him and with a brief 'Ta, Mrs P.,' she was gone.

Peggy was annoyed and frustrated, and looked impatiently at the man standing by the door. 'What do you want?' she said.

'I'll come straight to the point,' he said, 'I believe you are selling up, and my wife and I would be very interested in the possibility of buying the Stores.'

Colin Osman was an insensitive young man, an only son and used to pleasing himself. He was tall and gingery, and not bad looking – he had never had any trouble in – as he said – 'pulling the birds'. He had made up his mind to speak to Mrs Palmer, and would not be thwarted.

'I suppose you'd better sit down,' said Peggy, not having the strength to tell him to go away and ring the agents in the morning. But she could not concentrate on what he was saying, and found her mind returning over and over again to Sandra, defiant and defenceless.

'I am sorry,' she said finally, 'I am just too tired to listen properly this evening, Mr Osman. Why don't you ring Lambwith & Kitchener tomorrow, and then we'll take it from there.'

'No, you don't understand,' said Colin Osman, brash and uncomprehending, 'there would be no need for agents and all the extra expense. We heard about the sale through the village, not the agents, and we could do a direct purchase, just using solicitors. We'd both save quite a bit!'

Peggy's head began to swim, and she remembered she had had nothing to eat since lunchtime.

'Mr Osman,' she said, standing up, 'I have to ask you to go now. You must realise I have many things to think about, that I have had a hard day, and no supper. Will you please allow me to get in touch with you when I have thought the whole thing through properly?'

Pompous old bag, thought Colin Osman, but he reluctantly got up and left.

CHAPTER THIRTY-SEVEN

'So the Post Office is changing hands again,' said Joyce Turner as she and Bill sat over their tea in the dark little kitchen.

Bill looked at her in surprise. 'Is that your idea of a joke, Joyce?' he said.

'Ha, thought that would get you,' she said, pointing an accusing finger at him.

Is she making it up? thought Bill wildly, she hasn't seen anybody. Then he remembered her one and only visitor this week. 'Did you get it from Ivy Beasley?' he said. He stood up and began to take the dirty plates to the sink, to hide his anxiety.

'Upset you, that has, hasn't it?' said Joyce. 'I can read you like a book, Bill Turner. Not like you to miss a bit of news, Ivy said it was all round the village.'

Bill wondered why no one had told him, if it was true. Were they shy of telling him? He tried to calm down, to think who he'd seen.

'One of these days, Joyce,' he said grimly, 'I shall walk out of that door and not come back. You'll drive me to it, I swear you will.'

'Go, then, and good riddance!' Joyce began to shout, and with deadly accuracy threw a cold potato across the kitchen and hit Bill in the back of the neck.

He turned and glared at her with hate in his eyes. 'I'm going down the pub, Joyce,' he said, 'and I shall be back, unfortunately. See if you can calm down and clear this place up, do something useful for once.'

Bill put on his heavy jacket and pushed an old cap over his thick, unyielding hair. He almost never wore a hat, and looked rough, sinister even. But he didn't care what he looked like. He had to find out, right away. She wouldn't decide to move without telling him, surely? Not even mention it!

Well, Bill Turner, he said to himself as he turned the corner of Macmillan Gardens into the full blast of the wind, why on earth should she talk to you about it? She has Doreen and Tom, and her friends in Coventry, and she probably thinks you are just a village boy who's never been out of the village and can't see further than his nose.

Peggy opened the door and, seeing Bill, smiled broadly.

'Bill,' she said, 'come on in – did you get past Victoria Villa without being spied? I shouldn't think anyone would recognise you in that cap!'

She saw that he did not smile. He took off the cap, and came into the kitchen, standing with his back to the Rayburn.

'Do you want to go and look at them now?' she said.

'Look at what?' said Bill.

'The kittens, of course,' said Peggy, 'I got your note.'

'Oh, that was yesterday,' said Bill. 'Yes, I will look at them in a minute, but that's not what I came about.' He put his hands in his coat pocket and then took them out again, clasping them behind his back.

Ah, thought Peggy, he's heard.

'Are you selling up, Peg?' he said bluntly.

Peggy found she could not look at him. Why did everyone feel so affronted at her decision? She didn't belong to Doreen or Tom or Bill, or to any of them. She could make up her own mind, surely?

'Peggy! Look at me,' he said, 'please give me a straight answer.'

'Yes, Bill,' she said, finally looking at him, 'I am selling up. Lambwith's have been, and it will be on the market next week.'

'Peggy!' he said again, his face distorted with unhappiness.

Peggy began to feel alarmed. 'Come on, Bill,' she said, 'you know how it's been. I don't have to struggle to carry on – so I might as well give up now.'

'But you haven't given us a chance to think of a way round it,' he said, echoing Doreen's words.

'Us? Us?' said Peggy, getting cross, 'Who is this "us"? There is only me, as far as I can see.'

She was near to tears now, and sat down at the table frowning and trying hard not to lose her self-control.

'All right,' said Bill, speaking quite loudly, and thumping his hand on the Rayburn rail to emphasise his words. 'It's been rotten and 'orrible for you, and we all feel sorry for you. But just sympathy ain't enough, and you'll see, if you stay, the village will rally round – we'll think of something.'

'Sod the village,' said Peggy.

'Don't be childish, Peggy,' said Bill.

Peggy sat up straight and glared at him.

'You do belong to the village now, whether you like it or not,' Bill continued, 'and it isn't just me that cares what happens to you. Though,' he added more quietly, 'I care more than most.' He paused, but Peggy said nothing.

'Give us time, gel,' Bill said in a calmer voice, 'and we'll find a way. Good God, how long is it since Frank died? You can't go rushing into things so soon. We always say give it two years after a bereavement before you make any move.'

'I don't care what you always say, you and the rest of the village,' said Peggy loudly. 'I'm sick of "belonging", sick of having to answer for everything I do to a bunch of people who have never been further than Bagley. What do you know about me? Nothing. I've lived practically a whole life somewhere else. I was a completely different person, and I can do it again . . . Oh God, and I'm really sorry, Bill, I'm being unfair and stupid and ungrateful, and I wouldn't hurt you for the world.' Peggy sagged in her chair, all indignation gone.

They looked at each other without speaking, and then Bill's face cleared.

'Well, that's all right, then,' he said, and smiled.

Peggy got up and took down her anorak from the hook on the back of the door.

'Anyway,' she said, 'I've had an enquiry already – from the Osmans at Casa Pera.'

'Oh yes,' said Bill, unimpressed, 'let's go and look at them kittens.'

CHAPTER THIRTY-EIGHT

The telephone rang before Peggy had finished her breakfast the next morning, and her heart sank. If that's Colin Osman, she thought, I shall be really rude to him.

But it was Doreen, and her voice sounded different, stiff and formal. 'Will you be wanting any eggs this week?' she said.

'Of course, Doreen,' said Peggy, 'why on earth should I not want them?'

Doreen didn't answer, but just said, 'I'll be over later, then,' and put down the telephone.

'Oh dear,' sighed Peggy, 'I never thought this would all be so difficult.'

She opened up the shop, and stood on the step, looking out over the Green. The wind had changed, blowing softly over the village and hardly disturbing the high level of water in the Ringle. The river was still clear and ice-cold, keeping Warren and William at bay for another few weeks, except for the occasional lemonade can thrown in, and fished out again while Bill Turner stood over them with a threat of telling their dads.

There is almost a feeling of spring in the air, Peggy thought. I shall soon have to think about the garden. How am I going to manage that on top of everything else? Then, she remembered that it would be someone else's responsibility quite soon, and felt a pang. The daffodils, I hope I'm still here for the daffodils. She went back into the shop and unlocked the till.

'It will be a good while yet before daffodil time,' said a scratchy voice, and Peggy turned to see Ivy Beasley standing at the counter.

'I hadn't realised I had spoken out loud, Miss Beasley,' said Peggy.

'Comes of living alone,' said Miss Beasley, 'breaks the silence.'

Peggy nodded, and reached for the usual box of matches.

'And I'll have a tin of rice puddin',' said Miss Beasley, 'should make it myself, but I like the custardy taste of the tinned stuff.'

This was as near a reasonable conversation with Ivy Beasley that Peggy could remember, and she held her breath, waiting for the sharp exit line. But Ivy Beasley seemed to want to linger. She wandered round the shelves, picking up odd items and putting them down again.

'You still got your cat?' she said suddenly. 'I haven't seen her lately.'

Peggy hesitated. She had visions of Miss Beasley coming round at the dead of night with a hatchet and finishing off Gilbert and her little family. There were four kittens, and Peggy could see that two of them were ginger.

'She's got kittens, Miss Beasley,' said Peggy, 'so she hasn't been out.'

'Kittens!' said Ivy Beasley. 'She's not much more'n a kitten herself!'

'No, that's what I thought. But I'm told they get going very young.' Peggy busied herself with the Post Office, opening drawers and setting out books. Where was all this leading? It was a bit late for common-or-garden neighbourliness.

'Huh,' said the all-seeing Ivy Beasley, 'they're not the only ones.'

'What do you mean?' Surely she could not know about Sandra – she could only be a few weeks pregnant.

'Oh, if you'd lived here a bit longer, you'd know what I mean. Some families seem to think things aren't right unless the girls get going as soon as they're out of ankle socks.'

Ankle socks? thought Peggy. Miss Beasley was leaving, gathering up her matches and rice pudding, and heading for the door.

'If you like,' said Peggy, tentatively, 'you could see the kittens. Would you like to come round when the shop's closed?'

Ivy Beasley hesitated, gave a small grunt which could have meant anything, and departed, shutting the door quite quietly behind her.

Well, well, thought Peggy, it takes rumours of my departure for old Poison Ivy to be civil. She had not noticed the relief in Miss Beasley's eyes when she explained Gilbert's sudden withdrawal from circulation.

Her next customer was Pat Osman, not usually about the village at ten o'clock on a weekday morning. She was a pretty girl, with long straight dark hair and heavy fringe, like a modern Cleopatra. Her eyes were dark brown, almost black, and lively. Instead of her usual business-woman clothes, she was wearing jeans and a dark blue trenchcoat.

'Good morning,' said Peggy, 'not at work today?'

'No, I've taken the day off,' said Pat Osman, 'I am my own boss, more or less. I sell make-up – you know, parties, that kind of thing.'

'Ah ha,' said Peggy, 'maybe I shouldn't approve of you – competition for the village shop!'

Pat Osman looked around. 'You don't carry much in the way of cosmetics, do you, Mrs Palmer?'

'No, I was only teasing,' said Peggy. 'We just have a few basic brands for people who run out.'

Soon shan't have to bother with brands and stocks and new lines, she thought. What shall I bother with, then? Best not to think like that, I've argued it all out in my head so many times, and I know it's the right thing to do. Much better to make the break now, she thought, than struggle on getting older and poorer, and having to give up when I finally fail.

'Mrs Palmer!' said Pat Osman. 'Did you hear me?'

'Oh, so sorry,' said Peggy, 'I was miles away.'

'I said I was sorry that Colin burst in on you the other evening. He was so keen to see you, once we decided to have a go.'

I see, thought Peggy, so that's why you have taken the day off, Mrs Osman, so that you can come and attack me from a different angle. Well, we'll see about that.

'Have you had any interest yet?' said Pat Osman.

'It is not officially on the market until tomorrow,' said Peggy, 'and then it's for the agents to make appointments and so on. That's why you have agents, isn't it?' she added sweetly.

'Mm,' said Pat Osman, 'but I think Colin explained to you our plan for cutting out the middle man, so to speak, and . . .'

To Peggy's relief the shop door opened, and a solemn Doreen put a pile of egg trays down on the counter.

'I won't bother you now, Peggy, if you're busy,' she said, preparing to leave.

'No, no!' said Peggy loudly. 'Doreen, don't go – Mrs Osman has been served, so I can deal with the eggs now.'

She smiled firmly at Pat Osman, leaving her in no doubt that she was dismissed, and turned to Doreen, who stood uncertainly by the counter.

A reluctant Pat Osman trailed out of the shop, and the two friends were left alone. Doreen looked out of the window, round the shelves and across to the Post Office cubicle. She looked everywhere but at Peggy, and finally Peggy said, 'Doreen! For heaven's sake, what is it? If I've done something terrible, please tell me.'

'No, gel, it's not you, it's me,' said Doreen. 'I owe you an apology for being so sniffy, and not wanting to understand. I am sorry, Peggy.'

'Come and have a cup of coffee, there's nobody coming down the street so we're all right for a minute,' said Peggy, 'I think I need to sit down. My feet seem to ache all the time now.'

They sat either side of the kitchen table, and it was quiet and warm. 'I suppose I am worried that we've failed you,' said Doreen. 'When anyone nice leaves the village it always seems that it must be our fault if people don't like it here.'

'I do like it here!' said Peggy. 'But a very bad thing happened to me in Ringford, and I think it might be easier living somewhere else, you know, where I am not constantly reminded of Frank and the accident.'

'I know, I know,' said Doreen, 'of course you may be right. But if you look at it another way, you could stay and face up to it here. It would fall into its proper place in the end. Running away is never the answer, is it?'

She was quiet, afraid that she had said too much. Peggy's face was in shadow, but Doreen could see that she looked withdrawn and sad.

'I hadn't thought of it as running away,' Peggy said slowly, 'I truly had not.'

The shop bell jangled, and they stood up.

'Will you promise me to think a bit more about it,' said Doreen, 'before you finally decide?'

Peggy nodded. 'It is not likely to sell straight away, anyway,' she said, and then thought of the Osmans and their urgent proposal, and wondered if she should tell Doreen. But Doreen was already half out of the door, and shouting, 'Don't forget the Show meeting tonight!' and was gone.

'That comes round quick, don't it, Missus?' said old Mr Mills, lowering himself carefully on to the chair Frank had placed by the Post Office cubicle. Peggy counted out the notes for the old man, and agreed that no sooner was one year over than you were halfway through the next.

Mr Gray from Lambwith & Kitchener brought several possible buyers to see the Stores during the next few weeks. All exclaimed at the beauty of the village, and the quiet life they thought they could live in Ringford. So far, no one had made a firm offer.

Peggy found it difficult to be a good saleswoman. She hated strangers peering round her house. Her own excitement at seeing Doris's home was too vivid in her mind.

'Well, it wasn't long ago, gel,' said Bill. 'Why should you have forgotten?'

She showed a young couple from Birmingham the garden, and said, 'You should see it in summer.' And then she remembered Frank bending over his rows of potatoes, and hoeing his lettuces, and his pride in the straight runner beans. She told them about the walks along the river footpath, and saw herself and Frank wandering across the Green in the summer evening sunshine, arm in arm.

The Osmans were still pressing their suit, but Peggy fobbed them off with one reason after another. She had discussed their offer with Mr Gray and although his point of view was bound to be biased, he did stress that Casa Pera would have to be sold and this might take a long time. He was after a cash buyer, he said, if Peggy's aim was to move as quickly as possible.

The golden daffodils all came out at once, lured into bloom by one mild afternoon, and Peggy spent a lot of time looking out of her sitting-room into the garden, watching them dance.

She also saw Gilbert trying desperately to keep her four Beatrix Potter Kittens in order, as they strayed further and further each day. Ivy Beasley had still not come round to look at them, but Peggy caught her peering through the leafless hedge between the two gardens, catching a glimpse of them as they played.

One freak afternoon, warm as summer, but the air still clean and clear, when the school bus had come and gone, and Peggy looked forward to relaxing with a cup of tea, the door opened and young Sam walked in. Behind him, with her head down and a headscarf pulled forward round her face, came Sandra.

Peggy had not seen much of Sandra since that traumatic evening on the swings. Jean Jenkins had told her that Sandra had been to the doctor, and that she was at present determined to keep the baby. So far she had told her grandmother and mother, and they were standing by her.

'Well,' said Jean, 'both of them were expecting when they married. It's a family tradition, more or less, with them Robertses.'

Sam had been scared, Sandra said. But he, too, was prepared to do his bit – already done it, thought Peggy – and support Sandra as best he could.

Mr Roberts had not been told.

Now the young couple faced Peggy across the counter. 'Can we have a word, Mrs P.?' said Sam.

Peggy looked at the clock in the Post Office cubicle. It was just on half past five, and she nodded.

'Come through to the kitchen,' she said, 'I'll just lock up. It won't take a minute.'

She noticed Sam was holding Sandra's hand, and he gently pulled her through the shop into the kitchen.

'Well, sit down, then,' said Peggy, 'there's no need for us all to stand to attention.'

Sandra perched on the edge of a kitchen chair, and Sam stood behind her, his hand on her shoulder, unconsciously posed like an old sepia photograph. So far, Sandra had not said a word.

Peggy put on the kettle, wondering what this was going to be about. She turned to look at the young couple, and gasped.

Sandra had finally lifted her head, and was looking at her. Her left eye was black and yellow and red, and swollen so much that Peggy could not see the eye itself inside the puffy flesh.

'Sandra!' she said.

'I told me dad,' she said. 'Mum said I should tell him, and then she went out. So I told him, and he hit me. As you can see,' she added bitterly.

Peggy felt tears, and blinked hard.

'Have you been to the doctor with that eye?' she asked.

'Yep – told him I walked into a door,' said Sandra, 'but I don't think he believed me.'

Now Peggy noticed that Sam was pale and drawn, and she wanted to put her arms round the pair of them and make it better.

'We just came to say we're off now, back to my mum and dad in Tresham,' said Sam. 'They say Sandra can live with us, and have the baby, and Mum will help look after it until we can get married and have a place of our own.'

'Now?' said Peggy. 'You are going right now?'

'Yep,' said Sam, 'but we wanted to tell you, as you've tried to help . . . and that.'

Sandra stood up, and they walked slowly over to the back door. Peggy opened it and watched as they went down the side of the house and out into the road, where Sam had left his old van. At the little gate out on to the pavement, Sandra stopped and turned back to Peggy.

'We'll bring the baby over, when it's born,' she said, 'you'll still be here, I bet.'

Peggy made another solitary cup of tea and took it into the sitting-room. She looked out once more over the Green, and saw William and Andrew Roberts kicking a football round and round the bus shelter, until Warren

Jenkins arrived and dribbled it expertly away from them. Peggy drank her tea slowly, and thought about the shaky start for Sam and Sandra, and quite a lot about herself.

CHAPTER THIRTY-NINE

It was a fresh, sunny morning and the cuckoo had been calling from Bagley Woods since the first white light of dawn. 'Mocks married men, and thus sings he, cuckoo!' sang Bill Turner, getting his bike out of the shed.

Ringford had been taken over by birds. Newly dug gardens were given a second going-over by thrushes and robins and yellow-billed blackbirds. Dippers and wagtails were busy by the river, and the surviving ducks up-tailed and scolded, the females disappearing from sight now and then, almost drowning beneath vigorous drakes, resplendent and feisty in their bold plumage.

Doris Ashbourne was out in her garden, cleaning the big front window to a shining sparkle, and the Jenkins twins and small Eddie appeared in fresh, brightly coloured spring outfits, moving smartly off to the shop with Jean to buy new skipping ropes for the girls. Early daffodils appeared in sheltered corners, and rivers of liquid mud filled the farm tracks and sprayed over the verges as muck-spreading tractors rocketed by.

Tom Price walked across the Green, springy with new grass, and saw Bill cycling slowly down towards the Hall. 'Bill!' he shouted, 'can you spare a minute!' Bill had a scythe balanced over one shoulder, and found it difficult to slow down. Tom, mindful of his duty as a Parish Councillor, had been about to check the children's climbing frame and slide on the Green, making them safe for the summer, and he stepped out into the road, putting his hand on Bill's handlebars to slow him up. 'Watch out!' said Bill, putting his foot down as he finally came to a halt.

'What you doing, boy?' said Tom. 'You look like Old Father Time, with that thing over your shoulder. I haven't seen one of them off the wall for years.'

'Madam wants the dead stuff in the orchard cut back before the new grass is too high,' said Bill, 'this old thing can do it a treat, but it might be too wet still.'

'Is she back for good?' said Tom. 'I hope to God she is – Mr Richard was like the old ram without his yowes when she went.'

'I reckon she's back to stay,' said Bill, 'Old Ellen says she's taken on a new lease. Changing everything in sight, and finding fault all round. What's more, Ellen said she caught sight of them smoochin' in the boot room when they'd been out riding the other day.'

'Ah,' said Tom wisely, 'they do say horse-riding gets ladies all hepped up.' He winked at Bill.

'What bollocks,' said Bill, 'still, good luck to 'em, I say.'

'Anyway,' said Tom, 'I wanted a word, Bill – could you do us a favour tonight?'

'Depends what it is,' said Bill, instantly wary.

'It's the quiz team. We're going to be one short, and Doreen said to ask you. We're up against Fletching, and they're supposed to be mustard.'

'Me? That's a joke! I don't know anything about anything,' said Bill, 'why don't you ask Peggy? She and Frank got about a bit before they came here, and she'd know a deal more than me.'

'No, it was decided to ask you,' said Tom stubbornly.

Bill sighed. His good nature made him want to agree, but

he thought of Joyce and the fuss she would make about him being out all hours for the pub quiz.

'I don't know, Tom,' he said, 'it isn't easy, what with Joyce, and – well, you know.'

'Time you got a bit tough there,' said Tom. 'It isn't a life for a man, the way you're livin' it. Tell her you're going, and then go.'

Bill thought how easy he made it sound. 'All right, Tom, if you're really stuck, I'll be there – half past seven?'

Round Ringford team was doing well. It had not lost a game so far, and tonight they would come up against an ace team from Fletching, which included Mrs Layton, Ringford's headmistress, who traitorously lived over the hill.

Bill found the long tangled weeds and suckers too wet after all for scything, and after painfully slicing his hand on the blade, gave up and cycled back slowly across the Green. He propped his bike and scythe up against the wall of the Stores and climbed the steps to the door.

'Hello, Peggy my dear,' he said, finding the shop empty except for Peggy hard at work on her figures in the Post Office cubicle.

Peggy looked up with a smile. 'What can I do for you, Bill?' she said.

'Nothing that'll earn you a crust,' he said, 'I just need a bit of first aid. I nicked my hand with the scythe, and it is bleeding all over the place. Can you just lend me an old bit of rag to bind round it until I get home?'

Peggy came out of the cubicle and locked it behind her. 'Come on into the kitchen,' she said, 'and I'll see if I can remember what I learnt in the Girl Guides.'

Bill held his big hand under the kitchen tap, and Peggy watched blood and mud swirl round and down the drain.

'That looks nasty,' she said. 'Here, give me your hand and I'll sponge it clean.'

She took several pieces of kitchen tissue and made a thick

wedge which she wetted, and then took Bill's hand and gently wiped away the mud still clinging, until she saw a cut about an inch long down the ball of his thumb.

'Is that cut deep, Bill?' she said, bending over his arm to have a good look at it.

Oh God, thought Bill, what am I doing? He could smell her perfume, and the warmth of her body was too close. He knew he should have gone straight home, without calling at the shop. Well, why didn't you, you bugger, he thought.

He lifted his wet hand out of the sink, but Peggy held on to it.

'Stand still a minute, you idiot, while I dry it off,' she said.

But Bill twisted his hand round until he was holding hers, holding it tight and drawing her to him. He put his lips to her cheek, and for several seconds they stood without moving.

'Peggy,' he said, 'Peggy, my love.'

'Bill . . .'

The shop bell jangled, and they jumped apart as if the sword of Damocles had come down between them.

It was Miss Beasley, and she could see right through the shop to where they stood by the kitchen sink. She made a strange choking sound and, turning on her heel, almost ran from the shop.

Neither Bill nor Peggy said anything for a few seconds, and then Bill said, 'That's torn it.'

Peggy felt hot and confused. She made a big effort to pull herself together, and turned away from Bill to look out of the kitchen window.

'You must go, Bill,' she said finally. 'Here, let's put a plaster on it, and then keep your thumb clean until you can get it seen to.'

'Are you cross with me?' said Bill.

'Takes two,' said Peggy, 'as Ivy Beasley would say.'

She put her hand on his arm, and gently pushed him out

of the kitchen. She opened the shop door and stood to one side for him to leave.

'See you soon, Bill,' she said.

For the rest of the day, between customers, Peggy thought about Bill and Frank, and when she wasn't thinking muddled thoughts about them, she worried about Miss Beasley.

If only I could just pack up and go tomorrow, she thought, and escape. Ivy Beasley is not going to forget what she saw, and is quite likely to tell Joyce Turner next time she goes up there. And, of course, it will be chewed over by Ellen Biggs and Doris Ashbourne. Oh, blast it!

Then she thought of Bill's arm around her, and realised how much she missed Frank's body, warm and comforting next to her in bed, and the quick hugs and the occasional touch of his hand as she passed him in the house. But Bill belongs to Joyce, she told herself, he is not for you.

And what's more, Peggy Palmer, she continued to address herself, it is not just warmth and comfort you are after. Oh God, if old Poison Ivy hadn't come in when she did I might quite easily have dragged him up those stairs and straight into bed. And, she could hear them saying, Frank Palmer not cold in his grave.

'Bye, Ellen!' she said, helping the old woman down the steps, and going back inside to lock up with a sigh of relief.

That was the longest afternoon I've had in the shop, she thought. Now for a cup of tea and a sit down. Oh, but there's greedy Gilbert to feed first . . .

'Gilbert! Here comes food, come on, pussy!'

That's odd, thought Peggy, she's usually waiting for me. She went into the outhouse and the kittens were in a huddle on Frank's gardening trousers. When they saw Peggy, they began to mew desperately, as if they had not been fed for weeks.

She doesn't usually leave them for long, Peggy thought,

must be around somewhere. They were already old enough for new homes, but Gilbert was as devoted to them as ever, and was seldom far away.

Peggy called several times, but there was no sign of the cat. Maybe she's got shut in somewhere, she thought, and remembered when Gilbert had once before gone missing. I suppose she could have got locked in a shed round at Victoria Villa – maybe by accident.

There was nothing for it but to go and see, and Peggy walked quickly round to Miss Beasley's gate and swiftly up the garden path. If I go round the back, she thought, I might find Gilbert and not have to talk to the old trout.

She walked up the passage at the side of the house, and tiptoed past the back door. She was making for the outhouse where the coal and wood were kept, but she had to pass the kitchen window, and prayed that Miss Beasley was elsewhere in the house.

Ivy Beasley was not elsewhere. Peggy could see her quite clearly sitting in a chair by the range, and on her lap, curled up under Miss Beasley's stroking hand, was Gilbert.

As Peggy stood rooted to the spot in amazement, Miss Beasley looked up and saw her. She shot up, sending Gilbert flying to the ground, and rushed from the room. The back door opened, and Peggy saw the same bleak, twisted face that Frank had encountered that day, long past.

'Take your stupid cat,' she spat at Peggy, 'and be off with you, you . . . you . . .'

Gilbert came running out to Peggy, who picked her up. Before Miss Beasley could shut the door, Peggy found her tongue.

'I know what I saw, Miss Beasley,' she said, 'how long have you been enticing my cat into your house?'

Miss Beasley muttered that she was a fine one to talk about enticing, and Peggy added quickly, 'That just about makes us quits, wouldn't you say?'

But of course it did not make them quits, and Peggy was

apprehensive, wondering what Ivy Beasley would do. She knew enough about village life now to know that there would be no immediate repercussions.

It's not only the mills of God that grind exceeding slow, she thought, village retribution can be equally unrelenting.

'Tom's asked me to fill in at the quiz tonight,' said Bill. Joyce had her feet up on the sofa, and her fluffy pink slippers were matted and grubby. 'Oh yes,' she said, 'and is that just another of your excuses?'

'Don't be stupid, Joyce, I met him this morning on the Green, and he asked me then. I said yes.'

'That's it, then, isn't it?' she said. 'Don't bother to consult me. I can just sit here for another endless evening with nothing to do and nobody to talk to.'

'You've got the telly,' said Bill, 'and anyway, if you were better company I might want to stay in a bit more.'

Joyce didn't answer, but shut her eyes and pretended to go to sleep. It had been so long since she tried to do anything to please Bill that she wouldn't know how to begin.

Bill stood looking out of the window and across the road to the Roberts' house. Mrs Roberts came down the side passage and out of the swinging gate. Her shoulders were hunched and she looked defeated.

What a mess we make of our lives, thought Bill.

Joyce opened her eyes and sat up, swinging her feet to the floor. 'I'm not feeling at all well,' she said, 'I don't think you should go out and leave me.'

He assured her he would not be late, but she just repeated the same words over and over again, and rocked herself back and forth where she sat, knowing that this usually got to Bill, making him back down.

But tonight Bill felt numb towards her. She no longer moved him to compassion. When the time came for him to leave for the pub, he coolly changed into a clean shirt and trousers and put on his best overcoat.

'I'm off now, then, be back about half past nine,' he said, 'don't forget to make up the fire – it's a chilly evening.'

'I'm feeling very ill!' screamed Joyce, as he shut the door behind him and locked it carefully, as always.

The quiz teams were assembled and Bill was the last to arrive.

'Thought you'd got cold feet, Bill!' said Tom.

'Not me,' said Bill, 'but I don't know that I shall be much good to you.'

The questions were in groups, and it was a matter of luck if a team happened to have an expert on pop music, or sport or political history.

'Now, Mr Turner,' said the quizmaster, small, grey-suited, smoothly confident, 'the next round is local knowledge. Can you tell me the derivation of the word "Round" in the name of your beautiful village, Round Ringford?'

The rest of the team looked blank, and the schoolmistress from Fletching wriggled in her seat, the answer bursting to get out. Then Tom's face brightened as his memory dredged up long-neglected facts. He put up his hand, but Bill was ready for them.

'Comes from a round ring of old stones found up on the edge of Bagley Woods,' he said, 'they was going to excavate it at one time, but nothing came of it and nobody goes there now. And Ringford,' he added, getting into his stride, 'that comes from a fording place in the Ringle, before the bridge were built.'

'Good ole Bill,' yelled Fred Mills, from the corner by the fire, and there was a sprinkling of applause. It was a narrow victory for Round Ringford, in spite of the schoolmistress challenging the quizmaster's decision a couple of times, and Bill found himself a bit of a hero.

After a quick pint, and in spite of the fact that he was enjoying himself in the warm atmosphere of the crowded pub, Bill said that he must go.

'Right-o, Bill,' said Tom, 'thanks for coming – can we call on you again?'

'Why not, if you think I'd be of use,' said Bill. He said farewell to the visiting team, who gave him a small cheer, and was off on his bike back to Macmillan Gardens and the hostile welcome he knew would be waiting for him.

'He was like a different chap,' said Tom to Doreen, when he finally reached home.

Doreen guided her cheerful but slightly unsteady husband to his bed and said nothing, keeping her own counsel.

CHAPTER FORTY

Two more weeks of showing people round the Stores brought no firm offers – or even tentative ones. After another long day in the shop, Peggy was beginning to wonder if she could carry on. The thought of one more evening spent doing the accounts and checking stock filled her with gloom.

The telephone rang, and she lifted the receiver wearily. 'Hello, who is it?' she said.

'Colin Osman,' said the deep, confident voice, 'I am sorry to disturb you, but I have some news and wanted you to know straight away.'

'Oh yes,' said Peggy.

'We've got a buyer for our house!' he said. 'One of the blokes in my office is really keen and has the cash. There won't be any problems and we could go ahead more or less straight away.'

Peggy was stunned. She was too tired to think, and taken by surprise could not summon any reason for putting him off.

'May I come and see you?' he said. 'The sooner we get things on the move the better.'

'Hey, wait a minute!' Peggy said, pulling herself together. 'I am afraid I shall have to have a session with my solicitor before we go any further.'

'I thought you'd already done that,' said Colin Osman, with elaborate patience.

'Well, no, I haven't had time,' said Peggy. 'I'll see if he can fit me in tomorrow, and if Mary's free to look after the shop I should have some kind of answer for you tomorrow evening.'

Peggy heard his sigh, and a muffled remark made to his wife as he covered the receiver with his hand. Then he spoke again, and his voice had an irritated edge.

'Mrs Palmer,' he said slowly, 'am I right in thinking that you do want to sell the Stores?'

Peggy began to bristle. 'What do you mean?' she said.

'It is just that every time I talk to you, you do not seem at all sure,' said Colin Osman. 'My wife is still very keen to have a go at running a village shop, and if you are not really serious about selling up, then we could continue to look elsewhere.'

'That sounds like a threat,' said Peggy coolly. 'I have told you that I will let you know tomorrow or the next day, and that is what I will do. Goodbye, Mr Osman.'

She replaced the telephone and sat down.

Frank, she said, I don't think I am handling this very well. What do you think? No disembodied voice answered her question, and she did not really expect it. I just have to sort it out now for myself. After all, I've only myself to consider, so it should be easy.

There's Bill, though, she thought. This was the first time she had consciously taken him into account, and she knew that it was foolish. But was it? They had maintained an easy friendliness, and Bill had not touched her again, though she would not have minded if he had. When he looked at her his eyes were warm. Biding his time, I expect, thought Peggy, him being a Ringford man.

The solicitor was able to see Peggy, and congratulated her on finding a cash buyer herself, without the intervention of expensive estate agents.

'I didn't find them,' she said, 'they found me.'

'You do still want to move, Mrs Palmer?'

Why can't I just say yes, and get on with it, thought Peggy. But she said she would let the solicitor know what she decided, now she had all the facts. She somehow forgot to telephone the Osmans in the evening.

The next day was Saturday, and first through the shop door was Colin Osman.

'I don't want to hurry you, Mrs Palmer,' he said, 'but you do see that if I am to clinch my sale, I must know very soon that you are prepared to go ahead.'

Peggy felt genuinely apologetic. The Osmans had done nothing wrong. They were just keen and over-anxious; but thinking back, Peggy remembered that she and Frank had been the same, once they had decided to buy.

'Oh dear, I am sorry,' she said, 'but try to understand that I must be absolutely sure. I promise you there are no other suitable offers at the moment.'

No offers at all, thought Colin Osman, if I guess correctly. Poor old thing just can't make up her mind, I suppose.

'If you could just leave it with me for a few more days, Mr Osman,' said Peggy, and wondered what on earth she was doing, risking losing such a good buyer.

By Sunday, Peggy was no clearer in her mind. The pealing bells reminded her that she hadn't been to church for a week or two, and she hurriedly put on her coat for morning service. Maybe I'll get some celestial guidance, she thought as she closed the back door, though I doubt if it will be the answer I want.

The village was lit by hazy sunlight, the early morning mist not quite gone. It softened the edges of stone houses and pale green tops of trees reborn in new leaf. It's doing its best to seduce me, persuade me to stay, thought Peggy, as she walked along the newly mown Green, the smell of cut grass like perfume, and the willows swaying gently in the light wind.

'Hi, Mrs Palmer!' shouted Warren Jenkins from his new bike, whizzing past her and tipping at a dangerous angle round by the school house. He and William were having a race, and she called back, 'Watch the traffic, Warren!'

Not that there was much traffic, just a few churchgoers slowly bumping over the bridge and parking beside the church wall. 'Morning, Peggy,' said Doreen and Tom, Foxy Jenkins and Mr Ross. She sat in her usual place, next to Doreen, two pews from the front.

There was a christening during the service, and the parents and godparents, and all the friends and relations, crowded round the tiny infant and wished it well. Peggy thought of Sandra and Sam, and felt sad at the unfairness of everything.

The baby yelled without mercy as the vicar, his hands shaking, sloshed too much holy water over the angry little face. Poor old Cyril, thought Peggy, he's getting past it, and the baby went rigid with fury, filling the church with primitive anger.

'. . . and the blessing of God Almighty, the Father, the Son, and the Holy Ghost, be amongst you and remain with you, always. Amen.' The words are familiar, thought Peggy, but they're no comfort today. She left the church with Doreen, who said 'You look a bit middling – anything up?'

'No, not really,' said Peggy, doing her best to smile. The hoped for answer had not been given, and she felt frustrated and scratchy. She refused a glass of sherry at the Prices', and went on home.

The house seemed to press in on her, and after eating a piece of cheese with two soggy cream crackers, she decided on a walk up the Bagley road and into the woods to see if she could find primroses. I might not be here next spring, she thought, as she pulled on her boots and a grubby old anorak. Better make the most of it.

Where the church service had failed Peggy, the cool air

and ravishing smells of earth and new growth in the woods calmed her. She wandered about, leaving the path and finding little runnels of water running secretly under layers of old tree trunks and rotting leaves. In the grass she found a large clump of primroses, such a clear yellow that she caught her breath, and felt no desire to pick them.

On the far side of the wood, by the ring of old stones, Bill Turner, his gun held carefully at a safe angle, stood listening. Hazel branches moved gently in the wind, and drifts of snowy blackthorn blossom on the edges of the wood threatened cold weather to come. The afternoon sun, stronger now, dappled the damp ground, catching clouds of fragile white wood anemones.

A sudden clattering of wood pigeons taking flight in alarm set off a trail of lesser scuttlings and rustlings. The wood was vigorously alive, and as Bill listened for the sounds he knew so well, every living thing listened to him, waiting for something to happen, anticipating trouble, instinctively ready for escape.

Bill was looking for rabbits. Funny, he thought, I spend all that time fussing those rabbits at home, and yet I can come out here and happily shoot two or three for the pot. He saw a flash of movement through the trees and raised his gun.

Then he lowered it again, uncertain of what he saw.

'Oy!' he shouted, 'you're trespassing!'

The moving figure stopped dead. He saw that it was a woman, and as he walked rapidly towards her he knew for certain that it was Peggy.

If this was a film, thought Peggy, we would move towards each other in slow motion, arms stretched and hair flying. We would embrace and the scene would fade. Instead, she faced Bill with dirty hands, tangled hair and her boots heavy with mud. He looked at her unsmiling, then at his gun, and said, 'I could have shot you, Peggy, you stupid woman!'

Then he leaned his gun against a tree, and took her in his arms, mud and all, and kissed her with considerable feeling.

'I am so sorry, Mr Osman, but I have decided to stay and try and make a go of it somehow,' said Peggy into the telephone next morning. 'I wanted you to be the first to know, and I shall be in touch with the agents at once.'

Colin Osman was bravely polite, and put down the telephone quickly. Peggy knew he was disappointed, but nothing could dampen her wonderful sense of well-being. It wouldn't last, she knew, but just for the moment she blotted out all feelings of guilt and irresponsibility.

'I don't know how we'll be able to manage,' Bill had said, 'you can't keep nothing secret in Ringford. And I don't want to hurt Joyce, God knows I don't, though she's done her best to hurt me for years.'

'There'll be a way,' said Peggy, as they walked slowly back through the wood, hand in hand.

Now she patted the telephone, as if it had served her well, and went to have a quick slice of toast before Miss Beasley arrived for her Monday morning box of matches. Or maybe she won't, the old bat, thought Peggy, we shall see.